T0113801

Of Saints and Scarecrows

Ulysses Chuka Kibuuka

FOUNTAIN PUBLISHERS
Kampala

Fountain Publishers
P.O. Box 488
Kampala - Uganda
E-mail:fountain@starcom.co.ug
Website:www.fountainpublishers.co.ug

Distributed in Europe, North America and Australia by African Books Collective Ltd (ABC), PO Box 721, Oxford OX19EN, United Kingdom. Tel/Fax: 44(0) 1869-349110, E-mail: orders@africanbookscollective.com Website: www.africanbookscollective.com

© Ulyses Chuka Kibuuka 2007
First published 2007

All rights reserved. No part of this publication may be reproduced, stored in a retrieval system or transmitted in any form or by any means electronic, mechanical, photocopying, recording or otherwise without the prior written permission of the publisher.

ISBN 978-9970-02-530-5

In Memory of

Samaria Sarah Nakibuuka 1981-2005
God bless that brave heart.

Gratitude

To Mwalimu Austin Bukenya, Tonny Owana, Anthony Gatare and Tom Mugerwa for kindly perusing the manuscript and making useful recommendations.

To Pauline Nannono, who listened to readings of sections of this tale, ridiculed my chauvinistic and ignorant perception of feminine sensual arousal and offered helpful hours of detailed description.

To Fountain Publishers editorial staff at Makerere University campus for their unusual tirelessness.

To the FEMRITE group who were a major stimulant.

Principally to the unique companionship of – usually over *ndigi* and cards as Paul Kafeero closed off booze depots – Dahlia, Qvene Anne, Ziriana, Nakaliika, Flo Parma, Walugembe Kiweewa, Mubarak Nsabimana, Richard Mutaaya, Monsieur Richard Kabeya.

Dedicated to

Baba, Ajax, Grace Karungi, Kaasande, Andrew, Farouk.

Prologue

Kampala City, February 2006

I met Prophet Pacific Bantu high on Lubya Hill at the southwestern edge of Kampala City when Virgo Kabibi, bent double and grossly wrinkled with age, arranged with my boss to conduct me there in a hired car. The boss, Mr William Tunafish, editor in chief of *The Sunday Dawn*, had earlier that day summoned me to his wooden office and made me sit down comfortably before he shot a question at me: "Have you ever heard of the name Beelzebub?"

I shook my head. "I have met a Zerubabel, once; but a — Bez-what? No, sir, I have not."

Mr Tunafish, usually known as Mr Bill Tuna, picked up a heavy tome before him on his reading desk, looked through it while at the same time consulting a Toshiba Pentium IV laptop and checking things against stuff in the huge book. There was another book, bound in brown leather and its faded title could have been *Paradise Lost*, with the name of the author more legible.

"This is The Jerusalem Bible — unexpunged," he said without looking up. "And this is Milton," he patted the book with the faded title. "Beelzebub is a rare name here in Uganda. It has its origins in the Hebrew and Philistine cultures. It should have read Ba'alzebhubh — with aitches. It could mean Satan, satanic, child of the devil or even The Antichrist."

I waited for Mr Tunafish to say some more. When he didn't, I prompted him. "So, sir?"

He looked at me as though he had forgotten I was there, his well-polished pair of spectacles glinted in the fluorescent light. He was in his mid fifties and had ginger hair and a beard peppered greatly with grey. He was one of those rare genuinely kind *bazungu* people from England, who behaved as though he knew very well that only skin colour differentiated him from the black Africans he had interacted with on a day to day basis for the past couple of decades. "Ah; I want you to go to Nakulabye, place called Kiwuunya, I am sure you know of it. There is an important Catholic missionary establishment there — begun in 1909 I am told. There is a Reverend Father Anatole Kayiwa Kakande there — a friend of mine, of course. He will introduce you to an old girl, age probably late seventies; they seem to think she is beyond a hundred! You will go with her to Lubya Hill and, as you may already know, find there a horde of other journalists intent on interviewing the great Prophet Pacific Bantu. Since he is holding a press conference of sorts, attend that and afterward

— that is why I want you to pass by Kiwuunya first, so that nobody should beat us to her, get crucial extra data on the prophet from that old lady. I don't want her to talk to any other reporter before you have milked her dry of any information she should have. After that you may even go ahead to show her the unsuitability of talking to the other media men and women. Simply claim they will badmouth her in the media. I've been made to understand she is senile. And — oh, I nearly forgot, do not take any of the *Sunday Dawn* vehicles. Hire a taxi and bill Finance Department. Best luck and hurry up on it."

Most of the company vehicles were emblazoned with our name and logo in large black print, which went: *The Sunday Dawn*, and I immediately saw the reason Mr Tuna did not want me to go in them. Other newshounds would want to know what *The Sunday Dawn* was doing at a 1909 missionary establishment of the Catholic Church, particularly with the current bashing of that establishment by the rabidly anti conventional-religions movements bedevilling both conventional Christianity and Mohammedanism. The bashers were very fanatic vocal born-again Christians and even fiercer extremist Islamic gospel preachers referring to themselves as *Tablighs*, both of whom, when they weren't engaged in the ferocious battles for converts, castigated the older orthodox faiths for laxity and even outright paganism. The prophet I was meeting preached an altogether different spiritual doctrine which, to the fundamentalist Christians and Muslims, was proving simply too popular for their comforts, pulling mammoth crowds under its umbrella.

Prophet Pacific Bantu had been in the news for six consecutive months and seemed bent on keeping the headlines and bold columns to himself with the controversies that surrounded his title, his names and his pastoral ways. A number of reverend pastors, mullahs, and cultural seers — he brought many of these together in a sort of coalition umbrella that he claimed to represent worldwide, had recently come out to denounce his teachings, which consistently appeared geared at edging out the Middle Eastern prophets Mohammed ibn Abdullah of Mecca and Medina and Jesus Christ of Nazareth and bringing in African son-of-soil prophets with names like Kazooba, Jajja Muwanga and Mumbi of heaven and earth, Kibuuka *Omumbaale* of the skies, Musisi of the earthquakes, Kiwanuka of the thunder, Nyabyingi of the African spiritual cultures of Kigezi and Rwanda, Mukasa — also known as Mugasha of the seas and winds, Mayanja of the rivers and lots of other Black African God's representatives and messengers whose abode, several disciples of Bantu were beginning to proclaim, was Africa around the source of the Nile and the zones of the grand eruptions that formed the great Kilimanjaro, the Rwenzoris, the Kenya and the Elgon; zonal home to old Zinjanthropus. Opposing sects — which also included quite dangerous cults, accused Prophet Pacific Bantu of using witchcraft — a banned word in the prophet's congregations since he preferred to refer to such doctrines as Cultural Consultancies, and of being a Satanist; an Antichrist. Evangelists of all races, sexes and callings, who had come from all over the globe to see, hear, learn and scrutinize the prophet's teachings, had started writing to the general media and on the internet, calling Pacific Bantu a false prophet. But obversely, a multitude of other members of the human race from all over the world were willing to proclaim the same man as The Saviour since they claimed to be fortunate enough to be alive by his mere act of having touched them.

Bill Tuna himself had been contacted by the renowned Catholic priest, the Reverend Father Anatole Kayiwa Kakande, who also had been contacted by people who had brought the old woman all the way from Gikongoro, deep in Southwestern Rwanda, and which woman claimed to be a relative of Prophet Pacific Bantu and who, it was said, was willing to testify that the prophet was not only an actual prophet, but that she and Bantu's own mother — who had died while delivering him unto this earth, had known each other well. She was also stating she had been there at the christening of the baby prophet with the very name she was willing to supply to *The Sunday Dawn*. Mr Tuna himself would have wished to interview the old woman. But he was an Englishman and the old wench spoke only Luganda, Kinyarwanda and Kinyankore, in which languages I myself was fluent. How important and influential on the current trend in the media the revelation of that hitherto unknown name would turn out to be, I had no idea at the time.

I picked old Virgo Kabibi, a waiflike tiny woman, whose old age caused her to appear much shorter than she certainly must have been at one time, and headed for Lubya Hill, which was on the same stretch of road. Kabibi was talkative like old people are often wont to get and I encouraged her flow of words exploitatively. She was of a light brown complexion and wrinkles crisscrossed her entire exposed sallow skin. Her age-paled eyes had in them the well-defined rings of age but were as sharp as her chaffing voice was clear. Her puns were sadly of times long past but I laughed at them with cheer. I asked her why she was unable to meet the prophet herself and she said she had her secret reasons.

"I might go on to meet him in future. But you see, first I will have to see if it is he or if the newspaper pictures lied to me. Then I will gauge his attitude to his past if and when he lets me talk to him. You know he might wish to remain relationless, as he was brought up by entities that had told him so. But you can rest assured that if it is Beelzebub then I have the ability to reconnect him to the umbilical chord of his past and present. I lived with his father, his mother and most of his other relatives who, today, don't know of his existence."

"How will you identify him then?"

"Just by looking at him physically."

I got to Lubya in time and parked the hired car at a distance from the rest — there were several score motor vehicles all over the place, and I stepped out, leaving Kabibi behind. The great man came out to welcome us into the large single storied mansion that served as his See, as it was referred to, and conducted us to a large hall that was furnished mainly with extra-large Persian, Bokhara and other carpets and rugs. In the huge resounding hall with marble walls and wooden floor were gathered several large and small groups of people — you could not easily tell which belonged where but their various dress told you these were members of either religious or religio-cultural sects of sorts. There were clergymen in various garb and vestments denoting their highness of office — rich purple and equally rich black cassocks, snow-white soutanes and albs, Arabian desert dress in form of *kanzus, kaffiyehs*, tarboushes, fezzes, all manner of dog collars, strings of all colour of beads running round and round through the fingers of their possessors, flowing dresses and habits of feminine religious orders, strikingly colourful bark cloth-clad traditional seers and cultural consultants who were sometimes referred to as witchdoctors, with ages-old castanets and copper and brass trinkets gracing their necks, wrists and ankles. There were healers and consultants in fortunes, plain clothed members of the public — name it. They numbered perhaps three score, give or take, from all over Africa and the wider world, and all mingled with intriguing ease.

And there were, of course, the police and the secret service.

Our venerable host sat himself in a very large multicoloured, greatly upholstered seat — a throne of sorts that made Pacific Bantu to appear like a regal character from czarist Russia of the past centuries. He was most probably twenty-five to twenty-eight years, stood at six-foot-four, quite a giant of a man, strong and big boned, with long muscular arms and large hands with long fingers one of which, the middle one of the left hand, had on it a heavy signet ring in platinum. It was claimed the prophet contained a single bone, an undivided ulna, in either of his arms and that that made him a very physically strong man. His shoes could have been British size-fourteen.

His complexion was what some refer to as buffalo-black; something like over-roasted cocoa, and his face was fleshy, without traces of fat. The features were nicely planed — neither sharp nor blunt, which made him almost beautiful to behold. He had eyes that hypnotized in those aristocratic, near rude, *kumema* or mocking look of theirs. Women were rumoured to experience ecstasies of unprecedented orgasm by merely having him look deep into their eyes — and even more ecstatically, when he touched them physically. He was the most imposing human being I had ever stood before and even before he spoke you felt you were in the presence of an extraordinary human being — not like the great men of the clergy in church or mosque, but something enigmatic, electrifyingly and mysteriously present in the man. When he spoke his voice boomed resonantly like cannon but with great clarity like that of a cicada at high noon, and at the same time his voice contained utmost gentility in it.

"I will first tell you about myself and then I will field your questions," this was addressed to the horde of notepad-toting journalists. "That is the way it is done, I am sure."

We all nodded consent and several of the gathered humanity shuffled closer to be among the pen and camera wielding journalists, most of whom were foreign correspondents from as far-flung areas as New Zealand, the Koreas and Mexico.

The prophet then flourished a large beefy palm across the amplitudinous hall: "As you may have noted every member of the groups that proclaim God — that claim to represent God on earth, is here. *Yes*. Verily, God has representatives here, but God has no religion, as we all ought to have known by this era of human existence. God is above religion and faith and that is manifestly clear. God is the creator of all living and nonliving things and all substances in the whole Universe, and as you know those are as various and numerous as they are diverse. But do we owe God anything? Let me tell you what we owe to God, because I do know, as you should also. Almighty God wants of humanity only one singular thing of us all that live, all that think and all that act consciously. He wants us to never deliberately without justification do that which will leave the other displeased or harmed. This is not exactly like the Love Thy Neighbour as You Love Thyself doctrine of the Middle East. As human beings with our accompanying weaknesses it is not possible to just love everybody, neighbour or no neighbour. But it is viable never to deliberately without just cause, do harm to fellow man. As you may note, in such maxim of God Almighty lies all justice, all good, all generosity, and all holiness if you will. You may later see about the justification for some types of deed that displease others or may harm them; deeds which must not bear selfishness or harbour malice in their execution. Such deeds, even should they be involuntary, must serve good and must be directed at the worse entity that could harm the greater and better of humanity and other fauna. To determine the greater and better is easily through the scrutiny of our actions. Remember it is futile to attempt to dupe God Almighty, the God of the peoples of the world, which peoples include you and me as Africans. How can you dupe an entity that knows your thought several millennia in advance?

"You and others elsewhere have been made to believe for centuries that Jesus Christ and Muhammad Abdullah are the sole representatives of your

God — the God of all humanity, on earth. That only *they* can convey our lamentations to the single God. That those Africans that had died by the time of the advent of Islam and Christianity into dark Africa lived pagan lives and died as pagans and have no iota of opportunity to meet God on the Day of Judgment! That all our African ancestors before 1850 have no chance of salvation. That only a few black Africans that have known the Books according to Jesus and Mohammed may go to God's heaven as clean beings! That God, as discovered in Africa by the imperial crusaders that carried religion ahead of them as a masthead, was a god with a small g. Nothing more fallacious can be suggested or believed today, ladies and gentlemen, and that small g was and still is the figment of a snobbish and malicious imagination in the mind of a thieving opportunist imperial crusader. For where would such belief, if it were true, leave the combined billions of Chinese, Indians, Japanese and the other multitudes of the Far-East, who even as of today — let alone the recent and ancient pasts, never supplicated to God the same way the Monotheist Europeans and the Semites of the Middle East claim it ought to be done? You must, of course, know of Buddhism, the spiritual faith of the multitudes of China, Indochina, India, Japan, Vietnam, the Koreas and all Mongolia; Buddhism is our planet's most widely professed faith besides Hinduism, which is mostly confined to India and which is the mother of the Mantra-chanting Hare Krishna movement taking root right here in Uganda. What of Taoism and Confucianism, mostly practiced in China and Japan? You may one day hear of the Parsis or Zoroastrians of the Arabian Gulf states, more particularly Iran, who believe in Ahura Mazda as supreme God and in place of burying their dead — or cremating such, instead carry corpses into huge, walled enclosures called Towers of Quietitude, where vultures and the elements feast and act on the cadavers to leave clean skeletons. The Zoroastrian vows to Ahura Mazda and promises Him to always be clean of thought, of deed and of word, worships five times a day and does not need a prayer-leader — a *reverend* pastor or an imam, to communicate to God. In my endless spiritual journey I have interacted with all those. I have congregated with the Jains of India and Pakistan, the Bahai, the so-called Animists in most of Africa, the Asceticists, the Rastafarians, who believe in the late Emperor Haille Selassie of Addis Ababa, and the Ancestor-Spirit worshippers. These are great spiritual faiths in their own right but Christendom and Islam do teach that adherents to those religions, adherents who equal the numbers of all Christians and Muslims added together, shall all burn in 'God's' eternal, oil-stoked fire of Gehenna! Such belief, of course, is farfetched on the side of the pious Muslim and Christian teacher since it would be an extremely unreliable God who would destroy the bigger part of his useful population, whom moreover he would have shown the Christian-Islamic way in the first place if He had deemed it sensible or necessary. Why — these peoples, whose combined numbers as I have already stated, overwhelmingly beat the rest of earth's populations lumped together, don't view God in the same picture you have been taught to do. And yet God Almighty has seen it fit to bless these Orientals with the very overwhelming fertile reproductive systems he has so painstakingly begrudged those claiming to know Him better. Islam and Christianity would be a bit over-ambitious to have you believe that only they and their former *kaffir* — yes, *kaffir* is what you are derogatively called when you attempt to reach God through more logical means or when you don't pay the Christians and Islamites to do it for you — and gentile converts, will reach the Kingdom of God and that all those billions of Orientals and the Africans that have never heard the words Christ or Mohammed mentioned shall all perish in everlasting infernos! I need not remind you that an Eskimo and most citizens of Iceland would, logically, view a much chillier place as the truer hell and imagine such fires as described in the Bible and Koran as somewhat exaggerated fireplaces. Obviously God will roast or freeze the erring Chinese, as He shall the sinning Lapp or Jew. Is that not quite obvious? But all in all, I have found the two religions closest to us here the most devastating of all, in terms of respect for human life. Christianity and Islam are soaked in oceans of cold blood and are not bothered by it all!

"Know, all you gathered here, that all humanity originated a few miles east of here on the shores of great Lake Nalubaale and that means that God has been busier here, over Africa, more than anywhere else at any time in the life of planet Earth. Are you aware of that? It is true. The venerable Mahatma Gandhi implored his people to sprinkle the ashes of his remains at the point where the River Nile leaves Nalubaale, reasoning that those ashes would find their way to India and all over the world in the process as though he were aware all humanity started at the Source of the Nile to follow that river and scatter and populate the planet in the process. But then you should be interested to know that Indians know Hare Krishna to be a Black man! Much as they hate it all humanity who later became Semite, Aryan, Caucasian, Mongol, name it —all were once African and as black as you and I. All came from here!"

Of course I cannot repeat everything the Prophet Pacific Bantu stated in his sermon of that day but by the time he finished, none of us had questions for him. He had talked for a good one hour and forty minutes and all a journalist worth his salt had to do was use their notes to make a story.

Having noted a row of questions for my car guest, I ambled back to where I had left old Virgo Kabibi. I wanted to dig out things that the prophet had never spoken about himself. The world wanted to know what made this enigmatic spiritual ideologue the magnet that he was to so much of the God-fearing world. But within minutes I had discarded my questionnaire, for the old woman assured me there wasn't a possibility in the world for her to give me her story in just the few moments we snatched in the car seat. From what she was suggesting it looked like I might be required to travel far and wide, in the north and south of Uganda; traverse Rwanda and Eastern Congo — which she still referred to as Zaire, and always return to her to crosscheck things for confirmation.

"You say you are related to the prophet," I had begun, eagerly. "You came from Rwanda the other week and I have to assume you are a Munyarwanda. Would this mean Pacific Bantu is, also, a Munyarwanda?"

"Beelzebub ought to be a Muganda, just like you."

"Uh hum!" I grunted in mild surprise. "But then? What is he?"

"He has no tribe. His father loved a Munyarwanda Catholic woman with immeasurable ardour and yet he was supposed to be a Muslim Muganda who despised organized religion. He did visit local cultural consultants to have his fortunes told by *lubaale* and *mizimu* spirits and to him that was religion in its purest form. Both his mother and father died most tragically through the machinations — a fierce tug of war actually, between church and mosque. But this is a waste of time. You will have to travel south to where I just came from to have the feel of the atmosphere out of which Beelzebub evolved. You can also be assured I was the very first person to hold that prophet in my hands right from the womb of his dead mother."

One

Mbarara, Southern Uganda, July 1977

This was at a time in Uganda when Catholicism was the only other religion besides Islam and Greek Orthodoxy, that could be referred to strictly as *religion*; a time when Anglican Protestantism, a group not known to clamour to be regarded so much as a faith than as a political entity, was a force driven by political interests, greatly intent — as it remains today, on keeping the other *diinihs* from state power. Where General Idi Amin, a Muslim, had come from to hold sway over the region, everybody, including the thunderstruck but jubilant Muslims themselves, were still puzzling by 1977. Much later, after Amin's ouster from state power control, the Catholics were heard to mumble damnations at the British Government and Israel for trusting a Moslem over and above Rome's own flock, for by that time everybody seemed to have pinpointed the origins of Idi Amin's brutal barbarity to London's White Hall and Israel's Ha-Mossad. Suffice it to say that among the remaining faiths there could be found overt sin. Even the Islamic faith, whose members were deemed largely promiscuous with regard to their harem-like homesteads that teemed with numerous wives usually referred to by husband and offspring with numeric characterisations like Wife Number-One, Wife Number-two; First Mother, Middle Mother, Second-last Mother, and so on and so forth, was not quite as reverently looked upon as Catholicism. Islam was indeed secretly — and even sometimes openly, dreaded by members of the other faiths. The Orthodox Church, like Islam to some extent, was and remains much unknown, if not utterly mysterious to many in Eastern Africa. Yet the Catholics, with their solemnly dignified priests that shunned mundane familiarity and those saintly, quiet, veiled nuns, whose secret, mysterious and unsociable quiescence bordered on mystic cultism, remained the more *overtly* sinless besides boasting the greater numbers in spiritual adherents. To a huge extent it was especially those nuns that lent the Catholic faith that sedate, pious image. Indeed, the ordinary priest has metamorphosed considerably for the worse since, but not much so the Catholic nun — not even today.

* * *

The sixteen passengers had left the airstrip in a yellow airline minibus and cruised along the rough dusty road, gazing sleepily out at the mesmerizing

1

landscapes of the Kashari savanna grasslands that stretched off away to either side of the road, for it was not easy to do anything else with that beautiful panorama spread out there like baize. On her own side of the minibus, to Apollonia Kasangaire, the gently undulating smooth green hillsides lain out on the range like gigantic women on their backs with great breasts pointing up at the neat cloudless sky, were a breathtaking tableau of God's own fine art that struck a sudden nostalgic spell into her heart as she remembered her own land of origin a couple of hundred miles to the south of where they were, and where she hadn't set foot for close to half a decade. It had rained heavily the previous night to portend a clear metallic blue late afternoon sky with scanty wisps of isolated egret-white cirrus wallowing lazily across the vast canopy of azure blue firmament. The rain had washed the savanna meadows and pastures leaving the rectangular patches of ripening millet and sorghum fields and the larger expanses of uncultivated heath and heather jubilantly flashing a bright olive as they continuously swayed west under the gentle breezes, and a dark mysterious amethyst when they straightened out with a lull in the winds. Whiffs of air pregnant with the sweetness of the scent of grain crop and nectar from the profuse wild flowers whipped across their faces soothingly through the open windows and often awakened them from the illusion that theirs might have perhaps been a sweet daydream.

Through that vividly luxurious scenery a heavily corrugated, beige murram road carried them for four dusty miles, their vehicle nodding and bobbing its front like a heavy beast as the tyres hit the bumpy surface. They came to the west-easterly Mbarara-Fort Portal highway, a wide tarmacked thoroughfare whose smooth black surface shimmered whitely like a mirage under the harsh glare of the sun on the last leg of her occidental journey. The murram and tarmac roads formed a T-junction where they connected and at the neck of that T, where the savanna was momentarily interrupted, they found gathered a throng of people, mostly men and youthful lads, around what appeared to be a freshly occurred motor accident. The late evening sun burned hot and dry as could be seen in the scorched black sweaty faces of the small crowd of rescuers who, each, held the implements — metal bars, oblong pieces of steel and, in one case a pick axe, which they had used to get to the two mutilated corpses entrapped in the mangled wreckage which lay smashed against and was greatly dwarfed by a heavy ochre-yellow, compactly built Komatsu tipper truck. Besides the sweat and dust, the place was blanketed in a strong mixture of the fumes of diesel, petrol and oil. The rescue crowds, oozing the various odours that went with the dried and drying sweat, had had to abandon a relentless quest for flying termites, a renown delicacy in these parts of the world, that had like manna cascaded out of the angry night skies with the torrential rains during the night. The insects had fluttered in their zillions of numerity all over the land, darkening it from horizon to horizon and by the early morning all had lost their flimsy slivery plumes and now scuttled and scurried away to hide their nakedness under all available nooks. The rescuers had hoped to save the lives of the two lifeless men now lain out on the roadside mindlessly; formlessly, like carcasses of strange marine creatures. The termite hunters had heard the revved up engine of the small white Peugeot car and heard the titanic thump, and even as they hurriedly made for the scene of that carnage they knew no human being could have survived such a frenetic smash.

The airline minibus from the airstrip had crawled to a stop and several of its passengers disembarked to take a sombre close look at the nasty scene.

Apollonia Kasangaire remained seated in her place with her forehead pressed to the perspex window glass, the large brown-pupilled eyes slowly and calmly moving all over the scene, taking in the hideous details of the accident. The eyes, with lower lids moulded in sacs like oblong black grapes shaped like half moons, were set wide apart from the shapely strong bridge of her nose in the broad, softly curved *kiraalo* features. The *kiraalo* or rather Hamitic features of appearance were not the sharp aquiline lineaments typical of those nomadic cattle keepers of the Great Lakes Region whose diet comprised entirely of milk and milk products until they came of age. The gentle curves of Kasangaire's face were rather more softly planed than sharp, and yet, more blunt than soft, with her nose and its well-shaped pair of lobes curving in very gently to form the nostrils. With her sumptuous mouth with upper lip ever slightly larger than the lower and the cleft between it and her nostrils widish, she presented a countenance of curvaceous albeit also sedate, aristocratic majesty rather than of beauty. Indeed you could not have called Apollonia Kasangaire beautiful in the real sense of that word, or pretty. It was her mouth, supple, well curved as described, Venusian indeed, darker than the rest of her bodily complexion, wettish at the corners, that even to the casual observer would have been inferred to as, in the almost rude aristocracy it portrayed in her — sensually intimidating. She was expressionless, unsmiling, sulked, and her body was devoid of cosmetic makeup. She was a dark skinned woman in her late twenties, or even perhaps her early thirties, with a complexion like glossy old-millet bread — that millet that has turned roast-coffee brown with storage and which when milled and turned into flour and made into a hot round mound of meal, tastes strong and sharp and has a sweet pungent aroma in the warmth of its steam. The skin was soft, delicate and close to fleshy. Her dress was made up of a plain silver grey frock and an egret-white veil covering her head, with curly strands of thick-grained soot-black hair that reached to just her ears at the sides and at the nape of her neck at the back. To take her for a Roman

Catholic nun would not have fetched the observer any reproof, considering her dress. She even appeared sedate enough for that pious calling. But, even in her chaste, aristocratic appearance, there would have been those — even perhaps among the seigneurs and Superiors of the cloisters, who would have regarded with bafflement Kasangaire's presence in the convent considering the range of options apparently open to such a woman out in the wider world owing to that blunt, intimidating sensuality. She stood out immediately as a stranger to the land and had the wan look of travel exhaustion in her general appearance.

Kasangaire had indeed traveled with Pan Am Air from Chicago to London via New York and made the Sabena-arranged Gatwick-Entebbe hop through Brussels in about twelve hours. The Fokker flight from Entebbe to Nyakisharara-Mbarara, though quite turbulent and uncomfortable, had passed unnoticed to her, as she had resigned herself to the seemingly unending journey, which, by all indications, appeared bent on ensuing forever. And even as she quietly observed the distressful scene of death, her mind was not set on the jetlag she was experiencing. She was instead thinking of the country she had come to. She was also noting that for a third time since her arrival in the country a radio station, this time on a tuner in their omnibus, was pumping out the movingly melodious song *Soley Soley*. She found it an infectious tune that lingered on in the mind.

There was nothing romantic about Apollonia Kasangaire's journey. She had come to Uganda prepared for the worst, having expected to see death in Idi Amin country, as there was never a shortage of reports on that in the international media. She had imagined smoking Russian AK 47s, bayonets and sledgehammers, which journalists and refugees had occasionally depicted vividly. A certain fear sprouted inside her tummy when she began to realise that even this motor accident could have been staged. That fear had spread throughout her body as she remembered the narratives of the native rescuers whose language she was not too familiar with but which she had a smattering knowledge of. Those narratives and her suspicions gave rise to the notion that the killer truck had no business sitting at that spot, so awkwardly positioned at such a short distance from the road junction.

The dead passengers were an older graying man, evidently Caucasoid, in a brown camelhair jacket and a black African man, much younger, who wore blue jeans and a dark blue T-shirt, with a white cotton sock — the thick sports type — clinging to the right foot. Someone was pointing at the *muzungu's* face. Most eyes followed the pointing, and it was being inferred that a pipe the elderly Caucasian had been smoking lay rammed deep down his throat. The woman at the window could see each person bend forward to peer and then recoil in shock at what he or she saw. The African's body was intact and, save for the indecent immobility that is associated with death and the thick dark blood that had oozed into the thick coarse hair matting it into a ghastly oily paste, one would have been inclined to attempt to arouse him from his apparent slumber with a shake of the shoulder.

As the passengers of the airline minibus re-embarked, Appollonia's eyes went instinctively to the white writings stenciled on the cab door of the truck: *Kyera Stone Quarry*, and below that in smaller lettering: *Franciscan Rural Project*. The words sent a tiny shockwave through her entire body. There was justifiable cause. The sister she had traveled thousands of miles to see belonged to the Franciscan Order, whose headquarters and main convent were situated at Kyera. She found herself, by reflex action, taking up the silver-chain and mother-of-pearl rosary in her lap and running her fingers through its beads, while vigorously reading a silent Miserere for Julian Dominicus Kantarama. In a fit of rebellion brought about by annoyance and disdain, which she had experienced on and off since receiving two bad letters in one go, she declined to attach the title 'Sister' to her sister's names.

When the minibus started off, and several people began discussing the gruesome accident in tones — sad, excited, and anxious — she felt a trifle relieved. From what she could grasp of the mixture of dialects, she gathered, that Ugandans were so accustomed to the misfortune of witnessing violent death that they almost felt comfortable with — or were rather resigned to — it. But all this she had already known from world opinion.

As the bus cruised into Mbarara town, Apollonia, unsuccessfully, attempted to expunge the scene of the motor accident and the two lifeless figures from her mind. *Soley Soley* brought it back — and would now always evoke it.

Though she had been born 32 years ago in neighbouring Rwanda some two hundred miles south of where they now were, Apollonia Kasangaire had never ventured into this land of termite-eaters. Consumption of these insects amounted to an abomination among her own people. Several of her very close relatives were exiled in this very same land. She had been told long ago that in one of their flights from Bahutu pursuers, her relatives, while carrying her with them, had gone through Uganda from the Congo to sojourn in Kenya when she was a toddler. She knew her own country of Rwanda, tiny as it was in comparison to her neighbours', to be a collection of enormous hills, much like the mounds in potato fields, which had led to its being dubbed *le pays des milles collines* — 'the country of one thousand hills.' But Uganda, indeed most of what she had seen of it from high up in the skies, was a different land, stretched out flat like an endless baize mat with softly undulating hills. Terrible things were said about its military leaders, but she had to concede that Uganda was an exceedingly beautiful country.

She pulled out and peered at the letters from Julian. She found the name of the woman who would lead her to her sister. The woman worked at the Agip Motel on Masaka Road. To get there she had to persuade the minibus driver to traverse the town after dropping off the other fifteen passengers at the main taxi park. Julian had insisted that Kasangaire not head straight to Kyera to meet Father Giuseppe Mazinio. The contact at the Agip Motel, a woman with the immaculate name of Virgo, was apparently supposed to buffer her landing. And so the minibus delivered her to the Agip Motel, at the northern foot of Mbarara hill, which formed the main entrance to the town from the Kampala highway. The motel consisted of a filling station set back fifty metres from the roadside and behind that the low-lying slate-roofed cottages which made up the rooming area, and a bungalow-type house containing a bar, restaurant and a lounge — all spacious, airy and finished by an Italian interior decorator in knotted pinewood. At the time the minibus with the woman from Chicago arrived, there was no activity at the motel. The pump attendants sat sleepily in the shade provided by the eaves of a small concrete building, which served as the lubricants store as well as tyre-changing room. There were not more than half a dozen people seated at the lawn tables beneath large, wide, yellow-and-black Agip umbrellas, sipping away at all sorts of beverages. A cool wind blew the large eucalyptus trees standing among the low buildings. White-breasted crows cackled hoarsely as they fought playfully against the whistling wind to maintain their talonhold on the crackling branches. Other birds ambled carefully, attentively, heads turning this way and that so that their sharp eyes could discern the fat plumeless white ants in the lawn grass and among the pebbles at the roadsides. And bird and man competed in this extensive hunt for the termites.

A lean, very pretty brown woman in her late forties materialised from the bar section of the motel and walked hurriedly towards the minibus, the wind tugging fiercely at the flowing dress she wore. At first the visitor from America could not grasp what the hurrying elderly lady was saying as she approached the vehicle, consternation evident in her countenance. In spite of the fact that she had braced herself for the worst, another wave of uncertainty scythed through Kasangaire's insides, just the way it had at the scene of the accident when she had read the legend on the cabin door of that truck. But what it could be this time she had no means of telling. She appreciated she had come to deadly Uganda under clearly dubious circumstances, to assist in battling the crisis that faced the Catholic Church in the region. Dubious in that the church had sent her as a decoy in a scheme so subtle it might bewilder the sapient pontiff in Rome if he were to learn of it. But the pope's Pro Nuncio in Kampala had given it the go-ahead and that was what mattered. The crisis had to be averted, nipped in the bud before, like the hydra, it could replicate into a multitude of more dangerous monsters that threatened the foundations of the faith, particularly on this continent which, to Roman Christendom's wonderment, was now providing the church with hitherto unknown, unheard-of martyrs and saints of strange, not easily pronounceable names. *Kiganda* names like Karoli-Lwanga, Bazzekuketta, Gonza, Mawaggali, Kizito, Buuzabalyaawo, Muzeyi — and several others — were now full-fledged Christian faith appellations. Uganda was indeed Catholic-martyr country. But alas, what a jumble of crises!

It had all begun with the letter from Father Giuseppe Carenzi Mazinio. His gentle voiced, calm, uncomplaining, statement of a sad fact and the need for help issued forth from the dried Indian ink on the letter's flimsy pages. When Apollonia showed it to the Most Reverend Archbishop Jack Chord of Chicago, the prelate produced his own from Giuseppe, assuring her, with a heavy pat on her shoulder, of the urgent necessity for her trip to Uganda. Why, it was Chord himself who had offered the quarter of a million dollars to the Kyera Diocese to be offered to the Muslim man if he should denounce his apparently iniquitous intentions. Later there arrived Julian's own missive, thrice the length of the priest's, rambling, emotional, and full of complaints. It begged for humano-matriarchal understanding. As if Julian should not have known better than most!

Kasangaire had a chronology of crises to consider: the flight had exhausted her; the first sight to welcome her on land was a gruesome accident caused by a truck belonging to the faith; then she was told that the insects those rescuers were hunting for — small, dark-brown-backed, cream-breasted termites, fat as pigs — were food for human consumption! And now this agitated woman, apparently a Munyarwanda like herself, with tearful eyes fixed on her!

The woman was dressed in a brightly flowered yellow-and-purple maxi dress, one of those garments that covered the ankles and feet, which had been created after dictator *Field Marshal* Idi Amin Dada banned the wearing of mini-skirts and tight dresses. And she had on a pair of bright-red high-heeled shoes. Kasangaire could now hear the woman's voice and could tell she was speaking in Kinyarwanda, her own native tongue too, lamenting over a loss of sorts that she had suffered.

"*Ayi weh*, Kantarama!" she lamented. "*Ayi weh, mwana wa mama! Barapfuye bose. Barapfuye dii, mwene watchu! Duzakoriki Kantarama-weh, mwana wa'mawe?*"

The mournful laments of bereavement were directed at her. At first Kasangaire was dumbfounded as to how to confront this fresh crisis, before she realised with added shock that she was being addressed as the "Kantarama" of those lamentations. But how could that possibly be? At Kasangaire's reaction, which must have registered in her face and eyes, the elderly woman wailed even more and continued to mourn in her Ugandan Kinyarwanda, which Kasangaire could distinguish with sadness from the Rwandan Kinyarwanda — a beautiful language weakened, albeit lightly, by years of refuge in other lands: "They are dead, both of them," the mourner continued to lament, tugging at her hair and garments, her feet stamping the rain-washed tarmac of the motel parking lot in anguish. "They have died, oh, Mother of God! What will you do now, Kantarama, my mother's child? Why should this happen to you, *mwana wa'mama*? What is going to happen to you, Kantarama, child of my people? Why must the gods…? But — oh, Gracious Mary Mother of God!" The sworn words came abruptly, slow and spaced. "*You* are not... *you* are..." she clapped a hand to her open mouth quickly, as if to prevent more utterances flowing out, the fading pupils of her brown eyes rounding like perfect saucers.

"Oh, my Lord Jesus Christ!" Kasangaire started, jumping out of the minibus when she momentarily thought the old lady might faint. But, without knowing why, she stood back, with her back pressed to the body of the vehicle.

"Oh, Mother of God," interjected the lamenter. "So you are the *one*! So you have come! I did wonder — I was stunned that you could venture out here after all the furore. But – gracious Jesus! — you are the sister!"

"Yes, *I* am," Kasangaire nodded, still unable to move forward. "Tell me what is going on."

"Mother of God!" the elderly woman had not fully recovered from her astonishment. "What a striking resemblance! But this is terrible. They are dead — both of them. What will... oh, my God! I am sorry I am such a nitwit."

"Just which *both of them* are you talking about, my dear sister?" Kasangaire asked, showing her the letter Julian had written her. "Are you this Virgo Kabibi, also called Virigo?"

The woman's eyes still studied Kasangaire with unconcealed curiosity. She said: "You must have come from Nyakisharara Airstrip. Didn't you encounter the accident? People from that end have witnessed it."

"Yes. We *did* encounter a motor accident."

"You saw the accident?" She asked with added anxiety, as if she had wished for a negative answer from Kasangaire. "Oh Mother of Christ! You don't know who they are! But of course, how would you? That is — *was* Father Giuseppe and the other — oh, blessed Mary…!"

"So that is the fellow!" Kasangaire gasped. " That is…. Was…. Oh, Mary Mother of Jesus!"

"That *was* he. Father Giuseppe mentioned to me he would do it. And I thought he was teasing me as usual!"

"Father Giuseppe told you he would *what*?" Kasangaire inquired, tensely.

"That he would kill the — 'son of a bitch'; that white car you saw was the priest's. He was driving it when they left this place..." She paused to glance at a small wristwatch. "Fifty minutes ago."

"I don't understand," lamented the woman from Chicago. "You are intimating they were riding in the same car!" There was a trace of deploring disbelief in her voice. And then her mind cleared, in slow, shocked realisation. It went back to the wrongly placed Franciscan Order tipper truck. 'Jesus! An arranged accident! Arranged by — Jesus'! — She wondered silently in anxious realisation and aloud, said "Where is Kantarama?" — in sudden, urgent panic.

There was a doubtful look in the older woman's brown eyes. Then she muttered: "You want... to see her? Okay, of course... I'll take you to her. You can be certain she is safe. I'll send for a taxi at once."

At the mention of 'taxi', Kasangaire looked around to notice for the first time that the airline minibus had long left. Her panic vanished when she noted, too, that the driver had been kind enough to remove her brown leather suitcase which he had placed a couple of metres away on the motel's terrace.

Presently, the now recovered Virgo Kabibi beckoned to a motel casual labourer to whom she gave instructions to fetch a special hire taxi. Then she turned to Kasangaire and asked: "Your name is Kasangaire — Apollonia, I should believe? Kantarama has talked of you a lot. Your childhoods back home. She never told me you were twins. You're so identical — like newly minted shilling coins. And even the voice. But you have a distinct accent; your Kinyarwanda is Rwandan. That is the only feature that gives you away. Oh, how I wish Ssempa had seen you! He wasn't a bad man, you know."

"Where is Kantarama? It's her I came to see. The letter says to see you first."

Kabibi was quick to note the younger woman's apparent annoyance at her talking well of the dead man.

"Ah, Kantarama," remarked Kabibi, guardedly. "Poor, lonely soul. She had hinted you might refuse to see her."

"I shouldn't be seeing her," returned Kasangaire, a fire flitting across the eyes she had opened a trifle wider with those clipped words. "There is something evidently wrong with this land here. It has warped your lot. How can you dare to say you wished that Lucifer, Ssempa, had seen me and that he wasn't such a bad man? What has he done to my sister, to my family? .... To the faith? Are you happy, gloating over their actions?"

9

"He wasn't a bad man," Virgo Kabibi repeated, simply, stating her own personal conviction most casually. She had a unique simplicity of uttering hard things. "It was never entirely his fault either. He was manipulated — by people... by events. And he resisted them resolutely. That is why he is dead, of course. And to think that I have known him since he was a toddler!" Kabibi choked over those words, and she began to weep. Then she said: "You must think that I am too talkative," she sniffed. "And a fool too." She dabbed at her cheeks and eyes with a large cotton handkerchief, an action she performed with both eyes open even when she touched their whites. "I know I talk irresponsibly when agitated."

Kantarama had expressed so much about 'the man' in her letters to Chicago. Those missives were suffused with the attitude that the Mohammedan was a misunderstood *angel* of sorts. Somehow, Kasangaire felt consoled that she would always have an abstract image of 'him.' Her mind would always lift the denim-clad corpse from off the dusty hot tarmac, stand it upright and give it movement and words. Her preconceived picture of him had been different from that of the dead face with blood-matted hair and form in the blue jeans and T-shirt. She had visualised an Adonis — a tall heartthrob in designer suits; someone not too black, not too brown; someone tall, wide-shouldered with eyes that killed feminine hearts, and the suppressed thunder of a baritone voice that commanded feminine acceptance of his will. She would have felt overwhelmingly ill-at-ease having one day to face that kind of disarming Lucifer of a man as a sort of brother-in-law after all the damage he had wreaked. A Muslim that had the charm that not only made him attractive to and well spoken of by good, elderly Catholic ladies, but also got him into the marble hearts of perpetually avowed brides of Christ! She felt relieved she would never have to sympathise with Julian; to feel that perhaps that once holy, marble-hearted sister of hers had had a justification of some sort, say beauty in a human man, to break her sacerdotal vows. And Father Giuseppe, though he never termed the Muslim a Satan, had asserted that the man David Ssempa, good-natured though he was, was also a sly manipulator.

Her mind travelled back to Illinois, to the See of Archbishop Chord. She had had her own letters from her sister and the Italian priest, and she was not surprised when the great American Catholic church leader showed her the ones from the Italian padre in Uganda, and the very long one from Bishop William Kabigumira of Kyera. And the prelate had picked up the golden-yellow telephone and dialed the Kyera number. Even though he had switched on the scrambler he still advised her — an idea given him by William — to use Latin and Kinyarwanda but no English. The essence of the telephone conversation was most singular: to protect and save the image of the Catholic

Church in Africa — more especially in Idi Amin's Uganda, that land of heroic Catholic martyrs. Bishop William Kabigumira had outlined an ingenious, nay dubious, arrangement whereby if no other means became available or viable — and all manner of strategies were being sought and laid around the clock for better means — she, Apollonia Kasangaire, would have to take over Sister Julian Dominicus' position as the latter's understudy at Kyera convent. It was crucially essential for the church to prove to that country and region that she, Apollonia Kasangaire, was the true — indeed even truer — one and only Sister Julian Dominicus in existence, who had never ventured outside the convent at Kyera, which proof would strengthen the faith of those, even if they may be few, in whom it was greatly likely to disintegrate owing to the scandal that was already unfolding in Mbarara; the highly publicised marriage of Sister Julian to a Muslim man in a mosque. In one of Father Giuseppe Mazinio's letters he had written thus: 'The Mohammedan wants to cooperate with me. His reasons for that might be more outlandish than if he had utterly remained on the opposing side — especially if I were to read him wrongly. And my reading of him is in itself a circumstance only *I myself* appreciate. Africans rabidly hate and distrust their fellow Africans of the different religious denominations. Those Catholics that I have associated with over the past three decades in this country today doubt my intentions just seeing me confer amiably with Mr Ssempa. I still wish he were as bad as the rest of his own pack. That would make it easier — show everybody where they stood in this crisis. But alas, I have found it easy to discern an innocence of sorts in the Muslim man. I am only human and Ssempa could have been anybody's son... any Catholic man's son. He is not, unfortunately, and he ridicules us. It is important to keep that other alternative in mind and on the ready. We have made our own preparations here — quite drastic preparations inside the Muslim fellow's manour. Get Apollonia to remain prepared for — and she had better orientate herself to the possibility of having to come to Kyera in the person of Julian Dominicus. The point here is to have you point to her what *that* may entail; I mean what it would entail if she were to come here as a *replacement*.'

Long after the talk with Chord and the others, she had found out what going to Kyera as Sister Julian Dominicus actually meant. The thought of it! The sheer implication and significance of the scheme! It boggled her mind most mortifyingly.

In simple terms it meant there had to be only one Sister Julian Dominicus at Kyera, in the diocese, in the entire region, in the whole wide church; ultimately in all existence. The other Sister Julian Dominicus, the more genuine one; should never be permitted to surface to rescind that situation. And someone had to see to that: '*we have made our own drastic preparations — inside the*

Muslim fellow's manor'! The prospect was frightening. But the most crucial objective of the scheme, as Bishop William Kabigumira had told her on the phone in that Latin and Kinyarwanda expostulation meant to confuse would-be State Research Bureau eavesdroppers in the overseas telephone network, was to put to shame any side; any quarter suggesting that Sister Julian Dominicus was publicly wedding a Muslim man in a mosque, of all disgraces. It was very easy to prove in any event that she, Apollonia Kasangaire, was the genuine Sister Julian Dominicus if it ever came to serious contention; and more especially when there was to be no other *living* Sister Julian Dominicus to come up to cast doubts.

'Now the noxious Lucifer is dead,' she sighed inwardly, filled with profound satisfaction. 'And most of the crisis is over.'

With floods of relief filling her where fear and uncertainty had so recently and relentlessly lurked and wreaked havoc, she sat down at a terrace table, where the black-and-yellow umbrellas had been folded up, most of her tiredness gone, the jetlag also bygone. She let out another sigh — this one out of contentment — and turned to the older woman, who had just sat down herself. She said, almost sweetly: "But Kabibi, you yourself have to be a Catholic, and yet you talk so well of that dead man."

There was a triumphant sneering tone in Kasangaire's voice that Kabibi resented. Apollonia had said, 'dead man,' but her attitude suggested 'dead punk.' How could this woman be so callous? — Kabibi rued. How could she be so unfeeling with regard to her obvious bereavement? But conversely, what did she, a total alien to this land, know about Ssempa? *Nothing.* She could afford to express her apathetic, unuttered opinions.

She addressed the younger woman: "Because unlike you, my dear Kasangaire, Kantarama and I are refugees. Where we are, where we live and have lived for ages you can't afford the luxuriant enjoyment of that unholy, near-apartheid sectarianism. Did you ever realise that the name Ssempa wasn't even a Kinyarwanda name in the first place so that you could first blame your sister for cohorting with a foreigner before she would a Muslim? How many Baganda, tell me the truth my sister, had you met before Gregoire Kayibanda chased us out of our country? None, I must presume. Who did you think we lived with after Rwanda, my dear? Who do you think sheltered us in our most desperate hours of need and want? What if I told you it were Muslims, Protestants, and heathens — all types? Oh — and I have my opinions about my own Catholic church back home. I have personal recollections of stories told. We all heard stories of priests and superiors general not only grooming Gregoire Kayibanda to take over power, but actually encouraging the pogroms that followed that coup d'etat of a political election. Kasangaire, I have seen my people turn into things — turn into tribes and religions that they would never have dreamt of becoming or ever cherished to be if it had not been for this thing called *exile*. Do you hear me? A people changing their tribe the way others did their clothing and getting jeered at and ridiculed for it. I have witnessed the worst loss of pride that can befall a people. Imagine. Just imagine living among a people who — because you are a refugee and you need to stay alive, to survive and not die mentally — heartily believe you enjoy being called them...!" She broke down and started to sob. "The insults," her voice had turned thin and high-pitched, the words barely decipherable. "The insults are never in short supply. You would think they would grow less with the passage of time; that they would forget about you! But no! We were called 'over-eating refugees,' and said to be the ungrateful camel from the sandstorm that was bent on taking over the tent from its rightful owner. Those taunts, Kasangaire, are casual; when the indigenes are at ease. It is unbearable when some misunderstanding triggers it. What do you want us to do? What *did* you want us to do? Did you want us to stay behind and live in that shame like you?"

This last one did cut deep like a surgeon's scalpel into the body and soul and was meant to hold Kasangaire back from coming round the table to comfort the older woman, which she had been wanting to do. Kabibi's harangue had touched her where it hurt and revolted her very deeply. Did they, these exiles in Uganda, think that it was a bed of roses for those who had stayed in or returned to Rwanda? Or that she, Kasangaire had not tasted the ravages of being a refugee? What naivety in ignorance! 'Yes. She speaks out of ignorance. She speaks like that because she has never returned to the terrible country to see for herself how Batutsi are mistreated.'

"Unlike you, perhaps," she was able to say after a heavy interval of silence. "We live in the very eye of the storm of hatred and resentment, Kabibi. Whoever thought it was a life of ease and comfort out there can never know what true suffering is. You might be happier here. I've seen my fellow countrymen in America live as though they had never suffered or as if they had no living brethren back home, let alone a home. But that is just their outward body that I have witnessed often. And I know it to be part and parcel of the suffering. The inner soul agonises, Kabibi. Dies! You do see it in the best adorned, in the lives of those at recreation even. They are jolly on the surface, which is all. And it is even worse at home, in Rwanda. You must know it, *weh 'sheh*, that in Rwanda we are not allowed to progress or prosper in several professional fields and sectors of life. In the formal schools we are banned from studying beyond certain essential levels. We cannot be allowed employment in government or parastatal jobs. The few foreign firms and organisations that employ Batutsi — those mainly run by Europeans, North Africans and Middle Easterners — are ostracised when they become nice to us. Big government and Mouvement Rwandais National Démocratique ruling-party officials prey upon our sisters and top business people use them as breeding mares for producing better-quality humans and yet even those offspring are constantly reminded, in evil tones, that they are Batutsi. They call us descendants of a people who broke away from Biblical Moses' hard trek in search of Canaan to find the truer land of milk and honey that they sought at the source of the river that had served Egypt's and Palestine's survival needs for ages. They have called us direct children of Noah through his elder son, Ham, from whom we get that accursed tag, *Hamite*. They say we belong to Egypt, Ethiopia and The Sudan but not here. A Hamitic woman, they say, is only good in bed. Yes, they say so quite often. They hate Hamite and covet Hamite! Those same MRND party officials, like their progenitors of the Mouvement Démocratique Rwandais, dread to be seen publicly or known to consort with those same Hamite sisters of ours that they ravish perpetually. Do you imagine that? They call us Jews! Every big government official, including the president of the country, has a Hamite Mututsi consort tucked away in a mansion somewhere, hidden away from the eyes of those they tell to resent Hamitic people and never to cohabit with them. I tell you no lies, my sister, Kabibi. I haven't looked at your Ugandan identity papers, but on my Rwandan passport and all other essential Rwandan travel and public administrative documents it is spelled out clearly there: 'Apollonia Kasangaire — *Tutsi*.' It is like saying: Apollonia Kasangaire — *Felon*! My uncles, my mother, everyone, are denoted thus so that it becomes easier for you to be hated and shunned and ridiculed and heckled and harassed and insulted by — and at every level of — rural and urban protocol. In neighbouring Burundi, our brethren Hamite Batutsi do the same to the Bahutu there. You only see the mediocrity of it when you have lived in such a vast land as America. Yet even there you find a worse racial and cultural segregation! It is a bloody vicious circle, my sister, Kabibi, from which several felons benefit greatly and yet several others — you and I for example — suffer. And, mark you, it's not true that I don't know what it is to be a refugee, for I have been one myself. I was old enough when in fifty-nine and sixty-one it happened. I know as a result that nothing can be equated to the harshness of belonging to an endless human column of wretched people facing a neighbour, a colleague and an erstwhile playmate suddenly turned animal on one hand and an uncertain bleak destination on the other. Men and women that were once your jocular, smiling kin turn into Neanderthal creatures with all manner of weaponry — machetes, spears, ropes, sharpened objects and burning torches, threatening to destroy the very ground over which you fled to escape death, perhaps hating that ground because of the opportunity for escape that it offered you. They hated it for the escape that is offered you. They hated the ground that cheated them of your blood. And Kabibi! — That ground! — Oh, that ground...!"

"Stop," begged the older woman in a choked voice. "Please, do stop."

"That ground, Kabibi" Kasangaire might not have heard the older woman's desperate interjection. "That ground offered so much. It offered passage and escape from *kajugujugu* — those helicopters that belched thunder and flame over us. And yet, in the majority of cases, that ground opened up to offer eternal, albeit unchosen bliss, saving many from the uglinesses of fellow man. Yes, truly, I know how you feel, Kabibi, and I feel with you. But back there where you call home I have a mother who, like a habitual drunkard's hen, is never sure when the intoxicated brute of an owner may peep into the coop behind a sharpened knife. For to a Mututsi, dear sister, your beautiful Rwanda is a closed coop, a tightly closed cage."

She fell silent for several moments, during which both wept and sniffed, sneezing into handkerchiefs, their silence constantly punctuated by the frequent motor vehicles zooming on the highway and the detached free laughter of the pump attendants and mechanics, some of whom were busy eating living termites bought from the crowds that hunted for the insects.

Then Kabibi said: "Forgive me for my anger and for causing you tears. I have lost so much in life I know there is nothing in it for me any more. How I sometimes wish I were dead!"

"Don't talk like that," the other castigated her. "There is a great deal to live for. I always say all our people will one day return home whatever impediments those people in the Cinq Juillet put in their way."

"What is the Cinq Juillet?"

"Oh — an hotel. A swanky place near the city centre named after the date in seventy-three when Habyarimana ousted Kayibanda from power. It is the place they sit to decide on how to hate us even better, for hatred is the most important word in Hutu-Tutsi Rwanda."

"Well, you have the privilege to hope for that *great deal* to live for since at thirty-two, the probable age of Kantarama, you are young. At my own age there is nothing worth the effort of returning to Rwanda."

The name of Kantarama seemed to galvanise the woman from Chicago into wakefulness. She spoke with sudden fierceness and impatience: "I want to know where Kantarama is. Your Muslim is, in what was God's just decision, dead. Like a true Satan it is he that has brought us these tears. We are quarrelling over *him*. My mission has been eased so greatly by his demise, thank Maria the Virgin."

"I was attached to him," Kabibi asserted, as if to herself. "I watched him grow from a toddler into a man. I grew up in their home. My being a

Munyarwanda, a Catholic, a refugee and hopelessly helpless, and their being Baganda and Muslims of certain affluence did not matter or interfere with my life at all. I was never treated as an intruder and outsider. The family youth called me *Baaba*," she said that with the soft 'b' used by most Bantu-language speakers, without bringing the lips together. "*Baaba* means big sister, you see. Visitors were never made to realise I wasn't one of the Ssemagandas. And that is the kind of people I lived amongst during the first year after my arrival in this land. His father had five wives.... Ah, that is nothing," she added hastily when she saw the consternation on Kasangaire's face. "His grandfather, Abduwahid Zzinda, had had forty-eight wives. One of Ssempa's stepmothers had been a Munyarwanda Catholic, and a close relative of mine. You see when we arrived in southwestern Uganda in that hour of need, like Abraham and Saraai in Egypt, our parents were willing to give away their graceful daughters, and in some cases their own wives, for favours from the citizens. That was after the Banyankore had rejected our livestock, most of which, strangely, died on crossing the borders. But the daughter-wife-for-amenities barter system found snags. For some reason or other the Banyankore, a people with a strong xenophobia, dislike Banyarwanda to the extent that they refused to take refugee girls for wives or even for casual labour. I have been told they couldn't offer our people labour because they themselves laboured for the Baganda, their better-off neighbours to the north, but that does not rid me of my resentment of them for their mistreatment of us. You might also have heard that our people of old once castrated several of their warriors and leaders after burning to ashes the only symbol of legitimacy for a monarch to Nkore's throne — the six-century old drum, Bagyendanwa. Indeed between 1895 and the beginning of the twentieth century, tales of Banyankore's sad plight at the hands of the Banyarwanda were rife. This was the time when the angry threat or belligerent retort *urikashaahurwe*, which means 'may you suffer the fate of castration,' was coined."

* * *

Abduwahid Zzinda, Ssempa's grandfather, had come to southwestern Uganda accidentally. At the turn of the nineteenth century, the king of Nkore, Omugabe Ntare V Rugingiiza, knew he was dying. He was a most unhappy monarch. The commander of his army – who was also his first cousin, the prince Daniel Ruhwabwooba Igumira – had made successful incursions deep into Rwanda and captured thousands of longhorn cattle to restock Nkore Kingdom's own dwindled herds which had been decimated in a rinderpest pandemic. In a fateful action that would change Nkore's history forever, Igumira did an unforgivable thing – in the eyes of the Banyarwanda. Among the beautiful horde of Batutsi

16

and Bahutu women he captured as war booty from the hilly dominion was the very queen of the throne of Rwanda, wife to Umwami Kigeri Rwabugiri. It is a well-known fact that Rwanda has always had a customary policy of installing its kings either as warrior monarchs or peaceful ones, depending on the needs and moods of the times. Customarily, an *umwami* symbolically titled Mutara is a peaceful king, reigning to make peace with the kingdom's neighbours and to embark on making repairs to past or erstwhile political and economic damage. Mutara could by policy only, and most reluctantly, wage a defensive war — especially in case of a devastating invasion of Rwandan territory. On the other hand, to be awarded the title Kigeri was to me mandated — nay urged most emphatically — to wage wars crucially necessary to bolster the livestock and labour requirements of the kingdom. A Kigeri was a martial king, period. All Rwanda's neighbours, who were expected to know of that protocol, knew too when not to tamper with that small mountainous realm. They knew a Mutara could be invaded and ransacked with considerable ease – with perhaps only the consequence of a war to eject the invader from that territory's well-defined boundaries.

It has been suggested that the Banyoro seers and diviners who were at the time in the employ of Ntare of Nkore, might have advised the king badly with ulterior motives and malicious intentions. The kingdom of Bunyoro was a mighty power in those days and had as its chief enemies the monarchs of Buganda and Nkore, against whom it made regular and occasional wars. Moreover, just a few years ago, Bunyoro herself had invaded Rwanda and the king himself, Omukama Cwamali, leading the incursion. The Banyarwanda, as expected, routed the invader and slew Cwamali. On their return to their far-off kingdom sprawling against the snow-capped Rwenzori mountains to the southwest, the great Lake Muttanzige or Albert, to the west and the Albert Nile to the north, Cwamali's surviving warriors lied to the bereaved Bunyoro court that their brave king had defied their solemn pleas to return to his kingdom because a bunch of lovely Banyarwanda women had enchanted him with their enthralling beauty and elegance, thus preventing the king from returning home. Said their surviving commander: 'We left Rukirabasaija Cwamali ensconced among some of the most beautiful women your eyes have ever settled upon. It was hard enough even for us, to pull our eyes away to return to Bunyoro! Their melodious voices besought us to stay and be brought unto their boudoirs, but Omukama Cwamali, love-struck and all that, urged us to return to the kingdom to inform you to replace him with your choice of another. It was neither easy for him, nor for us, such a terrible decision.'

'My brother,' declared one of the more powerful princesses to the Bunyoro throne, 'does not speak the Kinyarwanda language. In what tongue, pray tell me, did this horde of heavenly beauties you talk of converse with Cwamali? As you all know I lived in that land for elephant-years and it was never possible for them to differentiate me from their own people! And I know their language to be indecipherable to the ears of our people.'

'Behold, your royal greatness, Princess Ikumbyanjojo,' the survivor commander laboured to explain. 'The women we tell you of seemed to have such divine power everything they told Cwamali, Cwamali understood well. As he commanded us to leave him where he sat in splendour, Rukirabasaija Cwamali spoke in a strange tongue with tones and connotations similar to those of those Banyarwanda women, and we were left in wonder ourselves!'

'You,' concluded the powerful, aged princess, 'are stating for all to hear that the Banyarwanda had divine powers that prevailed over those of Bunyoro! You are lying, of course. Away with you, felons; away to the sharp axe each and every warrior that left this place with the king.' The princess Ikumbyanjojo then turned to the palace guard. 'Off with the idiots' heads this very moment.'

All the survivors of the Bunyoro incursion into Rwanda were beheaded and Cwamali's eldest son was made king.

And now, after Prince Igumira's successful foray into Rwanda that had been carried out with advice from Banyoro diviners, Igumira had intrepidly brought to the court of Ntare Rugingiiza the favourite wife of Kigeri Rwabugiri.

Back in Rwanda the king, Kigeri Rwabugiri, trooped all the kingdom's warriors before him to one side. He placed a sizeable basket before him and ordered a march-past. Every single warrior that passed before him to assemble on the other side was required to drop just one seed of sorghum into that basket. Not until the basket overflowed with sorghum was Umwami Kigeri Rwabugiri satisfied that he had mobilised enough power to carry out his mission in Nkore. These troops he immediately unleashed on the plains to the north of his realm with orders to rescue his queen, return as many cows as possible and ultimately kill or capture — no less — the monarch that had slighted him so callously. He himself commanded a huge regiment of the army. The Banyankore had never seen or imagined such numbers of invading troops, *imigogo*, or such ferocity as was put into Rwabugiri's invasion. In the short run Nkore was more or less annexed, and for a good nine months Rwandan search squads moved all over the land, up to the borders of Buganda along the Katonga River, and up to the frontiers of Bunyoro and Karagwe in Rumanyika's land, where they sought to capture or kill Ntare Rungingiiza. And in the process the Banyarwanda soldiers, the *intumwa*, occupied and settled all land they deemed to be Nkore. They renamed places with names more familiar to them — Ruhengeri, Rwanda Urwera, Ntutsi, Lweera — names that stick to this day.

Ntare was eventually captured at Nyakakoni, not far away from present-day Mbarara, and, along with most of the kingdom's regalia, was dragged all the way to Kabeezi and on to the hills of Urukomo, where he was conducted before Kigeri Rwabugiri. The Rwandan king is said to have exhibited no anger when he called for *abashaahuzi*, those experts in the art of livestock castration, and ordered the removal of the balls of all the king's men as Ntare looked on! In addition — and in what would prove the bigger, unforgivable injury — Rwabugiri called for the best matchstick-dry faggots to be brought and, as Ntare looked on, the Nkore kingdom's regalia — including the chief item that legitimised a Nkore monarch, the royal drum Bagyendanwa – were burned to a cinder. It is said that even to the bewilderment of Rwabugiri himself, the drum Bagyendanwa hollered in a human voice filled with agony as the fierce fire licked at its ancient hide and wood. Ntare was then allowed to return home to Nkore, a devastated man.

Of course the affair of the royal drum and the mass castrations was hushed up most effectively, though significant and unusual things happened immediately in the aftermath of Ntare's return to Kaamushooko and later to Kaihangaara. Even as the best medicine men — Banyoro medicine men, treated the arcane wounds of Banyankore warriors, Nkore's top princes and their relatives fled the kingdom en masse. They were obviously appalled at the effective death of the kingdom with the destruction of the most guarded drum in that world. Ntare himself soon after suffered from a bout of pneumonia and, believing he might die soon, sent word to his powerful northern neighbour, the king of Buganda, Kabaka Mukaabya Muteesa, lamenting his woes: 'I am dying intestate. I die without heirs from my own gonads — a predicament the Banyarwanda have worsened for me. Nkore is going to spill rivers of blood in the people's search for a successor to me, now that top Bahinda princes have abandoned the kingdom in its blackest hour. I myself want my first cousin's son, Igumira's first-born boy Kahaya, to take the throne on my death. But Nkore's aristocracy, especially my cousin Kahitsi, are annoyed with my cousin Igumira and myself for bringing upon the kingdom the devastating ire of the king of Rwanda. They accuse us of the death of my kingdom. They also hate Kahaya for being the offspring of a Muhororo mother related to the Banyarwanda. I invaded the Banyarwanda because rinderpest had decimated my kingdom's herds. Now the Banyarwanda have taken over my land and are refusing to vacate it. I need your help. Banyarwanda are no match for Baganda, so send me troops to get rid of them. Haven't we always cooperated in all matters? I send you one hundred *ntsimbos* of the best mature ghee from my kingdom, ten pelts of male lion and ten of female, ten pelts of dark-night leopard and ten of moon, and two hundred elephant tusks from the stock presented to me in tax by the Banyabuhweju of Nsiika. I send you whole pieces only.' And he added: 'And tell Muteesa that I am dying. Tell him that is from my mouth — he will never hear of me alive again. Assure him that if I die and Nkore's remaining princes die off fighting each other over this empty throne, he will have no good neighbour south of his kingdom. He will be the direct neighbour of Banyarwanda, Barundi and the unruly people of Nyabyingi. He will be neighbours with Bahaya and Banyambo who harbour hostile *bazungu* tribes with pipes that make thunder, whose skins are like raw meat and whose eyes are like fireflies, who are not very good to look upon.'

Ntare then sent Kazini Akagina and Kanyabuzaana, who were regular travelers to Karagwe, to contract the best drum-makers there to proceed to Katete, where, at the palace in which he would soon die, a good replica of the royal drum Bagyendanwa, complete with the legendary scar – inflicted on Bagyendanwa by a Munyoro warrior who very nearly captured it several decades previously – was created. But many were aware of the forgery, closely kept as that secret was.

Soon after the messenger had left for Buganda, Ntare died, triggering another uncustomary event, to wit the mass suicide of the remaining princes, princesses, valets, consorts and aides. The entire king's harem — seven wives in all — without exception, hanged themselves or slit their bellies with sharp daggers. One wife, a close relative of Kahaya k'Igumira, who would soon be king, attempted to escape the suicide epidemic; but she was tracked like a wild animal and captured at the Kooga river crossing and helped to die. The last Nkore monarch to possess Bagyendanwa was dead! Igumira became a desperately disillusioned man. He ceaselessly blamed himself for the ill-advised invasion of Rwanda, for those bloody cows and the Banyarwanda's blasted women – an invasion which had claimed his eye even.

* * *

"And that," said Kabibi, pensively, "has been the main source of endless irreconcilable acrimony on the part of the Banyankore towards Banyarwanda. The Baganda Ntare sent for at that time, by the way, included Ssempa's grandfather, Abduwahid Zzinda, who arrived here with other troops in 1897 and went on to rid Nkore of the Banyarwanda *intumwa*. But why won't a people forgive or at least forget – some of the quirks of history? In any case, Baganda and Arab families offered their homes to our people, marrying them and offering them labour. Zzinda's son, Ssemaganda, already had my aunt with whom he had a child, as Wife Number Four. They took me on as one of the housemaids. Ssemaganda's brothers and cousins took on my other relatives severally with an enthusiasm akin to conquest. Several of our male relatives looked after the Ssemaganda cattle. And a dozen years later – when Idi Amin took power and gave them *mafuta mingi* businesses — shops, hotels and garages confiscated from expelled Indians, Ssempa's old man brought me to this town to help run an auto spares shop. David Ssempa and the brethren were still in junior school and I could count numbers and write figures, so I came in handy. Old Ssemaganda — currently in his late eighties — treated me as his own daughter. Do you not see now why I cannot blindly bias myself against a gentleman I knew so mutually, in favour of you or the church, for being ethnically or religiously related to you? Must I tell a lie to myself to please God and the Virgin Mary?"

"No, you needn't do so, of course. But Kabibi, Julian is a perpetually professed virgin bride. She cannot have committed this unutterable iniquity under normal circumstances. Baganda, like our own people, are renowned for a strong *ibiteega* voodoo culture. Is that what could have happened? Could your Ssempa have passed a lust-potion to my sister? You tell me since you seem to have known the fellow so well."

"I have shown you his neutral background. And it was that neutrality, I am sure, that could not have allowed Kantarama to realise his religion for all the time they were together, which is close to one year. He never revealed it to her quickly enough because he couldn't have considered the idea of what he always termed foreign faiths as important or necessary. He couldn't see the difference between her and himself because of what he always called trivialities of Middle-Eastern and European religions. I want you to imagine that the man Ssempa did not have the faintest leanings to any of the organised religions. He was also detribalised and quite utterly apolitical; a true rarity if any ever existed. And though I know what caused their entire problem quite well, Ssempa's free lifestyle is chiefly responsible for captivating Kantarama in the long run. For captivated she was. As for voodoo — yes, Ssempa held those local *Kabona* and *Ssenkulu* seers in very high esteem. He went to them before all his missions in the coffee smuggling rackets. He went to them — I want you to reflect carefully on this — even to bless his yearly pilgrimages to Mecca. I myself do know they did work miracles for him, or else he would have lost his life long ago like many of his fellow racketeers. I am also sure Kantarama does *not* know of that side of her deceased lover. Ssempa revealed himself to her gradually with great delicacy."

Kasangaire was staring at her face with a mixture of sadness and awe. Did Kabibi mean the dead Ssempa captivated Julian because she felt safer with a free, de-religionised person than with a fellow Catholic? She left that question to herself – unasked. She was already overly amazed by this woman's attached attitude towards the dead Muslim man and it frightened her so immensely that the prospect of returning to America without seeing her sister at all flickered across her mind persistently. 'How good', she mused, that Ssempa was dead since, obviously, Julian's own outlook on him must be worse than this woman's! Aloud she said: "I am yet to see Julian. My doubts are that I can stand her canonising a Muslim man with such a purely heathen side to him before my very eyes the way you are doing it. But go on, I am all ears."

Kabibi, whose countenance now exhibited impatience, kept looking up the road at the sound of every other car that came along, in anticipation of the taxi she had sent for. She had gotten up and started pacing the floor of the motel terrace, slowly but energetically. There was a deep urgent feeling in her heart that worked like the piston of a car engine, which pushed at her innards and at her limbs, propelling her whole being to Sister Julian Kantarama, whom she imagined seated on the off-white terrazzo steps of the house by the river. She suddenly wished, feverishly, that she could instantly, miraculously, reach the young woman six kilometres away in Kaburangire. And this overpowering urge forced her legs to move in small strides that she never consciously noticed. She then realised the awkwardness of her movements and, guiltily, sat down on the edge of one of the wooden seats but never ceased to shift uneasily before the morosely settled Kasangaire.

"Meanwhile, my dear Kabibi," said the latter, "you would do well to pull yourself together and relax. You are like a stretched rubber spring about to snap."

"Something is happening," Kabibi muttered, looking the other woman in the eye. "Something is quite wrong. I can feel it in me with clarity. Kantarama needs us right now. What in hell is happening to that goddamned taxi?"

"Don't swear, now. Pull yourself together. You were giving me the lowdown on your Muslim friend."

Kabibi threw a glance at her from the highway she had been watching steadily. She now appeared as though she might jump up and start to run off at the slightest provocation. She said, somewhat reducing the tension in her voice, "Yes. Perhaps if I tell you what happened here this afternoon, Kantarama — poor soul – might fill you in on her own part. I'll start with what happened this afternoon as we await the taxi. You see I have worked at this motel for two months, ever since Father Giuseppe threatened me with excommunication if I stayed on at Ssempa's garage where I had worked and lived for years. Giuseppe parked his car across the road over there. He said he didn't want the 'the son of a bitch' to miss it. Ssempa came an hour later, on foot. He said if he hadn't seen the car he might have cancelled the meeting. He had just turned thirty-six and at five-foot-eleven, was much taller than the Italian, was buffalo-dark and perhaps even buffalo hide-skinned, with a beefy, hardened face, healthy, big-boned and somewhat handsome — to women, especially those that sought granite in their men. He liked to dress casually for important occasions and almost shabbily — in jeans, T-shirts and dull-coloured short-sleeved cotton shirts — in daily life. He entered the motel and the two sat in that corner inside the restaurant and talked while the priest pulled at his much-cherished Bachiga pipe. The priest appeared haggard in his entire bearing, as if he had aged an extra score of years in the three months since Kyera had found out about Kantarama."

Kabibi paused and looking across the highway, pointed with a lean finger, "You see that horde of humanity milling around the roadside scrounging for termites? There is no single rotting piece of wood or other junk that they haven't shifted or turned over and over uncountable times in search of those insects. Ssempa said he was reminded of the biblical scriptures about doomsday: no stone would be left unturned. And Giuseppe taunted him in response that it was sinners of Ssempa's calibre that God would be hunting for on the Day of Reckoning. He went on to enquire whether Ssempa himself enjoyed eating what he called the ghastly grubs! I was seated with them, as had become my custom whenever there weren't many customers. Ssempa assured the Italian that he imagined termites to be a more palatable food than sea snails, which, he said, were slimy like snot or prawns that smelled like fart gas. And I remember at this juncture, word for word, Father Giuseppe's response: 'Eh, *bene*. Very good,' he had ejaculated in a sort of triumph in his hoarse smoker's voice. 'That's it, this choice in diets! Have you not noticed that it is not something that our contemporary generations ever had the powers to decide upon? It is easy to see that our cultural and religious forbearers chose and set our diets for us according to their own geo-cultural and spiritual backgrounds, tastes, beliefs and values. We were meant to toe their line without question since after all trying to explore what they had discarded could mean illness, death and other problems. You have it here in Africa: in Buganda, Ankole, Rwanda and Karamoja in the form of totems. If you eat this you die. You eat that and your body will develop scales like a salamander. You touch your mother-in-law and you get the trembling tarantism disease."

"But do those things happen? Those omens — do the transgressors suffer the said maladies for infringing them?"

"Yes and no. But it is more important to know that it has worked from time immemorial, because the fear of those consequences induces a kind of harmony, the requisite amount of discipline by which we live and interact as humanity. No upright person dares argue about such dogmatic norms; mark the reference 'upright'. The ancestors set these things out for us, full stop. They are taboos that have transcended time. But, of course, sometimes in the course of time, renegade mavericks — Lucifers in your case — come up setting their own ugly precedents by drastically straying, changing diets, contravening taboos set by millennia of hard thought and consideration. God's fruit tree is thus desecrated.

"Ssempa had interrupted him here: 'It's like kites whisking off complaining mother hen's chick'. He said this with mock kindness all over his face. And Giuseppe looked at him closely. 'You seem, rascal, to derive some dirty fun from those words of yours.' Ssempa shook his head, the sadness deepening on his face: 'No, Father. Simply some nostalgia at some thought in the past.' The priest nodded and said: 'We have that too in the Catholic doctrine. It is called *nostalgie de la boue*. An urge to bathe in the filthy sewer, you could say. The very affliction that hit poor Julian Dominicus!' Ssempa laughed at the Italian and told him a funny story that made the old man laugh too. He said: 'I like the way you missionaries; vending cultures you yourselves borrowed from Palestine, attempt to put the fear of the unknown into us by portraying several of our obviously superior traits as dirty and shameful. Several of you have come prepared to die for such lies for the sake of your own nationals' long-term interests because it is when we embrace your cultures like children that we may best pay for them — through the nose, since Europeans never give you anything free of charge. Today you sit here, Father, expecting me to internalise your Catholic cultural values better than I ought my own Ganda ones. You had virtually succeeded in getting Julia to do just that for a couple of decades. It is no wonder that it shocks you that I should eat flying termites. And that the genuine love between Julia and me is the equivalent of a bath in the sewage! When our forbearers selected our cultural diets and norms for us they never included the turning of our women into 'eunuchs' through doctrinal brainwashing. African women are strictly for marriage.'

"Giuseppe explained in detail why the church found it necessary to enforce celibacy and chastity, which explanations failed to convince Ssempa. I myself do sometimes find the Catholic religion a bit silly when I look more closely at its weak points and at what it has done to us, Poronia. But I do confess some of that is Ssempa's doing. Do you not see his logic, my sister? Anyhow, I returned to their conversation as Father Giuseppe said to Ssempa: 'How I wish that colonel and your sheikhs were here, to tell them how it wasn't such a big deal sleeping with nuns. Perhaps if they were to know it happened all the time they would be less excited by your foolish infatuation and help you give up the whole evil scheme. Priests and the faithful of the church do occasionally sleep with nuns, my dear Ssempa,' Father Giuseppe had stressed those words with strong passion in his hoarse voice. Having mistakenly thought he spoke out of excited unreasoning, I gave him an urgent look, which meant to warn him not to indulge in that kind of conversation. He ignored me completely, in all probability knowing Ssempa would never live to repeat anything stated this afternoon. He continued: 'Nuns and other faithful do occasionally suffer from fits of that *nostalgie de la boue* I talked of. But it always ends up between the sinners and us – the confessors and counsellors — when we get to know of their sins of passion. After all they are human beings first and foremost. The sinners are expected to repent and abstain when the enthrallment with the gutter has ebbed or passed completely. The cloister establishment may come in and banish the errant nun into seclusion so that she can do penitence. A sinful priest can be sent off to work in a difficult, usually far-flung region — even in another country. Women are much more difficult to bring under control, mind you — as my mother used to misinterpret the old adage 'hell hath no fury like a woman *unfinished.*' Believe you me, she had sense, that old Genoesa. Our counselling and penitential regimes have succeeded from time immemorial in combating these nuisance trifles. Thus your outlandish misadventure with Julian, David Ssempa, does not make you, in any way, special, as you or those other idiots may have thought. It is done all the time and is not new or even isolated. However, what makes your sin exceptionally evil is the politics that has been put into this conspiracy as though it weren't filthy enough the way it was; your people's scheme of the proposed wedding — any wedding at all, by God! A publicised mosque wedding! *Jesus Christ,* cannot your people see — are they blind to the fact that we, the Church, cannot allow that to happen?'

"Ssempa chuckled softly and said, very much to annoy the priest: 'You make the cloister sound as if it were teeming with characters from your Roman Empire era. Julian is no Popea, I can assure you, Father.' Here, I asked who Popea was and I was told she was a prostitute who sexually served the Roman imperial armed forces of one of their Caesars. He forgot which particular Caesar and Giuseppe supplied him with the name of the emperor of the times of the said Popea, whose name I forget.

"The priest then heaved a sigh and patted Ssempa's shoulder, gently, as one would his own son: 'Desist from that scheme, that is all I ask. I myself know Julian to have been above suspicion, so to say. But you are too green — you don't know it of course — to imagine what happens to a woman under the attack of carnal sin. As I have told you endlessly, everybody has wondered what satanic ploys you deployed to corrupt that child! Anyhow, just desist. That is all I ask. Leave Julian alone so she may return where she belongs. Desist from — have nothing to do with — those sheikhs and colonels. Even your own father, we are aware, is enraged about the whole scheme, to the chagrin of the mullahs and that felonious colonel. Be kind to your aged father and desist from this felonious conspiracy against my church.

"They talked for over an hour, sometimes with emotion and sometimes jocularly, mostly in Kinyankore, at which the Italian was native-fluent. They talked about picking you up from the airfield and even a little about the quarter of a million dollars the Archbishop of Chicago had offered should Ssempa opt out of the wedding scheme. Ssempa, of course, ridiculed the inducement, telling the priest he had rejected the sheikhs' money as well and wouldn't accept the Americans'. 'The only matter in my hands,' he told Giuseppe, 'is Julia. And the only spoilers are the sheikhs and you. If you both left us alone we would fade out quickly and quietly into our matrimonial future, without harming you or them. But you are tugging at us from either side. God Himself seems to be doing His own tugging from above. And each of your actions incenses the other side further. We are only human, mind you, Father'. I have thought of their conversation over and over in the hour since news of the accident reached us. It is my belief Father Giuseppe all along wanted to put Ssempa at ease so that he would have no reason or excuse not to enter his car to head for Nyakisharara when the time came. I was actually a little surprised when he accepted to go with the priest as easily as he did." She stared at the motel floor with intensity as if the answer to her wonder could be got from a point in the cement where her eyes seemed to be fixed. Then she looked to the northwest, across the highway, away in the direction of Nyakisharara. She said, slowly: "His day had come and he could probably have accepted anything from Kyera.

"I know, Poronia, you never met Father Giuseppe Mazinio in life. He was one of those nice missionary priests, seventyish, thinned steel-grey hair, thick grey-peppered eyebrows, reddish-brown eyes — bloodshot too this morning – Roman hooked nose, liver spots under the eyelids that a great suntan nearly obscured under its rust, a mouth that laughed and, today, with an untidy stubble for a moustache and all over the chin and cheeks for beard; a nice unhappy padre, Poronia. Today they were not rowdy in their exchange. There was a time, during the first days of the discovery of Kantarama's misconduct, that they exchanged blows, you know. Father Giuseppe's spectacles got broken then and I have not seen him wear glasses again. Today they mostly jested, with the priest typically losing his temper and Ssempa bemusedly laughing off what he called Giuseppe's overzealousness. They continuously glanced at their watches, timing the scheduled arrival of your flight. And all along I had expected the woman from Chicago to be an American *muzungu*.

"Father Giuseppe drank beer while at the same time Ssempa declined the coffee I suggested. He declared he would never again touch any Agip Motel food because it was an Italian establishment with, he told Giuseppe, possible Mafia connections and thus a capacity to poison him in the interests of Catholicism. That offended me greatly even though he may have meant it

26

as a joke, because he should not have expected me to comply or conspire with anybody that meant him harm. He then pointed out that I had easily placed aside the decade and a half I had lived with the Ssemagandas, just to please Giuseppe and Kyera — people I had just met, for religion's sake. And that smothered me out like death because my leaving the family business genuinely embittered him. But Giuseppe was pleased, stating he felt good knowing he was dealing with a man with a heart, a man who the hidden powers of Death, the unknown, did frighten. Sometimes I believe Father Giuseppe felt a great genuine liking for Kantarama's man."

"No, he didn't," said Kasangaire quickly. "He called him a scoundrel in one of his letters to me. He called him a *manipulating* scoundrel. That you attempt to endear me to such a man shocks me beyond words. In fact, I keep wondering whether you, Kabibi, weren't another one who may have willfully thrown aside her perpetual sacerdotal vows of poverty, chastity and conformity to embrace ordinary life. There is some piety about your posture, sprightly as it might have been at an earlier age, which is almost palpable. Did you yourself catch some contamination from this Ssempa whom you eulogise so ardently? Were you lovers?"

At that moment the taxi, a yellow Volkswagen Beetle, swerved into the motel parking lot and the two women shuffled into it in a measured hurry, Kasangaire returning to the terrace to pick up her suitcase. The driver asked them where they wanted to go and Kabibi instructed him to drive to the house by the river.

"Not another motel?" Kasangaire wished to know.

"No. Ssempa's house is some four kilometres out of town, deep in the village of Kaburangire."

They rode westwards from Mbarara town in silence, until the tarmacked road ended and they hit the rough pebbled murram, cruising through the dust-swept trading centre of Kakoba, which stretched for two kilometres with all types of houses, modern and ancient, tile-roofed and corrugated-iron-topped, interspersed with grass-thatched huts. And small shops. Everywhere you turned your eyes were men dressed in kanzus and kaftans, and with fezzes and skullcaps. And women with bright printed kitenges, mostly in greens, yellows and reds, wrapped around their lower halves, seated improperly in their doorways. And the endless stretch of banana groves so thick and dark it caused a sort of twilight. The hunt for termites, which had commenced with the dawn, had slackened and several pedestrians appeared to be on homebound treks, trudging with hurried steps along the dusty red-earth roadsides. Their number showed how intense the hunt for the white ants had been. They jumped off the rutted kerb to avoid the racing dust-spewing vehicle and hailed or whistled after it as the burping Volkswagen sped by. The interior of the car was hot and the dust swirled in freely through the open windows, the shutting of which had proven unwise because of the exceeding stuffiness of the cabin. The burping ruttut-tut of the exhaust filled their ears continuously, lulling their emotions into some form of tranquility.

Kabibi cleared her throat with a continuous persistence as if to decongest it of the coarse, gravelly dust, and said: "Your derogative rebuke, my sister, is appreciated. And you are correct — yes. Unknown to most, I was a postulant novice once, back in Gikongoro in 1959, before Gregoire Kayibanda and his monsters struck. I have known several novices and too many others who had taken their perpetual vows who had no way of continuing with God in that marriage unless they had to starve to death here in this country. But that should not get you to deem us as wanton, immoral lost souls. There was, for instance, no way I could sleep with the young Ssempa brothers. I told you their father brought me up as a daughter of his own and the boys and the girls of the homestead called me *baaba*, which, in Luganda, denotes something more significant — something weightier than mere 'sister.' But I don't expect you to imagine that kind of thing."

"I think I understand you perfectly."

"Then if you do," sniffed Kabibi in riposte, "let me — allow me to tire your ears with eulogies, the gospel of the man the church just murdered. I talk well of him because I knew and understood him better than most. I was fifteen years his senior in age, mind you, and there was no way for foolish affairs between the two of us. I had my last love affair over fifteen years ago when a fellow Munyarwanda, and a fellow Catholic at that duped me into committing an abortion and abandoned me after the act. It wasn't a very fabulous affair, I can assure you. I nearly died. That is how I ended up in the Ssemaganda family. It is only you that I tell this, of course."

The other woman elongated her mouth, pointing it at the nape of the taxi driver in a conspiratorial gesture.

"He does not understand Kinyarwanda, of course, or else I wouldn't be telling you all this. You see I would have loved Ssempa — carnally I mean, under different circumstances. I have known him to date women older than myself. And nobody — nothing — would have separated us. I would, I realise, have fallen into the same trap as other women did fall in. Ssempa was a women's man, I don't know why, but so many of them couldn't all have been that wrong about his whatever it was. But in the end only Kantarama, strangely, of the women he met, was ever able to hold that man to herself. Before that, Ssempa had been to women what bees are to flowers."

"I seem to see a butterfly instead," said Kasangaire, spitefully.

"Yes, truly a butterfly. He frolicked among them with so much ease, so much fun and relish that all hope in him as a future family man had been lost by his parents and friends. And the damsels that hankered after him with matrimony aforethought sought me out seeking his favourable ear. As you reflect over his jeans, Poronia, do consider my words too. Kantarama will eulogise Ssempa in chronicles worse than mine to your ears. And I forgot to say, his mother used to admonish her son in these words: 'Whoever bewitched you placed the fetish of your ruin in a Munyarwanda woman'. It is only recently that Ssempa interpreted his long-deceased mother's words to me to unravel his soft spot for our women. The woman that had helped to deliver him from his mother's womb was a Mututsi midwife in the county hospital, one Nyirandegeya, who happened to be my relative. She was an ageing maid who continued to care for Ssempa throughout his childhood and pampered him throughout his adolescence, always referring to him as her son. I have always suspected, as might Ssempa's five mothers, that old Ssemaganda had had a lengthy carnal affair with Nyirandegeya. Probably eighty percent of the women David Ssempa consorted with were Banyarwanda. Do I bore you?"

Kasangaire studied the sad ageing woman quietly, taking in the sharp, pointed Hamitic features and the tiny wrinkles that had already invaded the exposed flesh of her pretty long neck, puzzling over her nearly zealous attitude towards the dead Muganda man. An attitude so similar to her own sister's written laudations of the man! It disturbed her grossly. "No," she said. "You are giving me the whole nitty gritty. And I need it, much as I abhor it. Besides, you are such a very beautiful woman, Kabibi. It is hard to figure any man having abandoned you with ease."

"He did, too. But I am flattered. Of course, Kantarama says the same of me. Yet I am an old sad woman, tormented by abandonment, refugeeship and loss of the only ones that ever cared about my welfare. Beautiful and old is a terrible situation, Poronia. You feel awkward. You needn't dwell too much on how ageing feels though, for you will get there yourself in due course. I have seen men and women attempt to fight ageing, failing miserably, anyway. But you must know I miss nothing in life. I know I should have made another attempt at the convent after Gikongoro." She fell silent and watched the scrubby roadside rush by. Then she said, suddenly: "Don't tell me, Poronia, that you intend to go in for chastity yourself, do you?"

"Not after what I see you and Julian doing to the cloister," she said promptly with a pointed look. "I dislike hypocrisy."

"Hypocrisy!" Kabibi spat out the word like she would a gnat off her tongue. "I am not a hypocrite. Kantarama is not a hypocrite. Ssempa was not. Everybody else, I begin to see, is. Nobody else is true or genuine."

Kasangaire sat still. Her eyes watched the dark banana trees and their tall, broad aquamarine leaves whirl by. For about the thousandth time she asked herself why Julian had gone astray. And, her heart seeming to physically turn within her breast, a feeling that brought a sickly light-headedness to her whole being, she gave a prompt answer. Kantarama's letters and the woman Kabibi explained everything most explicitly. Both, letters and Kabibi, talked long and tirelessly. But on considering them more closely, Kasangaire saw no unctuousness in the authors of those feelings. She felt a horrible fear sneak around her heart. She became aware of an emotion that attempted to draw her towards the dead Muganda man in sympathy — or …Kasangaire closed her mind to the more salacious thought. Ssempa had been a true Lucifer, she decided. But she found herself digging up her other feeling, that the reason her own sister and now this ageing woman sanctified the dead man could be because he hadn't been so bad after all. He was lovable, that was quite clear. How else could Julian have fallen?

* * *

When they were children, their maternal uncle, Raphael Nyarwaya, now a prelate in charge of the diocese of Gitarama in mid-south Rwanda, had nicknamed Julian La Roche, which they used to laugh at. Raphael had seen a rock in Julian, to whom he had in the beginning given such fond pet names as Ambiance and Fantastique. Their mother, a once-upon-a-time catechist and teacher in a sub-grade school, would call her Coeur Marbre or Coeur de Rocaille, usually to annoy Julian when she had acted obstinately, which was often. Despite their parents' apparent belief that Kantarama was made of marble, she herself would occasionally castigate Kasangaire for being the more uncompromising of the two. And she would ask uncle Raphael why he hadn't given Kasangaire the nickname La Roche. Kasangaire, the younger of the twins, had no 'yes' in her vocabulary. They had laughed at her and added another nickname: Mademoiselle Pas Oui, which Kasangaire would write out in chalk on the large stone blackboards in the classrooms at the Kabgaye school where Father Nyarwaya taught and resided. The name had eventually metamorphosed into Mam'selle Paouis and would only leave her when they went into exile in Anglophone countries.

Apparently, Kantarama had noticed her own weakness even at that early age.

As for their priest uncle, Raphael Nyarwaya seemed to have resolved, as long ago as Kasangaire could remember, that Kantarama, who had been the more talkative of the twins, would go to the convent. She was brought

30

up to think about and believe in nothing else though this was seldom spoken directly.

Their father, Apolinaire Sebwitabure, killed in 1961 after a Tutsi group calling itself Inkotanyi had attacked Kibungo and Rusumo at the border with the then Tanganyika Territory, had despised European religion after seeing Belgian priests encourage and support Gregoire Kayibanda's murderers rampaging through Rwanda with spears, bows and arrows, and machetes — with crazed faces and reddened eyes — killing, pillaging, destroying with wanton abandon anything — livestock and crops — that they suspected to have Tutsi blood or sap in it, after ensuring that there were no more Batutsi men, women or children left alive on Rwandan soil. The Sebwitabure family was saved from sure death by the rare fact that a learned Presbyterian maternal uncle to President Kayibanda was married to a Munyiginya Mututsi granddaughter of Umwami Kigeri Rwabugiri, the late great warrior king. This was important for their salvation because that princess' daughter, Chantal Mugorewera Nzaza was the wife of Rufus Sinzagaya Gakinya, younger brother to the late Apolinaire Sebwitabure, who had been exiled in Kenya since 1959.

Sebwitabure was killed when the twin girls had just finished elementary school and Kantarama, now wholly decided, was blabbering, full of hope, about convent life. The family went into hiding. It had gone into exile before, in 1959. After weeks of waiting in vain for stabilisation of the political situation, Father Nyarwaya, a younger brother to their mother and who had kept Catholicism burning in the remnants of the younger Sebwitabure family and had returned to the country at the behest of President Kayibanda himself, took the girls with him to Bukavu in the Congo. There, another relative took Kantarama to Uganda where, shortly, she joined the convent at Kyera. Nyarwaya himself flew to Kenya with Kasangaire whom he handed over to her Mombasa-based uncle, Rufus Gakinya who, being a very practical person, had never attempted to return to Rwanda since the 1959 pogroms and had, at the time Kasangaire was brought to him, just converted to Islam. Meanwhile most of their brothers, cousins and close relatives who had survived the 1959-1960 massacres, were hauled off motor vehicles, grabbed from inside churches and picked from the bushes and hacked to death, some right in the centre of Gitarama *municipal*, which was then a small trading and administrative centre with a big Belgian gendarmerie encampment.

Kasangaire had found her uncle, whom she hadn't known much, a very interesting man. Rufus Gakinya, disgusted with the Catholic Church because of its open support for the mass murder of Batutsi, had become a Muslim soon after the slaying of Sebwitabure, his only brother, and several of his own sons and nephews who had returned to Rwanda. He took the name Issa, the

Arabic translation of Jesus. Islam was the natural religion to be in the humid, choking-hot, sprawling coastal city and he persuaded other exiled Rwandans to convert to it. His wife, Chantal Mugorewera Nzaza, niece to the late Umwami Mutara Rudahigwa, unable to stand her husband's new Afro-Shirazi wife and the clear desecration of her faith by belonging in a polygamous family set-up, left Mombasa to settle in Burundi where she became a renowned rich woman engaging in international trade. But in 1969, when the Americans placed men on moon's lunar surface to prove the Vatican erroneous in thinking God could not allow it to happen, Mugorewera Nzaza herself converted to Protestantism under the Presbyterian Church to which her mixed Hutu-Tutsi father and her Munyiginya mother had belonged. Nzaza had left with Kasangaire for Burundi to protect her from what she called spiritual contamination.

The twins' mother, Sabina Odette Mukamuhizi, lived for a time in Bukavu, where Nyarwaya had placed her at a French Protestant Huguenot establishment whose zonal founder and chief architect was Monsieur Honoré d'Aubervilliers, an old Christian-Algerian friend of his who passed for a Frenchman and had connections with Katangese secession guerrillas siding with Moise Tshombe. And when the thirst for blood had been quenched among the Bahutu politicians and agitators, she returned to the old Sebwitabure house, the first privately owned metal-roofed one in the whole *secteur* Gitarama. It had not been destroyed because it stood so close to the diocesan headquarters of the Catholic Church. A year later she sent for her daughter, Kasangaire, to keep her company and also to pursue her studies in the very superb Kabgaye *enseignement secondaire*.

Father Raphael Nyarwaya returned to Rwanda at the end of 1973 and was made monsignor that same year. He had returned on an arrangement worked out by Sinzagaya Gakinya, brother-in-law to his sister Sabina, who had himself returned to Rwanda from Kenya a few months earlier, after he had contacted powerful politicians in the influential Islamic leadership of Nyamirambo to enable the re-possession by many exiles of their own properties with a promise from the then new president, Juvenal Habyarimana, that there would never be a repetition of the crimes against them.

One year later, in late 1974, and thirteen years since she, her sister Kasangaire, Raphael Nyarwaya and others had been hounded out of their homeland together, Kantarama, now aged twenty-nine and a fully professed Sister Julian Dominicus, had returned to Kabgaye to reunite with her closest family.

"They should have christened you Petrus instead of Dominicus," Monsignor Raphael complained, in Flemish, still holding her in a fond embrace.

Their mother, now old, was happy to see her long-lost daughter, and she exhorted the nun to prevail over Kasangaire not to join convent life. At that time Apollonia Kasangaire had just done a certificate in theology and had, with her uncle Nyarwaya's help, obtained a scholarship to the Illinois Benedictine College in Lisle. Much as she attempted to convince her mother of the dissimilarities between her studies and the convent, the old woman would never believe her. In the night when the three were alone she surprised her daughters in an atypical outburst: "I had always seen more nun in you than in Kantarama. Let us face it, my angels," Sabina's tear-flooded eyes were blinking myopically. "You want me to be the ultimate terminator of the Sebwitabure progeny! That is much the same as spaying me. It is the equivalent of severing my old breasts. All your brothers — your own father's children — were killed. Others are hopelessly exiled and have even changed their tribe! Do you still have the minds to remember Mushekyera, and Karaveeri, and Hodari, and Viivi, and Innocent Rutagyengwa? Not to remind you of Ngoga's unexpected fatal bicycle accident in Bugande? And d'Ancilla who wrote me in bad Kinyarwanda saying she is now called Simollo 'the little one? Do you still know, or have you already forgotten, your own dead brethren? And are you not aware that all Gakinya's offspring were exterminated? His embracing of the religion of the *musulmans* and marrying so many wives, in its justifiable wisdom, has not provided him any other children. You are my only girls, my only children. You are the only Sebwitabures alive in this whole wide world, with the exception of Sinzagaya Gakinya. The very last Sebwitabures are in you and Gakinya, whom God won't give other children. What are you going to do? What do you want me to do? Don't you have sympathy for me? Don't you know the Bahutu are happy when they see us getting extinct?"

Shocked by their mother's words, the two young women had reassured the aged Sabina Mukamuhizi. Then they had gone, each her way, Sister Julian Dominicus back to Uganda and Kasangaire to the United States, leaving their mother a desolate, resigned old woman. Her only company were the children of Gakinya's two surviving nieces whom that old man, their own grandfather, never ceased to say were never Sebwitabures or even Batutsi as their fathers were Bahunde Congolese, related to the Batwa tribes of the mountains of North Kivu, the equivalent of India's Untouchables. These children would walk the three kilometres from the Muslim sector of Gitarama at Nyabisindu on the road to Kibuye and spend the days and sometimes nights, bringing her that greatly hankered-after noisy company of theirs and helping with household chores.

'Did Julian do what she had done', Kasangaire enquired of herself for the umpteenth time, 'to please their mother'? But that was impossible to envisage. For Kasangaire thought the old woman might even be madder than them all to hear of the terrible *faux pas*. She did not know that their mother had been one of the very first to discover the anomaly in her daughter.

What would that terribly sweet uncle of theirs, Monsignor Raphael Nyarwaya, do or think when he came to learn of it?

But why rue? she chided herself. Now that Julian had no more human suitors, Kasangaire's use to Kyera as her sister's understudy existed no more. The whole thing would have to be called off. The Mbarara municipal mullahs would be hard pressed to seek an identical David Ssempa. They would give up effortlessly too, she thought comfortably. She would talk to Kantarama and then, after seeing the Most Reverend William Kabigumira, might take a ride to the southern border and proceed to Rwanda, a country she loathed visiting because the Bahutu immigration officials, the most arrogant human beings that God might have ever had the impertinence to create, looked at her with upturned noses, as if she had the plague.

* * *

She turned to Kabibi: "Please tell him to turn off that thing. It is infectious."

"What?" Kabibi looked at her, in mild surprise. "You don't enjoy music?"

"Not *Soley Soley* right now. I want to cry. Its tune evokes tears in my heart and the Ugandan radio seems to have nothing else to play."

"*Soley Soley*," said Kabibi, rolling the two words off her tongue sweetly. "I don't understand. Those Middle of the Road chaps are my true favourites."

All the same she instructed the driver to switch the radio off, but the man had already tuned into a Dar es Salaam station with Congolese music where someone was singing Bavon Marie Marie's *Albertine Mwana ya Ndeke* very nearly like the original. The women kept quiet for a spell. Kabibi wondered if, after all, the driver did not understand the Kinyarwanda language as Kasangaire's request had been in that tongue.

And then Kasangaire said: "You were saying I was a hypocrite, Virigo."

"Oh well," the older woman pulled herself out of her own reverie. "Look — I am not talking to you of Ssempa to impress you. He is dead. And I am not trying to exonerate your sister of her imprudent actions. You yourself, when you get to know fully well what happened to them — both have each, in the long run, been able to recount to me their parts of the incidents — you will appreciate their predicament. You will concede there was no escape for them. There was no way in the whole wide world for them to avert the dilemma they found themselves in. Neither you nor I, my dear sister, would have deflected or survived such a dilemma."

She had in the long run noticed the younger woman's nun-like meditational silences, her economy of speech, her terse responses and the obvious curiosity that forced her to ask the continuous involuntary, probing queries. She was presently looking out the window on her own side of the seat, having noticed for the first time the Rwiizi, the river that rumbled down the valley in a green-grey easterly course almost in parallel symmetry to the track they chased. Youths and children swam naked in the steel-grey waters all along the river's course, drying their strong nubile, sinewy black bodies in the warm golden glow of the setting sun.

"If you say that the man Ssempa was such a good unscheming person, why did he go by a Christian name?"

"What? — A Christian name? What Christian name?"

"*David*," replied Kasangaire, turning her eyes away from the river.

Kabibi laughed. A dry, mirthless laugh: "You don't really believe that, Poronia, do you?"

"Look. Muslim names are obvious. Abdullah, Mohammed, Hussein.... I spent time in Mombasa years ago, you know. I even have a Muslim uncle. His Mohammedan name is Issa."

Kabibi was looking into her face with an inclined head as she counted off the names. She said: "Now we shall start fighting over their names, even."

"Whose names?"

"The Arabs and Jews, Poronia. There are no Christian and other-religion names. Names can only be ethnic or cultural. Although in the final analysis all names mean the same things universally when translated, they have more fundamental meanings to the tribes that invented them. Issa is not a Mohammedan name; it is the Arabic for 'Jesus'. There's nothing remotely religious about it. It is — think of it — like Banyarwanda and Ugandans refer to the border towns separating their countries differently, like in Kyanika and Cyanika, Katuna and Gatuna or Kisoro and Gisoro, you see? Neither Apollonia nor Virgo, are Christian names. Yours is Greek and mine Latin or Roman. They are names that existed before the birth of Jesus Christ or Muhammad of the Muslims and cannot therefore have much to do with Christianity or Islam. David, the King of the Israelites, was a Jew, not a Christian. David is not a Christian name, as you seem to believe. It is the ethnic Hebraic and Arab name Daoud. It is actually Semitic. Europeans changed it to fit their own vocabularies. As a matter of fact I have met more Muslim Davids in my life than Christian. Come to think of it, I don't recall a single Christian David offhand. Ssempa actually did have a middle name: Eddie or Ed. Nothing Edwardian about it, mind you."

35

"Well, what would Eddie or Ed be in their Arabic?"

"Ssempa was a pure Muganda — not an Arab. But Eddy or Ed can also be Edriss, Idriss or even Eid or Idi — like Amin, the president of this country. Ssempa was called Eddie or Eddy by most that knew him, or Daoud and David by others. In short, my dear sister, there is nothing Virgo about the Kabibi in me if, as I've occasionally been told, it means virgin. Look at me, Poronia — do you see a virgin?"

Kasangaire shook her head with a frown on her face. "You seem to know quite a lot of stuff, Kabibi. Again part of the ravages of being a refugee?"

Kabibi did not answer her immediately. They had come to the edge of a vast coniferous forest with sturdy straight, brown-stemmed trees grown in even, oblique rows that ended in an infinite grey darkness.

"It shows the abject ignorance of those — on both sides — that would have wanted to kill Ssempa. Actually, the more ignorant of the lot did commit the murder. Truly, both Islam and Catholicism — as opposed to Protestantism — ridiculously compete over obsoleteism."

The Volkswagen bumped its way towards the bridge and traversed it with a protesting engine as it had to mount the large, roughly placed palm tree logs that created a sort of hump. Some two hundred metres from the edge of the dense forest and a few strides from the stout log bridge that spanned the grey waters of the River Rwiizi stood a three-decade old, large, single-storied house with high sloping baked clay tegula roof and walls of dark, heavily knotted cypress wood. A mesh-wire fence, turned black with oxidation over the decades, ran round the perimeter of the wide compound, supported by unpainted palm tree posts. There were two smaller iron-roofed houses in the back, greatly dwarfed by the timber behemoth that had been built in 1948 by the Norwegian forest official who had created the cypress forest and who had left the country in 1962, soon after Uganda obtained her *uhuru* from the British colonists. The Norwegian's forest cast a deep verdant shadow over the high Scandinavian-style house and its expansive overgrown lawns with frangipani, bottlebrush and poinciana, all in bloom and, with a fire raging atop each short bright green-leafed poinciana in the scarletest of flowers any of the women had ever seen. Without any human direction, a cold fire of the greatest beauty burnt freely atop each flame tree and hurt the eyes. In the needle-pointed foliage of the conifers, velveteen blue sunbirds, bright yellow weaverbirds, cicadas and other fauna chirped spasmodic farewells to the setting sun.

"Jesus!" Kasangaire could not help exclaiming with a subdued moan. "In spite of everything, the place is beautiful. It is so entirely like a picture, a postcard picture. Is that the house?"

"Yes," replied Kabibi, watching the younger woman's appraising eyes closely without letting on she was doing so.

"You mean to tell me this Ssempa had gone to school? Muslims don't."

"Not your idea of *school*. He was a mechanic — learned on the job after his Primary Seven. He then went to an elementary technical college in Masaka where he did something in motor mechanics, but could not complete the course because he wanted to do trade more than anything else. He always used to say his own father had succeeded in it without ever going to school. He still owned a large motor garage but had found more lucrative incomes in smuggling coffee and other commodities. You like his place?"

Kasangaire looked at her reproachfully and deliberately stopped her surveillance of the place.

"You are a woman, after all," Kabibi pressed, needling the younger woman further.

"What do you mean?" Kasangaire enquired, edgily.

"I mean the dead man's *jeans*."

"You haven't forgiven me, eh? Let us not fight, please."

"If anybody had taste, Ssempa did. This used to be a Forests Department house. Ssempa's father got it in exchange for a mansion that now serves as the Forests Department headquarters on Boma Hill back in town. The dairy farm you see across from the southern edge of the forest belongs to the Franciscans at Kyera."

"Is that how they met? The proximity of...."

"No. But at the time before they met, a good friend of Kantarama's was in charge of the dairy farm. Both the friend and Kantarama taught at the missionary secondary school at Kyera. I think they were together at Bwanda and Nkozi for teacher training."

"Taught biology, of all things. Why didn't they give her mathematics? She was a wizard there. And what of that crowd of women? And men too! Do they reside here?"

"No, they of course don't," replied Kabibi as they disembarked from the car. "I don't know what is going on. It is improbable that they've already got news of the accident."

The crowd of people was converged around the main entrance to the lofty mansion. There were about a dozen and a half of them, of mixed sexes but predominantly female.

"Is any of them Julian?" Kasangaire asked. Then she realised the silliness of her query and took Kabibi's arm. "Come on, let us seek out Julian."

"I know she wouldn't like that crowd of people there. You know she's pregnant?"

Kasangaire started, releasing Kabibi's arm abruptly, as if struck in the face. She regained her composure very quickly and said: "Yes. Oh, Mary Mother of God, yes! It was all in the letters."

The cluster of people gathered outside the entrance to the house consisted of two dozen or so villagers, some of whom were children just arrived from a river bath. Kabibi knew some of them and they likewise knew her.

"What's happening?" she exclaimed, anxiously.

"There," the man she had questioned, a labourer at a nearby farm, pointed a finger at a cluster of women who appeared to be kneeling before a somewhat bulky-looking figure of a human being lying on the porch veranda. "Her husband has died, looks like."

* * *

The telephone had pulled her from the comfortable lull of a siesta she had indulged in soon after their lunch of hot *karo* bread, field-fresh cowpeas fried in raw cow ghee and, after cooling to some mild warmth, mashed in *eshabwe* — another cow-ghee sauce, milk-white, paste-thick and exquisitely tasty. She had prepared this sauce herself by mixing the ghee in crude caustic salt that had come direct from Lake Katwe, with tepid water and the invocation of her great culinary expertise. The housemaid, new and unused to the ringing of the instrument, had hurried to the bedroom and called to her in her incongruous, near-masculine voice, as if the house were on fire, and Julian wondered where this short, light-brown-complexioned, pudgy woman had plucked up the courage to pick up the receiver and place it aside. She had got up leisurely immediately the girl had left the bedroom and, standing languidly before the king-size bed, stretched out her long limbs, arms above head, and indulged in a low, languorous yawn. She was growing fat, what with the *eshabwe* and the pregnancy! Making a mental note of her new-found laziness, she brought her hands down to touch her tummy at either side, the long delicate fingers massaging the stomach and midriff in slow circular strokes. Her stomach had not protruded the way she had feared it might even though this was already her eighth month of pregnancy. She glanced at the old Blaupunkt tape recorder from which Congolese music — the truer cause of her erstwhile slumber, rolled, presently pumping out *Quand le film est triste*. Julian had gradually found herself falling in love with the music her lover loved, and this included terrible numbers like *Luvumbu Ndoki* and *Catherine*, in which Luambo Franco extolled witchcraft with a devil-may-care, fun-filled gusto. She walked out of the bedroom while at the same time pulling on a white-blue-violet cotton dress, her bare feet moving leisurely over the Bokhara carpets, towards the telephone at the bay window overlooking the river and the log bridge.

Ssempa had been gone some two hours now. Father Giuseppe had asked him the previous day to go to the Agip Motel for an audience concerning Julian and the imminent arrival of her twin sister, Apollonia Kasangaire, who would, if all went according to schedule, be arriving in the mid-afternoon from America. Giuseppe, that kind old padre, besides wanting Ssempa to meet and talk to Apollonia Kasangaire in order that the latter might attempt to melt the Muslim's heart with learned American persuasion, intended to introduce Bishop William Kabigumira to him as well. If that happened, Ssempa would be meeting His Eminence for the first time, something that the Muganda viewed more or less as meeting just any other man. The bishop would be part of the Kasangaire reception committee, too. After that the two men of God and Ssempa might want to have a face-to-face meeting with the two culprits — Kantarama and Ssempa — in the diocesan farmhouse just across the river on the other side of Bihunya Hill. Julian had been in such meetings with her erstwhile mentors now and then in the past three months, but she was not sure she could attend one with her sister and the bishop in attendance. Even a secluded meeting with her sister was not a prospect she very much looked forward to. Just to imagine how they would look at one another killed her heart and mind, so to say. Yet, she mused, as long as Ssempa was present, there was hope and assurance she might persevere. The very wise intercession of Virgo Kabibi might have eased things for her a great deal, too.

A couple of hours previously they had sat on the eastern balcony facing the vast pine forest, dark-green and covered by a thick mist in several places. She had greatly enjoyed the cold *karo* and *eshabwe*-in-green peas and the roasted cassava with the eshabwe and cold chicken, as they discussed the coming of Apollonia Kasangaire at length. The new girl, silent like a shadow, hung around them almost utterly unnoticed in her long old-woman's dress of a nondescript greyish colour that reached down to her ankles and the hood-like veil which she knotted at her chin so that only her face showed — the way some Muslim women dressed. She was short with an uncomely face whose main features were those round saucer-like eyes that protruded slightly. A nonentity — if any person could be described thus was that woman that Sister Gerald had procured for them from wherever Sister Gerald had picked her. Her name was Djamilla. Ssempa laughed at nearly everything she said in her deep, masculine voice. She referred to whisky as *bwisky*, getting one to wonder where that soft 'b' came from in such a simple syllable. Moreover, she insisted on making all her responses to vernacular questions in the English language, with her own extremely outrageous pronunciations of nearly every word she uttered.

The day she said 'I was wait for your arrivation before preparationing your bathing water,' Ssempa, aghast at her outlandish manipulation of the English

39

language, nearly strangled her in irritation. 'Silly idiot!' he admonished her. 'Arrive, not *arrivation*; people don't *arrivate*, they arrive. You don't *preparate*, you prepare.' When she had poured away some whisky that he had left in a bottle after a small party for fellow traders, he lambasted her for the action. Djamilla had put a hand to her mouth, wringing it with a force that lengthened the lower lip, and said in all meekness: 'I cannot do pouring away of bottle of *bwisky* again, sir."

The housemaid had induced into the nun the kind of shrill laughter that she had never believed she contained within her body, and by and by, they and the *shamba* boy had got used to the ways of Djamilla the new girl.

"The difference between facing Poronia and Reverend Superior," Julian had told Ssempa after the breakfast, "is membrane thin. I could even risk confronting Uncle Monsignor — but Poronia!"

"Come on, Julia," Ssempa had said, almost deprecatingly, his hand stroking her upper arm. "Apollonia is your sister not your Superior or Monsignor Nyarwaya. She has lived in America and may even surprise you by siding with us against the mediocre idiots."

She had laughed: "If only you knew Poronia, David!"

The new girl had cleared away the lunch things and left them holding hands as though they had just met each other for the first time only that morning. She had watched their every movement from the day, three weeks previously, when Sister Gerald Sebastian had dropped her at the diocesan farm and given her directions to the timber house, and just now she saw the man and the woman leave the balcony chairs to stand at the extreme southerly end bent against the polished mahogany balustrade. The woman was obviously disturbed by her sister's impending arrival and the man was doing all he could to reassure her of a probable positive reaction from her closest kin. The new girl, a woman in her late thirties but called 'girl' because housemaids were called that, remembered the long goodbye kiss between her employers well. Julian had straightened out the collar of the thin dark-blue cotton jacket he wore over the same-colour cotton tee shirt. Ssempa had left Julian standing at the balustrade, a sad smile on her face, a devil-may-care cheer in his, gone downstairs and driven off in the Peugeot pickup.

She picked up the telephone, which the girl had placed aside, her eyes looking out over the Kakoba hills towards the setting sun, then placed the grey bakelite receiver to her ear and, cautiously, said: "Hullo?"

The caller on the phone was Gerald Sebastian. She said: "Julian?"

"Hello, Gerald!" Julian's voice, expressing obvious relief, said in Luganda. "Do you know how much I wish you were here? Poronia is on her way in from Chicago. God, I am so lonely and jittery with David away. How on

Earth shall I confront Poronia? I am lost, Gerald. Kabibi won't come this end for fear Giuseppe might excommunicate her. This girl you gave to us isn't someone I can talk to, if I can avoid it; she only talks when she is practising English. Otherwise she gets so quiet sometimes one gets reminded of the cloister, and...."

"Julian, my very darling child," said Sister Gerald in a hushed voice, also in Luganda. Her voice was somewhat crisp, the way Sister Prioress or even Mother Superior herself talked, as though she wasn't the Gerald Namazzi she knew. "The bishop... just told me... he wanted me to give you the horrible news. Both Father Giuseppe and David have been killed in a car crash. They were on their way to Nyakisharara Airstrip to meet your sister."

"Nnnoooo! Oh, good God, nnnoooo!"

"Julian...!"

"Oh my God, you Gerald! They have killed — they have murdered my husband!"

"Julian, just listen...."

The phone went silent on Gerald Sebastian's side. Father Kajene looked at her with a wispy smile and asked with assertion: "What's her reaction?"

Gerald did not want to express any emotion on her face and she very well knew how not to do so. She looked taciturnly at the priest and said very quietly: "Shattered, you could say; from her voice. I believe I just killed Julian Dominicus for you. The housemaid thing was quite unnecessary."

"You were colleagues; you were *too* much attached — which nobody should have encouraged. But she will get through it, I know *that* woman. To imagine she had been nominated for Superior through unanimous vote!"

The fat nun gasped and fixed the priest with her large eyes.

"You didn't know, of course, but what I tell you is the truth. Many believe she has been a great loss to us as a Church. I don't, of course." Kajene smirked as though in disdain. "She'll survive her worldly husband's death, that woman. The fellow has taken her *place*, lucky wench. To the day of my death I shall always wonder what that Muganda man *did* to fell that Munyarwanda woman!"

The fat woman kept her eyes away from the priest. She waited patiently for him to dismiss her.

Back at Kaburangire, in the relentless grip of a frightening fear mixed with a hatred she had never imagined to possibly exist, Julian had banged the phone into its cradle, not having realised that Gerald had been compelled to prematurely cut her own end of the line, her mind filled with just one thing: to drive to the airstrip and she herself confront her sister over the murder of her man — her husband. For, quickly going back through her late conversations

41

with Father Giuseppe Mazinio — hints dropped here and there by that kindly priest — she was just now recalling Ssempa's description of a really evil person the way her own uncle, Issa Sinzagaya had told it to him, and was wondering if there was actually an iota of kindliness in any part of the person of Father Giuseppe Carenzi Mazinio — she had come to the conclusion that the Church had murdered him. But what of the padre himself, also killed? Could he have known it was difficult enough to murder Ssempa and decided to sacrifice his life alongside the crow-cagey man, which would in addition to having duped her 'husband' into not suspecting death, would also save the Church from the rage of the government that would not suspect the priest's suicide scheme?

She quickly pulled off the dress she had just put on and jumped into the pair of bulky woolen pantaloons Ssempa had bought for her in Dar es Salaam the previous month. Then she pulled on an equally billowy cotton blouse — garments meant to conceal her pregnancy. She picked the keys for the old Jaguar, that brute of a machine that they had traveled in to Gitarama and later to Bujumbura on a trip that had proven an embarrassment but that had at the same time freed her from the clutches of the kind of shame she had believed herself unable to confront — or surviving that terrible, terrible, terrible visit to her mother with her 'husband.' Oh, her mother!

"Oh, Sabina, *ma cherie mère!*" she sobbed out the name, and stepped out of the bedroom.

She went through the carpet-laid living room, glanced at its furniture, new and old — chairs, settees, mahogany and Elgon-olive sideboards and coffee tables — and walked out to the landing. She took a step — just one step — and in so doing turned her head to see the figure rapidly detaching itself from the wall, slightly to her right, and streaking like lightning towards her at a pace that overwhelmed her senses. It was the new 'girl' who had pulled the hood-like veil away from her head, letting it hang grotesquely over part of her face and shoulders. Julian threw her hand up defensively in a reflex response to the imminent danger from the intruder. Her eyes and mouth were wide open as a horrific realisation hit hard at her bowels. She was only able to utter one syllable in paralysed shock: "Dam...!"

As her heavy body fell awkwardly forward and down the stairs, she understood everything. She no longer wondered about those round protuberant eyes, the masculine voice, and the sporadic theatrics of the new girl. How could she have failed to identify the fellow whom she had known so long and whom she knew had hated her all the time they had known each other? How on Earth had she imagined she could survive *Them*?

By the time *Djamilla* leisurely got to the wriggling bulky form at the bottom of the staircase, Julian had lost gallons of blood. She bent over the squirming figure and her stout chubby fingers fumbled for the injured woman's neck, as if to feel her pulse. Her protuberant eyes looked furtively all around her and then came back to the scene of the accident. Those eyes had purpose in them.

The *shamba* boy responsible for tending the compound gardens was in the backyard when the quite agitated new *'girl'* let off an earsplitting scream and came out of the house running as though the house was on fire. She told the *shamba* boy, in unintelligible tones, of the tragedy that had transpired inside the house. He had so quickly gathered the village women who had earlier washed their laundry at the riverside and were now gathering the dried garments to return to their homesteads in the cooling atmosphere. And he brought them to the big wooden house by the river.

* * *

"This," rued Kabibi, looking about her suspiciously, her eyes even searching the twilight edge of the forest as if for a mysterious omnipresence, "must be God working." Then inwardly she said a special prayer: 'Holy Virgin Mary Mother of God, bless Kantarama, your true child, have mercy on her and forgive her all her faults. Amen!'

Presently, just as she finished the silent *prie-dieu*, there was the muffled sound of gurgling, followed by the sharp chorus of an infant crying. The baby's crying was so loud and shrill it sounded like a firecracker.

"Oh, my gracious Christ," Kabibi couldn't help reflecting on the number of times she had uttered that man's name in the last couple of hours alone. And she fell to her knees alongside the other women already kneeling there. Kasangaire, who moved more slowly — very slowly, as though held in a hypnotic trance — promptly followed her there, genuflecting before the prone form of her twin sister. She took her position at the other end where, with the open palms of her hands, she touched the face of her sister, stroking it with the most extreme tenderness. How could this be? How — why should this happen to her?

Apollonia Kasangaire had known she would never have forgiven her sister alive. But she had not at any point in time thought of Julian Kantarama dead. She could not see why Julian shouldn't have, at least, waited for her, to talk to her; to explain what had happened to that beautiful marble heart of hers! She wept, under control, silently with immeasurable hurt and bitterness, as she stared at her sister's dead, quite uncaring, unfeeling, unknowing face. There was in her mortified heart the horrible, merciless knowing that she would never ever get a chance to speak to that utterly indifferent face of the only human being that she knew she loved most because the two of them had come from the same womb during the same hour, nearly at the very same time, were identical to the

43

extent that even their mother at times had difficulty differentiating them, and belonged to a dwindling lineage of a clan now ultimately doomed to extinction. As she would later tell Kabibi, a newfound friend and sympathiser, there were plenty of Batutsi in the diaspora, but there were no more Sebwitabures now. Her clan had been wiped out under the worst, most unfair circumstances ever visited upon man. She verily, ultimately, wished to die there and then herself.

The women who had delivered the screeching infant finished up with their chores with silent, native professionalism and soon the tiny, noisy bundle was in the hands of Kabibi.

Did they, these village women, know that the dead woman had been a nun, a perpetually professed nun? Kasangaire wondered. She herself then stood up, her dark attractive face contorted in agony and smeared in a deluge of tears. Her stark white upper teeth with the tiny gap in them bit savagely into her lower lip, oblivious to the pain those teeth inflicted on its delicate fleshy tissue. She walked with heavy limbs to where Kabibi stood. The baby changed hands. Kasangaire looked at it closely through the flood of tears that blinded her. She had never touched the flesh of a freshly born infant, and it felt so hot, so energetic, like a powerful animal with a dynamo in its body. She nearly dropped it to her feet out of the fright it gave her.

Kabibi took her by the elbow and gently led her into the house, up the pinewood stairway down which Kantarama had tumbled to her death. Kabibi's own face was dry, for she had wept herself to exhaustion during the past couple of hours. They stood at the top of the staircase and Kasangaire, through her weeping and sniffing, was mumbling in a tuneless tear-filled chant to the infant baby: "Stop crying, Beelzebub; for I'll take you home, Beelzebub; to my own mother, Beelzebub. And she will succour you, my infant. You have grandma and me, Beelzebub. Oh, Beelzebub, my poor orphan boy."

"Beelzebub?" Kabibi enquired. "I don't know of any Beelzebub in the Kinyarwanda language."

"His name," came Kasangaire's soft reply. "It is Hebraic."

"It sounds awful. Where did you get it from?"

"It is actually an awful name that I got from my biblical memory, somewhere. If it is true there are no religious names then I think the Muslims will accept Beelzebub."

"Picked by you," said Kabibi, deliberately standing away from the younger woman in open animosity. "I hate to know its interpretation."

"Well, *il est quelque peu rageur; un petit démon!* A true son of the devil."

"Is that so? And is that what you will call your nephew?"

"Oh, my God! *Nephew* — eh?" Kasangaire looked thunderstruck at her newest discovery. Then, shaking her head as though to accept the terrible reality, she said, resignedly: "Don't forget he just killed my closest biological relative — the only one I had besides my mother and uncles Gakinya and Raphael. But never mind; Beelzebub is supposed to be a Christian name. My mother will most certainly rename him. Uncle Gakinya will probably get him another name too, something befitting the Muslim culture. Oh, my! — I hope I am not getting schizophrenic."

"Not when you are aware of the danger. Has it occurred to you that all this is so simply because we are a homeless people?"

"Yes. How else would I have a Muslim for an uncle, and now a devil's child for a nephew? And did it have to be a baby boy? A son! A true and certain imp." Kasangaire, less tearful now, still wept, her face still contorted with grief, her eyes never leaving the baby's screwed-up, meat-like face.

"If you won't show this infant all the love that it deserves," Kabibi was belligerent, "I will raise all hell to keep him myself."

"I'd never allow you to do that, Kabibi. This boy has the Sebwitabure blood flowing in his veins."

"Sebwitabure! Who's Sebwitabure? I don't remember that name."

"My father. It is the family name, inherited from my ancestors. I did tell you my uncle Gakinya and I had become the only surviving Sebwitabures. That was after the death of Kantarama and before Beelzebub's arrival."

"I don't know it like that, young woman. This here is true Ssemaganda blood."

"I agree with that. However, refugeehood dictates that the Sebwitabures intermingle with the Ssemagandas to recreate the dwindling Sebwitabure lineage. Call it a survival strategy — or even stratagem if you will."

"I won't argue with you. Just show love to the baby. Maybe Kantarama and Ssempa wouldn't have minded it that way. I know his family wouldn't come into this — his father, old Ssemaganda, was so much against the whole affair. What are we going to do now?"

"We will ask those people downstairs to help carry Kantarama into the house."

Kabibi's mind lingered on Kasangaire's referring to her sister by her Kinyarwanda name, which could have been indicative of some forgiveness. She peered down the stairs in the gathering twilight. The body was already on its way into the house between clusters of bent-backed villagers led by a short pudgy woman in a bulky buibui-like garb.

"Dry your eyes, my dear. They are coming up."

45

"I won't do that. Get the housemaid to direct them where to put her. I was wondering whether it is possible to procure a coffin."

"Poronia!"

"Yes. I want us to give her a decent burial by ourselves. I believe we can do it. We'll sink a grave with their help, eh? It can be done — even at night, can't it? I will pay them for the work."

"But, Poronia...?" Kabibi attempted to interrupt her again.

"The Church won't accept her, or had you forgotten! And we can't take her to Gitarama. You did hint Ssempa's own father disapproved of their actions. So where does my sister belong now, Virigo? But meantime you should get to the housemaid — or a good leader amongst those people downstairs and introduce these proposals. And we'll require some gripe water for Beelzebub. And we will bathe him; give him some appropriate nourishment. So you see I will not molest our dear Beelzebub."

"But I...." Kabibi began.

"And then, my dear sister, we'll sit down out there in the grass under the moon and the stars — ooo, my God! Look there," she cried in a disbelief filled with disdain, pointing with the baby at the dark aquamarine sky. A three-day moon with a large bright star a metre or two to its right, gazed back at them with a sort of benign glumness. "Does it have to be a bloody-fuckin' crescent moon? Damn the Mohammedans!"

Kabibi took her eyes from the sky to Kasangaire's teary face. "I am afraid you are schizophrenic. You must calm down, Poronia. Take it easy. Let us go and sit down in the living room."

Kasangaire spluttered into a soft laughter, which she cut short as abruptly as she had started it. "Schizophrenic, Kabibi? You cannot know what you are talking about. You just said I wouldn't be if I were aware of it remember? We will sit under the sky with the confounded crescent moon sailing, as you quite well see, to our own Rwanda, and you will tell me what has been going on here. You haven't told me everything yet, have you? Things like why I no longer have an only sister anymore. Why I remain with an aged mother, a doddery sterile uncle and, now, a crucially necessary but quite unwelcome Beelzebub for relatives!" Her voice remained soft and her attitude pensive, her eyes, screwed-up with burning tears, fixed at a point above the silhouette of the tip-pointed conifers where the moon sailed through the wisps of grey cloud. Then she turned those wide-set eyes to Kabibi and continued in that low, barely audible voice, her supple wide mouth slanting askew in chagrin. "It would have been fine to finish off their kind, their tribe; to cull it by snuffing out this brat in its infancy. But infanticide! Never. Mother would never forgive me. None of my people, my father and his father's fathers – no Sebwitabure indeed – would ever pardon me. I myself now have to strive to have children. But what if the gods — what if my God disallowed? Oh, poor me! I don't know what to do. Just what happened, Kabibi, my sister and mother? Tell me; you did say the two culprits had told you about it all. I need to know it *all* myself."

Two

Mbarara, southern Uganda, May 1977

Ssempa had driven his dark-blue Peugeot 404 pickup truck to Lugazi, a suburb of Mbarara town, and parked the vehicle a hundred yards before the posh residence of Donn Reisch because that is where he found his uncle, Shafiq Kakembo, the old sheikh. It was the *maulid* or birthday anniversary of Mohammed ibn Abdullah, the Muslim prophet, and at any opportunity of such a function, Mr Reisch usually made grand feasts where the biggest shots of the province, from the provincial governor, the commander of the zonal army battalion, the head of battalion intelligence and security — were all invited. Of the *maulids* and *ddouwas*, the latter events were the more frequent as they could be arranged even on the pretexts of praying for the state's wellbeing and the longevity of the 'life president,' Al Hajji Doctor Field Marshal Idi Amin Dada MC, DSO, VC, CBE, Conqueror of the British Empire. These events were grand, so full of festivity and fanfare, besides the solemnity of supplication led by the best of sheikhs from all over the nation. To miss them meant you were simply worse than a nonentity. There was a rumours that Donn Reisch, the greatest of the controllers of coffee smuggling in the province, called these *maulids* and *ddouwas* so as to concentrate security personnel in one place at his vast residence while his trucks ferried loads of coffee across the southern border into Rwanda and large specially built boats plied the great Lake Victoria laden with the dark grey beans that had been renamed black gold, on their way to Kenyan ports. Whether or not the rumour were true, Donn Reisch — a short stocky mulatto of M'nyambo-German parentage, a philanthropist in his own way, who lived grandiosely in a number of mansions, rode in uncommon American Ford Mustangs, Buicks, Lincolns and even a Cadillac the size of a small bus, dressed himself and his alluring Acholi wife Christina most fancily, and smoked cheroots like a Colombian drug cartel don — was one of the wealthiest men in the country. The nouveaux riches that had replaced the Katariyas, Guptas, Ladhas, Jansaris and Shantilals — those Indian commercial moguls that dictator Idi Amin had booted out of the country to give away their properties to the likes of Donn Reisch — were all expected to attend the festivities, along with the sheikhs, the colonels, the military intelligence chaps and the more sinister men and women of the two murderous state security agencies — the State Research Bureau and the Public Safety Unit.

With his uncle outside the expansive ornate gate of the tycoon was the municipal mullah and main mosque imam, a short light-brown man with

48

protuberant eyes and a severe affliction of acne, whose Pakistani outfit — a longish brown outer coat, stark white trousers and black leather sandals — made him to appear like a misplaced Oriental. He was a local Munyankore convert to Islam, one of Sheikh Shafiq's protégés and like most fresh converts to fundamentalist born-again faiths, was overzealous. He overdid everything he believed to be Islamic and had the genuine will to die for his newfound faith in which he was just six years old and in which he had educated himself most ambitiously. He had a name like Gullet or Gullid, which was meant to be an Islamic — or at least Arabic — name, having heartily paganised his original native one. And Ssempa disliked the municipal imam for that mediocrity that he exhibited with such assiduous enthusiasm.

The other man in his uncle's company was Anyanya Yoram. This man was dressed in a very smart jet-black three-piece suit with a light blue hard-collared shirt and a red necktie and was very, very brown, with prominent Hamitic facial features and generally running to fat. He was quite tall and big-boned, weighing some seventeen stone. His hair was brushed back from his high forehead with a force that maintained it in that harsh style as if a hot comb had been used on it, leaving the red-brown face quite stern. Anyanya Yoram, whose names should have been known in the reverse but were not, had the firm hard stare in his large brown eyes of a man well aware and confident of his power. Ssempa's knowledge of the man's reputation of ruthlessness did not stem from Anyanya's attire, stern face, eyes or severe hairdo. Every man or woman — especially in Busoga, that land spread on the northeastern shores of Lake Victoria — who had made big wealth on the roads and water lanes of Uganda through smuggling had met or at least heard of Anyanya Yoram, his mercilessness and his leonine hairstyle that so well fitted the interlacustrine region, for he was also known as Ntale, and sometimes as Simba, both of which meant 'lion'.

Irony of ironies, Anyanya Yoram was a mere army corporal! He drew his immense power and authority from his occupation as an intelligence officer of the dreaded Public Safety Unit, which was a paramilitary wing of the Uganda Police Force but had nothing to do with the safety of the public since it became responsible for seeing too many innocent persons to their premature and usually uncalled-for graves. Because the Uganda Army was, expectedly, clumsy in handling cases involving smuggling, Idi Amin had placed trusted police personnel in military intelligence units to assist in investigations that required empirical analyses. These investigations had come about during the big coffee boom that had followed unprecedented frost conditions that had adversely affected Brazilian coffee yields. The policemen had stayed on inside army intelligence long after that coffee boom was over, and were no longer regarded as policemen. Anyanya Yoram was one such operative. But his greater reputed personal authority, besides the fearful organisation to which he belonged, came primarily from his legendary incorruptibility. This implacable virtue in the man did not augur well for the smugglers, whose main safeguard against immediate death or harsh prison terms in military cells greatly depended on bribing the security personnel – the Anyanya Yorams that patrolled the highways, the lake routes and the frontiers.

Ssempa did not wonder or puzzle at this respectable, dangerous man standing outside the Donn Reisch gates with his uncle. The *maulids* and *ddouwas*, whether meant for good or unorthodox things; brought various — and even incongruous — people together. The rich and the poor attended them, the latter as long as someone going there knew them. There were no official invitations to these functions. The powerful and the meek came to them. The grossly pious and the profanely iniquitous would be found there. All the same, Ssempa might have driven by and entered the Reisch grounds and not given Anyanya Yoram another thought had it not been for the fact that from the moment the Peugeot turned into that drive, Anyanya's eyes had monitored its progress and escorted Ssempa all the way to his stop, as if there was a magnet in the pickup that attracted his eyes. However, Ssempa guessed he might have been mistaken about the intelligence man's interest in him for the latter left quickly — almost hurriedly — after Ssempa had greeted the trio. Now the two clerics faced him, their attitudes like those of belligerent poker players, palpable amounts of unease manifestly visible in both the imam and Uncle Shafiq Kakembo. The imam's protuberant eyes, which gave the impression that he was always puzzling at something, regarded his face slyly, like a toad's. His cheeks and mouth, which suggested he was always about to utter a protest at something, moved restlessly, again like a toad's. His Pakistani attire probably made the imam the only African man dressed thus in the whole country at that moment. Ssempa had the premonition, mixed with his dislike for the man, that he might hit Gullid in the mouth. There was such a mysterious urge in the knuckles of his fingers.

On his part, Sheikh Shafiq wore a white *kanzu* robe emblazoned with a thin-thread purple embroidery that ran down its front from the knee area, in a line that became a set of four oblong rings and connected by the thin line that did not cut through the rings, which design stopped just above the hem. The same thin purple embroidery went round the *kanzu*'s collar and ran down the breast to the heart, where the clear white glass buttons ended. Over the *kanzu* the sheikh wore a chequered tweed coat in black, grey and brown mosaic, which colours were, Ssempa thought, the very ones in the bands of age that ringed the pupils of the fellow's eyes. The coat was open with wide lapels.

His cheeks had begun to collapse especially towards the corners of his mouth. He was clean-shaven and his chin was rough where the razor had hacked at it every morning for some five decades. There were lines in his face, more so around his mouth, that showed Shafiq loved to smile and to laugh, just as he was beginning to demonstrate right then.

"Katabanye," he addressed his nephew with the pet name he used for all young people, which meant 'young son.' "You are obviously wondering why I am standing out here in this cold evening weather instead of sitting bent over a platterful of turkey-rice pilau in there." He crooked a thumb over his shoulder to indicate the main Reisch house.

"Not really, *kojja*," Ssempa used the Luganda word for 'maternal uncle.' "When I see two men of God standing together with a military man of Anyanya type, I get to expect better security terms and conditions for the weak citizenry. But you are right in the sense that the turkey pilau must be missing you."

The two clerics guffawed. "The turkey missing me! *Ya'illahi*, God indeed created these creatures that we normally eat so that they should hope for the best of us to enjoy them. But not even *I* can put the invisible Almighty Allah into Anyanya Yoram's life. It is well known he visits shrines of the earthly gods to enhance his success in the work he does so well. I have, of course, heard the same about you from time to time, but I doubt you would bring yourself down to such levels, Katabanye. We Muslims are lucky to have Qurr'aan'el Karim to solve each and every one of our problems. Witch doctors are for the weaker faiths, son. Come for a douwa with me one of these days, to add to your luck. By the way I have been waiting for you, Katabanye, for the past several minutes. You must have got my message to that effect. I want us to discuss a very important issue."

"If it should keep both of you away from the fleshpots of Donn Reisch's manor, then it must be a very important issue indeed. But I can make a couple of guesses. You want me... either there is an old hag you want me to aid with a ticket and provisions for the coming Mecca hajj; or, yes — I have it," Ssempa went on when the Sheikh shook his head mischievously. "As usual, you have a nubile, buxom village daughter of a Muslim friend of yours that you want to pressurise me into marrying. By the looks of it, I think I just hit it on the head, eh?"

"You are fixated on women, Katabanye, like every young man of your age these days ought to be. But being thirty-five and not even showing any sign or intention of introducing to us a lifetime partner is not very good. A fortunate rumour has, however, been doing the rounds lately. A very good rumour too. You know Mbarara is a tiny place. I was in El Kahira and in Benghazi, you know, huge cities where a rumour would be swallowed up by the waters of the Mediterranean in no time and before moving anyplace. You have splashed much sperm around, Katabanye, to no visible propagative result."

"I will marry, uncle, when the right time comes," Ssempa said impatiently, with visible displeasure.

"Don't tell me of right times, Daoudi. Every time you take a woman into your bed — or her bed — as long as that woman is not officially wedded to some other man, that is ample opportunity to keep her for yourself as a wife. Fortunately this time, so the rumour goes, such a woman — virtually unwedded to any living man — lives under your own roof, in your own bed. My question to you is, do you intend to keep her?"

"No."

"Why not?"

"Because, with all respect to you, Uncle Shafiq, it is none of your bloody business."

"But, Katabanye..."

"You are delving into a part of my life where I don't permit anybody. Let us talk of other things. Do you have that candidate for a free pilgrimage to Mecca?"

Ssempa hoped the sauciness of his responses would discourage further talk. He was quite mistaken. His uncle, obviously unruffled, quipped: "I do. But it is more important to me that you wed this woman that you keep at your Kaburangire home. I wish it. The imam here wishes to officiate at your wedding. He was a Catholic a mere five years ago and wishes to prove to himself and those he left behind ... that they have always lived in oblivion of the God that encourages multiplication of His populations. Colonel Lupai was overjoyed to hear of it. Your father, as expected of him, hates the idea — and vowed to talk you out of it. But I convinced them, even the top *kadhi* in Kampala, that I would put sense into you. After all there is an equivalent of five thousand dollars in it for your honeymoon and other things."

The old sheikh had talked with progressive urgency because with every suggestion he uttered Ssempa's countenance became ever darker with rage. The pimpled imam looked on superciliously, his eyes unable to meet Ssempa's, which made the latter suspect he knew everything the sheikh seemed to know.

"Uncle Shafiq...."

"You appear shocked! But it is a small town, Katabanye, not a big city like Ilksandria or Tripoli. Tell us if you think she will make a good fertile wife. I haven't met her, which I should, you being my most favourite nephew. But if you will keep her — and wed her in our provincial mosque — I will never bother you again with those rural beauties I've always dangled before your eyes."

Ssempa was mortified. The bloody cheek of it! He told himself, seething. He thought he might be trembling visibly with the anger he felt in every sinew of his body. So that was why his uncle, the old rascal, had summoned him!

But Sheikh Shafiq was innocent. He was simply an old fool. Legends from his clerical parish depicted him as a Don Juan of sorts, a cavalier who waylaid his female parishioners, usually wives of his mosque flock, by arrangement in the shade provided by the abundant coffee groves. The parish women on their part praised the sheikh's libidinous tact, an art they attributed to his military life in North Africa now three decades past. He viewed the subject of carnality, with or without love, as a game. Yet, ironically, he was one of the very few Muslims — sheikhs for that matter — who were married to a single wife who had borne him all his seven daughters and four sons. Sheikh Shafiq Kakembo had no peripheral biological children.

Among many other things, the sheikh, being a brother to his mother, was Ssempa's closest and friendliest relative. Many had suggested the young Ssempa had inherited his maternal uncle's lifestyle to the hilt. Shafiq had circumcised the boy Ssempa when he was five years old. The sheikh was then a handsome young man who still wore his World War II uniforms with an array of iron and brass medals suspended from multicoloured ribbons. The reverence with which Ssempa treated his uncle had nothing to do with religion or piety. The old man had no room for deliberate evil in his heart and to the younger man that was the ultimate good in any man.

"Uncle," Ssempa did not attempt to put a lid on the disdain he felt. "You are my most cherished uncle. Do not get me to hate you, please."

"What?" Shafiq Kakembo exclaimed, apparently hurt by the genuine contempt in his nephew's voice and bearing. "Would you hate your old uncle for wishing you well? Would you hate me for introducing you to a deal whereby you may earn yourself a fortune in American dollars?"

"Haa, Uncle," Ssempa's heart warmed up to the old man whose feelings he would never have dreamt of hurting. "A deal worth thousands — you said five thousand dollars! That is a joke. And even then...."

"Ten thousand dollars," the Sheikh looked in the imam's face as if to seek confirmation. "Ten thousand — and other things."

"It's a joke, uncle. But even then, talk about money, for I know you know I love money immensely. Leave out anything to do with my bloody private life."

"But you don't deny that the woman is there," piped the imam. "So the sister business is true. How truly...."

"Shut up your facial arse, you little horror," Ssempa's voice came out with acid sourness. "What is that perfume you are wearing by the way, Mr Gullet — Doom? Or is it formaldehyde?"

"Katabanye," his uncle sounded breathless. "You must always respect men of Allah. He means good, not evil, for you. How can you refer to his good perfume, bought by me for him in Jeddah during my last pilgrimage, as Doom, a stupid insecticide?"

"Then it must be formaldehyde," Ssempa said, looking in the imam's toad-like eyes. They were about the same age so he, being irreligious to a degree his uncle had no idea anybody could possibly be, had no fear of needling the imam.

The mullah unleashed a string of Arabic swear words.

"What is formaldehyde, Katabanye?"

"Khafiroun Christians inject it in the bodies of their dead in defiance of God," the imam told him, laughing falsely. "They don't want their bodies to turn back into earth."

"And you use it to keep away your own rotten, stinking bodily odours."

"Ya rabbil'alamiina, Katabanye! Do you understand that Sheikh Gullid is a representative of Allah in this town? Or are you not aware!"

"Allah has a job at hand seeking a better representative; if he needs one, anyway."

"Ya rabbi, Daoudi! Don't let your emotions destroy your future for you. When you are better off, I am better off. Your whole family — your relatives would benefit."

"My family, as you very well know, Uncle, is not exactly wallowing in poverty."

"The money on offer, for nothing actually, is the equivalent of ten thousand American dollars. Even with your family's renowned wealth that is no mean boost. We have arranged for you a grand wedding ceremony plus a one-month honeymoon in any country of your choice and in that country's best hotels. We want you to wed this girlfriend of yours according to our wishes, in the Mbarara municipal mosque, with enough fanfare to attract the international media. As simple as that."

"And then?" Ssempa, after a brisk, brittle silence, sounded like the grave.

"A-ha," his uncle laughed uneasily. "It nearly appeared like you didn't want the money." He was rubbing his hands together in expectation. "When was the last time you struck such a wonderful deal, Katabanye?"

The poor innocent fool!

The genuineness of the old man's wishes and his gullibility were not lost on Ssempa. To Sheikh Shafiq Kakembo, veteran of World War II, who had rolled in the hay with uncountable numbers of women, Ssempa's apparent defiance to his money-laced ideas was incredibly unreasonable if not grossly strange.

* * *

Sheikh Shafiq Kakembo was the brother to Ssempa's mother, who was the second among old Sulayman Ssemaganda's five wives. The sheikh and the trader had both been born around the beginning of the First World War and had found themselves fighting together in the Second, both in North Africa instead of Burma, where the majority of the 7th King's African Rifles had been taken to fight the Japanese. East Africa was then under the sway of Britain's King George V. Kakembo had been a cook and Ssemaganda a gun carrier for a commander under Bernard Montgomery of Britain. They, especially the sheikh, never ceased to narrate the episodes of the Kasserine Pass, El Alamein, Tobruk and the endless 'towns' of Tripoli, El Kahira and Ilksandria on the great River Nile and the boundless Mediterranean Sea. Whereas those Muslims who went to Burma loved to swear *'Bharatu'*, in what they regarded to be an Islamic sacred word, but which actually was the Arabic and Hindi name for India, Kakembo and Ssemaganda would swear: *'Ya rabbil'alamiina,'* which they believed was a more powerful and even more sacred Islamic swear word than Bharatu since the former came right from the Arab world. It actually was: *'Ya rabbi, El Alamein!'* — or, 'Oh good Lord, what we saw at El Alamein!' El Alamein had, in October 1942, seen the end to undisputed German supremacy in the North African desert when General Montgomery's Eighth Army defeated the armoured panzer troops of Field Marshal Erwin Rommel's Afrika Korps there in the fiercest and bloodiest battle of the war. To date, *'ya rabbil'alamiina'* and *'bharatu'* are standard sacred Islamic swear words among Ugandan Muslims. A non-Muslim may not, therefore, utter them without causing grave and even bloody religious conflict.

Sulayman Ssemaganda had married Kakembo's sister in 1939 and David Ssempa was born at the end of 1940, during World War II. Ssemaganda had been born into a Baganda family that had sojourned to Nkore at the turn of the nineteenth century. His own father, Abduwahid Zzinda, had been a big chief under Nuwa Mbaguta of Nkore and had had wealth in cows and a big house on Ruharo Hill on the western edge of Mbarara town. On the other hand, Kakembo converted to Islam soon after the World War and in turn converted from being a Munyankore to a Muganda complete with the clan totem of *njovu*, the elephant. It was the norm in Nkore for Banyankore Muslims to become Baganda because, it was Baganda Muslim converts running away from battles with Christian converts in Mengo at the turn of the nineteenth century, who had brought the religion south to Nkore with them. To be a Muslim in Nkore is almost automatically to be a Muganda as well.

When Ssempa was five years old, Shafiq, then a mullah of a neighbouring parish, came by and circumcised him. He also remained around to treat the penile wound with a crimson cream that he spread on the broad velveteen surface of a thin-split, musk-smelling leaf that he wrapped round the glans of the child's penis every day at dawn after washing that wound with boric soap and a cock's feather dipped in lukewarm water laced with a pinch of caustic salt. Throughout his childhood the people Ssempa loved most were Sheikh Shafiq — for treating him with kid gloves — and Nyirandegeya, the Munyarwanda maternity ward birth attendant at the county hospital, who had delivered him from his mother's womb. Ssempa did not know that it was that funny, jovial, talkative dark old woman who had helped to deliver him. But Nyirandegeya would prevent the medical assistants Ntungwa and Bagombeka from injecting him with big needles and she herself would choose a smaller one, show it to Ssempa and inject him herself. She would have substituted the smaller syringe for the appropriate bigger one without his knowledge. And he would not cry. This made Ntungwa and Bagombeka the two men he loathed most during his childhood. Nyirandegeya and Ssempa remained attached to each other until his late adolescent days when he went away to study in Masaka and Kampala.

A cousin of Nyirandegeya became the fourth wife of Sulayman Ssemaganda. And it was she, Virgo Kabibi's relative, who brought her into the Ssemaganda home to grow up there. His mother would often tease the child Ssempa: *'Abannalwanda balikuntwalira,'* in her good Luganda, which translated meant she had a fear Banyarwanda women would one day take him away from her owing to the fact that from the time Kabibi's relative married into the home, Ssempa deserted his mother and went to sleep in the bride's bedroom. This he continued doing until long after his circumcision and until he was in Standard Two at ten years.

* * *

His mind returned to his uncle. He forgave the old man for his naivety. For such an old man, even so experienced and once well-traveled, Sheikh Shafiq Kakembo remained an old village cleric going senile. To him, such large amounts of money in American dollars were beyond the wildest of imaginations. And all that money, Shafiq would fancy, for nothing! In the old man's mind, the idea would be likened to the proverbial killing of two birds with one stone.

In the younger man's mind, Ssempa saw one big, bad concept: SCANDAL in bold capital letters. And the scandal would hurt him a lot less than the other person involved. And that was what he could not stand. He would rather die than hurt that woman. Ssempa knew — had known from the start in that candlelit White Horse Inn room in chilly Kabale Town — that there would certainly arise rumours in the long run. But not that such rumours would come up this way, with a sheikh — an uncle he loved and respected — officiously imposing demands on him. He saw no other way out except one: to use a most effective means to stamp out the rumours, to terminate them — disable their dangerous tentacles from stretching and straying beyond these two men. He needed, and was prepared, to demonstrate that right here, to most resolutely, decisively and even rudely put his foot down.

"Uncle," he told an all-attentive Sheikh Shafiq Kakembo. "What I am going to say to you is not for discussion. It is meant to be so final I may otherwise never ever speak to you until my death. I don't ever want you to mention to me the subject of that woman — that nun — ever again either in jest or in earnest, if you are the true brother of my mother. I know that perhaps in your own way — in your good, kind heart — you thought you meant well for me to broach the topic. But I want to assure you that in the process you have instead shocked me, hurt me and distressed me most staggeringly. I feel insulted and disrespected by you, my own mother's brother. I respect the woman you are talking about profoundly. She has my untold sympathy because I hold myself responsible for having led her astray from her path. I respect and feel for her so much I would kill human beings for the sake of her wellbeing, for the sake of her already tarnished reputation. I would indeed kill myself before doing anything that would add to her misery. I would never do anything that would scandalise her further. I hope, Uncle, that this pimpled serpent here is not involved in this or I will do all in my ability to harm him. Do you understand that? There can therefore be no more talk or hint about marrying that woman. I have no intention of wedding anybody in the foreseeable future anyway. Bring me as many hijja pilgrims for free tickets as you can, Uncle, and bring me any subject, good or bad, for discussion — but never that woman. I'll leave you now."

"Wait," the sheikh was all urgency now. "Not even if we doubled that amount of money? I am your mother's brother and your father's best friend. Twenty thousand dollars is quite a lot of money..."

"What is this absurdity all about, my dear uncle? You are one of the poorest relatives I happen to have. Your whole parish would never raise a small fraction of that amount of money in several years. What is going on in your head?"

"We'd raise it," mumbled the imam, his pop-eyes unblinkingly fixed on Ssempa's forehead, as it seemed.

Ssempa looked the mullah straight in the eye and said through clenched teeth: "If you so much as utter another whine from your filthy mouth directed to me or about me, I will break all the teeth in it. And please take that very seriously."

Gullid, sensing the earnestness in Ssempa's voice, gulped, his Adam's apple working up and down like an agama lizard's throat.

"Colonel Ali Drony Lupai was promising to buy you an English sports car. He was told you entertain a strong desire for the British and their motorcars." Ssempa turned round to see the new speaker, who continued, "Your love for the British reverberates resoundingly in all corridors of government offices, David. Lupai's elder brother, Chief Razak Illeh, whom you know well of course, is paying the million and a half shillings — the equivalent of the U.S. dollars your uncle just told you of, for this important government project. He has forgotten — he told me himself — your impregnation and abandonment of his daughter, Zakiya, in seventy-two. Your son is now four years old. Illeh knows you say it is not your son, but he says the boy resembles your father like a mirror image. He resolved not to fight a son-in-law in any case and that is one of the reasons you still live. He has hinted to me you once seriously attempted to save a daughter of his in a foreign country and that his Wife Number-One regards you as one of the Illeh family. Everybody, besides the British, seems to like you as well, it appears. I myself do. Illeh mentioned something interesting just the other day. If you had died who would have brought up this grand project that you have created with such ease? Did I tell you that the car Colonel Lupai, Illeh's younger brother, promises you is a brand-new Jaguar XJS? The colonel calls it a bonus. I am told they cost somewhere in the region of one hundred thousand shillings before taxes. So you see, despite the echoes of your love for the British in the corridors of government, they still love you. And that is an extraordinary love too, as you can see. None of them — not to my own hearing anyway — has connected you with the imperialist Americans or the Zionist Israelis, yet. Just our old colonial masters, the British, which they seem to think is understandable; they were, until only recently, our masters anyway. I genuinely believe you will wed the woman, David."

Ssempa wasn't jolted as much by the money and Jaguar car talk as he was by the man sermonising him on the exhausted subject of him wedding someone who was customarily considered an unmarriageable woman. Anyanya Yoram's hard handsome face was smiling at him. Anyanya's connecting him so persistently to the British — *a love affair with the British* — was the main threat. It was an insinuation meant to imply that Ssempa was a traitor and a saboteur.

"So this is it?" Though his heart still thumped fearfully, Ssempa had regained most of his composure. "So Colonel Lupai will now have his back at Bishop Kabigumira? Using me as the whip!"

"Why?" Anyanya asked, as though he didn't know the answer to his own question already.

"Because the bishop wrote that damning report on the colonel's misconduct — his excesses in the district. President Amin never took much action apart from lambasting the colonel publicly at the stadium gathering last year. And it is because of Lupai, your direct boss, that you, Anyanya, are involved in this. Why, I took you for a Catholic. All the Banyarwanda I know are."

"I am Presbyterian."

"No wonder. So I wed a nun inside a mosque to the utter bewilderment of Bishop William Kabigumira! And if I don't I get killed as a traitor! Is that not so, Anyanya? And my poor uncle is helpless in the matter he sounds so enthusiastic about! He's a mere pawn being used in all this — just like the nun and I."

"You are not too far from the truth, I am afraid," Anyanya was jovial. "I envy you your plight you know, Ssempa. Quite a dilemma, eh?" The cynicism in his voice could kill on its own. "You are being coerced to marry a woman whom you love so greatly, against your will! I happen to know her family too, as you of course know that all Batutsi are somewhat related. So you get forced to marry this Julian Kantarama, daughter of the late Apollinaire Sebwitabure of Gitarama, and get coerced, you could say at gunpoint, to accept a large package in scarce foreign cash, an exotic car to boot and an offer of a great foreign honeymoon. You choose the country too, and the topmost hotel there! Give me a break, David. That sort of thing does not impress me. You are not a Catholic, are you?"

"I have no religion."

"This is not Russia, or India, or China. You are a Muslim here. Your father is a Muslim. Your uncle here is a Muslim. So you are a Muslim. If I were a Catholic myself — and I am already married as you know — and such a chance offered itself, and required the pope to intervene in a divorce, I'd use all excuses to divorce my wife and get that money. And that car."

"But even a man of the stupidity of Razak Illeh knows me very well. I lived with his family in Koboko and Arua long enough for him to know what I can and cannot do. If I couldn't marry his daughter when guns were held to my temples, he knows I wouldn't marry a nun against my will. Didn't he tell you he offered me a mansion with a title deed and a brand new Mercedes Benz just so that I take Zakiya, his daughter, for a wife? As for Colonel Lupai, he has an option. He can burn me up like he did Kapere at the petrol station last year."

* * *

The colonel had driven up to the Caltex petrol station where a long queue of motor vehicles had, as always during Idi Amin's years of scarcity, been moving slowly to get to the fuel pumps. On stopping, the colonel had espied a taxi driver whose plastic five-litre jerrycan had just been filled with petrol. The young, shabbily dressed man was just leaving when Lupai stopped by. There was a decree in force, passed by Idi Amin among many other decrees of his in those times, prohibiting individuals from carrying petrol or diesel in containers other than the car tanks. The colonel hailed the man, who trudged over to him gripped with fear. The army officer had taken the container from the man, unscrewed it open and, grabbing the taxi driver by his shirt collar, upended the small jerrycan over his head pouring the pink liquid all over him. It was a hot afternoon with a heat that made the air appear as though it trembled in the pale grey sky above them. About two hundred vehicles were jammed in the queue. Pedestrians and motorists stopped by to see what the trouble was. Colonel Lupai, charcoal black, slim and tall, with deep cuts sliced vertically in his cheeks in the traditional rituals of his childhood, asked for a box of matches or a cigarette lighter from among the gathered public. He entreated them to provide a fire, stating solemnly as if to a church congregation: "This man has defied the presidential decree. He is a fuel smuggler and must be punished. Where were you taking this petrol, you?"

The taxi driver had run out of petrol less than a kilometre from where they gathered at the Caltex filling station.

"Why didn't you push the car here?" asked the colonel. He then called over the two uniformed soldiers with whom he had travelled in his personal ivory-white Mercedes. "Search these people gathered here. Should you find any with a matchbox or a cigarette lighter, drag him out to me. I shall punish him the same as this petrol smuggler."

Immediately heads began to duck, people skulked away from the scene. A man came up. He was young, the son of a prominent trader in Mbarara town. He himself was coming up as a promising dealer in motor vehicle spares. He got hold of the colonel's arm, which had a very expensive Rado watch strapped on it, and knelt before him in utmost meekness: "Please, my brother, Colonel, do not do it. I vouch for this young man with my life. You know me to be an honest man, brother Lupai, and I take you for a true friend. This taxi driver is not one of those bad people. If he was taking away the petrol it is because his car got stalled somewhere without fuel along the way. Please, do forgive him for my sake."

"My friend," the colonel addressed the kneeling man, looking down at the top of his head. "Do you have a box of matches or a cigarette lighter?"

The kneeling man looked up at the face of the colonel. He did not like what he saw in that man's face.

"No. You know me very well. I am not a smoker."

"Then get away from my sight and always stay away from me. From today onwards you are not a friend of mine. You are on the side of those who don't like the life president of this country. How can he issue a decree and you ask me to disobey it? Go away from here at once before my temperature rises."

The appealer hurried away, just as one of the officer's two men returned with a box of mathces.

"Who did you get it from? Who had hidden this box of matches? Bring him here to me at once. He should suffer the same...."

"It is mine, *Affende*," the soldier lied, easily. "I had it in the glove compartment of the car."

All this time the condemned man, a short, light-complexioned, pudgy fellow in a grey collared T-shirt and very rough uncombed hair, stood facing away from the colonel, who still held him by the collar of his tee-shirt. The man's head was bowed in terror, his shoulders and his legs trembling spasmodically. The officer released him, ordering him to squat down on the tarmac.

"*Affende*," said the provider of the matches, uneasily. He pointed at the No Smoking sign in white against red. "Let us take him to the side, on the grass patch there. Here the entire petrol station could catch fire."

"Let it burn. Why did they give him the petrol? They are abettors of the crime. But all right, you move him away to the grass. Go with the matches and waste no time."

On the grass patch below the fuel pumps and away from the long queue of cars and omnibuses, whose owners looked on helplessly as their vehicles were lined up nose-to-tail and thus couldn't be driven away immediately in case of a raging inferno, the soldier pushed Kapere to kneel down in the recently mown grass. He then, with the detached quickness of soldiers, lit the match and hopped away to safety as the flames exploded all over the unfortunate man.

That incident was the most talked of event for months. And it was one of those the Catholic bishop of the region had included in his grievance report to President Idi Amin as Kapere, that hapless taxi driver, had been his parishioner.

* * *

"For us," it was now Sheikh Shafiq speaking, "we had hoped that you, being a son of your father, a good Muslim, without reason for a grudge against our government..."

"Save that for your fellow idiots, uncle. I just discovered I don't like you that much anymore. Get out of my life."

"That is not particularly patriotic of you, David," intoned Anyanya. "Your uncle means well. The president himself was pleased to hear about the existence of men like you... men of guts. He, of course, had hoped – had expected you to be more cooperative; to be even grateful for his personal involvement in the noble scheme. As you know he is cousins with both the colonel and Razak Illeh. He made an additional personal contribution to those offers to you. I am sure he would not believe his ears if he heard there was even a hint of reluctance on your part."

"Are you talking about the president of Uganda?"

"Yes," replied Anyanya.

"I don't believe you."

"You had better. I mean these people would have better things to do with such cash and Jaguar cars."

"Well, between you and me, Anyanya, if that money were multiplied a million times, I still would never do it. Idi Amin is your employer, not mine. Let him marry himself a nun if he so wishes."

"Between you and me, I was directed to suggest to you the offer. And that offer is the government position. I have, take note, not heard your statements and seen the expression on your face as you made them, about our dear president — not officially anyway. *Mark* my words."

"The government position," Ssempa pretended not to fathom the gravity of Anyanya's threat. "The government is actually involved in my illicit affair with a woman!"

"It is important for the government, you see. That church is not behaving friendlily towards the state either. You take the money and the car and please the government. I was directed to give you the position most clearly. I had wanted to remain out of it, with the hope that your uncle might find it easier with you, and that if you showed signs of reluctance I should report back on your reactions. Obviously you know what that may indicate. It places you with those Zionists ensconced up there in the diocesan headquarters of the church at Kyera. It will be said that those people at Kyera are paying you a lot more to frustrate the efforts of our fatherland."

"And then?"

"You are behaving like a fool, Ssempa. You are not who I was made to believe you were. All along, in the time I've seen you in your business, I saw nothing but shrewdness. I am personally very disappointed in you."

"I'll cry later, when I've gathered enough tears over that. You see, Anyanya..."

"A son of your father!" Gullid spoke softly. "A son of such great custodian of our faith, begrudging our government...!"

The blow thudded against the imam's mouth with a resounding crack. His head snapped back and the awkwardly dressed man staggered away several steps but was stopped from falling by a thick bougainvillea shrub. A few people looked in their direction, saw no commotion; and went on their way. Anyanya's firm grip on the wrist held Ssempa back from any other onslaught that he might have intended.

"I warned the little swine," he swore.

The imam's large square teeth were bared and they were scarlet with blood. A string of expletives in Arabic issued from behind those teeth. Ssempa was familiar with words like *himar* for donkey, *murrtad* for converter from Islam to other cultures, *nagis* for plain shit and *khafiroun* for heathen.

"You are in their pay," he shrieked. "That is why you travel abroad all the time. That is why you are always in the company of that Italian priest. You are a saboteur — let me tell you before this officer and your own uncle. That is what is known of you."

"You shut up the dirty viper, Simba, or I will kill it."

"But he could be right too," remarked Anyanya. "In fact, as though it were necessary, we will give you tonight to muse over the matter. We want an answer — a concrete answer — tomorrow at ten o'clock sharp. Give it to the sheikh here."

"Yes," interjected his uncle. "I am sure you have not gone too far astray. You still belong to us."

"No," Ssempa shook his head. "You will never understand this, Uncle. It has nothing to do with religion. I am not a Christian. To be a Christian is no different from being Muslim – both are dangerous, exploitative doctrines whose real owners hated us so much they wished and continue to enjoy seeing us squirm under their influence. They are happy that they have Gullet here as their effective agent to ensure we don't wriggle out of their imperial grip. Look at how Gullet is dressed! Look at how we are all dressed! Whose clothes are these that have turned us away from our own and continue to force our minds and intellects away from invention and discovery? Those two religions don't belong here. We have in both several contagious evils imported here and deliberately designed to keep us divided and on tenterhooks, to render us unable to operate or cooperate as an entity and unable to unite against the bloody imperialists. Christianity and Islam are the most fundamental form of imperialism; they are the chief instruments in our bondage to our enemies. You yourself, Uncle, are an epitome of the whole problem of imperialism. The invading gunmen followed in your wake into areas already softened by your lies; persons in special dress were deployed to spread religious falsehoods. Persons whose wise intentions were worse than the gunmen's because the gunmen were never necessarily intellectuals. On the other hand you, like hyenas after a pride of lions, followed the murderous plunderers through the ruin and smoke into regions subjugated by a brutal force worse than the Holocaust, to lie to the traumatised natives on behalf of evil converters that all the mayhem was in the interest of God and to 'please, embrace the faith of the thief and spread it across the continent for survival's sake.' And, of course, you got paid — are still being paid, in various forms of material wealth to preach imperialism. We can never rid ourselves of you — the cleric and the politician, the two equally essential overseers of neocolonial interests. You are, like the scarecrows we leave behind in our ripe fields of grain and fruit to guard against flying pests, the instruments that ensure the imperialists' economic wishes are kept safe and unchanged. You through your Korans and Bibles, the politicians through the gun and the threat of prison. But then that is politics — which is anathema to this regime. Yet again, you need to understand that I am not your type of..."

"You have performed the hajj several times, Katabanye and Allah...."

"Allah, Allah, Allah! The man ... the thing actually ... you refer to is our Katonda and their Allah. You want to say Katonda but you fear the imperialists' lies that our native name for Almighty God is inferior and even pagan! That is what I mean when I tell you I am not that type of Muslim. I am a reasoning man, Uncle. I refused formal school but have educated myself extensively on life and the dangers we face from our invaders. If you should know, I go to Mecca for an opportunity to trade in duty-free merchandise. Most of you do the same thing. But let us not let that cause confusion. I have your answer for you, your fellow sheikhs, Colonel Ali Drony Lupai, Razak Illeh and Idi Amin himself. My answer is a never in capital letters. I will not marry by force, and I won't fight Colonel Lupai's proxy vendettas for him. You, Anyanya, don't need a gun to arrest me. I shall willingly accompany you to Simba Barracks and there, lie down like a lamb for the slaughter. Never ever will I succumb to this idiotic scheme of yours."

"Katabanye — is your head all right?"

"Leave him to me," said the intelligence man, taking Ssempa by the arm. He led him across the asphalt drive to a spot opposite the two clerics, who stood gesticulating with considerable agitation. The two, Anyanya and Ssempa, looked straight at each other as the army man leaned with his back against the cabin of Ssempa's pickup.

Ssempa spoke first: "You are not arresting me?"

"No. I forgot my gun in my office."

"You need a gun to arrest me? I meant everything I told you. I will come with you most willingly to your blood-soaked barracks."

"The things you say! I have no escorts with me, anyhow. I would require the regimental police."

"You don't need them. I am not resisting arrest."

Anyanya laughed, a hearty laugh full of amusement. "I cannot believe my ears, Mr David Ssempa, but I am learning an interesting lesson. You are a very dangerous man, my friend."

"What is so funny about me? I told you I wouldn't marry that nun. It can only happen over my dead body."

"I am out to change your mind for you. I am only laughing at the sheer thought of arresting you without my gun! It would require a fully armed platoon of the regimental police for that."

Ssempa simply regarded the intelligence man with a sour face.

"I am not that foolish. I saw the way you hit the imam. I don't know what to make of you. Where did you do your training?"

"You must know, Mr Simba, that I very well am aware you need no funny excuses or pretexts to arrest me. That is no longer how it is done in Uganda. So you can keep that *training-where* bit to yourself and take me to your charnel house of a barracks."

"It is hard to believe. You want me to take you to Simba Battalion headquarters all by myself, do you? Do you want to kill me the way you did that M'gungu man with his comrades at the end of last year?"

It was Ssempa's turn to laugh, an uneasy dry staccato sound with no mirth in it. "What do you mean?" he asked the intelligence man. "Is that another tactic of softening me up?"

"Come off it, David. Come off your silly obstinacy. It all comes to the fact that only I will be able to talk some sense into your sawdust of a brain before a more practical man than myself blows it out of your cranium for you."

"You think I am afraid of death?"

"Far from it. I am beginning to dislike your clever evasions of what you know. You are enjoying me – making a fool out of me. I am no food, Ssempa. Nobody ever eats me and enjoys it."

"And you flatter yourself, mister. No amount of psychological or other torture will bend me, rest assured."

"We, as a matter of principle, never torture or kill the innocent."

"I like that. Does it mean I am free to leave? I have no more stomach for Donn Reisch's turkey birianis and mutton masalas. Not after this unfortunate appetite-killing encounter. Do not think I ever enjoyed hitting that twerp — much as I detest him?"

"But," said Anyanya. "We kill the culpable, after torture, of course. You are basing your defiance on your purported innocence. But your innocence is only relative and circumstantial. It is not genuine in the first place, or absolute in several contexts."

"You use bombastic English, brother Anyanya. How far did you go in school by the way?"

"I like you, Ssempa. And I respect your father most deeply. But don't take me so much for granted as to get flippant with me."

"Well, I never went far myself, as you must know. I am therefore not despising you. I am only impressed by your flowery English."

"I went far enough, traitor."

"You, a Munyarwanda, can call me a traitor?"

"I am obviously more patriotic than you as far as the state is concerned. I have never disobeyed orders from above!"

"I am a law-abiding civilian, Anyanya. I only take my own orders."

"If you are a civilian, how come you managed to kill four soldiers, including an American trained officer, last November?"

"What...?"

"Don't say 'what'? You know *what*, exactly. But it should go to show you we needn't torture you or get Colonel Lupai to burn you the way he did the Kapere chap to get you to comply. You can bet your pickup here that isn't Lupai's cruelest action from the time I've known him. Have you not heard of what he did in Masaka when he was stationed there as the Suicide Mechanised Brigade commander?"

"No."

"You have not heard what Lupai did to demonstrate his fondness for his Alur wife? And yet you are supposed to be a son-in-law of sorts to him! Let me tell you the story. You may then perhaps see why you ought to be a happy, grateful man for being handled with such otter-skin gloves. Lupai one mid-morning drove his large car into Masaka Hospital. I myself did some of the investigations into the matter but went off it when the president decided to transfer the then captain to Kidepo Game Park in Karamoja — 'to live with the animals with which he shares traits,' as the president put it. So this is what Lupai does: He parks his Toyota Crown near the entrance to the hospital. His twenty-year-old wife — Zoe Atimango was her name — is eight months pregnant and has come for one of her regular prenatal check-ups. In the car with the husband and wife are two army bodyguards. As Atimango prepares to get out of the car, a group of people — men and women — come from the far end of the hospital premises bearing a crudely made stretcher with the cloth-wrapped human corpse of an adult person. Mrs Lupai exclaims: 'What's that?' Lupai tells her that is a human body being taken away for burial somewhere. 'Really?' The young woman is genuinely appalled. 'How can it be — so straight, so stretched out and prone, and so thin? I cannot imagine it!' Lupai asks his darling wife if it is true she had never seen a dead body before! In her innocence the woman affirms she has indeed never seen one. The Toyota Crown is parked facing a large *mvule* tree, its engine idling. Under the tree are seated over a dozen persons come to see their patients, some come for treatment. There are three bicycles leaning on their stands there and an empty wheelchair. I found those items there later on that day. Without warning, Lupai engages gear, revs the engine of the car and releases the clutch. The Toyota bounds off suddenly dashing into the unsuspecting, yelling crowd of people. Lupai, according to my investigations, is adept enough not to hit the big *mvule* tree. But when he reverses, five children, three women and one man, are dead, in cash — I mean on the spot. Many are critically injured, so that four more are dead by nightfall. All survivors are in shock. Later the bodyguards testify that Lupai, after reversing the car turns to his wife, stating: 'There you are, love. A number of them dead....' He does not finish his sentence. The wife has been shocked terribly and gone into a swoon. Since she can't see the spectacle of mangled dead bodies he had favoured her to see for her very first time, and won't see the gynaecologist in her present state, he brings her round with a few light slaps to her face and drives out of the hospital grounds. The survivors are not sure what exactly happened. Most of them believe the soldier intended to kill them for whatever reasons soldiers decided to kill civilians. Others believe Lupai was a learner and had lost control of the vehicle after engaging the gear. Other bystanders have doubts. But the two bodyguards and Lupai's wife know. They tell me all about it."

"And you are proud to belong to...."

"Do you know what happened to that wife a while later?"

"You mean...?" cried Ssempa with genuine horror in his face. He knew exactly what had happened to Zoe Atimango, Lupai's Alur wife, five years previously but was looking for a way of prolonging the intelligence officer's tales while he sought means out of his fresh problem. "You mean that she is not alive?"

"You are supposed to know. You are the father of his niece's son. The story goes that he suspected Atimango to have had an affair with a recruit of Nsambya Police Training School — a relative of a big man in the Public Safety Unit wing of the police force, who had married from a militarily influential Koboko family. Lupai looked for the recruit all over Kampala with the intention of killing him and not only failed to trace the chap but also got a serious warning from Koboko — the place the president hails from — of dire consequences if he murdered the youth, who later vanished. In a fit of frustrated chagrin, Lupai put his wife into a Mercedes he had just bought, along with a little daughter of theirs — the product of that Masaka pregnancy had died in a miscarriage, you see. He parked them at a place before Cape Town Villas in Munyonyo, on Ggaba Road, with the wife handcuffed to the steering column of the Mercedes. He brought a tank from the nearby Bugolobi Barracks and personally drove it over the Mercedes. Four times. Do you get that? Four times Lupai turned that tank round and ran it over his brand-new Mercedes with his wife and daughter in it, so that the woman and child could not be separated from the metal wreckage later. He loved the three too much, he claimed later to a board of inquiry, to leave any of them to anybody. The three included the Mercedes Benz. He had expected no punishment short of a firing squad, of course. But his mother is a Congolese-Kakwa woman related to the father of the president. She is, more than that even, the president's chief witchdoctor. Lupai was posted to Mbarara as a form of demotion, in punishment for his uncouth deeds. He had been the erstwhile commander of the Malire Regiment in Kampala. Today, as you know, he commands a mere battalion. But he has since jumped the rank of lieutenant colonel to full colonel right from major. What else, foolish man, do you want me to tell you so that you may marry Kantarama?"

"That is already too much for my ears. I am actually unhappy that I am now privy to it all. But I still fail to see what it has to do with me."

"The murders you committed at Kyondo near Kamuganguzi are what it has to do with you. You were let off on those killings for three reasons primarily. Firstly, the commandant of the military police detach at Mwanjaari had an axe to grind with the officer you killed. Secondly, the respect your father commands in the Islamic and business community. And thirdly — and very oddly — because Razak Illeh Amin seems to prefer you alive and kicking, rather than dead. That is the impression I get whenever you are talked about up in those circles. But, of course, more than anything else, some people are simply lucky. Am I clear?"

"No, you are not. Of course, if what you are saying actually did happen, then you are confusing me with somebody else. I deny knowledge of all your false accusations against me and do reiterate my stand that you do whatever you want with me and later with my dead body. That must be clear to you, Bwana Simba."

"Two days after the killings," Anyanya Yoram continued as though Ssempa's detached response had never been made, "I was called in along with my colleagues, as would ordinarily be expected. I have been chief investigator for the army in southern Uganda right from 1973 even though I am just a corporal of the police force attached to military intelligence. There had been a fire at Kamuganguzi, at an impromptu military checkpoint erected to check fuel smugglers and other bandits. The preliminary information we collected and the circumstantial evidence we built pointed to a tall, stoutly built black-complexioned Muganda man traveling with a dark-skinned woman with fine hair which was visible even though she wore a wimple-like veil. A Munyarwanda woman in a leather-brown nun's habit, complete with a crucifix. They traveled in a tarpaulin-covered dark blue pickup truck, a Peugeot 404 pickup. This very vehicle against which I lean, I am afraid." He patted the vehicle's bonnet several times with his large open palm. "We adduced evidence that the two were saboteurs of sorts in disguise on a mission hitherto and henceforth unknown or identified. We were soon onto your pickup and even prepared a raid on your Kaburangire house. But a little later on, when Illeh got wind of it — from my commanding officer, Colonel Lupai himself of course — he hinted that he knew of your missions to Rwanda and Burundi and that you could definitely not be a saboteur. Imagine that from a man who everybody knows to wish you hell, David. And as you are aware, what Illeh says in this region — or any other region of this country for that matter — goes without much dispute. Now you know what I am talking about. And I begin to see the source of your haughty pride. You are quite well aware of Illeh's strange fondness for you."

"Same thing, Bwana Anyanya. I totally deny everything you state about me." But he knew the intelligence officer — his eyes studying every reaction of his face — had him in a tight fix. He was shaken by Anyanya's revelations because he had never had the faintest of suspicions that anything was known about his Kyodo checkpoint ordeal. He never had any idea that his old enemy, Chief Razak Illeh, could save — had indeed saved — his life by vouching for his actions. Now he had provided him with a kind of alibi in an obviously grave case of manslaughter as he preferred to deem it, though during Idi Amin's times such a legal term could not have been recognised in the courts of law. At the same time he was grateful to the gods for the wonderful feeling that Anyanya Yoram had no idea that he, Ssempa, had been the police recruit hounded out of the country by a Major Ali Drony Lupai, who did not know Ssempa's identity. His knees would have started knocking had the intelligence man remotely alluded to his name in connection with the Zoe Athocon Atimango Lupai episode. As it was, he had to lean against the pickup to steady himself against the shock of the mere reference to the 1972 incident of Atimango and her daughter. The limbs felt like jelly. It felt as though his legs had been replaced with a cushion of vapour. He could not help remembering that episode some five years previously when he became a direct victim of the feared man, Colonel Ali Drony Lupai.

He said, with a weak smile: "It is obvious you will go a long way to try to soften me up for the slaughter."

* * *

In 1972, without informing the family for fear that his strict father would disapprove, Ssempa abandoned a certificate course in motor vehicle mechanics to enroll in the Uganda Police Force. He left the Masaka Polytechnic with two other students who included his childhood friend and peer, Jee Salleh. This Jee had an older brother, George Mwigo Salleh, who was popularly known by his childhood pet name, Kacheeche, who was a senior superintendent in the police force. And it was Kacheeche who had made it easy for them to enlist. The superintendent lived with his wife Alwiah and two little daughters on Kisugu Hill between the Kibuli and Muyenga hills at the eastern edge of Kampala City. He had recently converted to Islam, just like several other Ugandans had done so as to feel more comfortable in Idi Amin's administration. It is probable that things would have happened differently if the police officer had not converted, for then he would never have left for the Mecca pilgrimage, and therefore Ssempa would not have gone to collect the two little daughters from school, where he would meet Zoe Atimango for a second time that fateful day.

They were in their fourth month of hard training at Nsambya, below Kibuli Hill, and had been given two weeks' leave whereupon Jee, who had no problem with his family over his joining the police force, returned to Mbarara to spend his. Jee's brother, ready for the Mecca pilgrimage, had welcomed Ssempa's idea of staying at his home during his absence. The cop was much older than Ssempa and Jee but they had all grown up in the same town, Ssempa in the town centre and the Mwigos in Kakoba, the famous Mbarara suburb.

The day he met Zoe Atimango he was driving in Kacheeche's bright yellow Isuzu Bellet car with groceries in the back seat. There were four large houses to one side of the short tarmacked drive that joined a large isolated road to form a T-junction, and a hedge of short oak trees and wild climbers to the other side, where there was a small old Anglican church with a rusted corrugated-iron roof. The Kacheeche house, a storeyed mansion with red tiles and whitewashed outer walls, was the second in the row as you entered the dark tree-lined drive. Ssempa drove the car at a gentle pace and nosed it into the drive just as a large jet-black Mercedes 280 SE shot out of it bucking like a wild bull on the rampage. A woman with a very light complexion was at the wheel. She was big and obviously tall and seemed to buck and bounce up and down behind the wheel with the movement of the big vehicle as she braked hard. The windows of the black Mercedes were tinted a cool green that seemed to light up the inside of the big car. But then Ssempa quickly noticed that the vehicle's sunroof stood open and the daylight fell on her directly from the sky. The woman, without wasting any time, leaned across her empty passenger's seat and rolled down the glass window. She turned down the volume of the car's hi-fi system, from which had just been gushing out Nsereko & Biriggwa's *Rocky Tonnenya*, and gestured with her head in a tacit inquiry — a gesture viewed as haughty by Ssempa, and which obviously said: 'Do you want me to reverse, in such an unmistakably expensive limousine as you see me in and such an important person as you must obviously see me to be, so that you, a mere mortal in an undisguisedly decrepit Isuzu Bellet, clad in a grey sweat-stained police training wing tee-shirt, may pass?'

Appreciating her implicit attitude, he put his head out of the window and said loudly in Luganda to the impatient woman: "Yours is bigger than mine. You could ease a bit onto the grass verge!"

Out of the blue, the woman laughed, flashing stark white teeth and her very dark Mongol eyes slanting even more. Her body complexion was a dark burnt yellow; the forehead was broad, her mouth wide and her nose small and quite short. She had exotically tousled jet-black hair. The laughter curved her cheeks gently and made her whole face a lot softer. She said, looking at him straight in the eye: "Just *how* do you know mine is bigger than yours — because you are a police detective?"

He did not get the joke immediately and showed a sheepish confusion on his face but when he did, he lit up and said: "Look, Madam. Oh, boy," he exclaimed when the joke filtered into his dull mind. His eyes made a cursory round trip over her body: "It's so obvious anybody with red blood flowing through his veins would sense it. And quite a beauty too."

The woman, in a melodramatic manner, peered at her body — her eyes going to her lap. She then looked at him and asked, a grave tone in her voice, "You know that, even?"

"It goes for your entire body, of course. You are the prettiest woman I have seen in quite a bit of time. I have been in training school four months to-date, and there are no women there."

"Sure, I can see that. You look big yourself."

They stared in each other's eyes for a very brief moment as if they gauged, in the psyche of each, what the other had stated.

She laughed again: "Okay. I'll ease over." She twisted the wheel away from the Isuzu and the heavy Mercedes' tyres crunched into the loam of the grass kerb, and Ssempa hurled the Isuzu forward, pausing for a second to say: "Thanks."

The woman said something like, "It's nothing," but her voice was drowned out in Euclas Kawalya's *Eseza* as her large car murmured its way off, away from the quiet neighbourhood.

As he eased the car into its parking space inside the walled-off enclosure, Ssempa was seething with an unreasoning anger. What would it have cost him to ask her name or address?

"I'm a proper ass," he said to himself. "I didn't even note the registration number of that Mercedes."

"What?" the gardener that had opened the car's boot asked.

"Nothing," Ssempa told him. "Her vehicle is unique, after all."

"She's his daughter," said the gardener, an old man in his early sixties. He used his head to gesture in the direction of the neighbouring house that stood behind a high brick fence.

"Who is whose daughter?"

"The woman you spoke to at the entrance to the drive. She's the daughter of the sheikh."

"What sheikh?"

"Sheikh Rajab Athocon – the house behind that; the last one. Married, too. The husband is on a pilgrimage to Mecca, with my boss."

Married! Ssempa pushed her out of his mind most promptly and, after the gardener had offloaded all the groceries, he returned to the steering wheel and drove out of the place. It was lunch hour and he had promised Mrs Alwiah Mwigo Salleh, who taught mathematics in a nearby day school, that he would pick the two little girls from the Norman Gordinho Primary School four kilometers away on the other side of the city.

He arrived at the school when most parents were driving off with their children and the din of the yelling pupils was reducing in loudness, and parked the car across the road at the public library. He sat there watching the shrill-voiced children, his eyes scanning the scene for the two little kids. There was a sudden sharp clap, like the crack of a sports pistol — three rapid reports obviously issuing from some person's clapping palms. Ssempa's eyes instinctively swerved to the sideview mirror and saw the woman. Her eyes were focused across the road, several yards away from the school's main entrance, where several little girls were engaged in a noisy argument. One of those, a tot of about six, detached herself from the noisy group and stood looking across the road, ready to cross it the moment the guard raised the red flag to stop oncoming motor vehicles from either side of Buganda Road. Ssempa's head came out of the window.

The woman stood at five-foot-five, dressed in a mostly yellow and purple flowing maxi dress printed with tiny white flowers on green foliage. She wore brown leather shoes with pointed high heels and held a smouldering cigarette in the left hand, which was lowered to her side. She had put on a pair of dark glasses since the time — forty minutes back — when he had seen her in Kisugu. Somehow, she sensed that his eyes were on her. This made her turn her face and she saw him staring at her. Thirty or forty feet separated them.

"Sorry, please," she said in English. "Just wanted to attract Zillah, my daughter." The little brown child had already darted across the road and grabbed her mother's hand in a frantic show of child-to-mother love. Ssempa deemed the 'my daughter' a little superfluous. Mother and daughter were identical except in size and age. Zillah was a cherub and the mother a replica only twenty or so years older.

"It's all right, Mama Zillah," Ssempa said, having stepped out of the car and ambled to her side. Euclas Kawalya was still at it on the hi-fi, this time crooning praise to Lake Victoria's powerful waves in *Yira, yira Nnalubaale*. "Your clap was a godsend as it attracted those two other rascals just crossing over. It's them that I came to pick up." He pointed to the Mwigo kids.

The friendly smile vanished from her face: "How do you know my name?" she sounded alarmed — and aggressive. Her eyes looked around the place apprehensively.

"Ah — I don't know your name. But you told me your daughter's, and everybody here names women after their child's name. Mama so-and-so. When I was a child my mother was called Mama Ssempa."

"That is your name? Mr Ssempa; a Muganda, eh? And those are Alwiah's kids! So that is where you were driving when we met, eh?"

"Yes; I live there."

"Ah, what is she to you? Or are you related to the husband?"

"The latter. We are family friends from way home."

"You frightened me," she said, having switched to Luganda. "I don't think it is good for you to stand and talk to me like this the way we are doing. Do you actually sleep at Alwiah's place?"

Her inquisitive eyes had such long lashes at first he took them for artificial eyelashes. They were such sad eyes in a person that drove a flashy Mercedes Benz!

"For the next ten or eleven days, maybe."

"And then?"

"And then back to Nsambya for five months of grueling drills."

She clucked her tongue sympathetically.

"So you are a police trainee. Then we should be able to meet again. What do you drink?"

"Tea and water or the other way round."

"Sure? You strict on Islam? Are you Muslim, anyway?"

"Yes and no. My parents and people — you know what I mean, believe they are Muslims. I guess I have to be one as a result, but I am such a rebel. Are you Muslim yourself?"

"From the strictest Muslim family in the whole West Nile province I assume. But if you do drink, I could arrange a wonderful liqueur... for both of us; something for beginners in sin, you know. Do you know why I got scared when you called me Mama Zillah?"

"No, you tell me."

"Well, my real name is Zoe Athocon. My father is your neighbour — Sheikh Rajab Athocon. My maiden name is Atimango."

"What impressive names — Zoe, Athocon, Atimango! The *mango*, especially."

"My husband, well, I am simply one of his wives — is Captain Ali Drony Lupai."

The shrieking of the school kids was abruptly broken by a heavy quietness which lasted a long moment.

"Oh, my God." Ssempa blurted the words out, his eyes no longer transfixed by her enthralling beauty but instead darting from car to car, from one adult to the next, within the entire precinct of Buganda Road, as if to record — to see how many eyes, if such recording was possible, had witnessed his reckless madness. This two-minute intercourse with the wife of the second most deadly army officer besides Brigadier Hussein Malera in the Idi Amin military hierarchy.

"Please, do not do that," the woman had opened the door for the daughter and shut it and now stood with her foot on the running board.

"You *are* the wife of Ali Drony Rapai!"

"Yes. But we are safe — for now. I know I am not being monitored. I would know it, of course. But we've met twice today — quite unexpectedly." She had taken off the dark glasses and fixed him with her sad — almost tragic — eyes. "I long for company, Mr Ssempa. But I will tell you all about that if you agree to my arrangement. I will drive a silver grey Iso Grifo to my father's house — the Sheikh Athocon mansion — at six o'clock. You'll be able to notice it when I arrive, if you care to look out for me. Then I'll send one of my brothers to fetch you. I'll bring a big bottle of good booze. Tell nobody, not even Alwiah, about it."

"That is simply not possible, Mrs Captain Rapai."

"Zoe Atimango," she laughed, as she had done earlier in the day. "'Rapai' is how he pronounces it when drunk, which is most of the time. But back to us; those Palestinian neighbours of ours will be partying as usual and there will be a *douwah* to pray for the pilgrims in Mecca at my father's place. I know we'll be safe with such a crowd around. You will come, won't you?"

The appeal in her voice and her sad eyes he had never felt in a woman before that day. It melted his heart — along with his sensibility.

"I'll try," he said.

"No. Promise that you'll come. Don't fear my Captain Lupai. He is away in Saudi Arabia."

"But. ...Okay, I'll come."

"Promise?"

The singer Fred Kanyike was lamenting '*Laba mbonabona, Dayiana maama, laba ndaaga, kululwo ggwe...*' on what must have been a record player in the car rather than a radio and Ssempa's head was going round and round in circles; how else could he be making those declarations and pledges to such a woman?

"Yes. I promise — I'll come."

"All right; I'll send Kajutant, my younger brother, to collect you. Look, I am aware we've stood together too long. Bye-bye."

Before he could bat an eyelid, the huge Mercedes was swishing past the little Isuzu Bellet with grace.

He found the girls already seated and in hot argument and sat behind the wheel. His eyes studied the surroundings minutely, using the mirrors and direct view. The din of yelling pupils had greatly subsided. He had not stood with that woman for more than four minutes, and if anybody had interested themselves in their brisk conversation, that somebody would now be interested in quite different issues. Which, Ssempa mused, meant that truly, their conversation could easily have been monitored. But what could he do now that he had already spoken — physically spoken — with the wife of the man who took very accurate potshots at people who, in bypassing his Old Kampala Hill residential mansion, happened to throw an innocent glance in the direction of his huge goats and fat waddling geese roaming the compound of the palatial residence. Indeed it was next to impossible not to turn to look at the querulous multitude of geese, stark white like new cotton wool. Of course, many a passerby knew not the temperament of the owner, who would be standing or seated somewhere in the dark portico of the large house watching the usually empty public street. Empty because many who had seen men, women and children fall never to rise up again after a single report of pistol fire chose longer detours to get to their destinations rather than risk the street in front of Lupai's house. It was known that Captain Lupai as a rule never shot at passersby who did not show an interest in his house, but citizens who had seen the occasional dead bodies of his victims preferred not to risk their lives when Old Kampala Hill was endowed with plenty of alternative streets and paths. Yet the odd stranger to the area would use the deserted road, usually wondering at the unique emptiness of it, and thus marveling at the large mansions and at Lupai's huge goats and noisy geese. Such a stranger could only survive a sure shot in the event that the mad captain was away.

The captain's residence was one street below Fort Lugard; and a half-mile street connecting two major thoroughfares passed by its front. Most of the houses — a dozen of them — were large mansions that had housed colonial officials before Independence and were now the residences of soldiers of high rank who were the new state administrators. The Lupai mansion was one of the largest since, even though he was just a captain, he was President Idi Amin's distant relative. He commanded the militarily important Malire Regiment, with its paratrooper battalion near the city centre and an armoured detachment at nearby Bugolobi, towards Lake Victoria's militarily strategic Port Bell. This trusted formation controlled central Uganda, which included the capital city, and this position made Lupai, besides Brigadier Hussein Malera, the murderous Sudanese who commanded the military police, the most powerful commanding officer in the eyes of those who knew the Idi Amin military hierarchy. Their power to kill did not end with unarmed civilians. The two formations, especially the military police, arrested soldiers of all ranks, and it was a known fact that the larger percentage of prisoners at the military police headquarters on Makindye Hill or at the Malire Regiment Headquarters, were brutally murdered and their corpses mutilated, usually by the brigadier or the captain.

In the meantime, visitors drove or walked in and out of the captain's residence mostly in military vehicles. The family, quite a large one since the soldier lived with all three wives, children, relatives and friends, went about its daily chores as if everything in the precinct was normal.

Ssempa had heard and knew the truth about several of those rumours. But his age made him a reckless person otherwise how could he have remained in Kampala as if nothing had happened, after talking to the wife of one of such sadistic people? How could he even think of considering — contemplating — that woman's callous invitation? For in Uganda at that time, women never proposed carnal affairs to men! But he had taken her invitation to heart. At Kisugu he got into the drive through a different entry, the side further away from the place where he resided. He paid new attention to the Sheikh Athocon mansion on its two-acre plot. There were many smaller houses and a couple

76

of large army-green tents in the large compound. The front and part of the backyard were divided by a well-manicured cypress fence with breaks here and there where strands of thick barbed wire were exposed. High brick walls separated the Athocon residence from the neighbours' at either side. A number of Palestinian military instructors occupied the house between Athocon's and the Kacheeche residence where Ssempa lived. There were half a dozen cars parked outside and two army jeeps inside the Arabs' compound and lots of jovial noise issued from within it. Ssempa estimated the distance between his residence and the Athocon gate at about one-hundred-fifty yards. His senses were excited by the image burnt into his brain of the burnt-ochre complexion of Zoe Athocon Atimango.

In the evening at tea, and quite casually, Ssempa asked Alwiah about the woman.

"*Ehh, Shemeji,*" she responded, guardedly, in Kiswahili, the language normally used in the house. Shemeji is Swahili for 'brother-in-law' or 'sister-in-law'. "Has there been something about that woman in the papers or over the radio?"

"No, *Shemeji*. I just wanted to know if you knew her!"

"Why? Let God turn me into this biscuit immediately, Shemeji, there's no earthly reason for you to talk about — to want to know anything about — the wife of Rapai."

"Well, she's one of a horde of them."

"Yes. But she's his favourite even though he chose to take to Mecca his newest one. He's dangerously jealous of Athocon's daughter. She can only move out with the women of the Rapai family as chaperons, you know. Even when she visits her father's home, which she does quite often, she's escorted there by the Rapai sisters or aunts. But Sheikh Athocon is even stricter than Rapai with women and the captain knows that. But please, never mention it to my husband that we discussed Zoe — indeed, why are we talking about that woman?"

"Your husband...."

"Powerful in the Special Branch as he is, George is frightened witless of Rapai, full-stop. She visited me once and my husband nearly strangled me."

"Get ready to have God turn you into a biscuit, Alwiah," the woman always swore by the nearest item to her. She would say '*Nikapinduke chupa hii*' to mean 'Let me be turned into this bottle', as a way of swearing. "I saw Zoe Atimango twice this afternoon."

"And by that you mean! So what...?" Alwiah looked more closely at him with unconcealed horror. "You even know her maiden name! You... And? And? Tell me! And what?"

"Well — we sort of exchanged niceties."

"Ehh, Shemeji!"

"What? Say — you woman. I am not easily intimidated."

"Y-o-u talked to t-h-a-t woman? In public?"

"Yes. We like the same kind of music, too. She plays hers very loud."

Alwiah digested his answer slowly, her eyes studying his face, to see if Ssempa wasn't merely pulling her leg. "Let God turn me into that light bulb right now, you have to die! Rapai is in Mecca, but that means nothing. It is like he is here — in Kampala."

"Shemeji..." began Ssempa.

"She liked you, did she? I know Zoe. She told you her name! She bloody well told you her lovely name! She was..."

"We talked for some bit of time — maybe a minute or two, and made an appointment."

"What?" Alwiah was not faking going out of breath. "What did you say just now, *Shemeji*? Let God immediately turn me into this teacup, you are a dead man. You are dead, dead, dead. How can you...?"

"Now, *Shemeji*...."

"Dead, I say. But really, what a waste! Why are they going to kill you, you man? Why did you come here — and for me to send you to that school, and for you to meet that woman? Why have you killed yourself, *Shemeji*, with your eyes wide open?"

"Shemeji, I...."

"Tell me, *Shemeji*," Alwiah was agitated and excited all in one. "What did she say? Who asked for the appointment? Did you know who she was?"

"She herself told me who she was. Then she suggested we meet at the father's house tonight."

"Oh, my God!" The horror in Alwiah's voice was total. "All along I wanted you to say you were lying to me. But something tells me you are in earnest, *Shemeji*. That is how people die. And trouble never seeks man — man seeks it. It could affect my husband — his career. If you do anything wrong, *Shemeji*, it can cause our deaths, even."

"I will not keep the appointment then."

Alwiah thought for a long moment: "Let God turn me into this tablecloth immediately, she must be very, very lonely — and hungry too — for a man. Why do you Muslim men use the stupid excuse of a lewd Koranic suggestion to do the impossible? — How can a man have — own in fact — so many women as wives when even fully satisfying one alone sexually is not that easy? How can a man — however naïve — mix up a woman like Zoe with other women? That girl is an Alur and Alur women are extremely sexy. But

78

why do I wonder? George just became a Muslim and soon I might find myself being referred to as Wife Number One!"

"He's not likely, ever, to marry another."

"Thanks for your comforting words, false as you know them to be. I would pack up my things and vacate his life forever. Poor Zoe. You said she proposed the appointment. What are you going to do?"

"I told you I am out of it."

"No please, for God's sake! She needs you. I can imagine what she's going through in that harem at that Old Kampala Hill house. It is those eyes of yours. She couldn't resist their bloodshot streak; eyes of a drunkard who is not that much of a *drunko*."

"Now, *Shemeji*...."

"Eyes of a ganja smoker who doesn't even do cigarettes. Do you know Zoe is a smoker? Not ganja, of course. Shows you how worried she is. Such a young girl!"

"What is your advice to me then?"

"You are going to have her! And she knows you are both safe — well, relatively safe — at her father's house. Do you know why Rapai knows no nonsense can take place in his father in-law's residence?"

"No, I don't."

"Long before independence, Rajab Athocon, then a bus driver, used a sharp razor to scoop out the private parts of his wife whom he suspected of cuckolding him."

"Good God!"

"The woman bled to death. And Athocon was sent to Openzinzi prison in Moyo-East for fifteen years."

"You don't say!"

"He came out of prison sometime after independence when he had converted to Islam. He went to Mecca several times, establishing contact with Arab traders who helped him start his transport and furniture companies. Today not many know of the sheikh's past. You can easily think he was born Muslim, even."

"What a brute! I hope I never get to meet him."

"Indeed, his domestic strictness — people of his household accept him as a slave rider of sorts — borders on the brutal. But like I pointed out about the tendency to polygamy, some of these things don't work. Most of the sheikh's children are into booze. How do you intend to go there?"

"She's sending one of the brothers."

"Let God turn... I thought so."

"You don't really mind me going?"

79

"I know you want to go. If I was a man, I would want to go," she made a dirty face. "How I would maul that woman — like a crocodile a fat zebra!"

"Ah, *Shemeji*...."

"I was with her at the airport to see our husbands off, you know. The way she walked, the way she talked! The texture of her skin — plumped, and the long look in those wide dark eyes. I got the impression she could rape a horde of men. Hassina, Mrs Captain Levi Kelili, said things to that effect and alluded to the idea that she might be pregnant! No man has a right — never let it happen to you, *Shemeji*, to marry more than one wife. I want you to imagine that Zoe is fully aware of the lethal dilemma she places herself — and you — in, by that desperate invitation. The Lupais of this world kill fellow human beings with less regret than we slaughter chickens for food, and yet their wives will risk all...."

"I won't go, *Shemeji*".

"No, you will. If you don't go, I'll deem you a coward and a weakling too. I'll deem you a man not worth any woman's respect. It is always chivalrous, as they say, to rescue a woman in danger — or in dire need."

* * *

There were over twenty cars and several revellers at the Palestinian residence. He had seen the big deep-throated Italian car slouch its heavy nose to the gate ten minutes earlier and, with much prodding from Alwiah, walked out of the house and down the drive in his grey tracksuit. He moved past several cars, left the main mansion to his left and followed the hedge to the Athocon gate. A young fellow introducing himself as Kajutant was there to receive him with a quiet 'salaam aleikoum.' It was seven-thirty sharp. They entered the Athocon grounds through a narrow heavy iron gate and hurried to a small iron-roofed cottage at the extreme back of the grounds. Ssempa was convinced nobody had paid much attention to him outside the gate. You could not do that with the crowds entering the 'Arab' gate. Inside it they met no one, and as they entered the two-roomed candlelit house, Kajutant vanished into the gathering darkness.

"Please, sit down." The woman came from the much darker room, bypassed him, the perfume she wore brushing his face. She shut the door quietly, and turned round to find him still standing.

"Daoud," she said, the light from the candle glinting from her evenly set, strong white teeth. Her hand took his arm — a very warm, soft palm and velveteen fingers. The name 'Daoud' came off her tongue as if she was using her teeth to nibble at it. "I shan't thank you for coming — because I don't have the words of gratitude for your very considerate gesture." Her body was before his, the warmth of it pulsating along with the fragrant perfume, hitting him in blasts. He trembled inwardly with the excitement of lust and with utter fear. The woman stroked the bridge of his nose with her finger and somehow without pushing, directed him to a seat. "I am going to offer — to give you a drink; a little alcohol in it! Please, don't say no. I know — no I don't know whether you are a brother to Kacheeche or to Alwiah, who are new to Islam. But even if you are a Muslim, I myself am the daughter of a top-notch sheikh, therefore you shouldn't mind. And this one is not all that alcoholic. It's made from oranges and is even sweet — very sweet. Not a whisky — or even a wine. It's liqueur — yes, Drambuie. I speak French too. So — ah… here you are. Try, Daoud — is it going to be your first time?"

"Ah — umh — yes. Argh — argh — argh. Atch — tch — tch; sweet, yes — and hot. Warm-hot. And… ahhh…" He had taken a small gulp — not sip — of the golden amber oily — orangey-tasting stuff and was now feeling the warm-hot ball of it descend ever so gently — but inexorably — down his intestines until it rested at the bottom of his tummy and burnt a heavy impression where it had settled. Strangely, he felt like he was sweating. And that woman's gentle satiny fingers stroked his inner arm and the other fingers a vein down his neck.

"You'll easily get used to this. And also, especially, to me." She took a sip from the same glass and offered it back to him for another sip. She then took hold of his head and brought her mouth to his. She did not kiss him; she simply made as if to kiss him. When he opened his mouth, her hot, Drambuie-sweet tongue slithered in and out of his mouth — like a serpent's perhaps, about a million times, very rapid movements that his mouth was unable to arrest or keep. And when she sat back, his mouth, his teeth, his mind — they all wanted her back doing the same thing again. But she sat back and regarded his face with her sad smile. "I know you must feel awkward — afraid of my husband. I want you to feel very, very safe here. Nobody will get to know about this, ever. And you'll go out through a back way. And as long as it is here — nobody will ever catch on. You should relax. You can trust Kajutant fully."

He knew and felt that getting drunk was the way he was beginning to feel. He had never tasted alcohol. But he also reflected that even if he was getting drunk, he remained intelligent enough to realise her naivety, on top of his stupidity for being in that house at all.

"I am relaxed," he lied. "And I'm really happy to be here — with you." That was true. "But, please, stop *matronising* me. I'm no slob or child."

"Oh honey," she grabbed him with a powerful passion and held on to him as if with desperation. "I know, I know. But in any case I'm older than you. Oo, how I'm going to love you! You are the only man I want to have, to love."

81

"You never saw me before today, Zoe. And you aren't anywhere older than me. I was born in forty."

"I was born in forty-six. But women are always older than men, didn't you know? And it doesn't matter that I only saw you for the first time this afternoon. We have always known each other without knowing." She made him sip more of the oily liquor. "Look, Daoud, I am a mere love-smitten woman. Your eyes penetrated my heart the very first time they looked into mine. Your eyes appreciated the loneliness inside me. They made love to me, Daoud — outside there, in the drive. You have terrible eyes. They are sharp, pointed eyes. And they probe. You know me more than I'll ever get to know you, Daoud." Her hot hand was inside his sweatshirt and his was exploring the most voluptuous body he had ever imagined. "I want to live for you, Daoud, and if I am to die, to die for you!"

"I would never let you *die* for me, Zoe. You have so lovely a body I'd first die before letting you. What are you made of?"

"What lovely, loving words to fall on one's ears in this life! I am made of the body of my father and my mother and myself, for you."

"Do you think someone could come here?"

She stiffened — her body muscles bunching themselves taut like coiled springs: "Daoud..." she sighed.

"Maybe I am drunk already, Zoe. But I can never rid myself of the feeling that we are courting the worst calamity of our lives — at least I am sure of that danger on my own part. We court danger in the stupidest way it ought to be done. You are the wife of a wanton killer, a murderer of a multitude of innocent human beings."

"If you don't relax fully tonight — for me — I'll kill myself for you. I don't want any feelings of fear to intrude into our new life — between us. I don't want any harm to come to us. I am sleeping with my second-ever man in my thirty years of life. Except that with my second-ever man, I am making love — not simply *sleeping*. Come, finish this. There's a bottle in the other room. And a bed." With both her hands under his shirt, she attempted to lift him up off the settee — but he was too heavy for her. So he eased her hands out of his shirt, stood up and hefted her off the carpet, the liqueur giving him a great boost, for the woman weighed beyond eighty kilograms. He took her to the bed.

They fornicated fervently, like pond fish that had not been fed for days fighting over unanticipated crumbs of fresh bread. And when they had exhausted themselves, they slept. For Ssempa, to whose body liquor had been an unfamiliar stranger, sleep bordered on the comatose. He was dead to the world around that bed in that small room. Yet his brain remained functional, free of the torpid body, and it stirred, prodding his subconscious to half-wakefulness. That subconscious talked to him — as if from afar, as if from a pall of the woman's perfume. Was it her loud moans of excitement — moans that had crescendoed into ecstatic shrieks — that the voices and loud thumps were in response to? Were those chaotic noises that assaulted his peaceful slumber real? Where was he…?

"Zoe," he called out to her, and their voices came out together, simultaneously, she too crying out his own name in panic.

"Oh, God!" she swore.

"Oh, shit." He sprang up, and within a jiffy had pulled on his tracksuit and sweatshirt. But his movements were too agonisingly slow; they were utterly unreal. His watch, seen in a surreal crystalline twilight, said one o'clock.

"Oh — my God! What have I done to you, honey! How can I do this to you?"

"Steady, Zoe. They are not coming directly here or they'd have arrived. They are still searching the other houses." But he was failing to move because some gargantuan cloud, which blanketed his head, held his whole body immobile. Something told him it was because of booze and he was cursing inwardly.

"If they arrest you, I swear in the name of Allah the creator of all living things — I will kill myself this very night."

"Nonsense, Zoe. I'll fight my way out. If you want to, you'll come with me for they could harm you too."

Then he woke up from the scary dream.

"You've been dreaming," said Kajutant – the woman's brother — when Ssempa opened his eyes and experienced the hardest headache he had ever imagined. He looked at his surroundings, the small twelve-foot-square room with the single five-foot bed with several pillows and a heavy sky-blue and pink comforter. He looked at the youth who had brought him into the place the previous evening, a chap aged about nineteen, with a small goatee; and the small, round grey glass-topped table with the heavy, thick dark-brown bottle — and the two crystal snifters, one of them half full of a crystalline amber fluid. Then he recalled everything.

"Kajutant," he addressed the youth. "You brought me here. Where is — er," he had momentarily forgotten the names. He only remembered the one he had initially addressed her by. "Where is Mama Zillah?"

"She's okay. She left at dawn and said to see you later this evening."

"You are her brother," he stated. "How do I leave this place without a problem?"

"That is why I came, of course. I'll conduct you through the fence at the back. And when I come for you tonight, you'll come through the same hole."

Ssempa, mind fully clear by now, felt a wild anger, fraught with jealousy. But he swallowed it.

"This is your residence?"

"Yes."

Ssempa's eyes wandered to the shirts and trousers on the hangers. They had already taken in the *Playboy, Lance Spearman* and *Drum* magazines — all male, teenage stuff.

The youth said: "Do you care for a bath?"

"No. But — how easy or difficult is it to reach the Kacheeche house?"

"Like ABC, why?"

"Because I will take a bath at home."

"You'll need to splash some cold water in your face. You look awful. And Zoe left you a toothbrush. Come."

Yes, Zoe. The name!

"Kajutant — that's the name you told me yesterday?"

The youth nodded as he indicated the grass footpath that snaked its way behind the houses.

"Kajutant, just how many persons have met Zoe in your residence, and left it through this very path in times past?"

"Ya'tarabana," swore the fellow, in Arabic or Nubian. "You take me — you think I am a bloody fucking pimp, huh?"

"Hey, hey, hey, Kajutant; don't let that excite you. But you see if I must be used, and your sister is using me, to speak the hard, painful Koranic truth, I must know whom I might bump into here for my life's sake. And I need a truthful person to deal with in such a situation... Otherwise, I wish you to appreciate the amount of shit that we, you included, could be mired in if anything went wrong."

Kajutant stared at him open-mouthed: "Tell me, whatever your name is, how long have you known Zoe?"

"I met her for my very ever first time yesterday evening as we collected the children from Buganda Road."

"But I heard you refer to her as Mama Zillah a while ago. That shows familiarity."

"There is nothing in that. Her little daughter is called Zillah, or so she told me. I can even refer to her captain husband as Papa Zillah."

Kajutant nodded in comprehension and said, "Let me tell you about my sister. She got married to Captain Ali Lupai three years ago when she was preparing to go to Makerere University. Our father chose the path of marriage for her like he has done for his other daughters and the daughters of the less affluent relatives and friends of his. It is my belief, naïve as it might be regarded, that my sister hadn't known a man carnally by the time of her marriage. No girl under this roof can do that and live. It was even harder in the past when my father was much younger and more alert. Father is such a stickler for domestic discipline. For the past three years the only places Zoe has ever visited are the greengrocers and the supermarkets — with a horde of her husband's womenfolk — a quite zealous and malicious Aringa lot from his maternal side. The only people she's permitted to talk to are fellow women, under the constant supervision of the said horde. She visits us infrequently, and even then either Lupai himself or his hyrax of an elder sister has to call Dad to send one of us to pick her up. We cannot — are not allowed — to stop anywhere on the way when we do that. We have to bring her straight here, where Lupai knows — simply has to know — that nothing immoral can take place. Here she would be safe even if she were to spend months, according to Lupai and our father. They don't know that things have changed a great deal. They are old fools. Obviously, you will never see my father's two youngest wives. They are covered up in veils and *kanga* sheets. Our older mothers can now uncover their faces because they are in their menopause. Yet they still cannot go out of the house unless they are chaperoned. Our father is seventy-eight years old now — having been born in 1893. He still believes — seriously too — that his codes of conduct for us still work. They do, of course, with a near-infallibility — with his younger wives, but not at all with his daughters and sons. Not anymore. But to the outside world — the Lupai's would be paralysed with shock to learn of our father's unwitting relaxation of those codes. No sin can take place in Sheikh Rajab Athocon's home. You see he was their teacher in Islam; he got them to cram the entire Koran. We, Atimango inclusive, all sing that huge book, every word of it, as easily as we do the most ordinary things. However, you must know that the fear you and Atimango have of Lupai is not the same as we have for that rascal. To us he's just another Kakwa like his cousin the president. And if I needed the money, which I don't, really, I would bundle Atimango into my Honda Accord and vend her to whoever cared to buy her beauty — Allah knows that woman is beautiful! And Lupai would never mention my name in his consequent tantrums. Lupai has a fear of my father like you have of Lupai. That said, if Atimango has slept with any man besides Lupai, and now you — then women have gifts in subtlety beyond those that made Nabbi Issa perform miracles. If a fly were to wander to her private parts outside this place of ours here, her husband would get to know of it if he interested himself in such event. If it happened here, most of us would know for sure except such foreigners as Dad's new wives and Dad himself. That is my word to you, whatever your name is."

"Daoud Ssempa," Ssempa volunteered.

"Well, Daoudi-the-Boozer-Ssempa. Do you know what my father would do to me if he were to hear, with proof, that a bottle of liquor had traversed any part of his compound?"

"You tell me."

"Believe this because it is true and he's done it before. He would simply read sections of the Koran known to him only — and I would die exactly the way he wished it to be."

"I thought he mostly used razors to mete out domestic punishment."

Kajutant looked at him with genuine shock in his eyes. Then he grinned widely, quite unexpectedly too, and said: "You are a fucking direct bastard. You don't shit people around do you now? Who told you of that incident?"

"Well, wasn't Rajab Athocon imprisoned in western Moyo for scooping out the genitals of his late wife?"

"You are talking about decades in the past, man. My father cut up that woman before he became a Muslim. He converted immediately he became a convict and spent every wakeful hour of his imprisonment mastering that great Arabian tome, the Quraan, and in the process learned how to use it to punish his enemies. He is said to have told relatives that certain officials — usually judicial fellows he deemed to have acted with malicious intent in judging him during his trial — would die by drowning and the event came to pass. A man, whom my relatives thought might drown in a lake or river owing to their faith in my father's words, was instead drowned when a deluge of water on the Kampala-Masaka highway swept his car off the road and kept it under its currents until they subsided. It had rained elsewhere and the flood had come along a dry riverbed. While still in Openzinzi Prison my father told all who cared to hear that his second wife and a lover taking advantage of his imprisonment to cuckold him would die, on separate days — both by lightening. My father specified the time gap between the two deaths and which of the two miscreants would go first. And — I know you have to find this hard to believe — the events occurred exactly in the sequence the sheikh had said they would. Do you believe me?"

"Of course I don't."

"You are right. I wouldn't believe me either. But, if even the simpler people he has taught so well can cause such things to happen — for money you know — then what of the grand master himself? Goodbye, Daoudi-the-Boozer-Ssempa. We make quite some company, don't we?"

"Wait. One more thing, chum. Zoe seemed well acquainted with booze..."

"Her husband is a sponge of sorts; could absorb any shit if it contained any alcoholic content. Of course he wasn't a Muslim until Idi Amin took power and gave him a chain of big command positions. She never drank in our home. But as you know, I am of a different generation from hers."

"She speaks French quite well, too."

"Atimango's mother was Philippino. A gaboon viper in the Imaramagambo forest killed the woman's husband, a Chinese road constructor, when he grabbed the serpent with intent to have it for dinner. He died instantly, it is said. My father, who worked on the same road, took the Philippino woman in, and when that road construction company moved on to Burundi, Atimango's mother went along with it. So my sister was born in Burundi and grew up there. The mother had given her the name Joy, which is said to have been the name of the Irish wife of a German foreman in that road construction company. She brought Atimango to Uganda when she was nine and deposited her in our ancestral home in Parombo, in the West Nile Province. She is called Zoe because the Luo people of Jonam usually pronounce Z as J and J as Z. So they named my sister Zoy. But when she was registering for high school she spelled it Zoe and the latter stuck. My father, strict Muslim as he is, never gave her an Islamic name. She has since forgotten all the Kirundi she spoke in Parombo to the amusement of the Alur people who knew nothing of Bantu tongues. She had forgotten the French too but sharpened it in high school."

"Where is the mother now?"

"She was said to have died — of old age — in Bujumbura."

"So Zoe is the only child of her mother!"

"Yeah. I myself am the only child of my late mother, but nobody is ever able to realise that when they visit our homes — here or in Parombo. Goodbye. I am driving my father to a *douwah* in Old Kampala."

* * *

They were caught on an Independence Day anniversary night. Taking it for granted that her husband would be too engaged in the big-day celebrations to pay heed to domestic matters, Atimango had sent Kajutant to the training school to pick up Ssempa in a hired taxi. They had driven to a house on an avenue just a street away from and above Kampala's Central Police Station on Nakasero Hill. The two foolish lovebirds were in the small guest wing of the house from six to eight p.m. Without particular reason, Ssempa had got up and stretched himself lazily and was in the process of going back to the bed, where Atimango lay on her back enjoying a cigarette. She appeared much plumper now, in her fifth month of pregnancy. A beige Datsun car, the very one that had dropped Atimango at the house, was moving up to the house at a slow pace, its headlamps off but its parking lights on. The main house obscured it momentarily and then it came into sight on the other side and stopped. The driver stepped out first — but he had not been driving. Four more men, two of them with dark glasses even though it was already dark, stood under the bright street lamp, looking up at the guest wing, which had been built on higher ground than the main house.

"Zoe," Ssempa told the woman in a loud whisper. "Do not panic, okay? Promise."

She dropped the cigarette onto the bedspread and Ssempa picked it up quickly and threw it into the ashtray. "I said do not panic, Zoe. Don't, if you genuinely love me."

"Okay," she said, breathlessly. "All right, David, I won't panic. What is it?"

"The man that drove you here is a prisoner of four mean-looking guys with pistols. They are watching this very house. I want you to remain calm."

"God, oooh, God, I've been very careless. What are you going to do?"

"It's for you that I fear," he said, while getting into his clothes, a pair of blue jeans and a collared dark blue T-shirt. "I myself can scale the back wall and fall on the other side. I've already examined it for just that purpose."

"He'll kill me, of course," she asserted. Her simple statement shocked him. "His fear of my father won't prevent him from killing me. My husband is simply a mad man."

"Then we can — but how can I even think of it. You cannot climb a wall in your state."

She had dressed up quickly herself, in a wide white calico dress with knitted designs of rose flowers and their thorny twigs in colourless fabric. Her tummy did not show her pregnancy. You only felt it in the extraordinary heat from her body.

"If you manage it — if you manage to get away, please, get in touch with Kajutant first thing and tell him that we've been caught. My father may not forgive me, of course — which is why I fear Lupai is going to kill me, but he favours me above all his daughters. He might prevail over my husband and save me."

"But there…"

A thunderous explosion cut him short. Somebody had somehow, to their shocked consternation, reached the back door without being seen and had kicked the door in with that one explosive blow. Ssempa grabbed a clothes hanger and smashed the light bulb and, perhaps because he had been drinking, rushed without thinking in the direction of the shattered door. There was another explosion — this time of a pistol shot — and he saw a tongue of yellow fire flick in his direction before his head smashed into the man's soft belly. His hands grabbed the sides of the man's jacket and pulled with savage force as he quickly moved backwards, fear lending him berserk strength. He stepped aside in his backward lunge and his burden bypassed him, falling headlong into a nearby wall. In a crouch, he kicked at the legs of the second intruder, his boot connecting with the ankle of his enemy. The man stumbled and fell, his chin hitting the concrete floor and the dark glasses shattering with a small tinkling sound. Ssempa sprang up and picked up the pistol — he didn't know to which of his adversaries it belonged but the light from the street lamp several yards away had shown him the large gun lying on the corridor floor. He smashed its butt into the back of the head of the man he had tripped up. As he did this a shot went off. According to the yellow fire in the muzzle, the bullet must have missed his face by a whisker for he had hit the man with the butt with the pistol facing upwards.

The man who had fallen first was groaning and a man barked from outside, in Kiswahili: *"Kitu gani nyiye?"* (What is going on, fellows?)

"Hakuna," Ssempa shouted back, making an attempt at a northern Uganda accent, *"Tunamleta mjambazi."* (Nothing; we are bringing the thug out)

"Haya, basi. Muharakishe." (Okay, hurry up)

The man groaned again.

Ssempa moved cautiously to the back door, rounded it and saw the other person, who stood with a pistol pointed down at the grass. He aimed carefully and fired at the man, who staggered a bit and tumbled over without a noise. The pistol clattered over a steel manhole cover, went over a concrete outcrop and fell some feet below to the back of the main house. He turned around, intent on pulling the woman out of the house. But she was already standing there, her white dress conspicuously exposing her as an easy target.

"Why did you fire — what did you shoot at?" Atimango asked, anxiously.

"Come on, let's go down. There is another man there — and the driver."

"Uncock that thing. It can go off at a mere touch."

"What?" Ssempa looked at the pistol.

"Uncock it. It's dangerous."

"How do I do that? This is the first time I'm holding a pistol."

She took it from his hand, gingerly, and did something to the hammer, which had stood poised to crash back into the back of the firing pin.

"Oh boy, that is why it went off when I hit the other man?"

"When you fire, it automatically returns to the cocked position."

"And now what if we are attacked?"

She showed him. "You ease the hammer back with your thumb. Like this, and this, and fire."

They found the other man right at the main entrance. Zoe was in his back and Ssempa came face to face with his foe, their eyes meeting in the dim evening light. The man was not armed so he turned round and sprinted to the car. Ssempa shot at his fleeing figure, twice, without aiming with the eyes, and saw the Datsun leap forward and zoom off.

"Quick," he got hold of her arm. "Let's move on. It will not take them long to return. Whose house is this?"

"My husband's. He just renovated it to lease it out to an embassy. As you can see this is embassy zone. That is the Nigerian High Commission, that is the Rwandan embassy, Cuba there, Yugoslavia.... The Sudanese military attaché is taking my husband's soon. Well, I stole the keys knowing he wouldn't miss them."

Ssempa looked around them. The area bristled with fluttering flags of foreign countries.

"How on earth did they get to us?"

"The taxi man, of course. Do you think the man you shot is dead?"

"Who said I shot a man? How can I know, anyway?"

"I have never seen a dead person in my life, Daoud!"

"With Rapai shooting them dead now and then outside your residence ...?"

"It never happened in my presence. Do you think you killed a man, Daoud?"

"For God's sake I am not thinking of the bloody fucking thugs. Let us hurry up, or do you want us to return and take a good look at the man I shot at?"

"Our first quarrel! What nasty circumstances!"

"How can you think of such things now? We'll get a taxi for you at the International or the Grand Imperial. The police will have heard all the shots that went off and might decide to investigate. But they might not if these fellows informed them in advance of their operation to catch us."

"You must not show yourself with me," she said as the lights of the Shell fuel station at the Grand Imperial Hotel came in sight. "Here — you'll need money. Do you think the other man recognised you?"

Ssempa took the money Atimango offered him and pocketed it. "At the entrance? I doubt that he could have recognised me. You know him?"

"Juma Tretre, an intelligence sergeant with Malire Regiment based in the old palace at Lubiri. You can never be too sure with such people. He might have recognised you. I want you to take care of yourself. I want you to be safe."

"And you?"

"I'll go to Kisugu — to my father's house. And give him a cock and bull story about what happened."

"What will you tell him you were doing at that house?"

"It's my husband's. I had gone there to rest. Pregnant women do usually develop strange habits and needs. There was no other individual in the place, and I don't know why those men were shooting at each other."

"Sounds good enough."

She grabbed his left hand and was doing something to his fingers. She put something in her mouth — to wet it, and pushed his little finger through it. He looked at the finger. A large ring embraced it. It had a blue stone the prize of a cowpea, that twinkled in its face. "My husband told me he looted if from the Congo in 64 when he was a corporal commanding a section. The blue stone is sapphire — genuine too. An Indian in Drapers, on Kampala Road, was offering him five thousand shillings for it recently."

"And you are giving five thousand shillings away like that!"

"I am not. You and I are one. If I hadn't been pregnant already, I should have wished to have your baby. Goodbye. I'll take care of myself."

"Goodbye, Zoe."

* * *

During that week, an army tank trundled its way from Jajja Villas on the shores of Lake Victoria and ostensibly met with a brand-new black Mercedes Benz 280 SE near Ggaba. The tank ran over the Mercedes, blending it with the tarmac. At the wheel of the Mercedes, it seemed, had been a light-skinned woman and in the passenger seat, a little girl aged five, part of the family of recently promoted, Major Ali Drony Lupai — poor man!

The voice of John Johnson Kibajjo announced the tragic incident on the seven-o'clock news on Radio Uganda. But Ssempa would only catch a chance glimpse of it in the *Voice of Uganda* newspaper, which ran a dozen lines of the unusual accident in a standard column. Yet the more reliable Radio Katwe — the grapevine of Kampala — clarified that the woman in the driver's seat, though not easily identifiable, had been handcuffed to the steering wheel of that new Mercedes car.

* * *

Two months before the end of the course, a drastically thinner Ssempa, quite obviously saddened by the despicable murder of a woman he had begun to deeply love, took a quick stroll with another trainee to buy groceries at

Nakasero Market, less than two kilometres from the training wing. It was a humid hot afternoon during the lunch break. The trainees were prohibited from going to town at any time without permission and transgression could be punished with dismissal from the course. But what Ssempa and his colleague were doing was not unheard of. They walked over the railway line and the wooden bridge across the Nakivubo Channel, coming up to the sharp triangular intersection that branched off Entebbe Road to join Rosebury and Salisbury roads on the east side. They sweated profusely in the humid heat. As they stepped into the inner market they came face to face with two uniformed soldiers and a man in plain clothes. The man in civvies was in new-looking blue jeans, trousers and jacket. Ssempa recognised the man immediately as the nocturnal intelligence sergeant, Juma Tretre, and he turned round and, followed closely by his colleague, blundered his way out of the marketplace.

There was the expected uproar as traders and buyers yelled, all at once. The soldiers, along with the plainclothes man, gave chase, but were no match for the police recruits whose chief daily course was a six-mile jog, every morning and every evening. They left the shouting behind them — not one civilian would intervene in a contest of any sort involving uniformed soldiers, and that gave the two police recruits an opportunity to move through the crowds of shoppers and pedestrians. Ssempa looked back over his shoulder only once, to note that his colleague was close behind and the man in civilian dress, a man in his forties, was a good deal ahead of the two uniformed soldiers, who were obviously giving up the chase. Their minds seeming to work in concert, the two trainees chose not to take the Allidina Visram Street that went past the Swaminarayan temple, their feet leading them towards Entebbe Road. They crossed that road, a Ford Zephyr taxi missing Ssempa by a hairsbreadth, and headed for Ewa-Hussein, flew over a fat old woman vending boiled dry coffee beans in dry banana-fibre wrappings and the *mulondo*-root aphrodisiac. She cursed them colourfully in the Luganda language, most of whose meaningful adages were picked by the fleers' ears. They soon left Salisbury to the upper left side and dashed into Rosebury Road, a street dominated by typewriter repair shops, stationery and the business of bulk printing. A few feet down Rosebury, they veered off to their right into the bushy junk-strewn area behind that road, approached the bridge below at high speed. Their boots drummed on the stout planks. Soon they were crossing the railway lines and, to confuse their pursuers, continued up to the police residential quarters below Nsambya Hospital. Between the borders of these quarters — then the largest police barracks in East and Central Africa — and the hospital, was a vast slum, where the two trainees headed. Ssempa knew well that police trainees in training garb were the commonest sight in that area.

"What's this all about?" Ssempa's colleague asked, at the end of the three-kilometre sprint.

"It could be nothing," Ssempa had thought out his response in advance. "I thought I recognised one of our instructors."

"Sure?"

"Yes, sure. Did you recognise none?"

"I was behind you and may have missed him. But those soldiers!"

"Ah, the soldiers decided to run after us for fun, I think. The blundering fools."

They laughed heartily about the whole thing after waiting for several minutes and seeing no more pursuers. They returned to the training school.

That same day, when the recruits trooped in, one after the other, from the evening run instead of heading for the mess for their porridge, all were ordered onto the parade ground. As they stood there wondering about the change in routine, two army Land Rovers drove in from the side of Kibuli Hill Road in the wake of a flashy red Range Rover. The three vehicles parked before the administration building and several men, mostly in army uniform, alighted. The men from the Range Rover entered the office building and came out again after about five minutes. About a dozen of them walked leisurely towards the four hundred assembled police trainees.

Ssempa recognized two men. One was the elderly, tall, slim commander of the Malire Regiment, Major Ali Drony Lupai, whose very dark face gleamed blood red in the crimson light of the setting sun. He swung a large dark-grey pistol in his free hand. The other hand held a thin black cigarette. He was talking as he moved forward, laughing genially and nodding. A jovial man! His companions were also elderly, but younger than the major. One was the commandant of the training wing, an assistant commissioner of police from eastern Uganda, and the other was the very man that had led the two soldiers in the sprint after Ssempa and his colleague earlier in the day; the man who had run away from him on Nakasero Road the night of the shooting. There was no question about it: here was Intelligence Sergeant Juma Tretre out to identify a man he had accidentally encountered in a grocery market. The intelligence clue? Nsambya Police School fatigue tracksuits. Ssempa felt he was a dead man this time.

The parade of exhausted men consisted of three equal rows of men, one in front of the other and each row stretching one hundred or more yards.

The commandant commanded the recruits to attention and invited the army officer to address them.

"You recruits," he began in Kiswahili, "stand at ease. Did you leave your homes to come to Kampala to fight Ali Drony Rapai?"

Four hundred throats echoed a resounding "Noooo!"

"But some of you are criminals. I am a very unhappy man because of some of you. It may be two, three or more of you. I have come here to find out which. Of course when I do, we will settle our score here. Do you hear me? To save time and to ease my anger, such persons should come out voluntarily or else they will be killed immediately I get to them."

There followed a dead silence in which only the heavy breathing of men just back from execise could be heard.

"Well. The person I am looking for was not with you in this school on the night of the anniversary of Independence Day. He was out of this place, busy enjoying himself with — with the wife of a friend of mine. I myself, I was away at Entebbe State House. But my friend here, Sergeant Tretre, of military intelligence, got wind of what one of you was involved in and took policemen to arrest the culprit. That culprit is one of you and that culprit shot dead one police officer and badly injured two others. Do you hear that? One of you is a police killer pretending to like you, do you hear that? If you know this culprit report him to me here *india-mike-mike*. I will give you exactly five minutes to show me the fellow. If you cannot, I am coming in to identify him myself. When I do, I'll kill him at once, along, of course, with the two men standing to either side of him."

The ensuing silence was even deader after the major had spoken. He looked at his large watch and, frowning, said, "I start to count now."

Ssempa knew he had to give himself up for the sake of the two men standing to either side of him. It did not matter that they were not his close friends. He had a moral duty to save their skin for they were innocent men. Nobody in or before that parade doubted a single utterance made by the major. Nobody came out of the parade to report anybody.

"All right," said the major, impatiently. Then changing his voice into a screech, he thundered, *"Nyooote mguuu-ssaw'a!"*

All stood at ramrod attention.

The major nodded appreciatively and beckoned to the man, Sergeant Tretre, who fell in step with him to walk to the beginning of the first row. A small entourage of soldiers fell in at the rear. They moved very slowly, peering closely into the faces of the men they came by, at times stopping to peruse and scrutinise those faces. Ssempa stood in the second row, through which the face-inspectors were now moving slowly. He was sure, and his anger caused him to stop caring, that he was a dead man. There was no way out this time. The man would look at him only once. He had grown much leaner with training, but mostly because of the death of Zoe Atimango, yet his visage remained unchanged. The inspectors were fourteen men away, moving from one recruit to the other, carefully perusing faces.

94

A radio in the Range Rover was playing the BBC World Service signature tune, 'sixteen hundred hours Greenwich mean time'. That meant seven o'clock East African standard time. Four persons away, Lupai having moved ahead, was standing just before Ssempa, whose legs were beginning to tremble. His nose smelt the man he would always hate. There was a heavy thud. Although they were all at attention, they turned their heads to look at the third row. A large, tall recruit had fallen on his face in a swoon.

Major Lupai roughly pushed Ssempa aside and strode to the fainted man, as did the other inspectors.

"Turn him over," ordered the major. "Is he the one, Tretre?"

"Hmmm, let me see more closely. It is getting darker, you see. But... he definitely is our man."

"Well, bring him around quickly," said Lupai, himself bending over the fallen form. "Do this — like this." The man lying on the ground stirred, coughed and sat up. "Coward, huh? Tell me, where were you on the night of Independence Day?"

The man looked sheepishly around him from his sitting position.

"Hey, don't pretend with me," said the major, giving him a sharp slap to the cheek. "Where were you on the night of Independence Day?"

"Sir, I had gone to the slum quarters for a glass of something."

This was followed by murmured laughter.

"A glass of something!" Lupai himself was amused by his victim's euphemism. "You want to say a glass of crude waragi, don't you? He's our man, all right... what a foolish alibi! Who were you with?"

"I was alone. I am a loner. I...."

"Did you get permission? Say."

"No, sir. Forgive me, sir. I am not the person you are talking about."

"Then why have you urinated on yourself? You thought you were brave, eh? Bring him to the front of the parade at once. People — police recruits must learn not to misbehave. Remove his T-shirt."

The frightened man was dragged to the front where he stood trembling like a leaf in the wind.

"You shot my man dead, eh? Let me show you how they do it even better. Brother Commandant, I beg your permission to rid your force of a most dangerous enemy. What's your name, you?"

"Kayombo. Julius Kayombo, sir. But I am going to die for no reason, sir. I swear to God Almighty, sir, I...."

"Where are you from? You talk like a Congoman."

"I am from Fort Portal, sir. I am innocent, sir. Do not kill me, sir."

"You are dangerous. Actions speak louder than words. You cannot confess, yet your body confesses for you. You fainted at the mere sight of me, yet you were not afraid to cuckold me — because you had never looked at me. Now you pee on yourself! Stand there and don't move."

Major Ali Drony Lupai did a most extraordinary thing. He moved away from the trembling man, swinging his pistol in his right hand. A dozen paces away he shifted the pistol to his left, and still walking away, and without turning his head around once to look, he swung the pistol over his right shoulder and fired once. He walked on and turned round at about the twentieth pace. As all assembled there were wondering what the purpose of that shot was, suddenly they saw poor Julius Kayombo tumble over onto his back. The commandant rushed forward, followed by the other part of Lupai's entourage.

"He's fainted again," said someone in the parade.

The major heard the words and said, laughing, "No. That man can never faint again. He's dead this time. You men have not seen Fernando Sancho? No? You should watch him closely if you want to become ace shots like me."

And truly, as everybody would find out soon, Kayombo had taken a bullet in the centre of the forehead. The commandant of the school appeared as though he might fall over with shock himself, but a fake, twisted smile warped his face in a grotesque grin. He and the rest of the men must not be seen to disapprove. He was a most unhappy commandant.

As the major and his people started moving away there came the sound of a confused scuffle near the dead body and a voice said: "Major, the other one."

Ssempa, was moving furtively away, ready to vanish into the gathering gloom when he heard the next words uttered by Sergeant Tretre: "If you are innocent, why did you run away from us?"

On hearing that question, Ssempa started moving towards the more remote area of the gathered crowd of police cadets.

"We did not run away from you, sir. We had seen one of the instructors in the market — and we had left camp without permission."

"Are you sure? Who were you with? Show us the other recruit you were with. He was much darker than you!"

"But he's that man Afende Major just shot dead."

"Really?" Major Lupai's voice joined in as Ssempa sneaked farther away. This time he vowed to himself that he would be shot running. It was dark enough. "Where were you on the night of Independence Day?"

"I was in the dormitory with everybody else. They will all confirm to you that I'm not lying. I have never left this place at night from the time I enlisted."

"What were you doing in the market this morning?"

"We went to buy avocadoes but we did not. Soldiers ran after us when they saw us running away from the instructor."

"You are a lucky chap. You should never play around with people's wives. Never antagonise the army, do you hear, boy?"

"Yes, sir."

"Sometimes I wonder why the police enjoy antagonising us so much! What did the army do to you, police — tell me. What did we do to you?"

"I think he's lying, sir," said Sergeant Tretre. "The man with him was much leaner than the thug you just shot. I think we should take him with us to the Public Safety Unit headquarters. By midnight, this young man should have talked."

"Ah, why not, if you think so, Sergeant. Good idea, my dear fellow. If you won't tell us what we want to know, young cadet, we shall take you to Naguru — to persuade you to talk."

The last thing Ssempa heard in that place was the recruit's next words, "No sir. Don't take me to Naguru. I'll show you the man. He is right here on the parade ground."

Ssempa never returned to the dormitory. He hurried through a yam plantation, found himself behind the slummy Kibuli trading centre shops and walked on without looking back. There were numerous sandpits, most of them quite deep and with dirty stagnant water at the bottom. But his mind never dwelt on the idea of a hiding place. Instead he thought of just one thing: a change of clothes — any clothes. And he knew he would get those in the vast slum area from anybody unfortunate enough to be found drunk that night. He could get transport money in exactly the same fashion — mug somebody and take his or her possessions.

Three days later, he was in Kigali City.

* * *

Ssempa's mind returned to the present — to the intelligence officer standing before him, leaning with his back comfortably against the Peugeot pickup truck. To the best of his knowledge, Lupai had never connected Ssempa with the case his intelligence operative, Juma Tretre, had so diligently tracked and nearly unmasked on the sports grounds of Nsambya Police Training Wing at the end of 1972. The Muganda trader felt safe there, for the moment. Across the asphalt drive, his uncle Sheikh Shafiq Kakembo and the town imam still conversed, occasionally throwing impatient glances in the direction of the pickup and the men who argued before it.

"Anyhow," Anyanya Yoram was saying to him, "Razak Illeh Amin or no Razak Illeh Amin, you would have been picked up several months ago if it had not been for the commandant of the military police detach. At first I had suspected Illeh had had a chat with him to cover up for you. But I found out other things later. The commandant was then a major but is now a full colonel. He had just come from jail where he had done time for embezzlement of unit funds. On returning from prison his wife had informed him that the man you later killed had raped her during interrogation as they tried to find out if she had stashed away some of the cash embezzled by her husband. It was decided, with the encouragement of the commandant, that a certain dead corporal lied to the board of inquiries about a killer man with a woman disguised as a nun because he wanted to cover up a petrol smuggling racket in which he and the M'gungu lieutenant were involved; a racket from which the commandant had allegedly been warning them to desist. It now appears neither the lieutenant nor the corporal was ever involved in fuel smuggling, and that the dead corporal never lied to us. That commandant was bent on protecting anything — fire or man — that had been responsible for the sweet revenge he himself hadn't had the opportunity to carry out against Lieutenant Manuel Musinzi."

"Manuel Musinzi?" Ssempa echoed.

"Yes? That is the name of the officer you murdered; any memory of the small handsome, smartly uniformed officer?"

"No. I am just wondering that a man with such a dignified Christian name can at the same time be such a felon."

"Tell that to the birds, David. But you quite well know we don't need any concrete evidence — any evidence at all for that matter — to charge you with the murders. On the morning after the lieutenant's death everybody that had kept quiet about his misconduct began to talk. It turned out he had slept with nearly every other soldier's wife, usually after putting the victims in compromising situations. He was, you could say, a serial rapist. You see he was also in charge of special investigations within the district. Thus it was not surprising that when he died there was widespread jubilation in the barracks. When we went in to set up that board of inquiries we received little cooperation. I remember feeling that the commandant talked of *that* fire that they had decided to give as the purported culprit, in amicable terms as though it had been a friendly — in fact even a sort of kinsman — thing to him. All that is unnecessary now, anyway. To remove any lingering doubts from your mind, I can add that the staff and clientele of the White Horse Inn, including two respectable Russian expatriates, saw you that night in a suspiciously, disheveled state. There was a curfew and yet you were out and about. They never saw the woman dressed as a nun, though. Where had you hidden that woman, David?"

"If you talked until the next millennium, Simba, I would still give you my one good, truthful answer. I deny all you say about me. You are not one of these other soldiers and officers whom I would bribe to buy their silence, even if such silence was about things of which I was innocent. So the ball is in your court, my friend. I have for the past ten minutes urged you to get on with whatever you have in store for me, and I am still waiting. I shan't resist arrest; no wise man ever does in Uganda any more."

"One of the men you killed talked afterwards," Anyanya said, unruffled by Ssempa's sphinx-like attitude.

Ssempa barked out a laugh. "That's very funny, you know. A man I am purported to have killed *talking* afterwards."

"You heard me talk of a dead corporal. That pudgy ugly soldier, Corporal Bingwa, did talk."

"Corporal Bingwa?" Ssempa's apprehension returned as quickly as it had receded.

"Yes."

"Talked, you said?"

"Yes. He died later of his wounds — mostly burns as only one shot had caught him in the right shoulder, smashing the collarbone badly. It is the fire that he died of; first-degree burns. But he did talk nevertheless, or else none of us would ever have wised up."

Ssempa was staring at his feet, furtively. He looked up at Anyanya: "So now you think you have me fixed, *do* you?"

"I don't think it; I know it. And I also happen to know that your father-in-law of sorts, Mr Illeh, won't interfere in the matter this time. He would not stand a fellow Muslim snubbing his own faith the way you have, the way you are looking down your nose at the president of our nation! You will marry that woman just the very way the state wishes or I will arrest you immediately since I have already told you too much. You will be charged with treasonous murder and malicious damage to government property — remember the brand-new Land Rover V8 that you had no compunction in setting alight? It is a case the state will be proud of, as it is never easy to stumble across genuine ones. You are beaten I must say, David."

"Oh, shit!" swore Ssempa, moving away from his position at the pickup. Anyanya's eyes studied his movements closely, like a hawk. "If I hadn't acted quickly enough, Bwana Anyanya Yoram, if I hadn't killed that filthy bastard, he would have raped a nun. Not that that was that important to me — I am not that type of believer. The crook intended to murder us after his heinous crime, quite obviously. It was in self- defence, man, that I shot the fools."

"That is a lot better," Anyanya Yoram was jovial. "Keep on talking."

Ssempa regarded him sourly, opened the passenger door of the pickup and slumped down in it, with one leg out, quite a tired man. He said to the intelligence officer: "It is that very scoundrel lieutenant who caused all the trouble that keeps me standing here instead of finalizing my deal with Donn Reisch inside there; may God stifle his chances of reincarnation permanently!"

Anyanya Yoram shook with laughter: "Never swear at dead men, David," he chortled, dabbing at his eyes with pink Kleenex. "What happened?"

Three

Gitarama, Rwanda, 1976

The nun arrived in a tiny Citroen car with her uncle, a big, tall, bespectacled man of dark- brown complexion with grey hair brushed back from the forehead the way Banyarwanda men did their hair. The man was clad in rich, fluffy, almost glittery vestments — a raven-black cassock and a dark purple chasuble with a silk dog collar at his throat — that exuded a certain spiritual smell that enforced a sense of power and respect in the wearer. A great solid-gold crucifix suspended from a thick, dark-purple ribbon dangled about his midriff. Ssempa noted that the nun wore a miniature of the monsignor's insignia round her own neck, though hers was of sterling silver, and it was held by a chain of similar metal. It only reached just below the point at which a wimple-like head-and-shoulder dress covered her flat chest. A car radio in the Citroen played a melancholy tune. The music sounded French, something like '--- *soleil, soleil,*' 'sun, sun.' It could easily have been mistaken for a Latin American or Spanish song if not for the English vocals: '*Just a little bit lonely, Just a little bit sad.... I was feeling so empty, Until you came back.... Ohhh — Soley Soley....*' it went. The priest put a hand over his brow and gave the dull-grey clouds sailing low over them a cursory look. To the northeast, where Ssempa was headed, the heavens were a flat smoky grey.

"It will rain," said the prelate in Kinyarwanda before turning to Ssempa as if to seek an opinion.

The man of God was the Monsignor Raphael Rugambage Nyarwaya of the diocese of Gitarama headquartered at Kabgaye, a kilometre southwest of the town of Gitarama on the road to Butare. It was he who had contacted Issa Sinzagaya Gakinya, his brother-in-law, about the possibility of getting the Muganda to offer a lift to the nun. Monsignor Nyarwaya's having a Muslim for a brother-in-law was not strange. Several years ago, Gakinya, now a sexagenarian, had been exiled in Mombasa, that famous port on the Indian Ocean coast of Kenya, and became a Muslim to fit into the coastal community that was predominantly Mohammedan. Moreover it was not Gakinya who was married to the relative of the monsignor. It had been an elder brother of his, Apolinaire Sebwitabure, killed in 1961 during the worst upheavals in Rwanda. At that time he had married Nyarwaya's younger sister, Sabina Odette Mukamuhizi, who was also the biological mother of the nun.

"We will have made it," Ssempa told the priest in his broken Kinyarwanda, and then switching to English, added, "I am not stopping anywhere."

"She is Sister Julian Dominicus, my niece, and I am Monsignor Raphael Rugambage Nyarwaya." He spoke good English with a faint Kinyarwanda accent rather than a French one. "Are you a Mugande?"

Banyarwanda do not only originate from Rwanda, that tiny former kingdom-state, but are found in quite ample numbers as indigenes in the countries surrounding that country. He did not pretend to take Ssempa for fellow Munyarwanda the way most Banyarwanda did. And though *Mugande* could refer to his nationality, Ssempa knew the priest wanted to know his tribe.

"Yes," the Muganda acknowledged with an accompanying nod. "David Ssempa." He always anglicized his first name among his non-Muslim friends and associates. His own family members would address him as Daoudi or Daoud.

"Good. I like Bagande. They are cordial people." The priest casually turned his long thick neck this way and that to see if there were any other people fluent in English or interested in their conversation. He seemed to find none. "Your people have accepted us in Bugande more than any other Ugandans. Your Southerners are not happy or very receptive to our people." He gave his niece, the nun, an exaggeratedly pitying look. "Some ancient political contentions and glitches you know; they look at my niece with contempt. But I want her to continue with her calling there. God's work can be done anywhere on the globe. And Julian has helped many of our people to leave the refugee camps."

"But Uncle Raphael," the nun spoke to him cautiously in a lilting voice. Ssempa was unready for that singsong cadence. "You won't go telling everybody that. They will think I am an agent of sorts. It can be very dangerous for me and the others."

"You are right too, Julian. But you see I am a student of character; I am a very good judge of men. This young man here … Ssimha… is a very trustworthy person. It is written in him. Why else do you think Nzaza gives him messages for your uncle? You are sure you won't stop over in Kigali, Ssimha?"

"My name is Ssempa, not *Ssimha*," the younger man said, quite effectively concealing his irritation.

"Ah, Ssimha — that's what I just called you myself...."

"Ssempa — with a *p* not *h*.' He proceeded to spell it out. "It is spelt double-*es, ee, em, pee, eh*. Pronounced *s-s-e-m-p-a*."

"Yes, sure; Ssimha like I said exactly. Where am I in error, young man? All right, I shall call you David, okay? So that we may remain on good terms even in future."

"That's a lot better. What would you like me to do for you in Kigali, Reverend Monsignor?"

"I want a personal letter delivered to a colleague in Christ on the Avenue de Rusumo, that is all."

"Then I will stop by there and drop it for you, Most Reverend Father." That was how Sinzagaya Gakinya had told him to address the man of God.

"I told you the young man is nothing but good, Julian. Bagande are people after our own heart."

"And with all due respect, Monsignor, I don't care much for your ethnic sentiments. I don't believe in that sort of stuff."

"You do, son. You cannot afford not to. You see all people with a monarch to rule over them are tribalists."

"We lost our king — the *kabaka* of Buganda. He died in exile in London some seven or eight years ago."

"*Exactement*. It is especially those people who lost their king in such circumstances who are most tribalistic. Ah, do not argue. I know Uganda has managed to live in a semblance of harmony with many tribes and ethnicities. But I also know Bagande to be the most tribalistic of the lot. Without their *kabaka* on his throne at Mengo, they don't feel included in the general Uganda. They are always Bagande as a nation and Ugandans as countrymen, am I not correct, Mugande? On our part, we cannot be anything but Banyarwanda, yet politicians who hate us for very trivial reasons have attempted to exclude us from our own country."

"How did the Baganda help your people?"

"Ah, David, they married them."

"What?"

"Married them, I said. The southerners did so most grudgingly; long after much of the suffering had subsided. It is a historical animosity between us — as we don't share borders with your Bugande. An ancient grudge that refuses to go away."

"And we are Baganda, not Bagande, Monsignor."

"Never mind my pronunciation of your names, David. There are things — words that Banyarwanda tongues and throats cannot bring out of the mouth. The Belgians attempted to force us to speak Flemish like them — I doubt a crueller people exist than *les flamands*. They failed with us, anyway. Then the French attempted to assimilate us as Frenchmen; they still complain of our incompatibility. In any case, a rose by any other name still smells just as sweet, as they say. You are always Bagande to me. And as for tribalism, I hate it probably more than you do. But you cannot pretend you haven't seen it being used here and there. Indeed, somebody here is practising it most grossly

103

to keep me oppressed till kingdom come. However you will find Kantarama — ah, by that I mean *Soeur* Julian Dominicus here — quite detribalised. Says she cannot afford to be tribal as she lives permanently among foreigners."

"*Says*? She says nothing at all. You are not talkative, Sister," remarked Ssempa facing her.

"Ha! You won't get much out of Sister Julian. I am the ancient mariner of the family. Always have been. And she took to me more than any other of our kinsfolk. Quite chatty during her adolescence, too, like a magpie; never could keep quiet for a minute." He was looking at her fondly with craned neck and oblique face, with eyes laughing. "But you will need to get used to her silence. Brides of God spend the best parts of their lives in conversation with Him only for lengthy periods. She is a teacher by calling too, which has — I am sure — killed several faculties in her, like custody of the eye. But she has quite a strong custody of her marble mind, mark you. And I say she must talk a great deal in the children's classrooms at Kyera. You will find her fluent in your Ugandan languages, perhaps not the northern tongues; and in English, of course. You aren't returning to Sinzagaya's, are you?"

Ssempa threw a glance in the direction of the eucalyptus-lined dusty murram road that sloped away to the northwest on its way to Kibuye. A mile ahead stood the commune of Nyabisindu, the tiny settlement dominated by the Muslim community of Gitarama. Most of those Muslims, like those in Nairobi's Kibera or Kampala's Bombo — had served with the colonial Belgian gendarmeries, had come from other parts of the Great Lakes region and had to be settled separately from the indigenous peoples. They slowly coalesced with the citizenry and became indigenes themselves. The Sinzagaya the prelate talked of was an indigenous Munyarwanda and an in-law of his.

"No, I cannot return to Nyabisindu. I've already said farewell to his family and he himself is in Kigali. I will start off at once."

"Better do that for I am a true ancient mariner and would never be the first to say adieu to you." The priest went on to embrace his niece the way the Banyarwanda did, by putting a hand across her shoulder and another behind her back – she doing quite likewise, and each patting the other's back most affectionately, cheeks pressed hard together. "Never mind the Mugande, Kantarama, *dii*. He is one of us. Anybody who can carry letters from Batutsi exiles living in Burundi to Batutsi subjugated in Kigali through the loathsome *douanes* of those Bahutu immigration officers is a true friend of ours. And let him not deceive you; everybody practices tribalism."

"A vast number of my closest friends and associates in Rwanda and Burundi are Bahutu, Monsignor. And I convey love letters, not..."

"Ah — the majority of my pastoral congregations are none other than Bahutu men and women, Mugande. I take months without the benefit of seeing a single Mututsi citizen in this place. Strange country this is, no? But as for those missives you convey — well, it is safer, of course, for you to carry *billets doux*, David. Do you read mail entrusted to you?"

"What you say gives me second thoughts about this letter to your *Mon Père* Honorè d'Aubervilliers. Am I supposed to transport it inside one of the spare tyres? Eh — *Mon père...*" swore Ssempa under his breath, studying the envelope critically. "*Mon père....* Father Honorè d'Aubervilliers!"

"What is wrong with the name, Mugande — you've heard of him before?"

"Short, stocky fat fellow who lived in Congo – Bukavu or Kamanyola — before? Arab or Algerian who passes for a Frenchman? Dealer in... Oh, my *jajja* Zzinda!"

"Nobody ever discusses Honorè d'Aubervilliers' past; but he it is that you talk of. You must have met him through Sinzagaya. He knows too many people, that *beau frère* of mine. By your facial expression, you cannot have parted well with the man of God. But as I said, nobody ever discusses Honoré d'Aubervillier's past. It is not safe to do so in Rwanda."

"I am agreed. I only discussed it once, in Koboko, and five or six years have gone by since. Some things are safer undiscussed, I concede, Most Reverend Monsignor."

"How I wish I had more time with you, Mugande. You are a man after my own heart. Do, please, find time to drop by my place at Kabgaye *Sacré Collège* whenever you drive by on your way to Burundi in future. A lot we can expostulate upon. I would tell you, for example, that that d'Aubervilliers priest looked after my sister, *Soeur* Julian's mother, in the best of ways during our worst tribulations. You needn't hide the letter inside your spare tyre, though; this particular one is innocent. That man was a Tshombeist back in Katanga. Then he became a Lumumbist. Then a Kimbanguist — the latter is more or less a religion in Zaire today. He was with Ernesto Guevara both in Congo and in Angola. He assisted Agostinho Neto in ousting the Portuguese from Angola. He built a large mission school that still stands in Dilolo and yet another church school in Lobito, on Angola's Atlantic coast. The Congoman he despises most is Joseph Desire Mobutu. He is, besides, a supporter of my enemy government, the MRND regime of Habyarimana, but he does this on principle, and I understand him clearly though I hate communism and so-called revolution. Having been ruled by the French, Algerians have a considerably low opinion of monarchical rule. You must have heard what the French did to their own royal family during their savage revolution. It is unfortunate that Father Honorè d'Aubervilliers regards all Batutsi as monarchists."

The nun had looked at them quietly all this time, expressionless, unpuzzled by their talk, her hands clasped at her front, just below the crucifix, and her eyes uninterested in what went on around her, or so it appeared. Ssempa would soon learn that this nun didn't miss much. When she was sure their talk was over, she went round to the driver's door and stopped short of yanking it open. "Ah la lah," she exclaimed, hurrying back the way she had come. "You get too easily used to these wrong-sided Rwandese cars."

The monsignor turned to Ssempa, smiling cheerfully. "I used to get tired telling her not to swear. And to make it worse, she even tribalises my car." He patted the small Citroen's top. "She harbours a most healthy hatred of Rwanda. But her mother lives here, she has never lived anywhere else for any length of time. All her people now live here, thanks to the church — and to Gakinya's mosque, too. She even thinks that those of us who returned and those who stayed behind to be ruled by Gregoire Kayibanda and, later, Juvenal Habyarimana, were treacherous Bahutu sympathizers. Would you like me to show you Gregoire Kayibanda's home?"

"Is it near here?" Ssempa showed mild curiosity.

"Over the hill there." The priest pointed at a bearing slightly west of Kabgaye.

"No time, Monsignor."

"Of course. It is just behind that hill." He still pointed westward, vaguely, his face distracted by a traumatic past. "From behind that hill I would point out that murderer's home. It is a mere few kilometers that way."

"Uncle Raphael," the nun, now settled in the passenger seat, said in a scolding tone. "That death wish stalks you again, it appears. If you were only to be overheard!"

"There is no danger to me. These dreadful people would in this era think twice before committing crimes against people of the cloth."

"You think so?" the nun said. She secured the silver grey terylene seatbelt across her torso, the mounds of her breasts barely discernible against the breast flap of her dusty brown habit. Ssempa would have been bound to make a witty comment about or even ogled another possessor of such breasts. But he saw no sex in the woman's broad, dark-complexioned, smooth face. He saw only a nun, a sister, *Bikira* Maria — as the Baganda Catholics referred to the Virgin Mary. To him she was neutered by the antimacassar breast flap. "You think they know what religion means when you very well know why uncle Gakinya became a *musulman*!"

"The politicians are the truer danger, but the people are very deep believers who verily extol God Almighty."

"When they want to misuse Him," she corrected him. "You don't know well the people among whom you live. Reverend Superior General at Kabgaye — even as she raised her hand to give me benediction for the journey — could not effectively conceal her antipathy toward me; her eyes studied my throat the way butchers view *ihenes'*. And I always perceive a lust to kill us all whenever I visit Mama and the *villageois* and *villageoises* come to look at me from their village homes." A shivering fit visibly ran through her body. "Oh, how I fear for you when I imagine the animals behind the masks of their faces."

"I forget what *ihene* is," Ssempa said.

"Goat," said the monsignor. "She means goat. She thinks the worst thing a person — a nun, of all people — should think of a Superior General. You must, my dear, Soeur Julian Dominicus, confess your faults the moment you get to Kyera." He seemed to have recoiled inwardly at the imagination of what his niece had said about the Reverend Superior's eyes. The monsignor looked away from the two and again viewed the sky through his thick steel-rimmed spectacles. "If your roads weren't tarmacked I would strongly discourage this journey. It is going to rain the proverbial English cats and dogs. I hope it does not get you before leaving Kigali." Then with a gesture of his open palm he dismissed them. "Don't forget to give my highest regards to my brother, Bishop William Kabigumira, my dear Kantarama. If it weren't for your other crucial work with the refugees I would take you away from him. You can tell him that for me. You are of such great value to me here. And such a great cook too. I will miss your goulashes and cassoulets. So will poor Sabina, of course. And, Mugande, don't let her lecture you on time consciousness. I want you to drive and arrive safely. And, oh, Julian — how I wish you were wrong about la Generale superieure!" He gave her a sad look and made a wide sign of the cross to bless the journey. "God be with you."

"Au revoir, Oncle Monseigneur."

* * *

And just as Monsignor Raphael Nyarwaya had predicted, it rained cats and dogs. It never rained in Kigali itself, but for hours it appeared that a torrential downpour had hammered Byumba, Rubaya and Urukomo, all of which were mountainous highlands north of the capital city. They got to Murindi, far below the steep hills of Byumba, at the mouth of the Mironko tea estates, and found a fifteen-foot section of the tarmac road entirely washed away. Reddish-brown water churned violently across the road into the once green fields of tea, creating a foamy lake the colour of yellowish-brown milk tea.

Tops of tea bushes that were normally a lush green appeared black against the tea-brown, on the surface of the new lake. They saw the dislodged concrete culvert pipes that had supported a bridge under which the eponymous stream hurtled east to fill up the River Kagitumba, which also ended up into the Akagera to form the natural frontiers of Rwanda, Uganda and Tanzania. Some stood upright, others at right angles to the currents from the hills to the west. If they were to return to Byumba town ten or so kilometres behind them, they would have to take a murram road that would carry them through Urukomo and bring them to a spot a mere six metres ahead of where they stood stranded on the other side of the washed-away patch of road. Ssempa estimated the detour to be thirty kilometres. The only choice was to drive back and take the mountainous Byumba murram road since the trader was mindful of old Monsignor Nyarwaya's apparent wish that the nun get to her Kyera convent that very day, or night at latest, so as to *confess her faults*. He would have, on his own, opted to return to Kigali and spend the night there or make the Rwamagana-Kamwezi detour right from Byumba in an opposite direction to the mountainous Urukomo route. But that direction was where all the rivers converged and the storm could be worse there. Alone, he would have risked it, but there was the sister, silent and seemingly indifferent to the highland cold, already an encumbrance to him and his trade. He turned the pickup and followed several other motorists to Byumba where he would take the Urukomo pass. He later wished he had not done so.

After the town of Urukomo high above Rwanda, the murram turned into a red-mud dough of winding track that snaked its way on a strictly downhill course. At several points the track hurtled down nearly vertical gradients and at others vehicles careened at impossible angles, their sides nearly touching the red mud. About a dozen trailer trucks and smaller lorries whose load-laden springs were no match for the inclines simply sidled off the track and slid down the grassy slopes. Their dangerous progresses downhill were arrested by the sporadic large-boled pine trees through which the road had been hewn decades ago. The other heavy commercial vehicles sat with their arrays of double tyres caught fast in the fine, soft, red dough of sticky mud. Ssempa's pickup managed to get through primarily because of his adeptness at the wheel, the accelerator and the clutch but also because the villagers had pushed the pickup over and around ditches, laden with heavy enamel-coated utensils as it was, and from potholes and sometimes out of the bush onto the road again. The villagers, whose thinly coated animosity towards the Mututsi nun was not lost on Ssempa, eagerly directed them onto a rutty, rocky groove that no motor vehicle could have ever used, along which the pickup trundled blindly until it brought them to a point directly above the washed-away tarmac road. But there was a precariously precipitous slope — a sheer drop, actually — to the tarmac road at Murindi, where confused motorists turned their heads to look up at the pickup as though it had come there from some star out in space.

"Ah la lah," the nun exclaimed and clucked her tongue in resignation.

Ssempa made his own exclamation inwardly. But they were happy in the comforting idea that they were standing on the good side of the gushing river with an unobstructed black ribbon of road that would see them in Kabale if all went well. But they had to drive back up that rocky rut a whole bushy kilometre before another slippery path and, pointing the car northeastward, where they sensed the tarmac road to be, they trundled on. By the time they got to Murindi it was seven o'clock. The atmosphere was bleak. In the grey gloom the sun appeared to be lost for good. They sighed inwardly with relief now that they were on firm black tarmac again. Ssempa parked and got out of the vehicle, checked that the nylon tarpaulin had protected the cardboard cartons from moisture, gave all the tyres a few resounding kicks and returned to his seat.

"I'll still get you to Kyera before the day is out. That means, of course, before midnight Uganda time."

"Monsignor told you to drive carefully, remember?" Sister Julian's condescension was for real for on several occasions Ssempa had spoken, sometimes simply to make conversation, at others to comment on some place or feature along the way and sometimes to hear himself talk. And her responses were always a nod, seen through the corner of his eye, or a laconic chuckle. Most times she ignored his voice completely.

"Yes, of course, I recall the ancient mariner's advice. Careful driving will get us to Mbarara at around ten o'clock."

When they had cruised along the nearly corkscrew twists in the mountainous road, Ssempa turned to the nun and asked her: "Why do you think those villagers helped us through? Their antagonism to you was almost palpable."

"Monsignor Raphael was correct when he told you the Banyarwanda are a deeply religious people. The fundamental function of all the religions of the earth, is to create a fear of the unknown so that we may not do things that will harm the next person."

"Is that all?" Ssempa asked, puzzled that this big piece of stone beside him on the upholstery could have in her such a salvo of words. But it was also a sermon on religious thought. "Do you really believe that is *why* they helped?"

"No; there was also an urgency to see me out of their *bourgades* — they were pushing me off Rwandan soil."

"I did think so," Ssempa conceded.

As the evening gloom slowly became more dense and the colour had left the vegetation and the rock outcrops by the steep roadsides, they left the hairpin curves behind them high in the *secteur* Byumba and were presently within view of the lights of the *douane* at Gatuna, on the Rwandan side of the frontier. Ssempa stopped the pickup at the entrance to the customs offices.

The *douaniers* were sympathetic — to the driver, whom they knew well. But if the villagers' hatred for the nun had been somewhat concealed because of her sacred cloth, the learned men of customs and immigration were different. It was always the erudite whom she feared and blamed for distilling hatred among the bourgeoisie and the proletariat.

"Kuch'ufite ipasseport yu'Bugande, sheh?" The immigration officer held the nun's Ugandan passport gingerly as if it were a serpent that might strike at his fingers.

"I am a Ugandan." Her responses were sombre, and a bit too courteous. Ssempa thought he detected a deliberate superiority that didn't come off or if it did, bounced off the haughtiest officialdom he had ever encountered. Nobody he had ever met could manage to be as arrogant as a Munyarwanda immigration or customs official.

"If you are a Mugande, then what brought you to Rwanda?"

"Because you yourselves allowed me in."

"That was because you were traveling with that Englishwoman and the other religieuses on their way to Bujumbura and Kigoma. I remember well the Volkswagen car that brought you in two weeks ago."

"But I told you where I was going, too."

They scrutinized her passport, making dissatisfied and disapproving noises and apparently wanting to make sure she understood their disdain. "The religious orders will one day destroy Rwanda," one of them said.

When an official made a comment in Kinyarwanda, the nun responded in that language, and when they turned to the French language, she did likewise.

"We are told they once almost did," said the nun in the cold tone that Ssempa should have expected her to use all along. In the electric light from the small stone building that housed the customs and immigration offices, stores, a jail and residences on a precipice of granite rock, Ssempa looked at the profile of her face and heard the cold anger in her voice. If he had not known her paternal uncle, Monsieur Issa Sinzagaya Gakinya, and had not met her maternal one, the Monsignor Raphael Nyarwaya, whose features she had inherited most, the Muganda would not have readily guessed the nun, with her softly blunted facial features, to be a Mututsi. But she and her fellow Banyarwanda had ways of discerning such things in their worse-than-apartheid hatred of each other. And the nun now seemed to have set out to make a statement with her cold attitude, that she was an aristocrat — love her or hate her.

"You are told, *shahu*! Who by?"

"We in Uganda being your neighbours do like to listen to historic narrations at the fireside. We read a lot of your civics too."

"Is it written in Kinyarwanda?"

"Why?" the nun asked.

"Because if the civics you read in Uganda isn't written in Kinyarwanda then it cannot have anything to do with Rwanda."

"Indeed it is not a history of Rwanda. It is a history *about* Rwanda. We read it with much gusto." This she said in French.

"*Ari'ko* Mugande," the chief customs officer asked Ssempa as they went through his cargo of tableware. "*Uyuu nu'Muhima wanyu changwa n'Umututsi wachu?*"

"Me, I don't know whether she is a Muhima of ours or a Mututsi of yours. I know that the women from either tribe are stunningly beautiful. You will agree with me that even though she is a nun, she is not ugly."

"Yeah," the *douanier* conceded grudgingly. "You Bagande are sympathisers with our enemies. *Bien entendu*, we are too small a country and we cannot confront your Idi Amin. *Afite ama'charblende n'avion z'helicoptere.* We don't have a single tank. And I am told every Nubian army officer has a Mututsi consort."

"What of it? Even in Kigali every Muhutu top politician, all the colonels and businessmen have a Mututsi concubine ensconced in swanky mansions and retire to them more often than to their official residences and wives."

"How do you know that, Mugande?" the man asked full of overt suspicion.

"Who does not know it? Your president and his close relations have several female Batutsi companions in Kakiiro and Remeera. I am well aware that Colonel Lizinde has a great beauty of a Mututsi woman in Gikondo-Magerwa. The other powerful fellows, Rwagafinzaho, Bihozatsinzi, and nearly all your big business magnates — to the chagrin of their very close relatives — have Batutsi consorts. Your ordinary women are said to be incensed most with your *Animal Farm* ways than the men — these women refuse to have anything to do with Batutsi men. I bet you know of *Animal Farm*; I saw a French version of it being sold in a *Karitas* bookshop in Kigali the other year. I would not wonder if you yourself had a Mututsi woman hidden away, considering that Lizinde is renowned as the greatest Tutsi hunter-killer of all time."

"Yoh, yoh, yohh! Is that what you think of us? Well, well, well; on my part, I don't associate with those women who sell themselves to all and sundry in Kigali. You know that is what Batutsi women — and men too – are best at. Selling off their bodies. That is what they do even in your Kampala, is it not so?"

"In Uganda they are exiles mind you. Exiles and refugees haven't much choice in what to do for a living, my dear friend."

"Alright, tell me the truth — is this *religieuse* a Muhima or a Munyarwanda?"

"I gave her a lift from Gitarama, that is all. She was in the presence of a top prelate. They only spoke English and the prelate struggled through some Kichiga, which as you know, is like Kinyankore."

"Ah — Habyarimana's language too. But you would know, certainly."

"Know what?"

"You know fairly well what I mean, come on, Mugande."

"How, by the way, do you identify someone to be a Mututsi or a Muhutu? There is nothing specially unique about my passenger."

"Aughh," the man made a typical French exclamation. "Look at her eyes. Hers are not very chinoise. You see what I mean? But those bulbous pockets under the lower eyelids, that overfull mouth of hers, the jet-black gums — those gums point to over-consumption of milk. That is how we identify them. That and their open hostility towards us, especially when they come in from their countries of refuge. The ones here — the indigenes — would never have the audacity to backtalk me with such insolence. Do you see, Mugande, how easy it is for us to identify our enemies?"

"I don't see them fighting you even though you hound them all the time."

"You don't know what they did here twelve years ago? They came in with heavy guns from Tanzania and nearly finished us off."

Ssempa laughed: "You see friend officer, where I come from it is different. In Uganda you don't become my enemy merely because we come from different ethnic backgrounds. Remember we have more than one hundred languages in Uganda, including indigenous Banyarwanda. All Banyarwanda everywhere speak the same language. Why you pick on someone's bodily features to nominate her an immediate enemy beats me. You could rethink your attitudes, perhaps?"

"You say that because no tribe mistreated the other in Bugande. But here it was bad. It was very, very bad, Mugande. And *la petite rosse* claims she reads our history; bah!" He spat on the ground. "If she hasn't read of the heinous crimes they committed against us what can she know?"

"So; how long do you intend to go on reminding yourselves of your historical acrimony? Even the French have forgotten they once had monarchs at Versailles."

"You yourself are an historian, eh? Well, you are not being so cooperative. It is important to me to know if your passenger is a Muhima or a Mututsi. You see she keeps coming back."

"That could easily be because she has a share in your country equal to yours."

"This country is too small now for us to share with *inyenzi* cockroaches."

"Well, as you very well know, such things are not issues of importance in my country. I hate someone attempting to indoctrinate me into hating my fellow countryman because of ethnic differences. Why, we don't even segregate the many non-Ugandans that live amongst us."

"Yes. You have married Batutsi refugees from here so that their offspring should invade us some day. That is why you are never cooperative with me, Mugande. But I like you. You and I are friends. If you weren't a Muslim I would give you a crate of Primus beer to take back to Mbarara with you."

"Thank you very much. I'll take it if you give it to me, though I go in more for the harder things."

"I know, I know. I'll have for you a bottle of Johnnie Walker Black Label on your next crossing here, rest assured, Mugande." The customs official walked with him to the cab. "But all the same strive to find out for me."

"Find out for you what?"

"I am not a *manehko*, my friend, if that is what you are afraid of. But this woman crosses this border every once in a while. As you see she cannot be touched because of her cloth. We are very deep believers in God. So you find out for me, eh? We reward information with big *cadeaux*, Mugande. You never know — they always return; like cockroaches, you cannot stop them effectively. But like with cockroaches we have discovered a good insecticide. The locals call it *perdu*; in Anglais-h you would call it doom. And it is people like you, Mugande — people of thriving *affaires* — on whom we rely to maintain our country in the sort of tranquility you always find it in. You must admit Rwanda isn't anything like your Uganda, even without ethnic problems there. We also hear things about your country, mind you. Some of those things we can view right from here where we stand. Mass killings and cadavers thrown into the rivers for the crocodiles to feed upon; a necessary evil, such killings, no? *Perdu* insecticide for the cockroaches, I say. I will await your next visit most eagerly, Mugande. Remember your Johnnie Walker Black Label *cadeau* will be awaiting you."

"The Baganda have a saying; in your language it would translate: The doom intended for the ewe may kill the ram."

"Why should someone want to kill sheep unless they were Batwa people from the hills? Oh, but I forget easily. You people eat the damnable beasts!" He then bent over the nun's window and asked pointedly: "*Mbese*, Julian, have you learnt to eat mutton among your Bagande keepers?"

"Ah, mutton? — That is nothing. We eat grasshoppers and white ants," she said and the customs officer jumped away melodramatically as if in genuine horror, contorting his face in the utterest disgust expressible. And he made noises in his throat, pretending to be threatened with a vomiting fit. "And Jesus Christ cleans all our food too," she added jubilantly.

"Drive her away, Mugande, at once. She puts bad things in the mouth of God."

"Mais mon passeport," protested the nun.

"You'll find it ahead of you, mutton eater," the official told her in Kinyarwanda.

Relieved at the sudden unexpected jocularity in the man's attitude, Ssempa cruised the pickup down the slippery murram to the edge of the swamp that marked the beginning of the no-man's-land. An armed customs gendarme raised the boom, holding the nun's passport out. Ssempa grabbed it and drove through. The road through the swamp was extremely slippery and he had to drive very carefully.

"Do you know why I keep my cool?" the nun asked unexpectedly.

"Yes," Ssempa replied to her question when he had gotten to the no-man's land stretch of road with flooded swamp to either side. "It would be unnunlike to explode in anger."

"No, no, you are wrong. I have to be in Mbarara without fail tonight so that I am at my duty by prime, or at least before terce, tomorrow."

"What are prime and terce — meals like breakfast, or some types of prayer?"

"Time, the way the faith counts it. Prime is around seven o'clock. Terce is around eight, after breakfast."

"And so what does your getting to Kyera at those times have to do with your immigration friends at Gatuna?"

"Come on, Mugande — that is what all Banyarwanda have called you since the time we met. Those men possess the malicious power to refer my exit visa back to Byumba *prefecteur* or even to Kigali. And remember there is that washed-away road at Murindi."

She was correct too. Ssempa had seen them do such things to other travelers occasionally — over quite trivial matters too.

* * *

At Katuna, on the Uganda side of the border, it was even more uncertain, more treacherous. The immigration desk was manned by men of the State Research Bureau. Ssempa always felt a sense of shame returning home and finding that it was usually in his country that things were so wrong. The angry grey cumulus thunderheads had hastened the dusk and one would have expected them to send the SRB chaps hurrying off to their houses and Nissen huts. They did not. The men lingered unscrupulously long on the nun's patent leather valise, fingering her rather austere garments in a deliberately obscene, manner. Again Ssempa knew such nuisance would last, and they would be allowed to proceed to Kabale some fifteen miles to the north. But the security goons, some of them already drunk, started their sick antics. Some said the pickup should proceed to Kabale and report to their barracks near Mwanjaari, while others insisted that there was a nationwide curfew and that the nun, whom they now dubbed a spy, and her collaborator, should sleep in the frontier jail. Ssempa could not help sympathizing with the woman of God: her own people across the border ostracized her because she was a Mututsi, and the Ugandan side dubbed her a spy because of the cloth of her faith.

The security people, apparently, did not seriously mean all they said about the two travelers and never even attempted to sound serious. On the nun's part, no trip to Rwanda had ever been without these *minor* incidents on either side of the border. The Rwandan side always made it a point to show her she was a foreigner there; unwanted. Do-not-come-back-please attitudes in all the officialdom she encountered at the douanes, and very uniform too, as if orchestrated all around the country. The immigration officers lingered on her passport, which they invariably handled as if it had slime on it. The customs officials over-checked her valise. Even the gendarme who lifted the barrier would have a bad word for her to take wherever she went — into or out of Rwanda. She was meant to know, and tell those of her ilk, that Rwanda had stopped being their country — full stop. The Ugandan side, since General Idi Amin came into power, represented, theatrics more than a bother to her. Now they were threatening them with jail without really meaning it.

A couple of weeks previously, when she traveled to Rwanda with three other nuns, she had witnessed a comic event at this very place. One of the nuns was a Makonde from Tanzania and the other two were Irishwomen; all three were from Tororo Diocese in Eastern Uganda and were on their way to Bujumbura. The customs and immigration people had released them but, intimated a distrust of them that you could not miss. When they reached the steel boom before the no-man's land, a soldier deciding on his own to make a last check asked the driver of the azure blue Volkswagen Beetle to kill the motor. The soldier had gone to the back of the car, opened the hood and immediately closed it, and come to the window to talk to the driver, the ageing Sister Remigius Shaw, usually called Sister Remmy and a frequent sojourner at the Kyera cloister. In Kiswahili he assured the nun he knew she had greased the palms of the officials back at Customs so as to overlook her crime. Unless she gave him something too, the nuns could not proceed to the Rwandan side. The soldier was cordially grave about his demand until the driver asked him to reveal the crime she had purportedly committed. The soldier then proffered his hand: "Give me the export papers for the engine."

The nuns gawked at the soldier's declaration. But old Sister Remmy was unruffled, having gone through too much in her long life to be surprised by just anything.

"We don't, my dear *askari*, export things." Said she. "We're the four of us women of God, going into Rwanda, and your own folk have just cleared all our travel documents. I cannot even think of tipping you, young man, if that were your stratagem, because you have suggested we are criminals."

"Then, madam," said the soldier as calmly as the Irish nun herself, "I shall have to call the chief collector himself to countercheck you. The men he trusts to do the job for the state prefer money, it seems, over the economic war waged by our great president. Here come some of the customs people." He looked up at two men who had come from the customs checkpoint, walking hurriedly to where they stood parked. "All you need to do is give me a little something and I'll let you go before they get here."

The customs official and an immigration man got to the crossing point where the nuns were parked and the tall soldier hulked above them. One of them asked the soldier what the matter was.

"Both of you," said the soldier; "know what the matter is. These women wear the dress of God, yet they go on to engage in smuggling."

The two officials had looked at each other. "Is there something that was missed? Gold! — What?"

The nuns wore glum faces.

"Don't pretend with me," the soldier was now livid with anger. "How can the whole lot of you miss an entire car engine being smuggled in the boot of their car?"

"What! Take it easy now soldier. We can easily get to the bottom of this. Did no one check the boot? Do you, Sisters, have a spare car engine in your car boot?"

"Not on your life," said Sister Remmy, her wide bespectacled face puzzled and belligerent in one single expression. "We have our suitcases and things there."

116

"That is not true," said the soldier. "Come and see for yourselves; a whole, intact car engine. Do these people take me to be blind or plain foolish?"

"Oh, Holy Virgin — he means...." Sister Remmy issued a very irreligious shriek of laughter. "He does not know about Volkswagens," she instantly ignited the motor and struggled out of the car. She was very fat. "Come," she took the reluctant soldier's arm and waddled her way to the rear of the Volkswagen with him. *"Ebu njo, askari; njo nikuponyeshe....* Come and see for yourself." Sister Remigius Shaw's Swahili was impressive as she attempted to emphasize every letter of each word.

At the back of the car she yanked up the hood. The fan belt whirled furiously as the motor burped away. The soldier did not appear crestfallen until one of the customs officials took him to the front and opened the hood there. "In Volkswagens," he told the man, "the engines are in the back. The luggage is stowed at the front, as you can see. Know that from today."

"Where is he from?" Sister Remmy, a veteran nun who had spent more than thirty years in Uganda, was thumping the soldier's back with her gout-afflicted hands as she led him to her door. "Where are you from? You tell me."

"I am from Keri in West Nile. I was transferred here last month from Arua."

"But there is a customs post at Keri, isn't there my dear? I have worked at the St Lwanga Mission in Koboko before. You ought to know these things, my dear. Here; this is not a bribe," she handed him a cash note. "It is to always remind you of me. And others like myself. People dressed like us never steal or smuggle. Be a good boy and always remember that."

Today it was nearly the same with these goons to whose dark faces behind the dark glasses that were worn even in the deepest of darkness the twilight had lent hideous shadows. They wanted money and Ssempa eventually managed to get them to accept the bribe that they went to much pain to get him to force upon their leader, who also took a set of very good enamelware baking utensils. They cheerfully sent him off in the light drizzle that appeared to be turning into a serious downpour judging from the accompanying gale-force wind that shook the crests of the surrounding trees and made the branches of those giants creak in turgid protest. Ssempa felt content. He had not liked or planned to cross that border at such a late hour. Dusk seemed to evoke evil in soldiers. But then he had not anticipated the storm that had washed away the road at Murindi.

* * *

The roadblock caught them by surprise. It had been established after a very sharp bend on the murram road before Kamuganguzi and they came upon it with a jolting suddenness. But Ssempa was so familiar with the road and his driving was so good that he managed to brake the Peugeot gently before hitting the large lorry-tyre, complete with steel rim and a wooden pole with a piece of red cotton cloth that fluttered flag-like in the evening wind. He promptly extinguished the headlamps, leaving the parking lights glowing. A lone sentry in a military police uniform with red beret and red-and-white lanyard and webbing belt superfluously signaled them to halt using the open palm of his hand. When the darkened sky lit up with a bolt of white lightening they saw a large army-green military tent a few metres away to the left of the road, the canvas awning over its entrance flapping erratically in the raging ante-storm wind. So the curfew those State Research Bureau goons had talked about could be real! But roadblocks during the Idi Amin era could sprout up anywhere and at any time. Another flash of lightening showed them another soldier emerging from a cluster of scrub where he might have been relieving his bowels. This one had on the same beret and belt as the other but his trousers and tunic were darker with leopard spots. He wore canvass ranger boots.

"Where are you going to, big man?" the first soldier asked in Kiswahili.

"I am headed for Mbarara, if I can make it. I hadn't expected a roadblock here. I nearly hit the tyre."

"Don't you know there is an emergency? There is a curfew — all over the state. Where are you coming from and what do you have on the truck?"

"I am from Kigali. Actually I left Bujumbura at dawn. The sister is from Gitarama."

"And you weren't told back at Katuna that there was a security alert?" asked a newcomer, a man with a lieutenant's insignia on his shoulder epaulettes.

"I was told — I heard someone mention there was a curfew. I didn't believe him. He said it very casually, and he let us through anyhow. He allowed us to proceed this way."

The officer nodded in the darkness, his small, clean-shaven black face illuminated yellow by the dim parking lights of the car. The only other glimmer of light came from a parting at the tent's entrance, which the harsh evening draught closed and parted occasionally. The officer switched on an electric torch and flashed its beam in Ssempa's face. "Do you know what time it is and when the curfew commences?" He asked in impeccable English. Then he turned to the man in the leopard-spots uniform. "Corporal Bingwa," he barked in Kiswahili, "Search the pickup."

"Sir," Ssempa attempted to mollify the soldier. He had always wondered where soldiers got their anger. They went to a place singing most jovially, jumped off their ugly trucks most cheerfully and, becoming angry all at once like sadists, they grabbed at and whipped people they had never met in their lives as though they had been lifelong enemies. The whiff of a freshly consumed, locally brewed potent gin known as crude waragi wafted across Ssempa's face as the lieutenant spoke. "Sir, they searched us at Katuna. You see we were cleared out late. And there were no lodges in Katuna."

"There were no lodges in Katuna," the lieutenant mimicked Ssempa's words. "Of course there are lodges in Katuna. There are lodges for the likes of us but not for the likes of you. For you, you want to sleep in the White Horse Inn and the Highland Hotel. For you, you despise us who stand out in this cold weather. And you try to trick the state by dressing this raving beauty of a spy like a Catholic nun." He looked up suddenly, as if startled by the blue-white lightening that streaked across the pitch-black evening sky and the explosion of rumbling thunderbolt in its wake. "And the rain too," he continued grumblingly, his eyes darting from Ssempa to the nun, from the nun to Ssempa. "Do you have any idea why we are here? Do you, big man? Do you know we are here to safeguard — to protect your rich, precious lives with our own discomfiture?" He paused again, as if he was busy inventing things to say in a fabricated bitter voice. He suddenly snapped on the electric torch, hitting the nun's face with the sharp beam. She had not expected the man's action and her mouth fell open revealing a small gap between the upper teeth behind the deep purple spittle-laced labial flesh. She closed her mouth quickly and crinkled the corners of her eyes. The reflex action gave her countenance a severe look. There was a mixture of apprehension, fear and anger in her face as her eyes bore the unrelenting brunt of the beam of light. Ssempa now saw what the undisciplined army officer had, in the dimness of the night, seen that more sane men would have missed or not cared to seek in such people. The dark-skinned nun was not a beautiful woman in her sedate way; she was not beautiful at all, but there was a striking quality — an attitude to her appearance that demanded notice but at the same time urged the observer to look away. The look her eyes lent to her face was almost rude and mocked those that her eyes appeared to disparage. It was a look of near aristocratic pride that must have enhanced her untouchability as a nun as it defied the observer, challenging him to take back his stare. Her face was broad, fleshy, and had a natural glossy sheen that was manifest in the skin of her entire exposed body. Ssempa noted the features he had not bothered to see before; the outer corners of her eyes went far towards the cheekbones and the inner ones were cast a bit too far from the bridge of her stout nose. Her mouth was wide and firm and her chin was well curved and not pointed at its base, with her jaw long and curved up gently towards the ears. Visible strands of her pitch-black hair were thick and naturally curled in longish strands that regular trimming kept under control. Such hair is generally uncommon but normal among the black Hamite tribes of the lacustrine region of Central Africa. The features of her face were not aquiline as is typical of most Hamitic peoples but were instead, like most of her other features, more softly curved than chiseled. She had a pretty strong-bridged nose. A shallow groove ran from her nostrils to the upper gentle curve of her firm meaty mouth, the pertness and vulnerability of which were exposed briefly in the electric light. When he had told the immigration officer at Gatuna-Rwanda that the nun was not an ugly woman he had not meant what the army officer had exposed. He had perhaps meant she was not the typical permanent servant of the Church and the Christian God.

"Why are you doing that?" Ssempa asked sharply, yet betraying helplessness.

The soldier switched off the torch. He laughed, derisively as one pretending to be dead drunk. As though to indicate it wasn't Ssempa's almost reprimanding voice that had made him switch off the flashlight, the lieutenant snapped it on once more. "A raving beauty, and a spy. She is even prettier masquerading as a nun, by God. At first I had thought she was a mulatto of sorts; she even so dark. Look at the hair, *Sponse* Madonna! And what a mouth — Santa Maria... reminds one of a certain actress. Are nuns, by the way, Sister, permitted to hot-comb their hair these days?"

"It is not disallowed, officer, but this is my natural hair." The nun had slightly lowered her eyes. Her voice had so much headmistress firmness in it that Ssempa trusted, that it and her imperiously dignified looks would always keep her out of trouble with bullies. She never moved her head out of the beam of torchlight.

Probably because of the confidence in her voice, the lieutenant switched off the flashlight again. "Adds to the prettiness," he said, to remind them he was not beaten or finished.

"Jesus Christ wants me that way," said the nun in her granite-hard voice.

"Jesus Christ; Jesus Christ!" There was impatience in his voice. "Yes. Jesus Christ is the guy to be. Don't tell me," he said snapping on the flashlight again and directing it into Ssempa's eyes, "that you are traveling with a Catholic sister at this ungodly hour of a stormy night for — well, for nothing. Unless you want to tell me you are a priest yourself. Which is it, big man?"

The nun chuckled uneasily; Ssempa laughed wearily at the army officer's callous jokes. To the ears of a person who didn't know the workings of the minds of criminal security personnel this lieutenant was a jovial and even amicable army officer. But Ssempa had been in too many fixes with Idi Amin's soldiers in his unending smuggling rackets to be fooled by it. He had lost friends at roadblocks in situations that began innocently and on many occasions comically. He knew when a soldier simply wished to carry out his assigned duties and would not touch a bribe. He knew when a soldier wanted a bribe but wouldn't take it for fear of offending those present who held him in esteem or because he did not want to share it with the others. He knew when a soldier was good-hearted and when a soldier had no power to handle a dicey matter but would not want it to be known by those he handled. He knew when a soldier meant evil. On several occasions after selling truckloads of coffee to Kenyan or Rwandan businessmen across the borders, the smugglers would return with sackfuls of the greatly devalued Ugandan currency notes. It was always preferable to be caught taking out the coffee — which was bad enough as Idi Amin had given orders to his anti-smuggling units to kill anybody found illegally taking even a single kilogram of the beans out of the country – than returning with cash. Here you had to be armed with AK47 carbines to occasionally fight it out with the soldiers. Paper money was several tons of coffee greatly reduced to pocketable size. It was quite a good-hearted, morally upright detachment or check-point commander that set his eyes on bulky amounts of cash and satisfied himself with a small fraction of it, given that he had the power to liquidate the smuggler, take everything for himself, and never face an investigation. These situations taught Ssempa one important thing. The premeditated killing of a human being remained a very tough act even for an Idi Amin soldier. Ssempa had lost colleagues in the coffee capers, but not only to evil-minded soldiers. Partners murdered their colleagues after the sale of coffee. An evil mind was an evil mind. The lieutenant standing outside his vehicle right then possessed a mind more evil than most that Ssempa had met and for that reason he did not like the man's jokes in their pretended over-drunkenness flow.

"I am not a priest, officer. This lady — umm, nun actually, was given me by her uncles to give a lift to Mbarara. One of her uncles is the imam of a mosque in Gitarama." He said that on the off chance that the officer might be a Muslim and sympathize with Issa Sinzagaya Gakinya. "We were hoping to reach Kabale town early so that I could drive her to the Bishop's residence. But you say there is a curfew. If only it hadn't been for the blasted rainstorm back in Rubaya! But in any case, officer, I could drive back to Katuna, with your permission of course."

"There is a curfew, so says my commandant at Mwanjaari Military Police Zonal Headquarters. You civilians are deliberately funny. You pretend to be ignorant of crucial matters like this curfew, deliberately again." Here the lieutenant switched to Kiswahili. "Spies are usually funny, pretending, deliberate characters. They pretend to sleep when they are awake and pretend to be awake when they sleep, like the clever Mr Hare. Spies are dangerous people, not so Corporal Bingwa?"

"Of course, affende," the short, stocky soldier in leotards yelped back in Kiswahili.

"And it is our sole duty to find them out, to unmask them. To see whether or not they are pretending. Where did you say you came from, bishop – or did I get your title incorrectly?"

"I told you I am not a priest."

"Hard voice. I should be careful, eh. You could swallow me. I am so small to you I am swallowable. Let's take a look at your identification papers for I heard you mention the 'bishop' somewhere." He had again switched on the flashlight. Ssempa did not find that demand preposterous. He expected it at the very moment it was uttered. But who knew, thought he, the quicker this was over, the better. "Brother officer…?" he began.

"If you are going to declare to me you don't even have identity papers I will faint right here before your eyes, Father."

"Alright then, officer. But I am not a priest, *please*."

"And how do you expect me to know that without looking at your passport?"

Ssempa, followed by the nun, proceeded to hand over his passport. The officer's dark, handsome face followed the beam of the torch, roaming the pages of one of the passports, unbothered that rain droplets pattered on the pages.

"Aha!" the soldier exclaimed. "She has a Ugandan passport, even. My! What beauty," he took his eyes off her passport photograph and peered at the nun, but not with the flashlight in her face this time; a Peugeot's dashboard instrument panel is unusually bright in its green light. "And a true Nyarwanda; with a Ugandan passport! My, she has a mouth! Brigitte Bardot — yes! I found it. That is my actress. Brigitte Bardot — if you weren't so big bodied. I've seen *And God Created a Woman*, and *A Private Affair*, and…. well, many others — in the deserts between Arizona and Nevada, where I did my intelligence course. But a Nyarwanda with a Ugandan passport!"

"I am a naturalized Ugandan, officer."

"I don't know about naturalization. You mean like I read on milk packs — pasteurised and homogenised? Spies everywhere, particularly within the church. And what were you doing in Rwanda you? — You make for her a good, big, mean Jean-Louis Trintignant, or Jean Gabin, see? I wanted to know what you were doing in Rwanda, big man."

"I was in Burundi, not Rwanda."

"You hear that, Corporal Bingwa?"

"I hear it, *Affende*."

"Didn't you just say you had come from Kigali? Did I hear him right, Corporal Bingwa?"

"He said so. I also heard him with these ears," Corporal Bingwa pulled at one of his ears with finger and thumb.

The lieutenant bent low, in a comedic posture, with an ear directed at the corporal: "Something.... There is something you missed Corporal Bingwa."

"*Affende*, sir," the Corporal said.

"Yes. Don't forget that." He then turned to the pickup. "You were in Rwanda?"

"I came from Bujumbura through 'Kanyaru, through Kigali and Katuna." Ssempa's voice had assumed a sauciness — an impatience the thickness of which could be sliced with a razor blade.

"I wasn't asking you this time, big man. What are you doing in Uganda, Brigitte Bardot?"

"I am *not* that name. I have never met any Bardot in my life with Christ. My names, as you just read them off my passport, are Julian Dominicus. I am a bride of God. I am a Ugandan of Rwandan origin." The stoniness in her voice made her words concrete. There was no trace of fear in her voice and it pleased Ssempa that way. Bullies were cowards when confronted with confidence.

"I am a Ugandan of Rwandan origin," the lieutenant mimicked her. He was a superb mimic for he made out the nun's voice and intonation quite well. No wonder he talked of movies and actors — actors and actresses foreign to Anglophone Uganda at that — in a way you wouldn't expect of an Idi Amin soldier so deep in the middle of a dark nowhere. "There is no such animal. Maybe you are a Rwandese of Ugandan origin. Get out of the car, both of you." His voice had suddenly transformed, became a thunderous shout. The cordial attitude had been replaced with a grave anger. But when he spoke again, he sounded as cool as he had been all along. "The thunder gets louder." It was as if he was reciting a written piece. "The storm will be here soon, and the deluge. I want you two to enjoy the effects of the rain with us lesser creatures. What do you think of this strategy, Corporal Bingwa?"

"The best tactic to catch spies, sir. You know you are a genius. Don't I always keep reminding you, sir?"

"I know. Bring them inside the tent for a search."

Ssempa's heart sank to the soles of his feet. He knew there was no need for them to be taken to the tent. He believed the lieutenant wanted to rob them. In the tent any plan of escape, if it came to that, was ruined. On the road, even with the purported curfew on, a lone traveler or an army patrol vehicle was likely to come by and that could change things most drastically for them. But it was very different away from the road on a stormy night. Moreover, if the lieutenant's mind was on robbery it would require him to have to kill the two civilians. But perhaps, the lieutenant merely wanted to take them into the tent because of the violent rain that was clearly about to pour out of the sky.

The two other soldiers were now standing at the tent's entrance. One of them held a French G3 carbine with a rocket-propelled grenade. The other had a light machine gun slung carelessly over his shoulder. The fingers of his left hand, Ssempa could see from the slice of light coming from the tent, nervously played a tattoo on its hanging bipod legs. The lieutenant had a heavy holstered pistol belted at the left hip and a tortoise fragmentation grenade on the other. Corporal Bingwa, who had a mischievous smile playing on his ugly light brown face, pushed the two travelers brusquely forward to step over a ditch and walk through the short, wet grass to the tent, which stood at least a dozen metres from the roadside. Sister Julian Dominicus touched Ssempa's arm nervously and her fingers were cold and trembling. The mountainous Kabale area, stretching into Rubaya and Byumba in Rwanda, is the coldest zone in the two countries of Uganda and Rwanda. "Come on, Sister," he mumbled to her in his poor Kinyarwanda. "They cannot harm us. You will be safe. After all we have done nothing wrong." He believed himself and somehow that made their situation feel a little bit less dire.

A powerful bolt of lightening lit up the heavens rendering the sky an inkier black and bathing the entire surroundings in light that appeared much whiter than earlier, perhaps because the atmosphere had become much darker. Ssempa saw more clearly a plantation of mature sorghum across the road, its dark grain-laden fingers swaying and a few straggly banana trees where the sorghum field ended. They were careening furiously and erratically in the raging wind that was saturated with a thick spray of wetness that stung the exposed flesh like tiny arrows. The wildly flapping awning at the tent's entrance slapped at his face, smearing it with a cold dampness that lingered. Ssempa hesitated to enter the tent; the nun stuck to his arm. He turned to the lieutenant: "Listen, I can give you a gift." His voice was low, which was a superfluity. Nobody else besides the lieutenant would have heard those words, and he doubted the lieutenant himself had heard them. Big rain raindrops hammered into the canvas tarpaulin of the tent so cacophonously that they drowned out his voice even to his own ears.

But that devious lieutenant was endowed with unique aural powers; he had heard Ssempa. And he said, shouting so as to be heard; "Don't worry. We shall come to the attempted bribery bit later. Do you carry guns on you?"

"You must know we cannot have guns, officer."

They were now inside the tent. A groundsheet covered the grass, which Ssempa felt crumple under his feet with an unheard crunch, and a canopy made of thick white calico offered a ceiling of sorts that somewhat reduced the noise of the hammering rain outside.

"How would I know? Tell me. You a priest, by the way, or did you say you weren't? — Because," he gestured to Ssempa to shut up. "Because we are told Catholic priests are trained soldiers, commandos, actually. Take your seats there." He indicated piles of grey packing cases. Here the smell of the crude liquor was quite distinct and the culprit bottle that at one time long ago had contained a litre of Cinzano Rosso stood guiltily on a grey foldable iron table.

Ssempa glanced around the tent's interior. It was not a small tent. It was about ten feet high — some of the piled boxes touched its canopy and gave a general dimension — and about fourteen feet broad. A hurricane lamp with a soot-blackened globe stood on one of the bigger boxes, a weak yellow flame uselessly struggling through the soot. A Primus pressure lamp, its globe also blackened on one side with a dark brown glutinous substance, hung burning and suspended from a metal wire at the extreme end of the tent. Moths of all sizes and some black beetles zoomed round the lamp, and a number of them lay on the floor directly beneath it, some completely knocked out, several scrabbling over the floor dazedly and yet others, usually on their backs, barely moving. There were three army-green four-gallon metal canisters standing upright in another corner where the soldier with the light machine gun had settled himself and mounted the gun on its bipods. Its ominous dark-centred muzzle peered bleakly at the tent entrance. But for the soot on the lamps, the interior of the tent would have been brightly lit. It was instead cast in general shadow except for the side where the unblackened globe of the pressure lamp faced, which was towards the hurricane lamp. Ssempa's eye did not miss Corporal Bingwa picking up his own G3 carbine and slinging it over his left shoulder. Another rifle, an FNL, leaned against another pile of packing cases. Ssempa looked at the lieutenant, whose eyes watched the nun as she stood there, unsure where to sit.

"Are we going to be made to spend the night here, brother officer?" He was doing his best to suppress his apprehension and outrage.

The lieutenant first gave him a sidelong look, and then turned to stare squarely at him in clownish bewilderment. "You quite simply cannot fathom the effrontery, eh, big man, of the possibility of a mere mortal like myself interfering with your White Horse Inn frolic, can you?"

"Look here, brother...."

"Corporal Bingwa?"

"Yes, *Affende?*"

"When you search the bishop keep in mind that priests are well trained in martial arts. They are commandos. Big man here is even worse. He is after all a bishop: think of a black-belt."

"I'll take note, sir," Bingwa was gloating.

What made Ssempa suspect the worst was the army officer's pretended seriousness of voice and superficial calmness, plus, of course, his genuine tipsiness too. It bothered him that the lieutenant sounded so officious. Ssempa's instinct discerned some felonious intent. A normal person would have believed the lieutenant had no ulterior motives. But Ssempa felt in his gut that something was very wrong with the soldier. He perched himself on an oblong packing case facing the lieutenant while the nun, following Ssempa's example, sat on a lower box, feet in brown leather brogues tucked in, knees pressed together, hands clasped in her lap. There were two chairs in the place and the lieutenant had taken one, sat on it and rested his ranger-booted feet on the other. In the better light from the hissing pressure lamp, Ssempa studied his detainer at close quarters.

The lieutenant was a medium-height, slender man of above thirty-five and below forty years of age, clean shaven, handsome, with a light chocolate complexion. Only his bloodshot eyes, suggested he was a habitual drinker or perhaps had suffered from trachoma during childhood. The strong smell of *waragi* in the air, and the empty bottle made the former seem more likely. He was very smart in his plain green uniform and red beret, the black leather band of which touched his eyebrows. The Uganda Army insignia, a golden metal emblem, glinted whenever the officer turned his head. It was not easy to tell his tribe or origin from his good English, Uganda-Army Kiswahili or facial features. But Ssempa had detected some influence of Bunyoro or Toro in his English. He would find out several months later, under even more touchy circumstances, that his guess had been, very close to right. Ssempa knew that criminals became most deadly when they noticed you studying their faces. They hated, more than anything, to be pointed at positively in identification parades. The lieutenant seemed to have caught on that he was the subject of a close, albeit subtle scrutiny and he turned to the corporal.

"Corporal Bingwa, search the priest."

"I am not a priest, officer. I am a trader," Ssempa said, patiently.

"You are a spy," the lieutenant spat. "You," he snapped at the nun, who almost jumped the box at the crack of her caller's voice. "Get up and come here. Who is this man? Is he a priest or is he a trader as he claims?"

"I…. Well, I d-don't say I know."

"Come on. Come here; come on, come on. Move closer here. I want to see your face closely as you deny things."

"I am not the type of person to deny things, officer." She sounded unsure of herself. The strength and confidence her voice had exhibited outside the tent were gone inside it. The army officer's voice and attitude had changed from pretended camaraderie to harsh authoritativeness.

"You are the type of person to ride at ungodly hours with smugglers who don't even pretend to be priests. Why is that so, if you'll tell me? What is his name?"

"This man — er, this man." The nun sniffed several times, probably trying, Ssempa thought, to recall the name he had told her uncle back in Gitarama. "He is Mr David. He is a friend of my uncles — Monsignor Raphael Nyarwaya and Monsieur Issa Sinzagaya Gakinya. Ssempa is his other name. He came from Bujumbura this morning and my uncles requested him to give me a lift to Mbarara."

"What were you doing in Rwanda?"

"My mother lives there, at a place called Kabgaye in the commune of Nyamabuye."

"What is your mother doing living in Rwanda?"

"My mother is a Rwandan. She was born in Bugarama, in Cyangugu. Her husband — my father — died more than a decade ago. I visit my mother in Kabgaye twice every year."

Ssempa, watching the officer, could see his facial features soften — apparently in embarrassment. The nun had again spoken firmly, fearlessly, and most truthfully. One had to be a sadist to query her further.

"You seem to speak the truth, woman," he said, and Ssempa noted the reference to the sex rather than to title, which should have been *Sister.* "It is your boyfriend here, whom you say is not a priest, in whom we are most interested. Have you finished with the priest, Corporal Bingwa?"

"Just about, sir." The soldier's attention had all along been engrossed in the exchange between his superior and the nun. Now he grabbed Ssempa's shoulder and shouted: "You. Off with your shoes."

"Gentlemen —! Brothers —," stammered Ssempa, in anxious protest.

"Remove your shoes," shouted the lieutenant. His bark was drowned in a heavy thunderclap. The heavy raindrops ceaselessly pummeled the canvass of the tent. As Ssempa speedily untied the shoelaces, the officer was saying, "Sister, are you sure you don't carry a gun?"

"Why should I carry one? I only travel with *Bikira* Maria the mother of God." Her fingers were clutching the crucifix at her breast, unconsciously stroking it.

"Then of course you wouldn't object to a search, would you?"

"A what? A search? Of me?" There was a mixture of scorn and disbelief in her voice.

"Yes; a search of you, a close-body search."

Ssempa now conceded his suspicion had been right. The lieutenant was up to great evil. If he committed a crime of passion, he would never allow his two prisoners to remain alive. He raised his voice above the heavy drumming of the rain on the taut canvas: "Officer, now please, leave the person of God alone."

The lieutenant's eyes darted his way and even in the cold rain outside, there were beads of sweat on his fine eyebrows and bridge of nose. He said in an unnaturally high-pitched screech: "I said it, didn't I? Your voice spells it out. You were headed for the comforts of the White Horse Inn — together. Together alone." The soldier let the words roll off his tongue softly, as if the mind that composed them had gone to sleep. His eyes remained fixed on Ssempa's in the dim light. "Together alone! As I always say, after Curiosity's creation of God for man's psyche, Loneliness created woman for him, though most tend to believe woman mothered all and else. You see, *Sponse* Madonna, I caught you out, didn't I? It is a very, very lonely night. Come close — closer here, lady." His eyes left Ssempa hurriedly for his crime-impassioned mind had turned him into a zombie. A crazed grin twisted his face, turning it into a little ugly mask. His voice had acquired a tremulous twang. His eyes were mad with unholy lust and they stared up at the nun's face unblinkingly. She took another heavy step closer to where he reclined in the metal chair. He sat forward, extending his arm and his right hand, edged like a machete, and touched her knee. Sister Julian Dominicus stood ramrod above her tormentor, her eyes looking down on his bereted head. Ssempa felt something like a cold-bellied viper edge up his spine and he shivered.

"Stop it, officer," he growled.

The lieutenant seemed at once to be awakened from a trance. He turned round. He blinked several times and cleared his throat. There was a dead silence in which, besides the almost hushed raging of the storm, only two huge nocturnal beetles assaulted the blackened globe of the steaming lamp with metallic clangs.

"My God, Corporal Bingwa! Corporal Bingwa, my friend! What do you want me to do? Do you begrudge me my officer's pips? Ah, no, if you want them, here they are, on my shoulders. You simply come and rip them off and take them. Place them upon your own shoulders. And, of course, my job too. You want it, don't you, Bingwa? You've always coveted my position."

"No, never, sir," the corporal said in frightened meekness. "I am a corporal, sir. I am a born corporal. No officer stuff in me, sir. I beg your pardon, sir."

"Do you know my pips were given me by the commander-in-chief of the armed forces?"

"Yes, sir."

"And who gave you your corporal's chevrons?"

"What are chevrons, sir?"

"Your two corporal's bars, Corporal."

"The commandant gave them to me, sir."

"Can the commandant place even one single officer pip on your shoulder?"

"Only the commander-in-chief...."

"Enough. Then why do you, Corporal Bingwa, seek to demote me? Why do you want me to do your — a corporal's – duty?"

"No, sir."

"Again?"

"Yes, sir. I mean, sir — no, sir."

"Then, Corporal Bingwa, why do you want me to do a corporal's job — tell me?"

"No, sir."

"Then, Corporal Bingwa, why do you let a civilian idiot — a spy who pretends to be a bishop, address me as if I were his subordinate? Why do you let him give me orders? Oh, my grandmother Maria-Theresa — he told me to shut up! Did you hear that? Oh, Maria-Theresa, the spy ordered me to shut up. And, Corporal Bingwa?"

"It shan't happen again, *Affende*."

As far as Ssempa could recollect, all he had said was for the officer to 'stop it', not to shut up. He wondered and worried what else that lieutenant was up to.

The lieutenant, eyeing Bingwa, his stare slowly taking in Ssempa and then Bingwa — completely ignoring the woman who towered above him — sighed, tiredly, melodramatically. He appeared to quickly regain his composure. "I am quite convinced it shan't happen again, Corporal. I assume you have your gun."

"Yes, sir," came the superfluous reply.

"Is it a G3?"

"Yes, sir."

"Made in France?"

"Yes, sir."

"Made to kill?"

"Yes, sir"

"Is it cocked?"

"Yes — no, sir."

"What, Corporal Bingwa?"

"No, sir."

"Cock your rifle, Corporal Bingwa."

"Yes, sir. Of course, sir." There was the harsh grating noise as the carbine's mechanism slotted a cartridge into its breech.

"You aren't Catholic by any chance, Corporal Bingwa, are you?"

"No, sir. I am Protestant."

"Catholics, Corporal Bingwa, don't love Protestants very much — I don't know if you are aware of that."

"Ah, I know that very well, sir."

"If they were ever to rule the country, they would torch all your churches. That is why, Corporal, we have a Muslim president rather than a Catholic one. Even Rome knows it. The British and the Americans ensure it."

"Yes, sir."

"We shall never, despite their superiority in numbers, allow a Catholic to preside over us."

"Is it so, sir?"

"Are you disputing my... er, well — orders, Corporal Bingwa?"

"No, sir. How ever can I, sir?"

"In Britain it can never happen. In America John Kennedy and his brother, Robert, were killed for assuming the possibility of it. Do you hear that? A Catholic cannot rule Britain. A Catholic cannot rule America in tranquility. Believe that, Corporal."

"Yes, sir. No Catholic presidents here, sir."

"Did you know Uganda has never had and cannot have a Catholic president?"

Bingwa cleared his throat, bravely: "There was one, sir. Benedicto Kiwanuka. The name is typically Catholic."

"Not a president, idiot. He was a chief minister. And where is he? I shan't task you over that. But that priest standing there against that box before you is a Catholic. According to information we received earlier on, he wants to be president of our country. If he so much as twitches a muscle — even accidentally or by reflex action, do you hear, Corporal Bingwa?"

"Yes, sir."

"It will mean he is succeeding in his ulterior ambitions. I don't need to remind you of the dangers of such outcome."

"Yes, sir"

"Shoot the bastard."

"Right away, sir." Bingwa promptly took two steps back, leveled his carbine at Ssempa's stomach, his lips peeling away from his teeth as his nervous index finger touched the trigger.

"Not now, you idiot." The lieutenant jumped up from his seat.

"Yes, sir," Bingwa spoke breathlessly, his eyes opened very wide and darting all over Ssempa's face like a lizard's.

"Only when he twitches a muscle." The lieutenant sat back slowly. "I told you *only* if he twitches a muscle."

"Oh yes, sir. Sorry, sir."

"Don't be," said the lieutenant, anxiously. "If he twitches a muscle and you let him get away with it the next thing you will know, the priest will be president. And did you know this?"

"What, sir? No, sir."

"Catholics are never allowed to read the Bible — by His Holy-Self the Pope. So they never forgive, for they don't know how to."

"Yes, sir."

"Now, back to business." He turned his attention away. The corporal and the other two soldiers became more alert. "Sister — that gun we were discussing. Where is it? Is it a tiny pistol, like those that female spies carry in their underpants as shown in cinema?"

"I have no gun." Her voice now trembled. "If you do anything evil to me, army officer, God will concentrate all his attention on you in the worst punishment you can imagine."

"To guard the nation against foreign spies is a God-ordained duty, lady. God never contradicts Himself. Come closer and let us get on with it."

Ssempa's troubled eye followed the progress of the lieutenant's intentions with a mixture of anxiety and rage. He momentarily forgot their more dire peril: certain death after whatever crime that lieutenant was bent on committing. This time the man stood up and, theatrically, felt under the nun's veil, his hands going to either side of her face and ruffling her thick short hair and then coming out suddenly. As he did so, his eyes stared into hers and because his were filled with a certain rabid madness, she looked above his head, as she was taller than him. Still looking up at her face, the soldier proceeded to pat her body downwards, his face following the progress of his hands. Doing all he could to show he was disaffected with what he was doing, the man's open palms patted the nun's breast cover, felt beneath it, lingered there, and went on down. The other four men in that tent, the two soldiers, Corporal Bingwa and Ssempa, looked on. The soldier in greatcoat lay down behind the bipod-supported machine gun that faced the covered entrance of the tent. His colleague half sat, half leaned against a pile of packing cases. Bingwa's mouth was half open, his teeth unseen but the tip of a pink tongue quite visible. He might often have witnessed this kind of spectacle, Ssempa thought, his mind alert and scheming.

"You are committing a grave offence, officer," Ssempa heard himself say.

Bingwa took those two steps backwards: "Can I shoot him now, affende?" His voice was urgently expectant, eager for an affirmative answer. His eyes had momentarily left his superior's exploring hands and concentrated on the center of Ssempa's stomach.

"Yes, of course," replied the lieutenant. "If he utters another sound. I mean that, bishop," he added for Ssempa's benefit.

The lieutenant's voice had come out in gasps, as if from afar, a breathless, husky loud whisper. He slumped into his chair with a small crash and pulled it forward, closer to the nun, who had refused to take another step forward. His hands patted her rather wide hips, and then patted her buttocks in the same theatrical, callous manner. And she stood in one place, her eyes riveted at a spot in the empty grey wall of the tent. And in the hammering noise of the rain on the canvas, the pressure lamp hissed on, and the beetles, now quite numerous, plunged their armoured bodies at the hot globe with explosive knocks. In her silence, tears glistened on the nun's cheeks as they flowed slowly down her set, broad face.

Ssempa kept his eyes away but turned to look whenever the lieutenant expelled a breathy sigh.

"If you have a gun anywhere," the felon was saying, as if his words were addressed to his right hand, towards which his head was slanting sideways. "I will find it, lady. I am very, very thorough."

The man's face was grotesquely twisted. He was no longer the handsome man with the confident poise. His mouth was open. A quiver twitched the flesh of one cheek, just above the mouth, pulling part of that cheek towards the ear in little violent spasms. An eye awkwardly attempted to seek out Ssempa. His hand was traveling up the woman's inner legs, the hem of the dusty-brown skirt caught up between his fingers and thumb.

"Ah, now, Corporal Bingwa, are you searching that priest?"

"Yes, sir," lied the corporal, whose breathing had become even more rapid as he watched his boss's atrocious deed with glee. "I am searching him, sir."

"I — I want... I want to ... to see you d-d-do it," he was unable to turn his head or eyes fully in Bingwa and Ssempa's direction. His whole attention was now glued on his right wrist, the hand of which was already invisible on its progress up the woman's inner thighs. "I myself am about t-t-to search in

132

regions that you don't have the man-d-d-date to witness. Which makes me wish we had curtains. Or f-f-f-female personnel for this dastardly ch-ch-chore. How I d-d-detest it! Remind m-m-m-e to make a note of it to Affende Comma-mma-mmandant when we return to base, will you, C-c-co corporal?"

"Yes, sir."

"We must recruit f-f-f-female searchers for female spies, d-d-don't you agree, Corporal Bingwa.

"Er – er, yes, sir."

"Ah, never mind. Th-this will be my last f-f-f-f-female search st-t-tint. And because of that, I'll p-p-lace my everything into it."

"Yes, sir."

Then Ssempa heard it — the unacceptable! The protest gasp. Her voice was low, anguished, and full of tears: "Oh no, please, Mother of God, nnnoooo."

"Bingwa, do you hear that?"

"Yes, sir."

"You hear it b-b-because you aren't concentrating on your job. I ordered you to search the b-b-b-b-bloody p-p-priest."

"Stop this crime immediately, lieutenant."

An ominous silence blanketed the place in the wake of Ssempa's tightly spoken, well-spaced command.

Corporal Bingwa, knowing his superior would turn to admonish him over his negligence of duty, bent down quickly so as to appear to be searching in the trouser legs of the so-called priest. He had been so engrossed in the evil goings on, so excited indeed that he couldn't remember his orders – or he would have promptly shot Ssempa. It was the latter reaction that Ssempa had expected and prepared himself for. Bingwa made things easier for him by bending to his trouser legs, grabbing one stockinged foot and fumbling with that. As he did so the muzzle of his rifle pointed to the floor. The other two soldiers' attention had been transfixed on the lieutenant's sinewy wrist. As the lieutenant's twitching face started to turn to his corporal, Ssempa's elbow thudded downwards at the base of Bingwa's neck. The soldier began to unfold upwards furiously and in so doing, met with a second, more powerful downward elbow jab. Ssempa had the sling of the G3 in his grip and the two fought for the gun. As they struggled, the lieutenant's visibly trembling right hand came out from where it had been pushed and fumbled with grenade and holstered pistol at the same time. Ssempa, unsteadily as he fought the indomitable Corporal Bingwa, pointed the G3 at the lieutenant, his finger finding the trigger guard. There was a great bang of exploding shells. The recoil of the carbine pushed Ssempa backwards, hurling him against the packing cases, Bingwa coming along with the gun because the sling was still looped round his shoulder. The two other soldiers got over their initial shock when they saw their superior fall off his chair. They both charged forward as one unslung his gun from his shoulder to bring it to high port while the other dived behind the light machine gun and swiveled it adeptly to face the enemy. He started to adjust the chain of shells as Ssempa's eyes sought the nun who had fallen backwards along with the lieutenant. He knew he had killed her in his inability to aim the gun properly with Bingwa's shoulder pulling erratically at the sling. He now knew the trigger worked and prepared himself for the backward thrust. He squeezed at the trigger, swinging the muzzle from the upright soldier to the one adjusting the chain of cartridges. With amazement, as he himself was pushed back once more, he saw the upright soldier fall back away from him. He saw the flashes from the mouth of his rifle pointed at the tent's ceiling and even saw the rain spraying over his own head. The machine gunner was spun on the floor and fell with part of the chain of glittering copper-jacketed ammunition crossing his neck and part of his face. Ssempa cleared the sling from the shocked Bingwa's arm. The corporal sank to his knees in a kneeling posture with his face pushed into the ground sheet of the tent's floor. He was trembling like a pneumatic drill.

Ssempa's eyes traveled to the nun and the lieutenant, and he immediately realised his mistake. The officer had not been hit by any of the bullets. He had sat up, successfully unbuckled his belt, pulled out the heavy pistol from its holster and in that seated position, pointed it in Ssempa's face before the latter could steady himself. He saw the soldier's thumb work the hammer back at the same time as he saw Sister Julian Dominicus spring up and without much ado grab the officer's gun hand. Ssempa saw fire in the pistol's mouth, followed by a dull crack. His ears weren't good after the cacophony of the G3s. The lieutenant pushed the nun away with a hand to the left of her face and stood up groggily, his mad eyes darting around. He took three steps to where Bingwa lay and kicked him unceremoniously, to arouse him. Ssempa held Bingwa's gun uselessly as he feared to fire lest he hit the nun who had also stood up and began to move towards him. The lieutenant bared his teeth in a derisive smile and aimed at the nun. As he fired, he staggered because Corporal Bingwa was getting up, his hands using the officer's legs as supports. He fired another slug at her and the nun shouted inaudibly as the lieutenant staggered again with Bingwa heaving up and standing with fingers tentacled in the officer's red-and-white lanyard. The nun turned and flew out of the tent as the lieutenant, debated on whom to shoot first. The thrall that had immobilized Ssempa's trigger finger released it the moment there was no Sister Julian in harm's way. Almost reluctantly, and as though the lieutenant himself, after balefully looking at Corporal Bingwa, was being held by some power not to fire at him, Ssempa squeezed the trigger of the G3, which had all along been pointed at the officer' chest. He saw the crazed face screw itself up in unconscious agony as he threw up his arms, the pistol tossed sideways and cluttering away among the boxes, his body rushing back but his face and torso falling forward in a grotesque slow dance that kept him up on awkwardly moving legs that carried him in a forward-face, backward-midriff progress right into the wall of the tent. Bingwa, to save his superior whom he must have liked, had grabbed the G3's barrel at the last minute to yank it away, but released it just as quickly, spitting into his scorched hands as that barrel had turned very hot. He began to run out of the tent with a frightened-animal look. Ssempa even considered sparing him but immediately realised that the nun was out there in the hammering rain. He touched the trigger as Bingwa got to the entrance and there was a shot — just one shot — the very last one. It hit Bingwa between the shoulders and hurled him into a pile of boxes. He fell on his face and his left booted leg began to twitch and kick spasmodically like a slaughtered animal's. The leopard spots completed the beast image. Ssempa stared at the carbine in his hands and was horrified to note a straight line of pieces of pearly-white stuff stuck against the hot olive-green metal; they stood out like cogs or the serrated edge of a carpenter's saw. There was a sickly rancid stench of burning flesh mixed with the sharp one of cordite. "Oh, my God," he swore under his breath, looking at the dead army officer's body. Somehow, the man's flesh, bloodless like that of lean fish, had gotten onto the hot gun barrel! How that had happened he would never know — and the picture of it would never leave his mind. He threw the gun away to the side. His eyes went around the tent quickly. His ears, made temporarily deaf by the blasts, hummed hollowly, but he could still dully hear the hammering rain. Draughts of wind swept in sprays through the several parts of the damaged tent. He went to the tent fly and edged aside the stiffened wet canvas. The inky blackness was total, and the rain in his eyes further exacerbated the tenebrosity. He returned to the boxes where he had sat and quickly pushed his already soggy stockinged feet into the suede working shoes. The light of the pressure lamp was flickering and it would splutter with dull explosions after which the hissing of the pressure gas lowered. He went out into the rain and he saw the greatly dimmed parking lights of the pickup as his eyes adjusted to the darkness.

He found the nun already seated in the passenger seat, the instrument panel throwing a greenish light in her face. He opened the driver's door and the woman threw her hands up defensively and screamed in his face.

"Come on, easy, it's me."

She sat back, trembling and whimpering. When he pulled the door shut he discovered the absence of the windscreen. Shards of its glass remained at the edges but ninety percent of it had been shattered away. Without word he rummaged through the glove compartment and pulled out a box of matches. He jumped out of the cabin and pushed his hand beneath the tarpaulin at the back of the pickup, took out a twenty-litre plastic jerry can full of petrol and ran with it to the tent. He could now see a great deal better in the deep darkness. He entered the tent, went to the dying steaming lamp and released the pressure. The interior of the tent was now cast into total darkness. He blew at the lamp several times to ensure it was fully extinguished and then unscrewed the jerry can lid. He stood in the centre of the tent and doused the place in gasoline, ensuring most of it went to the metal canisters which he suspected to contain petrol. He threw the container on the floor and rushed out. The rain had eased but still inflicted pain on impact. He ran back to the pickup and started it. He drove it fifty yards up the road with lights off, dreading the possible appearance of another motorist, whom he had wished to appear less than an hour ago.

"What are you doing?" the nun asked in a raised voice to make herself heard as the rain had again intensified. "What are you going to do?"

"To do God's work," he shouted in her face. "You made a promise to that officer, remember?"

She looked at him in the green glow of the light from the instrument panel and seemed not to understand.

"God does it with fire," he shouted at her again.

"I did not mean fire. I meant thunder."

"Then," he yelled, "I will make thunder. Those boxes in there contain grenades and ammunition."

"Wait, Mr Ssempa...."

But he had already jumped out of the vehicle, heading back into the blackness.

Mindful of the way petrol fires ignited, he hesitated before striking a match. When he did, it fizzled in the wet gusts of wind. He went closer to the tent's entrance, stood to one side of its awning and, cupping one hand round the box, scratched another match against the sulphur. He knew very well that the canvas walls could not protect him if the flare-up were to be sudden and powerful enough. He placed the burning match into the half-open matchbox — a foolish thing to do since he had no extra matches — and touched it to the sulphur of the other sticks. The pack began to flare. He threw it into the tent and sprinted off. He jumped in the car and turned to look back.

"Oh, my great ancestors of Nnalubaale," he swore. "Nothing has happened. Oh, *Jajja* Zzinda; nothing is happening, and I have no more...."

The tent walls lit up yellow and then suddenly flashed a reddish white. A great fire defied the torrential rain and shot up in angry yellow and orange soot-tipped tongues. He looked towards the nun eagerly, to see how she was taking it, but the pickup faced away from the fire and her face was shadowed. As he watched the fire, he heard her open the car door and turned to see what she was doing. She did not respond to his query on where she was going. But just outside the cabin, by the door, she squatted and he heard, above the rain and the crackle of the flames, the cascade of her urine gush out of her in a strong spray that had a peculiar tiny, high-pitch, swishing whistle to it. He imagined a small unevenly rounded hole, jetting out the pressurized cascade. Soon she shuffled back into her seat and shut the door. As he started the pickup off up the road, they heard the first deafening explosion. He turned to her and found her eyes on his face. He turned his away to the road ahead and stepped on the accelerator.

They rode against the rain and, without a windscreen, gushes of chilled wind and sheets of ice-cold torrents of rainwater buffeted their bodies, pinning them against the upholstery. Needles of it missiled into their exposed faces like shrapnel. At Mwanjaari, Ssempa reduced speed and drove the pickup with all lights off. But he had nothing to fear. Only a soldier or person of uniquely malicious steadfastness to duty would be out in this kind of weather to catch transgressors. He went past where he sensed the military police barracks to be located, a site with which he would have been quite familiar on normal days and at normal hours but which he was unable to glimpse in the stormy darkness.

Twenty minutes of very chilled, wet driving brought them to the steep incline that ascended to the celebrated White Horse Inn.

There was a power blackout throughout Kabale town, not because of the purported curfew the soldiers had claimed to be in force but because of the heavy storm, which had now eased into a steady heavy thundershower.

* * *

The hotel, which consisted mainly of huts with tall conical tops and thatched with coarse, age-greyed meadow grass, was shrouded in deep darkness greatly accentuated by tall eucalyptus and conifers, dripping of heavy raindrops that hit the grass lawns and the cobbled parking ground with continuous thuds. These trees were as old as the huts, which meant something close to slightly more than half a century of life. The place had the feel of an impenetrable jungle with the large raindrops that fell from the foliage above the huts adding sufficiently to the effect. The sky was not discernible in the ink-black atmosphere. Ssempa eased the pickup into the spacious parking yard and, telling the nun not to move, went in search of George Mwigo Kacheeche, the hotel manager, who had been retired as a top-flight police detective for a few years. Kacheeche had been a senior superintendent of police when he got involved in a serious road accident in seventy-three — an accident that literary broke him into pieces that were reassembled in an East German hospital. Here was the only person — beside his wife, Alwiah — who knew the location to which Ssempa had vanished from Kampala in 1972, the year he first set foot in Rwanda, and the horrible reason why! He found the short, stout middle-aged man in the bar where, being a non-Muchiga, he had to wear a thick sweater under a mackintosh, knee-high brown leather boots and a brown-and-black chequered homburg pulled tightly on his head. It appeared to Ssempa like the wrong hat for the time and circumstances. Kacheeche had done most of his police training in Europe and Eurasia and, as a result, dressed in garb you did not see daily on the streets. His dark rotund face with the greying sideburns showed that tonight he would have preferred to be elsewhere, say somewhere in the extreme north of the country where it was hot all year through or, at least, under wraps at his ancestral home in Kakoba, a suburb of Mbarara town. The chief bartender, a Muchiga native of Kabale and two tipsy Russians, were trying to cheer up the former cop with continuous chatting. But all three knew a worse-off man when they saw one for Ssempa did not have to put on an act to show he had an affliction that could be likened to St. Vitus' dance. The hotel manager, who had virtually become a client of the smuggler in profitable merchandise like whisky and good foreign cigarettes that the government no longer imported, was more closely related to Ssempa than the secrecy surrounding the latter's 1972 escape from Uganda allowed him to exhibit. He attempted to assist his friend up the steps but the latter shrugged off the helping hand.

"I am seeing the true literary meaning of occupational hazards first-hand," said the hotelier. "Not that it perturbs you in the least, you son of a gun. You aren't supposed to be alive."

Ssempa fixed him with a sharp stare: "Hey, hey, hey, George. You aren't even drinking — so what gives?"

Kacheeche chuckled good-humouredly and patted him on the shoulder in an avuncular manner. "I know, I know, my boy. But your fear of the past borders on cowardice. We, too, have seen the worst of life. As you know, my assistant has not been seen since he was taken away in the trunk of a car on New Year's Day. It is coming to five, six months. I have stainless steel rods in both legs for bone! Nothing will ever convince me my chief at the Public Safety Unit did not stage that accident in fear that I was a threat to his position. But what does one do? There is no longer much in this good old hotel, but this being Kabale, especially when the weather doesn't get so unkindly, I do enjoy myself most tremendously. Alwiah will be here with the girls over the weekend, and what more can I wish for?"

"You are not in any danger — or fear of danger." Ssempa also spoke in Nubbi, a language he spoke haltingly, unlike Kacheeche, who was as fluent in it as any Nubian. "I have justifiable reason for my fear."

"Those people don't know you, anyway."

"Not that. You know how I suffer being reminded of Atimango, do spare me those bloody memories, George."

"Well, you are in need of a good antidote for your shivering, man. But unfortunately, as you can see we can't get you anything in the line of hot beverages like coffee. No fire or cook. It is not difficult to get the bloody hotel staff, but it is a rotten atmosphere out there. And that was the very last spirit in the bar. The storekeeper left early this evening to attend the funeral of his uncle's neighbour if you can imagine that! One could have secured you a Johnnie Walker." Kacheeche spread out his arms in hopeless exasperation.

The last spirit in the bar was an empty Uganda Waragi bottle settled between the two Russians perched on facing high stalls. Ssempa nodded his plain regret and asked for a room.

The manager gave him a key on a ring and said: "Unfortunately we can't provide you a lamp. You will find a candle or two and matches in the suite, though — I hope, anyway. We were so unprepared for this sort of thing, this sudden blackout."

Ssempa thanked him with a jerky nod and trudged to the passageway that led to the thatched suites. He had been given number twenty-seven, which was conveniently at the furthest end of the long, winding cobbled aisle. He unlocked the door and entered. On a normal night he would have experienced the comparative warmth the sumptuous place offered with a sigh of satisfied relief. Not tonight though. His hands sought the matches and candle on the glass mantelpiece and, with difficulty, his fingers managed to strike the single matchstick in the box and to light the stick of candle on a stainless steel two-branch candelabrum. He placed the lit candle on the ornate glass-topped table and looked around the place as he collected his thoughts.

The Scotsman who had built the hotel in the first quarter of the twentieth century had considerately taken into account the almost temperate-zone climate of the Kabale region and furnished every suite with an ample stone fireplace. The sitting room and the bedroom were made of one circular and two straight walls. A big terrycloth-covered settee with a rounded back fitted perfectly into the circular area. Another settee, a smaller one covered in the same fabric, was adjacent to it. The ornate glass-topped table had two smaller ones that you pulled from underneath to expose a rack with magazines and the customary paperback Gideon's Bible. A thick silver-grey rug protected the feet from the cold concrete. It covered the floor from wall to wall both in the sitting room and the bedroom. A drinks stand stood against the left wall, empty for the past two years, when the effects of Idi Amin's Economic War had began to bite. A quartz clock encased in copper hung on the wall opposite the entrance and gave the correct time at a quarter-past-ten.

Ssempa turned the handle and peered into the bedroom, which had two three-and-a-half foot beds separated by four feet of carpeted floor space. The beds were made of thick mahogany wood and had mattresses filled with cotton lint and a pair of large pillows. A terrier cloth bedcover of the same material and colour as the settees in the sitting room was neatly folded at the bottom end of each bed. A thick woolen blanket with green, red and greenish-blue checks was wrapped tightly round the mattress on each bed as if to keep imprisoned any warmth. He did not have to open the bathroom door to see its contents. It opened off the sitting room at the main entrance and had an iron bathtub and a plastic-sheet-curtained shower and a section with a pink-and-red terrazzo shelf with a stainless steel sink for ironing and other laundry work.

The Scotsman designer of the hotel and other Europeans had long left the country, firstly with the country's attainment of national independence and then later because of General Idi Amin and his Economic War. Apparently with some nostalgia, the concierge had maintained the fireplaces. They kept them filled with well-trimmed logs of cypress and pine. Contemplating the logs as if it were his first time to see them, Ssempa thought he might disappoint management by being the first client in a very, very long time to set fire to the precious, well-preserved ornamental relics. He left the suite, locking it behind him.

He took his time at the steps of the hotel vestibule where everything was in darkness. The small party of men he had found there a few minutes earlier had left. He carefully made his way towards the parking lot, which stood below in a flattened out, tarmacked area with a wide grassy space bordering a mesh wire fence. Large icy raindrops still pummeled the earth from the tree boughs.

When he was sure there were no watching eyes he stepped onto the tarmac of the parking lot and walked to the badly beaten pickup. He found the nun in a doubly worse state than his own. He had been away for nearly thirty minutes and in that time the woman had developed an illness that he could liken to the tarantella dance of medieval Southern Italy. She looked up at him in the darkness, her face barely distinct. He was aware of her malady from the way her teeth knocked and the seat on which she sat shook.

Without saying a word he shut the door again and undid the tarpaulin on the pickup, pulled it all the way so as to cover the whole vehicle. He pulled a part of it aside and opened the passenger door, got hold of her upper arm and gently pulled her out. His other hand holding her valise, he led her, almost dragging her along, up the steps, along the opaque-black zigzag aisle to hut number twenty-seven. At their door the hand which had lifted the nun's valise all the way from the parking yard to the hut, was unable to open, the fingers having gotten locked due to the numbing cold. Seeing the problem from the faint light that came through the transom of the door, the nun helped to pry his fingers open. She also, with her own difficulty, unlocked the door to the hut. He directed her to the larger of the two settees. Her teeth continued to clatter and her body to gyrate in a near ridiculous *dingidingi* dance — the famous dance of the elegant Acholi people of northern Uganda. Her face remained smooth and glossy, as she wore no cosmetics. But with the shaking of her body she looked beaten, dishevelled, weak, lost... totally dilapidated. And he felt for her as he would his own younger blood-sister. If he was aged thirty-six, he guessed she had just gotten to her thirty-year mark.

"Do you have matches in your valise?" He found he could only use his lips, not mouth, to speak.

She shook her head, a gesture that wasn't easily discernible from the general shaking of her entire body. She could not speak, not with her jaws and teeth working with such violence. His own jaw felt as though it might lock, never to part again.

"Well, just in case the candle goes out, for there was only one matchstick in the box, I will have to place the stand on the floor, away from the draught."

She kept her eyes on him, following his movements. He stepped into the bedroom and scooped the covers from one bed and brought them to the settee, wrapped them roughly round her shoulders, noting the beddings themselves would become soggy from the sodden habits she wore, and went to the door. "I'm locking you in. But I'm pushing the key under the lintel back to you. I'll call your name when I return. That means you shouldn't open for anybody who does not call your name — let us say, Kantarama. I will not add Sister, just in case anybody is already looking for us. Please, do not move unnecessarily. Try to absorb some heat from those things." He pointed at the blanket and white sheets. "Open for no one who does not call you by your one name, okay?"

She had her benign eyes on him. If she nodded, he could not tell from the *dingidingi* her body was performing.

"Well, then," he said, sadly. "I will have to take the keys with me. I will open the door for myself."

He left the hut.

He found himself at the door to the maitre d'hotel's residence nearly half a kilometre up the hill to the west of the hotel, though it was within the hotel grounds, and knocked several times before Kacheeche came out dressed the way he had been in the bar except that he had replaced the homburg with a brown-and-black woolen balaclava which made Ssempa suspect that was how the hotelier intended to enter his bed.

"Uh-hm," said the man. "I expected you to be under wraps already. What can I do for you? Come in and sit down."

There was a hurricane lamp burning and a *Newsweek* magazine with someone called James E Carter and one Roslyn, smiling nicely at the camera.

"I cannot sit down," Ssempa looked down at himself. "I need help. I know I can trust you."

"You should read this." Mwigo patted the *Newsweek*. It was Ssempa himself who sometimes brought the hotelier the news magazines from Busia or Eldoret in Kenya as they were banned in Uganda. "This man is a groundnuts farmer. Only president who went through their naval academy; top-flight scientist — nuclear physicist, it appears. It also says here Jimmy Carter is the only American president who was born inside a hospital. Imagine! Were you born in a hospital, Ssempa?"

"Yes; obviously. Let's hope he won't be as crooked as Nixon. Hospital or no hospital their hiccups affect us, you know. My problems, George, are quite huge at this very moment and they have completely nothing to do with American politics."

"Coffee?"

"If you have it ready," Ssempa answered, expectantly.

"No," said the man." I cannot make you any. No means of doing it, much as you obviously need it. Man, you can hardly open your mouth to talk! I meant…. I thought you had coffee — *beans* — that you want hidden."

"Come on, George," Ssempa's disappointment was plain. "Coffee goes to Kenya these days; not to Kigali. Can I keep my pickup in your garage?"

"What's wrong with it?"

"Nothing. I'm carrying stuff on it, as usual."

"Whisky or cigarettes?"

"Enamel kitchenware and dry batteries." He was pleased Kacheeche was leading him on as he was in no state of mind for much talk or explanation. The hotel manager, besides being an old friend to Ssempa, was a man that minded his family and the running of the mostly out-of-business White Horse Inn. He was in his mid-fifties. His family lived in Masaka, where his wife, Alwiah, was a headmistress of a big school. After his accident and quitting the police force, George Mwigo had reconverted from the Islamic faith he had temporarily embraced and gone to a sect of Christianity that prohibited the use of clinical medicine so that when Ssempa had just returned from his Rwandese sojourn and had given Helen, the Kacheeche's ten-year old daughter a tube of medicinal cream to heal a scabies infection, they almost became arch enemies. "I want the use of your garage. I hope you do not have a car already there."

"You hope wrong. My Bellet is in there. But as you know, since my deputy was whisked away by the State Research Bureau late last year and has never been seen again, his fully furnished house is free. I have the keys to it too. You can take your load there. The night sentry is ill – as if we needed one! It is the house next to this one as you go along. I will get you the keys."

* * *

He got the keys and walked back down the hill to the hotel. In the parking lot, using his hands, he scooped water from a puddle of clear rainwater that had collected there and splashed handfuls of it against the body of the vehicle. The water was warm to the frozen hands. The one-kilometre walk had brought his body from frozen to just chilled. He readjusted the tarpaulin cover, drove out of the parking yard, and round the hotel buildings up to the staff residential area. The sky had lightened to paler blackness. He got to the abducted and certainly murdered deputy manager's house and drove right into the garage, which he had left open for the purpose. He then covered the whole vehicle from nose to tail with the tarpaulin and locked the door. He sought his way to his hut.

He found the nun in the very posture and position he had left her: seated in the settee with her feet up in it as she leaned against the back with her head erect.

"Are you okay?" he asked her. "Sorry, what a stupid question!"

He had a silly idea that she was perhaps performing a religious ritual of sorts in her silence. Then he thought the idea unfair, as he himself was not finding it that easy to speak or move. Moreover he himself had the added advantage of moving up and down, generating some considerable heat in his body. He wondered if the tiniest amount of heat had had the ability to enter his body at all, remembering with longing the warmth of the water he had scooped with his hands to wash the vehicle.

"I'll do something," he said, partly to her, partly to himself. He peeled away the other beddings and threw them on the bed he had earlier denuded. He returned to the living room and bent over her, hoping this time she would respond to what he had to say: "I have made you something more comfortable."

She nodded her head, uttering no sound. He helped her up, out of the settee, her wrist nearly twice as chilled as his fingers. He thought of the warm water again, while seriously wondering why the hell he shouldn't light a fire in the ready fireplace! But he knew the problem with that. The smoke from the chimney would raise several eyebrows, and the cleaners would also become curious at the unusualness of a fire in the fireplace. He led her, and she walked as stiffly as he expected zombies to perambulate, to the edge of the bed.

"Well, can you remove these?" he asked, looking her in the face. He expected to see her elbows fold and her hands go to her veil and, eureka! — pull it off. "I am afraid I am going to have to help — to help undress you. Your garments are practically waterlogged."

She nodded disconsolately, a look of desperate, anguished hopelessness in her eyes.

"I am very sorry about all this," Ssempa felt grimly awkward standing before her. "I should never have brought you across that awful frontier into all this. It makes those animals behind the faces of your Rwandan countrymen appear very amicable creatures."

She did not respond. He had expected a smile, even if it should be sardonic.

He put his hands carefully to the edges of her dusty-cream veil and removed it, placing it on the other bed. He then got hold of her crucifix, the rood with Christ heavy in its sterling silver metal, and, passing a hand behind her neck, unclasped the chain. He held the argentine Christ in his palm and, with an obviously mock reverence, placed it onto the veil on the stripped bed. He then bent down, touched the hem of her wet dress and lifted it gingerly, gathering its edges at either side and pulled upward, noting its resistance at her breast, until he pulled it over her head, which she could not bow owing to the stiffness in her body. He put the sodden clothes over the mahogany bedpost and, not wanting to look again, took up the cotton wimple which he had dropped onto the bed and, still not looking, placed it round her small, fully rounded breasts which, even in that chill, stood out erect and angry. Lifting her upper arms, he tucked the edges of the cloth there to keep her breasts covered. He knew why the woman had no use for brassieres. Her breasts were almost level with her chest and the bosom flap that fell from the neck and shoulders of her dress in the same brown fabric like an apron made her seem flat-chested. She had on a dark brown half-slip that went up above her pushed-in navel and was held there by an elastic band. Ssempa had in fact expected to see starched khakis or calico but the material turned out to be something like crepe de chine with a white acrylic Christian Dior label. He unbuckled the dark brown leather band of her tiny Tissot wristwatch, which he placed beside the crucifix. Then he noticed the tiny black leather-bound book, her missal or breviary, which had fallen down on the rug from a pocket of her habit. He placed that close to the crucifix and watch. The veil he had tucked between her flanks and arm biceps fell to one side, re-exposing her breasts when he took her arm to help her lie on the bed. He tucked her chilled feet in beneath the covers and pulled the blanket up to her ears and chin. He then went to the living room, got the other beddings, brought them and spread them over her too. Her right wrist protruded from under the blankets and her fist opened. He bent down and picked from it a small rosary of iron chain with mother-of-pearl beads. He placed that with the crucifix and other stuff.

"Now, Sister," he spoke to her knelt on one knee. "This is just not enough for your condition. I am going out to seek some aspirins — or whatever tablets I can get hold of. You will only get better with something like that or else you could contract a nasty bout of pneumonia."

She stuttered a pitifully distorted "Yes." She added something, which was meant, to mean; "I will be okay."

"Don't strain yourself. I'll go out and seek the aspirins, and some coffee, if I can."

"You are worse off yourself. You just don't notice." She pushed the words out with great effort.

"Don't strain yourself talking. I have to go out anyway. I cannot rest. That pickup — I washed it and hid it in a friend's garage. I want to go out there and sweep away some broken glass. Somebody seeing it tomorrow might become suspicious. I cannot afford to leave any clue that might connect the Kyondo incident to this hotel."

She nodded spasmodically. She had no arguments to make.

"Now I want you to absorb all the warmth you can from your inner body and those covers. That means you don't move. Don't open for anybody even if they call your name."

"I'll only open for you."

"Not even me." He showed her the key. "I will open for myself."

"You are worse off than me."

She could not be correct, he mused as he closed the door behind him. The bed on which she lay was vibrating like several devils were shaking it.

*   *   *

The White Horse Inn is a reputable hotel and even during Idi Amin's dastardly era it would have been quite odd for a person not to get a good cup of coffee at any time of day or night. But this night had sent man and beast to seek the warmth of their cradle. So Ssempa's feet carried him through stagnant puddles of water to where he knew to be the cradles of most hotel staff — the workers' quarters. They were asbestos-roofed cottages that lined the crest of the hill under eucalyptus trees that sang, groaned and moaned eerily in the wind. The cottages had been built around the same time the hotel was put up and they had concrete walls painted a no-longer-recognizable cream colour. Ssempa knocked at the only door where he saw a yellow glint of light seeping from under the lintel. A heavy-set elderly man opened up for him. He stood in the doorway comfortably, his bare chest covered in large coarse curls of hair. His eyes were peering myopically in the darkness.

"Who is it," the gruff voice asked in Kichiga, the language of the area.

"I have good money for a pot of coffee and a bottle of Uganda Waragi," Ssempa announced.

"Ha, ha, haaa," the man laughed. "How much is that good money that you have on you?"

"How much would you take, five hundred shillings?"

Kabale was and has always been a smugglers' town. Ssempa's offer would not be found strange. A pot of good coffee would have cost twenty shillings in the hotel restaurant and a bottle of Uganda Waragi two-fifty. Bachiga, the natives of the highland area, are a cordial people with a knack for trade. Large, burly people they are nearly immune to extreme cold, a trait that earned them the tag 'Scandinavians of Central Africa.' The man in the doorway did not waste a minute on queries. He shouted back into the cottage, "Did you hear that, Byangye?"

"Yes, I heard that," came a booming voice from within.

"Ah hah? Then what do you wait for? Make the coffee. Do you think Banamba could be home?"

"Banamba is a sensible man. All sensible people are home tonight."

"Don't insult our guest-client, Byangye; he is *out* here. But he obviously has an unquestionable reason for being out, too. He trembles like the *akacugamuyaga* buzzard up in the sky fornicating with the wind."

Byangye laughed and came out, peering into the darkness: "Eh," he exclaimed. "Do you want medicine? I happen to be a doctor, too."

He could have been a younger brother or elder son of the bare-chested man.

"He is an illegal doctor, no doubt," commented the bare-chested man. "A quack. Has been to prison for it not once. But nobody with the nobler of the gonorrhea strains gets cured in the government hospital. They come to Byangye, also known as Five Mega Fred. Do you want him to treat your malaria?"

Ugandans refer to all fevers as malaria. Ssempa contemplated taking the young man to have a look at Sister Julian. But he discarded the notion.

"What of some aspirin?"

"I don't stock those; they don't fetch money. All the same I'll treat your malaria like no other...."

"Not on your life; not Five Mega anyway. The coffee and the Uganda Waragi will do fine," Ssempa assured him.

"I have other stuff — Togamycin and Kosyginozolle from Russia, Castrocycline from Cuba. Also Chiang-ching capsules from China."

"Huh, huh-huh," laughed Ssempa through clenched teeth. "You cannot be serious?"

"Cross my heart and hope to die. I even have Qadaffin from Libya; cures grenades like no other thing on the market."

"And what are grenades, man?"

"They are huge nice lymph nodes that develop under your armpits when a venereal disease grows quite bad. I have things for syphilis...."

"The coffee and Uganda Waragi, my friend, nothing more. As you can see, you must not torture me with laughter; it hurts the muscles of my mouth."

"Okay, okay. But Banamba does not have Uganda Waragi. He has whisky — Teacher's, Hennessy and Johnnie Walker. Napoleon Brandy too. And, of course, Pompidou sherry from Paris."

"That's not bad for me," Ssempa assured him. "Any good spirit will do me fine. Not the *sherry*, please."

"I'll rush to Banamba's then. My old man will be slower. You make the coffee, Mzee."

"How long will you take?"

"Ten minutes," Byangye said and ran off barefoot into the wet black night.

"And the coffee?" Ssempa enquired of the man.

"Twenty minutes, if you want it White Horse Inn standard — made by myself, as per my profession." Considering the way he stressed his words, he sounded like he was a connoisseur in the art of brewing coffee.

"Make it one-hundred shillings standard."

"No. You said five hundred."

"Yes. That will be for the whisky. Remember I had said Uganda Waragi."

The man laughed. "You are a true Muganda. No wonder the weather has battered you so bad. Come and sit near the *sigiri* charcoal stove."

Ssempa stepped up into the warm cottage. He was wondering whether there were many who could have gone through his ordeal and remained as cool as the bare-chested man was.

* * *

Half an hour later he was back in the hut with the coffee, a one-litre bottle of Gilbey's Gin, several candles and a box of matches. Sister Julian had not changed her position in the several minutes he had been away, her teeth still clattered but the shaking of her body had reduced in violence to sporadic jerks.

147

He lifted the Thermos flask to her.

"Coffee."

"*Urakoze*," she said quietly, her voice and words slightly more coherent.

"I'm sorry I could not get you the aspirins." He told her of Byangye's assortment of injectables and capsules with their weird labels.

"It is quite alright. I've never taken an injection in my life. The gin will do."

Sure in himself she had mixed things up, he said: "You mean the coffee. The gin is mine."

"The coffee too, of course. But the gin will be the better, more effective remedy for me."

"You mean…!"

"I see where you are headed. You want to know whether nuns do booze. They don't. My Order, in fact, is strict on that one. But the Benedictine Order in France makes one of the best liqueurs in the world. To imagine outsiders tasting it for them for quality for the hundreds of years they have been producing it would be fallacious. But for remedial purposes anything will be permissible to me tonight."

"I did not know about that. Not too many people know much about you people I guess."

"No," she conceded. "Many Ugandans, even the Catholics here, understand Catholicism differently. It is a problem in most Anglophone countries, actually. Francophone ones are a different kettle of fish, like they say. You should meet a Zairian nun — or priest."

"What of them?"

"They are alarmingly naughty — may Virgin Mary save their souls!" Her prayer for Zairian nuns, and priests, sounded like she had closed the subject on nuns.

But he wanted her to go on talking as he poured out the coffee in the large, ribbed glass beer mug that Byangye and his progener had provided him with. Talking seemed to revive her, to calm her body and stabilize her voice considerably.

"Are you sure about the whisky?" He asked as he stirred the sugar in her coffee with a tablespoon, its aroma lulling his mind.

She nodded. "Of course I'm sure. You make me feel guilty, but there is nothing to it, really."

"How much?" he asked, breaking the seal and unscrewing the bottle of gin — and tipped it over her glass mug.

"There. That's enough."

He handed the hot mug to her and she held it pressed in both hands, her long slender fingers the colour of the hot beverage. Her well manicured, long nails the colour of pale rose-petal pink trembled against the thick glass. She placed the rim to her mouth and took the first sip carefully. When she had swallowed the coffee, she spluttered into a series of coughs that watered her eyes. But she rejected his attempt to take the glass mug from her unsteady hands.

"I am quite fine, thank you. I'll be all right."

He poured his own coffee into the larger of the dark grey cups that were part of the lids of the Thermos flask, half coffee, and half gin. She frowned at him.

"That's too much," she warned.

"Not for me. I'm not exactly an alcoholic, but I am well acquainted with booze. And I quite well need it."

"You haven't added sugar."

"Not now. Sugar isn't my strong point." He sipped the gin-laced coffee and, following the nun's example, swallowed carefully. It burnt its progress down his alimentary canal like a knife skewing through the nerve system. He did not cough, but it scorched his throat and he screwed up his face as in pain. "Would you drink gin under normal circumstances?"

"I wouldn't broach the subject of nuns and my religion at all under normal circumstances, if you should know. It is much beyond compline and I should not be talking at this hour — not even to a fellow sister."

"I'm sorry for prying. I'll not introduce it again."

"These are quite abnormal circumstances, though," she said over the rim of the glass. "It is not really that religion prohibits drink. Alcohol is used at our altars all the time, wine actually — as though wine were the more innocent of beverages. Indeed even wine, when taken in liberal amounts, is impermissible. Our sacerdotal vows, the whole ecclesiastic establishment is archly against intoxication, of course. Drinking in moderation is allowed among many orders. We Franciscans are the strictest of them all. Your name is David," she added that in without a break in what she had been stating. "You aren't Catholic, of course?"

"No, I am not Catholic. I am...."

"I am sorry for asking that; to think that such trivialities should turn good men into automatic antagonists!"

"Religious talk turns me immediately into the ancient mariner your monsignor uncle is on politics of tribe and ethnicity," Ssempa began, slowly. "I never tire of explaining my bitter feelings towards the divisive foreign religions that imperialism brought to our lands. I am absolutely divorced from foreign religious doctrines, Sister Julian. I happen to know God very well. He is not a Christian, a Muslim or Jew – or even a man. How can a person seriously follow priests and sheikhs that believe fervently in the creation according to the Bible and the Qur'an? How can we allow ourselves to believe in some fools' mythological pasts as though we had no mythologies of our own? Being a Muganda I, and of course my long-gone ancestors, those who never heard of Christ or Muhammad, have always believed in a powerful God who always saw us through the thin and thick of life. It is the imperialists, with robbery aforethought, who, having picked Semitic doctrines from Palestine to use in subduing their own European citizens later brought the same to our own gullible chiefs — along with threats in form of the sword, the gun and an obviously dangerous, sadistic god that delighted in frying humans in great fires under influence of childish anger. Both the Bible and the Qur'an revel in the hoped-for holocaust of the human race by the god they portray and his horn-blowing archangels. The God that Africans had known through millennia was not an evil, jealous, avenging, warmonger dictator. He was part of the Sun, called Kazooba, and brought food to the homesteads, insisted on good manners and showed his people the medicines to cure their ailments. Without Kazooba life could not continue, you see? These foreigners, along with their dangerous books and guns, brought trinkets for the chiefs' wives to wear round their supple waists and necks, for they knew of the wife's capacity to influence a powerful man in avarice. These trinkets are still being employed by the same robbers in collaboration with neo-chiefs, this time called Their Excellency Misters President who preach a good anti-imperialist doctrine as their spouses, the busy bodies of paramount greed, undertake charity campaigns and preach in voices sweeter than the clergy but are rotten to the core with untold corruption. They, with their husbands, go to bed with the robber colonist at twilight. In that way, peasant natives turned Their Excellency keep us subjugated for their imperial masters for pay in rotten overvalued trinkets. It is the only way that the imperialists, empowered by our native collaborators — political and religious whores, ensure our deadly, artificial divisions. It is those divisions that are exploited in robbing us more than doubly — first by taking away our God-given wealth in diverse forms, and second, by getting us to believe that their doctrine, evil and satanic as it obviously is, is the better doctrine. And we must pay for it dearly in hard-earned cash and more often than not, believe it, with our blood. We buy their books so that we may become more brainwashed, their dress, their food, their cultures, their guns, all of which, please believe me, they themselves do not like. They prefer our own lifestyle — or haven't you seen them moving about close to naked on our streets? Your dress, your habit, automatically does not allow me to talk to you normally and yet there is no enmity or good reason for suspicion between you and I. You know your uncle Raphael's Citroen car to be French and thus suspect it to be an enemy — as though you were an English carmaker's daughter. The lieutenant at the roadblock says Uganda would rather be ruled by a Muslim man than a Catholic even though the colonial master, busy ensuring that situation through the supervision of his proxy, His Excellency, is himself as Christian as any Catholic. Do you see where I am getting?"

She laughed. It was the first time he saw her do so. The laughter stretched her wide mouth, folding her checks into gentle curves, accentuating the bulbous half moons that were her lower eyelids and exposing stark white teeth with the tiny gap between the upper incisors. "I see where you are headed, and I do not like the path. But *you*? — Not religious — with your kindness?"

"I am highly religious, Sister Julian. I pray to God all the time that I am in trouble. But kindness has virtually nothing to do with those Middle Eastern gods, their prophets or your Roman Orders. They are the most selfish, most murderous, most villainous...."

"You are still too generous to be irreligious," she interrupted him as if unable to bear such verbal assault on her own faith.

"I am *not* irreligious. Not every religious person is a Franciscan, as you must very well know. Look at the selfish divisiveness of the imported faiths: why the existence of Franciscans, Carmelites, Benedictines, Mill Hills — besides the Lutherans, Anglicans, Shiites, Sunnis, Ismailis — uncountable sects claiming to believe in the same deity — but one better-armed group of the richer nations tells us to follow one of them or else! Do you see what I see? Religion — Europeanized religion and kindness — do not go together. Kindness and generosity are personality traits, I guess. Above all, the more refined sectarian hypocrisy exists mostly among the extremely religious. And there is a lot of that everywhere. Just as there is lots of so-called religion-organized foreign indoctrination everywhere. The lieutenant and Corporal Bingwa, back at the roadblock — were — could have been Christian."

She continued to regard him over the rim of the beer mug, with that laughter still in her cheeks, the hands clasping the glass snugly and no longer trembling, and she said: "Yes, he was a Catholic too. He wore a rosary with blue beads on a silver chain under his tunic."

"You don't say!"

"Yes. He had a crucifix. He saw me staring at it and adjusted his collar to cover it up. But by then it was too late for him."

"Too late..." began Ssempa.

"Nnno," she shook her head violently with that sharp word. She had closed her eyes, taken an unusually large gulp of her coffee, obviously agitated with the recollection, swallowed it and kept her chin pressed to the glass rim of the mug and her eyes shut. The nails of her long fingers had gained an even purpler colour in them as her blood flowed more freely with the warmth of the coffee and the beddings. Her mind went back to times past partly as a way of getting rid of the present. Father Damien Beemereire, popularly called Dam, the priest in charge of the diocesan education department of Kyera had often got her and her teaching colleague, Sister Gerald Sebastian Namazzi, drunk on Chianti and Rufino wines during the days he had shamelessly and persistently attempted to coerce her into a sensual affair. The man had gotten to know of her interest in the Mabonwa Dispensary and Sanctuary, where she arranged the exodus of capable and eligible Banyarwanda from the refugee camps into the urban areas. There they were helped to find work, and given papers that showed them to be citizens. This she did with a little capital she amassed from friends of refugees abroad and within the country. Her efforts helped the refugees to live better lives in a part of the country that had not welcomed them with open arms. Dam, the priest with wide-ranging powers in the education department, used sister Julian's interest in the refugees against her: 'You bend to my wishes or I transfer you to a diocese in a place so remote that you won't know what is happening in your people's refugee camps.' That he forced sister Julian into his company and fondled her breasts at any opportunity he got was an open secret among the other teaching nuns. But priests, so unlike the nuns, could get away with murder, so to say. Sister Gerald had once told Julian she thought Father Dam had felled her at last. When Julian told her he had not, sister Gerald praised the Virgin Mary for the rock in Julian's heart. Sister Gerald, with that flamboyance unique to the Baganda people, had herself fallen and was in her second year of sin, but she was unwilling to admit any regrets. The two sisters would sleep away the night in the residence of the priest at The Martin Lobo Recreation Centre, also known as The Marlorec, in Mbarara town, and Julian was always worried that one morning she might awaken to find herself defiled by the brutal little man. Fortunately for her, for a non-sexual offence committed with a novice, the lecherous priest was transferred to another diocese, in Burundi. In any case the only fear she had harboured was defilement during sleep; she never worried that her marble heart would fail her even if she became tipsy.

Now as she sat up in the bed, humid with her own body heat, she regarded the man before her: his dark buffalo-skin complexion; the sad, solemn, lonely eyes that looked at her own with a kind of benignity she had believed absent among the worldly community; and the way he sipped at his strongly gin-laced coffee as though there was no alcohol there. Other drinkers would take a sip, screw their faces as though in agonizing pain and wait to take another. There was some quality about the Muganda man that she wanted to reach out for. Though his perambulations were slow and cramped now because of the chill in his body, his earlier quick and skilful maneuvering had betrayed an enigmatic presence. Remembering the failure of his fingers to open the door of their suite, a sympathetic feeling arose within her breast. She knew she had to hold him to herself, to show him her innermost gratitude for his suffering for her sake. He had killed dangerously armed men for her.

And then there was the other feeling she abhorred so much.

She did not wish to consider for even a microsecond that which she had constantly, with such poor results, been attempting to expunge, from her body and mind for the past two-and-a-half hours — the goddamned feeling of a satanic arousal so ruthlessly awakened by.... She closed her mind to the thought that dug at her so cruelly! She closed her eyes for a long minute.

When she reopened them and had taken another sip of the strongly sugared gin-coffee, she said: "You are a preacher man; a Protestant preacher man. A Lutheran. You would make someone doubt the fundamentals of the faith."

"That would be terrible. The word *religion* itself means firm, unquestioning belief and faith in something for which we have no proof. Yet without those fundaments, several of them false as I know them to be, your Bahutu in Rwanda, the lieutenants at the roadblocks, Micombero in Burundi and Idi Amin here would be the rule — the majority rather than the exception. Judgments in courts of law and tribunals where crimes of man against man are decided, are based on solemn oaths upon those so-called religious books. Relics indeed, but the suspected malfeasants and their alleged victims all believe in them and while the former hate to be forced to swear upon those books, the latter — the victims, grab at them in desperate conviction that they shall enforce the mundane justice they seek. That is how crucially instrumental these faiths of yours are. If there were no such faiths there would be no peace or tranquility on earth. My concern with all that is that nobody here seems to recall we in Africa lived under such rule — under an even stricter, more effective, unwritten moral code of laws that were less costly than these importations of yesterday. Our judicial systems could function a lot better with our own customary laws than with the usually unfair alien ones that leave native eyebrows raised. I am not opposed to religion *per se*. I am only opposed to the alien religious culture of usurpers who despise and insult my own ancestral spiritual values. I support religion fully and am willing to accept and tolerate conversions as long as they are not being used to maintain our mistrusts of one another. You see, I don't see Idi Amin entrusting crucial military duties to a suitably qualified Christian military officer if a less competent fellow Muslim man is at hand and likewise your Juvenal Habyarimana would view a Muslim commander in a more suspicious light than a Catholic one. Tribalism is a hugely comfortable trait compared to religious division, Sister. As I have already shown you, it does not mean that we had no better systems of justice before the European robber entered into our affairs. I still know that alien religion is meant to serve the weaker minded, the less experienced in this life full of good and evil, of which the fabric of the world is chiefly made. One needs no organized, foreign God to know which side to fall in at. The god-fearing man is made weaker than the so-called heathen when the former commits an offence equal to that of the latter, though Christianity and Islam want us to think that a habitually sinning church or mosque goer who confesses every other day to a clergyman is a better person in the eyes of God than the atheist who may not offend at all. By 'offend' I mean sin. The heathen has no Fridays, Saturdays or Sundays to go troubling God; the so-called pagan always thinks seriously of his Maker when he is in a tight corner. Oh, you should hear me lamenting and beseeching God to redeem me from a fix just *that once* — and my solemnest pledges never to forget Him ever again! But do you know what happens soon after all my troubles are no more? Well, nothing happens actually. Indeed I sometimes engage in impolite and argumentative dialogues with the same God, lambasting Him over certain injustices. To live what is called a heathen as well as morally upright life is the ideal way to live, in my opinion. I see no good in hating someone for his belief in a different, invisible, *alien* and divisive God. God is here, right in this bleakly lit hotel suite inside our psyches; so is Satan. He needs no iconic messengers to communicate, and what He decides neither you nor I can stop or change or undecide. If He needs messengers then several must exist here, but not only among those Semites of Palestine who exhibit moral and other weaknesses greater than mine. God was present at the Kyondo roadblock and personally saw to the demise of those who pretended to safeguard the lives of the non-lethally armed."

She did not respond for quite a time as her eyes studied him in some sort of wonderment. She had never heard any person talk so disparagingly of religion, although she had met many that ridiculed it. She said: "Did you sweep away the broken glass?"

She had decided to steer clear of a subject that touched, blasphemously, on doubt in the Catholic God.

"I shouldn't be talking to you like that, of course. To shut up my type of person your clergies would call me a mad man. Well, I did tell you religion incenses me. What did you ask? Oh, I swept the glass shards in the grass."

She kept her eyes on his face, which she seemed to study in her mildly deprecatory stare. 'A real heathen if any ever lived,' was her mind's chief notion as she sipped her gin-coffee. "How did you think of that?"

"What?"

"Washing the car, hiding it, sweeping away the glass!"

"It was the logical thing to do. I did not think of it. I just did it."

"Just like that?"

"What is so amusing about that?" He had seen the sad laughing smile again, which, without her exposing her teeth, mocked. "It is a survival gimmick of sorts."

"I think you are not a killer," she said as if with a faraway thought that perturbed her. "You are too wonderful a person to be."

"Nonsense. I just killed four men. You were there, weren't you? No amount of religious thought can change that or obliterate the deed. And, if you want to know, I am not perturbed by it. I would repeat it any time under similar circumstances, even though two of those men were relatively innocent."

They were silent for some moments. Then he said: "The man with the light machine gun was quite as dangerous as Corporal Bingwa. It was his gun, always pointed at that tent's entrance, but easy to swivel towards where we were, that I was most scared of."

"You? *Scared?*"

"Of course I was scared like hell. That lieutenant intended to kill us after-- after...Oh, well."

The nun shivered severely and, clenched her teeth against the glass rim of the mug.

"Sorry," he said to her, as he replenished his cup of gin-coffee. "I should not broach that subject again."

She said: "That was God-ordained killing. I am more than equally responsible for tonight."

"What do you mean, *more?*"

"You killed for me," she stated plainly and fixed him with her level gaze. "You killed *because* of me. You would not have killed otherwise. You would not have used such violence if it hadn't been for what that — that dreadful soldier was doing to me."

The gin-coffee had rid her cheeks of their sickly appearance and strengthened her voice. She no longer stuttered constantly. She had pushed the covers away from her shoulders to leave one of the white bed sheets covering her upper part.

"Are you afraid of death, Sister Kantarama?"

She laughed, nearly choking on the mouthful of coffee she had just sipped. "How did you get that name? Oh, from my travel documents. No, I remember; Uncle Raphael, of course. You must never complain to Monsignor whenever he calls you Ssimha again. The way you say my name is wrong. We Banyarwanda don't pronounce hard consonants after an *en* or an *em*. You could say Kan'harama or even Kanarama in Kinyarwanda. It is spelt with a *tee* but that *tee* is muted. And if I was to say Kampala the Kinyarwanda way I would have to skip the *pee* and say Kam'hara or Kam'ara — as you must know Banyarwanda substitute their *el* with an *ar*."

"Oh, I know all about that. But your uncle, Sinzagaya — the way he has discarded the Kinyarwanda intonations in his English and Kiswahili is intriguing. Banyarwanda cannot pronounce the letter *oh* in speech either. You say ooh for oh. And then there are your *cee* and *kay*; you, like the Jews, pronounce them *gee* or *gay*. This I found in a book I read a long time ago — Scott Fitzgerald's The *Great Gatsby*, I think, where a Jewish character said *Ogizford* instead of *Oksford*. Most Banyarwanda refer to doctor as *dogitor* and to introduction as *introdugition*."

"Don't they always say we are related to the Jews? Except they say it of us derogatively. Only Uncle Raphael and my mother ever call me Kantarama. Poronia calls me Julian."

"Who is Poronia?"

"My Sister. We are twins. Her name is Apollonia Kasangaire. But everybody calls her Poronia. We skip the *'eh'* at the beginning and, as I told you of our *els*, use an *ar* instead. But the way you say Kantarama — it is nice."

"Poronia," Ssempa spoke the name slowly. "We — I mean the Baganda, would say *Polonia*. What does your name mean?"

"Names don't have to mean things. Mine would imply something like 'of Ntarama,' who could be a person or place. There is definitely a place called Ntarama a few kilometres south of Kigali. Does yours mean something?"

"Ssempa is a shortened proverb the meaning of which is obscure to me. It is a male name of the people of the *nte* or cow clan of Buganda. A woman of my clan would be Nnampa. Your natural name is a lot more beautiful than your other names."

"Natural name? What's wrong with my Christian names?"

"I don't find Dominicus particularly savoury, or even Christian, perhaps Roman. Even Julian is very masculine. You could have been named Julia or Juliet; and of course Domina."

"Juliette was my first baptismal name. Although it is not such a rigid rule, sisters of the cross usually go by the names of male Christian saints'."

"I figure that by necessity that is a way of making such names less sapid so as to enhance the element of chastity."

"You wanted to know whether or not I feared — if I was afraid of death." Julian disregarded his interjection with a little shrug of her shoulders. "Yes, of course, I hate death; I am afraid of leaving my mother, my sister Poronia, my uncles Sinzagaya and Raphael to this world. I just cannot imagine them coping in this ugly place. Uncle Raphael would be okay, of course. He is tough and strong in Christ. But my death would deprive them most greatly. My mother would be devastated. I don't see how she would recover. I view myself, selfishly, as their guardian angel. I am not supposed to, mark you. Life and death are strictly God's turf and we Christians must submit fully to God's will and His wishes. Are you afraid of death yourself? No," she answered her own question promptly. "At least I am certain you don't fear it. You challenge death. I don't know how often you have encountered that angel of finality! Your wife must be very proud of you."

"I am not a married man."

"Eh! You are not married! Why?"

"Because I am a bachelor."

She laughed: "Alright. Your future wife will be a woman most proud to have you around all the time. God Almighty, you are ruthless! I saw you turn lethally armed men into skulking rats. Where did you learn to shoot so accurately?"

"Oh, my ancestors! – Me? Shoot accurately! You cannot be serious, Sister Julian. That was my first ever time to fire a gun in anger."

"And — oh, my God! Are you saying you might have hit me?"

"I *did* believe I had killed you too – until I saw you get up to foul that army officer's aim at me."

She laughed – a real, true loud laugh – and said: "You don't say!"

"I own a gun; an AK47, Russian thing with slightly smaller bullets than those of the G-3s those men toted. My occupation involves smuggling. I take coffee, crude *waragi*, gold and *bogoya* bananas to Kenya; tea to Southern Sudan; dried *makayabu* fish to Zaire. I return with gold from Zaire and Sudan, whisky and cigarettes from Kenya. I cross to Rwanda quite occasionally too, and Burundi — I have lived in Kigali before, for a year. But for the coffee, tea and fish you need to be armed with a gun. The smuggler's trouble in such case is not chiefly from the government anti-smuggling units but from fellow smugglers. I have always managed to get out of tight situations through negotiations." He then explained, falsely, how he had learned to handle a firearm. "Someone, the man that sold me the gun years ago, taught me how to use it, how to strip it apart and reassemble it. He told me he hoped I should never have to use it. I never did. I doubt I ever will. To think I had to practice shooting in anger in something so silly!"

"You think what that man did was merely silly?"

"I am extremely sorry, Sister Julian. It must have been; it was definitely dastardly. There was nothing trivial about what I shot those goons for."

"You have no idea how bad…. Ooo blessed Virgin Mary! As you said, God Himself was present there at Kyondo. God was present there in you. But I want you to know I do not believe that that was your very first time to handle a gun. You are not telling me the whole truth about that and I am wondering why!"

Some thought that rushed to his brain made him narrow his eyes in the candlelight. He then recalled old Kacheeche's reference to his unreasonable fear of the past, which he had said bordered on the cowardly. He relaxed and said: "Why do you say that?"

She sensed the tension in his voice. "Well, I'd have thought you did things there like a trained combatant."

Ssempa sighed tiredly. He shook his head and murmured, "But how can you know? Only good old Kacheeche knows."

"What's that? And who is good old Kacheeche? Don't say you are drunk already."

"No, I am not. But if you had said what you just uttered to me about my apparent knowledge of guns under different circumstances in another place, I'd try to get as far away from you as my legs would carry me. But…. Ooo, my God!"

"And this Kacheeche…!"

"I am very sorry, please, Sister."

"You don't want to talk about it, so don't."

"Yeah. It is only that — you see, Kacheeche is the manager of this hotel. He is an ex-policeman. He helped me to get recruited into the Uganda police force in 1972, a year after Idi Amin had captured power in that bloody coup d'etat. But I left the training course quite prematurely and had to run for cover in Kigali. It is very possible I would never have ventured there or met your uncle Sinzagaya if it hadn't been for that. But I do beg you not to ask me more about all that."

"I shan't harp on it. I am imagining you trying to get as far away from *me* as your legs can carry you."

He remained silent, observing her over the rim of his plastic cup the way she liked to do herself.

"And I have seen you smile only twice since the first time we met in Gitarama. And your smile has sadness in it. One wishes to touch the — what shall I call it? — the enigma of you. There is some simplicity about the way you do things, in the way you move, the way you talk and the set of your jaw. The way you look, one would not think you noticed much, or saw anything for that matter. But — but, I think you even planned and timed the deaths of those four men. You knew the one called Corporal Bingwa would bend down to fumble with your shoes in pretended searching when you chose to admonish my tormentor. You knew Bingwa would expect my tormentor to turn to look at him, and that Bingwa would want the lieutenant to find him busy carrying out his orders. I think your mind never rests in your seeming aloofness. It is a little calculating mechanism; I am a trained mathematics teacher, mark you. And when you look at me the way you are doing right now, with the bloodshot eyes of a drunkard, I am happy I am with you on the same side. You could easily be counting away at my heartbeats, serializing my thoughts. I know you are seeing right into me, into my heart. And you know all my feelings." She sighed, like one very tired after a long trek, and took a gulp at her coffee as if she did not expect any response to her analysis of him.

"All along at that checkpoint," Ssempa said, smiling, "I thought your mind went through that canvas tent wall at which you stared. I thought your mind was traveling through space in search of the holy Virgin Mary, to whom you kept mumbling divine citations. I never once saw you notice the corporal or myself. But when you say you were watching my every reaction in that tent it leaves me to wonder which of us is the worse. You are the mathematical computing mechanism, not me."

"I was noticing everything. That is why I ducked out of harm's way when you fired at the lieutenant."

He winced and shivered: "I feared — I knew I had hit you. When did you see me smile, twice, you said."

"Actually you smile all the time. You can remove the fake one playing on your mouth presently. I think it was thrice; but the third one was faked. And at that time you were negotiating with the Ugandan immigration officer to whom you gave the baking set. That was when I realised you were a smuggler. Your fake smiles are the most charming, the most convincing, and they are the reason he allowed us to go off in spite of the curfew."

"Up to now I am not sure of that curfew claim. And the other smiles?"

"When the tent eventually lit up. You had thought the matches had failed you. The lights from the dashboard highlighted your face and I watched, first your anguish and then, when the tent lit up, your smile."

"You are not serious," Ssempa laughed. "You are suggesting I smiled with euphoria at that?"

"With rapture. And also when you brought in the coffee and gin, when you lifted them up for me to see."

"When you talked of a mathematical mind, Sister Kantarama, you meant yourself. Yours never lost track or rested. Mine did, somewhere."

"Where?"

"When we got to Byumba and found the pass strewn with trailer trucks in that mud, I should have returned you to Gitarama or, at least, to Kigali. To that Arab Catholic priest's place in Rue de Rusumo."

"Yes," she agreed, offering him her empty glass mug with black coffee dregs at the bottom and at one side. "One of the times I saw you desperately angry was when you mentioned that very thing to me an hour ago. Then you had just rendered me nude before you. And I had no brassieres on. I never wear a bra because my breasts are almost flat on my chest. The habit covers them sufficiently."

"You make me feel like the English cat that swallowed the canary."

"You are a very shy man, too. But you see, it ought to be obvious to you, I had never dreamt of a man undressing me, the way you did, with such delicate gentility, like a lover."

"The gin has gotten to your head, Sister Julian," he said to her cautiously.

"You think so? It is just that I am very happy and grateful to God to be alive. I have never had guns fired directly at me, mind you. You haven't added any gin to my coffee!"

He attempted to hand her the second mug of steaming coffee with sugar. "Not on your life." He indicated the ring on her left hand's middle finger. "I am busy calculating and serializing my probable answers to your husband for getting you tipsy."

"Husband?" She looked and sounded startled at the word. Then she laughed, shaking her head again at the hot coffee. "Oh, you mean God! You think I am tipsy, do you? Maybe you are right. Do you know I have not spoken so loudly, so continuously for so long in the last eighteen years? Just add a very little bit of the gin, that's all."

He took the glass and added a bit of gin to it. "Eighteen years!"

"Yes. From the time I joined the cloister as a novice shortly after entering Uganda from the Congo, to which we had initially fled from Kayibanda's murderers. That was at the beginning of the sixties and I was barely fourteen. Please, a little bit more of that gin."

Ssempa was thinking back to Monsignor Raphael Nyarwaya's eagerness to take him to the other side of the hill to show him *that murderer* Gregoire Kayibanda's home, at Kabgaye. He knew about these people's suffering as from his childhood he had lived with those who had taken refuge right under his own father's roof. He poured himself a third cup of coffee and gin, placed it on the glass-topped table and removed his canvas jacket. There was still a feeling of chill on his skin. He went to the other bed and patted the bare mattress.

"How are you now? — Because I am going to have to take away one of the blankets from you."

"No, you won't," she said. "Look," she added when he made to protest. "I am not afraid of you as you might fear. I already trusted you with my life. You, of course, cannot see how devastated you appear. Only a woman's body heat would resuscitate you."

"Sister...."

"I said I trusted you absolutely, didn't I? Unless you wish to say you don't trust me! In such case I won't argue with you."

"I am honestly flattered, Sister Julian, but — in all fairness — I cannot even begin to try to imagine myself starting to trust myself with you. It was bad enough getting you undressed."

In undressing her, he had detected a heady scent from her hidden body, the smell of a lass' disturbed anatomy like fresh soil brought to the surface by the hoe. The scent had filled his lungs and sent his chilled blood corpuscles on a wild swirling safari through his veins. He had gone out, back into the chill of the night, and gratefully had the elements wash the devil out of his system.

"Was undressing me that bad, really?" she asked. "I never noticed. But don't bother about your lack of self-confidence." Her eyes mocked him in their lazy, nearly aristocratic drop-dead gaze, as if there was anger in them. Her long fingers curled round the hot mug. "I am now fully revived, which cannot be said for you. Uncle Monsignor did not entrust me to you for you to abandon me. Why would I desert you to your plight?"

"Are you aware that I am already tipsy?" Ssempa pointed at the nearly empty bottle of Gilbey's Gin, a good percentage of which was now busy chasing the blood corpuscles in his arteries.

"Tipsy! — You could even be dead drunk, judging by your mistrust of me. I am in full control of my own bodily faculties. I will restrain you from any scandalous deviations your tipsy senses might devise; have no doubt of that."

"Sister...!"

"I won't in any case let the man that rescued me from that beast suffer any further inconveniences from this devastatingly cold night when I am well equipped for his remedy."

"I have to remind you Sister Julian," Ssempa did not dislike what the woman was getting at, and indeed hoped she meant all she said, "that I have none of your type of religion in me."

"You don't trust me, obviously!" There was now genuine hurt in her voice and a majestic scornful annoyance in her aristocratic eyes. She bowed forward and took the large bottle off the table and looked at its label more closely with a frown. "You think it is Mr Gilbey talking in me. You think," she bent forward again and placed both half-drunk coffee and bottle on the table, "that I am seducing you?"

Still her eyes mocked. She sulked and her mouth pouted. He now looked most closely at that mouth that had probably begun all the trouble for the army officer back at Kyondo, and repeated in his mind her words... 'When I am well-equipped for his remedy.' He did not find her mouth at all like Brigitte Bardot's, but it was still a chunky, intimidating, mouth with an almost obscene beauty about its wet corners. And a tremendous carnal urge burst in his loins and drowned him in terrible hot currents.

"I am very sorry, Sister."

"For not trusting yourself, David? No man does, I believe. Blow out the candle and come to bed. You are grossly ungrateful but you will thank me with the sunrise."

He took his time, unlacing his shoes, removing the soggy stockings with gravel in them. His feet had turned a sickly grey and were severely wrinkled from the dampness they suffered all the way from Urukomo, up in Byumba. He picked up the plastic cup and finished off his coffee, eye lingering on the remaining gin settled at the bottom of the one litre bottle. He then blew out one candle and placed the other in the other room atop the glass table, so that the bedroom remained in a faint yellowish glow. He peeled off the tough water-hardened blue jeans, which he piled at his feet. He went to the bathroom and pushed off a gush of hot strong-smelling urine, washed his feet in the trough, dried them with one of the crisp-dry towels, and tried to look at himself in the wall mirror but could not do so clearly in the very faint yellow light from the candle out in the other room. He left the bathroom with one of the towels wrapped round his midriff and walked to the bed, sitting on the edge.

She got up and in the golden gloom he saw her pull down the brown *crêpe de chine* slip. She then went out to the sitting room, her big shapely body momentarily framed in the doorway against the yellow candlelight, and he heard her open the door to the lavatory. He unscrewed the lid of the gin bottle and emptied it in one gulp. He entered the beddings; his head was considerably clear but his body yearned for repose. Soon she returned, stark as the day she was born, the mounds of her breasts larger than he had imagined them, and lower below, at her groin, another mound, suppler than any he had ever seen. She stepped agilely over him, lifted the coverings and slithered her body next to him. He had not realised how cold he still was until their bodies touched. The covers and the gin-coffee had created so much heat in her that her body burned his flesh like hot charcoals.

"What is it?" she enquired breathlessly.

"You are hot."

"Is that bad?"

He laughed: "No, please."

"I told you, didn't I, that I was well-equipped for your situation. Hold me like this — oh, no! What's this? You won't be allowed to bring sodden unmentionables into my bed. Take it away to your own bed, will you!" Her commands were breathless, husky intonations.

Soon they were clad in nothing, just like termites.

Her mouth was hot with the coffee and tasted sweet with the sugar and had the faint aroma of the gin. The satin-soft fabric of her flesh scalded his own rough skin. His body in that untaught old-old ritual guided her lumbering, frantically tremulous movements as the arms and hands sought out each other and intertwined in a frenzy of movement, their faces crushed together, softened tongues probing. In Kantarama the man found an absolutely genuine African woman not a vestal spinster who had relegated her physical and spiritual being for nearly two decades to a harsh, uncompassionate and dogmatic desuetude. The utterly powerful, sweet, pungent scent from her flayed body was far more intoxicating than the coffee-gin he had imbibed, far more overpowering than any ecstasy he had ever experienced. The ripe, wild scent transported him to his father's vast banana plantations in Murema-Bukanga, where he and other adolescents rushed through the cut, dried and tattered banana leaves lain at the foots of the fat smooth green, black and purple and sometimes pink stems of the banana trees. The leaves were meant to rot and create compost manure and mulch. As the youths fell and rolled on them; the deafening crunching and shuffling, frightened away wood pigeons, lizards, magpies, and the large, beautiful locust-like hoppers with thick armoured bodies and indigo-to-violet spurs on their hind limbs. The youths pursued these insects, fixing their sights on the yellow and sometimes bright red or even dark glittery purple inner plumes that burst out of them until they exhausted them for easy capture. They would roast the fat, tough-bodied insects in outdoor fires and munch away at them outside the house as they were prohibited from eating such things inside the house. Growing sporadically among the straw-brown dry leaves was a mushroom with the glossy dark-chocolate colouring of a woman's skin. The *kassukussuku* only grew in banana plantations and its name hinted at *nsuku*, or banana plantations. The first person to discover the phallus-like head breaking the black loamy earth and dry banana leaves shouted out for all to hear: *'Nkasse!'* ('I have made a kill!') He then covered the mushroom up with a dry banana leaf to hide it from other hunters. The mushroom would not penetrate through the new leaf as it had the firs, and it was rare for those present at the first kill to return to steal the find from the initial owner. By evening it would have matured, fully unfurled its *café au lait* brown gills. At supper the youths pushed the mushrooms deep into the steaming hot, doughy matooke lump apportioned to them by their mothers. *Akassukussuku* was never cooked on a fire. It cooked within five minutes inside the hot *matooke* lump and when re-exposed suffused the dining area with a strong, sweet aroma that women were said to find disgusting. The more mature mushroom, the one that had not been discovered on the first day that it broke through the earth, was never eaten by young boys because it smelt too strong. It was the older youths and mature men who preferred the older *akassukussuku*, whose smell, similar to that of the genitalia of nubile girls, was intoxicating. The *akassukussuku* was the more genuine of the claimed aphrodisiacal mushrooms. Ssempa remembered the words of his maternal uncle, Shafiq Kakembo, a mullah of a parish mosque who, not expecting the youth to grasp the subtle contents of his conversation with other men at a mutton barbecue, had described it thus in his sermon-like whisper: 'It is the smell that becomes rarer and rarer in our modern woman. I did find it among the Nuba and the Zande of the Sudan Bahr el Gazal – perhaps the most unmodern people with whom God populated His endless Earth'. Here Shafiq Kakembo had looked around and lowered his voice even further. 'Here in our own land you'll find it in the village lasses and in women who have not encountered penicillin and other European drugs because they haven't been contaminated with gonorrhoea and the other diseases of the pudenda. In those who haven't swallowed birth-control pills that deepen their voices into heavy bass and bring out hidden beards, and those who haven't rubbed petroleum jellies and lotions in their secret bodies. For the cleanest of women, my dear brethren, is not the one who washes herself sterile before coitus to expunge smell, but the one who contains that unadulterated scent of the over-mature *akassukussuku* mushroom. Such a one need not bathe for sex'.

Ssempa suddenly realized that only now at thirty-six years of age was he experiencing what that rascal uncle of his had experienced in innumerable encounters. Tonight in a chilly candle-lit Kabale hotel suite, that very powerful, ripe aroma suffused his senses as the two lost souls held one another, she sobbing in husky soprano, uttering things in the Kinyarwanda tongue, and he sighing in the bass, grunting like a pig in no language at all. Their cries merged in a mangled tenor. The two lost themselves to the passions of their forgotten bodies. They sinned together, fornicating until the gold of the sun flung the curtains asunder through the big sturdy stems and boughs of the tall eucalyptuses and touched their skins.

* * *

In the red gold of the rising sun the woman touched the dark crimson smudges in the white linen and watched the man's relaxed sleeping face. The hidden power behind that sleeping face, she thought alarmed; had drawn her blood! She shook her head slowly against the pillow, a tender look touching the languorous brown eyes in her face. There was no gin in her head now, just the faint, dull ache of a hangover, and her heart beat assiduously. There was the dull bruised feeling to her body and another ache she could trace with the index finger of her right hand to a part of her that had been contently inviolate. She withdrew her hand from beneath the coverings and stared at her fingers. Her pupils remained dilated in the red gloom of postsomnus relaxation. She spoke quietly: "I have sinned! I, Julian Dominicus; I, Juliette Kantarama, Paouis, Coeur de Marbre, Rocaille, Petrus, of all people, have fallen!" She touched the fingers to the sleeping man's face and caressed it as he lay like one who had been given laudanum or belladonna. "I, Kantarama, am no longer chaste! I am a weakling. Nobody can believe it, but I am weak. Apollonia would be shocked unto death to imagine this," her eyes peered pointedly at the sleeping face. An expression of mild shock unfurled on her forehead: "Gerald Sebastian will laugh me to hell because of my own scorn over her deeds with the diocesan vet. She should laugh at me to death and nickname me worse than my own nicknames for her. At least the vet is an insider, a failed Brother of Christian Instruction. But this!" She touched the rough hair above his right ear. "A foreigner, a true outsider — a man of the world if any ever were. A man of the world with whom Gerald Sebastian Namazzi, would trust her own indulged life. Gerald would understand my dilemma."

Ssempa stirred in his sleep to her lullaby-like soliloquy. Though in the convent, she would have been up two hours previously, Julian felt sleepy.

"At least on that Day of Judgment which will certainly come, David, like he so tiny against Goliath, will be there to calculate responses to Him whom he has called my Husband and Whose bride he so buccaneeringly deflowered."

With such consolatory thought, her eyes gradually closed and she fell asleep once more beside the foreigner.

* * *

They spent the day in their suite, getting room service that Ssempa arranged with Byangye the bootlegger and quack doctor of Kabale.

Ssempa had brought out the smaller of the settees and the ornate glass-topped table to the hedge-enclosed lawn of their hut and placed them under one of the ages-old eucalyptuses with enormous cracked-bark bole, the gnarled roots of which provided an ample seat. Each hut, he had noted, had its own backyard, wide, grassy and capacious with a tree or two to provide shade and ambience. The hedges were of thick, short, impenetrable, sturdy cypress. The woman had been in the lavatory-cum-laundry for a good hour giving a wash to their clothes. After stretching out the laundry to dry on the separating hedges she joined him in the cool shade of the tree whose foliage sang mournful serenades in the highland winds. She had wrapped round her hips one of the green-yellow-and-white batik curtains that Ssempa had stripped from the bedroom window and pulled on a light long-sleeved, topaz-brown sweater that did not hide her breasts the way her habit had. She sat on the settee, looking fresh and vivacious after her bath and laundry work. Behind her the flowery verdure of tamed shrubbery and climber vines accentuated her charm, the elegance that the dead army officer had discerned even in unfavourable light and that had tempted him into a fatal crime of passion. Love making appeared to have bruised her lips to a purple-black cherry. They were prettily puckered and luscious.

A thought intrigued Ssempa and not for the first time. What made women want to become nuns? Women like Julian Kantarama! Did their parents and relatives force it upon them? What of the men who became priests? Some thought that impotence or frigidity sent men and women into celibacy and chastity, but Ssempa couldn't buy that. Here was one woman who had lived wrongly for the best part of her life in a dusty brown uniform that scared away natural feeling. A woman of extraordinary sensual fervour whom the Baganda would have aptly described to as *akatula keebisse*, or 'she of the veiled *other* things.'

"You look at me like a bird of prey at a fledgling, you man!" she said in Luganda. Her Kinyarwanda accent made the words exotically beautiful.

"I feel exactly like such a bird right now."

"And yet you know it leaves mother hen crying and lamenting?"

"Yes. Eagle glides away puzzled by all the naggings of mother hen. Did God create pullets so that needy eagle should endlessly roam the skies hungry?"

"The typical thief's reasoning. There are mice and smaller nestlings to forage for all over the desolate earth."

"Ha! Are those without their own mother to lament after good old eagle? — I doubt it."

She laughed, a laugh that crinkled the outer edges of her eyes, making the bulbous lower lids appear swollen, or like those of Mongol peoples. "Must you always seek rhetoric for everything that comes your way? Anyhow, this was a chickling ripe for the thieving kite. If only Gerald Sebastian could hear me talk the way I am!"

"Gerald Sebastian!" Ssempa's eyebrows shot up, furrowing his forehead. "Who is Gerald Sebastian?"

"Look at the way he looks at me! Hey, hey, hey; take it easy; Sister Gerald Sebastian is my teaching colleague; don't be jealous of her. There are no other kites or eagles to whisk this chickling off now."

"Except — God; or is it Jesus?"

"I won't accept blasphemy. I stood up to it last night because you were drunk. Besides, those two, who are one, have a different kind of love. A very, very deep and eternal love."

"And you don't think humans are capable of such penetrating love?"

"Penetrating! Penetrating yes. Ravishing, yes. But there it ends. Human love, even for God the creator of man, is ephemeral. Man only grasps for it in the mind in times of dire need for immediate salvation, for rescue of his spirituality. It is extremely easy to sin, to fall from the grace of God the Creator the moment a person like myself steps out of the sphere of her Mother House, of the cloister, which is God's fortressed bastion for us. You become like the fledgling out in the open. And, the fledgling finds herself up in the sky where she does not belong, in the claws of a deadly dangerous life. If she grieved forever her grief would come to naught. That is why I laugh at myself. And look at mother hen, my House; my mother, Sabina; Reverend Superior General; Uncle Raphael; Poronia; Gerald, ah, Gerald! — Not many can survive the peregrine falcon."

He did not respond to her, not immediately. Julian's heart was crying unseen within her. She was expressing her disgrace for him to hear and probably understand, but it was more to herself that she spoke. She wanted to convince herself — and her now distant Mother House, that her sin had been an inevitability. She had stepped too far out of her clucking, cautioning ambit to remain safe. He looked at the sky where her eyes had strayed, as if looking out for eagles and kites. Instead, there were sparrows skirling and twittering as they dived this way and that for tiny prey. Eagles had already fed and gone away sated. The sun was setting but still hot. Towards the horizon, where the red ball was rapidly heading, furious sooty clouds loomed like charcoal dust. To the south the sky was bright yellow, to the northwest, malachite green. The rest of the sky was a beautiful lapis lazuli mottled with bright pink wisps of strange cloud that reminded Ssempa of the side of a large tilapia fish in clear water under strong light. These pink clouds had marine shapes: submarines, sharks and whales, walruses, otters and seals. And then there was the very deep bright red that shot out from behind the boiling dark red beyond. Ssempa imagined sparks piercing the heavens above the horizon. In their adolescence he and his peers pictured God, dressed in regalia like Kabaka Edward Frederick

Luwangula Mutesa of Buganda busy barbequing great fresh chunks of meat, tears streaming out of his eyes because of the sour smoke, and sweat oozing from his face as he stoked the great fire with logs bigger than the biggest trees they had ever seen. And Ssempa had always visualised his own mothers — seven of them, the wives of his father Sulayman Ssemaganda — preparing the evening meal. He even had images of nun-like damsels or those dressed like *hajjatis*, busying themselves making God's bed with a mattress of fluffy clouds the colour of silver-white cottonwood.

From a hi-fi phonograph somewhere in a suite two or three huts away from theirs, yesterday's car-radio singer was crooning: *'Just a little bit closer, can you lay by my side; can we get it together, lazing in the sand; Ohhhh – Soley Soley...'*. The nostalgic tones intoxicated him.

"Would you wish this — this thing, to end?" Ssempa asked her, delicately.

"To wake up from my dream? — No, alas; it is wishful thinking. This is reality herself."

They fell silent.

"What will you eat, Julia," he asked her, as much to break the silence as to change the subject. "Byangye's big brother happens to be the acting assistant chief cook of the White Horse Inn. He believes I am alone here and wanted to get me the best the kitchen had on offer."

"Do you want to find out what nuns eat in the convent?"

"Don't tell me you eat ambrosia, like the gods. I do recall Monsignor Raphael referring to your cooking, Julia. Do you prepare ambrosia, by any chance? — For I would then say to hell with Byangye's big brother's written menu."

"Ambrosia, ambrosia! What ambrosia do you talk about? I am your ambrosia," she stopped abruptly and spluttered into soft laughter, opening her eyes wide, as if what she had just said bewildered her. "Do you hear how I can talk? — I do believe that is how humans — I mean people of the world outside the cloister, talk. You say truthfully what you think and feel, isn't it so? You don't train yourself how to say things, how to feel!"

"People out here are terrible, Julia. We think subtly before we utter things; which keeps us safe from things like our own governments and even our own better-off or more authoritative relatives. We lie alike to the security personnel and to our parents so as to evade, or, in the case of government, to save our skins. You must never forget that."

"I have an idea of it, you know. You see, my being a teacher and the Church's unofficial representative of Banyarwanda refugees in Orukinga Valley and Kashojwa, in Nakivale, means I meet a lot with worldly people."

"Oh, hell! — It is difficult to tell whose life is worse!"

"At least I never missed life outside of the cloister, which ought to show you that the life we lead, though austere, is not bad at all. Indeed it can really be paradisiacal, believe me. But for the stomach, we Franciscans eat whatever we are served, and that is frugal... and good too. Of course, out in the world, like at The Marlorec in Mbarara, where I so often cook, we eat anything as long as it is immaculate – or kosher, as the Jews say. Tomorrow being a Friday, for instance, I cannot eat any meat. Do you know The Marlorec?"

"Yes. The place where padres booze themselves into stupor, we are told. A very close acquaintance of mine frequents it. But, surely, you eat the same food as us mortals, don't you?"

"I guess we do since we are, like you, mortals. But our meals are measured; you could even say weighed, with scales. And our eating hours are more or less fixed. Supper is at a time we refer to as vespers, and our lunch, whenever necessary — it usually isn't — at nones. I cannot go into all that for you of course as most of it must be Latin to you."

"But today you can eat meat? — Because Byangye's big brother wanted to make special things."

"I don't know meat to be such a special item of food. I don't care much for it, anyway."

"When I met the fellow last night in the darkness, I believed him to be the hewer of logs for the hotel's firewood. He has a *cordon bleu* — can you imagine! — from Paris. He showed me the framed award. He is only far down his section's ladder because of a drink problem. The man lived in France for fifteen years."

"All the same," said Julian. "If we had a kitchen to ourselves I would do the cooking for you myself. Uncle Raphael was not jesting about my culinary abilities. I am very good at it, in the eyes of The Marlorec's patronage. It is a grave sin for me to talk like that, David, praising myself. But I am now a human — we call outsiders humans, in our circles; so let me talk the way Uncle Raphael told you I used to, like a chatterbox. Father Mazinio, everybody from Mbarara knows Father Giuseppe Mazinio, that old Italian priest, drives forty miles from Mushanga Parish every Friday to eat my *au maigre* dishes."

Ssempa knew of Father Giuseppe Mazinio, of course, like just everybody else did. The Italian priest had lived in Nkore and Kigezi for more than four decades, had written the only grammatical book in the Vernacular of the region, started a typewriter repair workshop which gave birth to a full fledged printery assembled from scrap equipment he gleaned from here and there in Europe, created a carpentry and joinery workshop cum institute, and set up a secondary school later named after himself. Father Mazinio was not bent by his years or weakened in the head. He was known to shout back at the top of his voice at men and women who waved his old Peugeot to a stop for a lift: '*Nyoko niwe yaaginguriire?*' 'Did your mother buy me this car?' And, of course, that worthy would drive on since he was always in a hurry, something the lazybones of the villages never seemed to understand.

"Is it true priests have affairs with nuns?"

"Is that in direct response to all I've laboured to explain? — Or is your mind in some other place? You are such a jealous boor!"

"Really, of you, Julia? How can I be jealous over a ...?"

She had gotten up in a flash and slumped into his lap to clamp a hand to his mouth. They sat there, he rocking and swinging her gently from side to side. She was saying: "Thank you, David, for not finishing such a stupid remark. I think you are very stupid, too. But a very, very good stupid man. Uncle Raphael said it of you, remember?"

"You think that for all my life I can ever forget any bit of yesterday and today? I can never, except that I don't remember the good old monsignor calling me stupid. He did not, as a matter of fact. Listen to that *Soley Soley* playing again! Listen.... do you not hear it?"

They listened to the song as they rocked lazily.

"Sounds French."

"It is in English, and very popular nowadays. It will eternally remind me of our first encounter. It was playing on your uncle's car stereo yesterday, if you remember. Look, see what Byangye's big brother wrote here. That I should tick off what I want. They don't prepare local dishes in these government-owned hotels. I cannot read most of it, but can you?"

She took the notepad sheet from his fingers: "Ah la la lah!" She clucked her tongue softly. "He can do all this? What did you give him David, for...? — Ah la lah! The man is offering you ... did you say ambrosia! For a *chaufroid hors d'oeuvres* he offers *quenelles*, with tilapia as the chief component, very well that. And *noyau*! Great liquor that; you said they didn't have wines and spirits last night."

"The storekeeper had gone for a funeral or something. That could mean he is a smuggler and gave that classic Ugandan excuse for job absence. He must have returned."

"I will only believe when I see the bottle. Uh hmm, *bouillabaisse* — I believe from the same tilapia. This man does not seem to care for meat; he must be Catholic or...." she gave him a sidelong, suspicious look. "You didn't tell him you were ensconced with someone's bride, did you, David?"

"You never know."

170

"Would you do that?" she asked with a little jump, shock in her voice. She knew how to be funny and humorous, like most Francophone Africans he had met, though she herself had, seemingly, lived most of her life in Uganda.

"I am such a chatterbox, you know."

"I would happily kill you, of course." Her eyes were back on the sheet of paper. "He certainly lived in France, your Byangye's big brother. He offers five choices of main course. *Chateaubriand, coq au vin, duchesse* with *foie de veau, nasi goreng* — ah, this is too good to be true, and risotto, again with fish rather than meat. All are *à la fermière* too. Give me that pen. Think of pilau for the *nasi goreng*. He must have asked of you about your susceptibility to paprika unless he knows your culinary ways well. I overdo my own peppers at The Marlorec; I doubt your mouth would take what mine is capable of, David. Your Byangye's big brother has noted it here as *diable*, you see? — Now, *diable* means quite... diabolically hot. I am noting here *medium hot*."

"For my mouth's sake?"

"Yes. Unlike you Baganda, Banyarwanda do love their hot peppers. Our only equals may be the Indians. But give me matoke, Irish potatoes and posho with beans and groundnuts at any time."

"One requires some change sometimes. Let's see; what are you hiding from me here?" He took her left hand from her right and prized her fingers open. She covered her eyes with the released wrist of her right hand clutching the biro pen, the way she had done during their sexual intercourse, and fell back against his chest.

She said in a small, shy voice: "I removed it with the help of soap. It hurt me and drew my blood. I sinned in it, imagine! I want us to get to Mbarara as quickly as possible so I may confess my faults, David."

He fixed his eyes at the pale area, where a metal band had embraced her finger for nearly two decades. He felt tears sting his eyes, recalling the tears in her voice about that ring. He thrust her savagely against his bosom, covering her face with a million kisses, munching at her supple, mouth: "Ohhh, my poor little girl," he cried out on releasing her face. "I am so, so sorry. Forgive me."

"No, I cannot forgive you. If I do, we'll part."

"Never," his fingers stroked the pale area where her ring had been, with utmost tenderness. "But I want you to relax and take it easy. We can never pretend to undo what happened. And as you did correctly realise, this is no dream. I myself have for the past several hours expected myself to wake from its sweetness. I am happy it goes on. Let us talk of other things. Tell me how you learned to cook and to speak French directly from the aesophagus instead of off tongue-tip."

She removed her hand from her eyes, and said: "You have solutions to all my life, what remains of it anyway."

"I'll always strive to have something up my sleeve for you, honey. That great French of yours...?"

"I don't speak it as well as Poronia. But as for cooking, our Uncle Sinzagaya and his former wife; your friend Chantal Nzaza, taught us much of it. Poronia is even better than I."

"And Sinzagaya got it all from the Coast?"

"Yes, they — Chantal and Uncle, worked for the various Mombasa hotels during their exile. There is nothing under the sun that Uncle Sinzagaya cannot cook."

"I had a stepmother who used to say there was nothing on earth she couldn't cook except stones."

"Through his adept culinarian hands you might enjoy a good meal of rocks from Uncle Sinzagaya and afterwards say you never tasted anything better. I want to know how you got to know Chantal and my uncle. I've been curious about it since yesterday when Uncle Monsignor introduced us."

"Ah that! Your Uncle Gakinya made me such a meal, a meal of stones, you could say. But not even he could convince me of any sweetness in it afterwards. It chased me out of Rwanda and I never returned there to settle."

"You lived in Rwanda?"

"Yes. I think I did tell you before that I did. For nearly a year, some time before Juvenal Habyarimana took over power in July seventy-three. I nearly got killed too. It is a long, bad story."

"Worse than last night?"

"Last night was good. It culminated in you for me."

"You rascal, did you orchestrate last night?"

"If I had imagined it would turn out the way it did, I'd have done all in my powers to engineer it. But, in all honesty, I only saw your dull brown cloth and the crucifix. There was no woman in you at Gitarama yesterday. That is honest, Julia."

She looked at him gently and said: "Is the genesis of your encounter with my uncle so bad — too bad for my ears?"

"Yes. But it probably can be softened by Byangye's big brother's cooking." He glanced at the notepaper. "You ticked off *nasi goreng* – with medium-hot pepper, and *noyau*. Let me take it back to him. And before what you called vespers — or are we already in compline — I shall tell you all about how your Uncle Issa Sinzagaya Gakinya, he is my uncle too now.... Hey, hey, hey, don't strangle me for that, my dear Julia! — how Uncle Issa Sinzagaya Gakinya placed me in a bloody deadly fix whereby I should have died."

Four

Kigali, Rwanda, July 1972

Issa Sinzagaya Gakinya was a short smallish, charcoal-black man of quite sharp aquiline facial features whose hard dark eyes had seen hard times. In late 1972 he returned from exile in Kenya, where he had sojourned in the coastal city of Mombasa. Gakinya rarely smiled and never laughed in all the time Ssempa knew the man but at the same time, the Muganda hadn't met many better-hearted person in his travels. The Munyarwanda returnee wore chequered flat top caps, of which he seemed to have quite a supply. These were intended to cover the bald patch that had replaced the short thick-grained curly hair of his head. He drove a hire van for a generally English-American clientele hotel, the Hotel Internationale, on Avenue de Paix in uptown Kigali.

On the other hand, the Muganda had arrived in Kigali one dawn, dirty and smelling of a rough overland journey, which he had made mostly on foot. He had a stubbly beard all over cheeks and chin; his bloodshot eyes looked over his shoulder all the time in a fear he strove too poorly to conceal. He was new to the country where his first impression was of motor vehicles that drove on the wrong side of the road and all the steering wheels were on the wrong side of the motor vehicles. And he had immediately embarked on seeking out a nephew — a son of an aged cousin brother, who worked in Kigali as a mechanic in zone Gikondo-Magerwa. There were not many Baganda in Kigali, so the moment he mentioned the name of his nephew, Ssempa was taken to Rwanda Mechanique, the repair garage where the nephew worked as a trainer of mechanics. The nephew was openly happy to receive a rare Muganda visitor, who was moreover a relation of his, and conducted him to his shack, not far away from the place of work. To the nephew Ssempa gave a tall story about family troubles that had caused him to abandon home. He got a promise from the relative that nobody would get to know of his whereabouts. Being a mechanic himself, albeit one who had abandoned training at a polytechnic, Ssempa got a job as a trainer in the same garage. But after a few months someone recommended him to the state-owned transport company, which was in the process of importing Nissan Diesel buses for public transport. The company was setting up a modern maintenance garage and the Japanese contractors responsible for the project found the Muganda to be an exceptionally good mechanic, though he had abandoned the certificate course in motor vehicle mechanics to get recruited into the Uganda Police. But that work was over after four months. He would have left Kigali soon after the state garage stint, having wished to get as far away from Uganda as he could. His mind was fixed on Bujumbura. But another man, a top business magnate, was establishing an assembly plant for Toyota vehicles and with a recommendation from his erstwhile employer, Ssempa joined the Toyota man to teach his local people the fundamentals of mechanics. He had left Uganda with the sapphire ring he had been given by the late Zoe Atimango Lupai on the night they separated on Kampala's Lumumba Avenue, never to see each other again. This ring he had sold for several thousand Rwandan francs, which he stashed away in a nook in his nephew's house. With that and more money made from his work in the two big garages, he bought a Volkswagen Combi van from an auction by the hotel where he would soon acquaint himself with the transport officer, Monsieur Issa Sinzagaya Gakinya. At that time in Rwanda, used motor vehicles were never returned to the road, and thus he got the fairly sound van for peanuts. Quite a small town in early 1972, Kigali, built on a single steep-sided hill, had few Africans but many vain Belgian and French citizens. Many Germans in the mining concern SOMIRWA and the radio-relay station Deutchwelle lived in Kigali. Then there were the highly promiscuous Lebanese Arab traders running the *boulangeries* and confectionaries. The latter offered him roles that changed his mind about leaving Rwanda. They contracted him to transport their black market merchandise within Rwanda and between Rwanda and Burundi, and occasionally even between the two tiny states and their gigantic neighbour, Zaire. Occasionally Gakinya tipped him off on tourists who wished to pay for hotels in Rwandan francs instead of US dollars or French francs, as required by the finance ministry. He would transport such tourists to Ruhengeri, Kinigi and Kidaho at the foot of the M'havura Mountain Ranges from where the tourists would start off on the climb up the mountains to look at the rare gorillas in the mists of the ancient bamboo jungles. Meanwhile the nephew at Rwanda Mechanique, who had been instrumental in bringing Ssempa and Gakinya together, continued to give shelter to his step uncle. He found the Munyarwanda former exile an amiable, talkative man who never laughed; a man who took his job seriously. In addition to heading the transport section of the hotel, the man also occasionally took tourists around in a Volkswagen Transporter van. And because he provided excellent service, tourists came from overseas with Gakinya's names noted in their diaries.

On the evening the giant Laban Sorrozo gave him the deadly job, Gakinya had found Ssempa at La Vedette, a popular nightclub in Nyamirambo, and parked his van at the kerb. Ssempa, on seeing him, had left his own group to join the newcomer.

"I have a customer for you, Muganda." Gakinya spoke English fluently without the typical sibilant French intonations of the Banyarwanda, and spoke

Kiswahili like a Mijikenda native of Mombasa. "A Senegalese man — but
as you know, that could mean just any West African. He could even be from
Congo-Brazzaville for all I know. He wants to hire a van."

"Where does he want to go to and why a van? I don't like transporting
West Africans, with the stiff laws here."

"Same old story, my friend. The man does not want to pay the hotel in
regulation dollars and claims he's time-barred. But, West African though he
might be, you will find him a most civil gentleman. Don't expect to meet a
more cordial person."

"Ha; cordial! That is worse in a West African, especially a Francophone
West African. He will have ivory to take to Burundi, I can assure you of that;
ivory from Uganda or from Tanzania. That is what it will turn out to be. Have
you not told him I wouldn't touch a game trophies smuggler with a twenty-
metre pole?"

"Why not talk to him first and hear him out?"

"Where is he? At your hotel?"

"No. Look across the road, to the left, under the streetlight post. That is
him in the car."

"And what car is that? It looks like a Peugeot 504 ... but — it actually is
a Peugeot 504!"

"*Cinq cent-et-quartre* coupé. My very first, even. It has Gabonese
registration."

"*Tant pis*, my friend Sinzagaya. Maybe I need an even longer pole to touch
your man. What did you say his name was?"

"Monsieur Sorrozo. I do not think you need that pole. He'd disarm you
in no time, even if only by his very first words to you. You will certainly
like the wife. She is the dream of most Mombasa citizens: dark, big and lithe
— emerging out of the deep blue Indian Ocean at Nyali Beach, with or without
a fish tail."

"I hadn't seen the connoisseur in feminine beauty in you, Sinzagaya. You
sound like a love-bitten poet."

"How can you say that, Muganda," cried Gakinya with accusation in
his voice. "When I showed you my former wife, the princess, just the other
day?"

Ssempa had been shown Princess Chantal Mugorewera Nzaza in Bujumbura
the previous week when they had driven a batch of tourists there in a convoy
of a dozen vans. At forty-eight years of life, six foot of height, and an impala's
neck, Princess Nzaza was a concoction of Queen Cleopatra of the Pharaohs of
el Misr and the Empress Sheba of Abyssinia, in her sheer beauty.

"Still dark, big and lithe emerging out of deep blue waters can also fit cobras, wouldn't you agree? But I will talk to your man and promptly reject his deal. Even from here, you can see a smuggler in bad stuff."

It was a warm late night with the sky over Kigali hill bedecked in beautiful twinkling stars. A band called Kwashamankoi had just finished a number from Docteur Nico. That master guitarist's cicada-serene solo had been performed in what Ssempa deemed utmost perfection. As they headed for the chic Peugeot 504, a throaty voice like a night bird blared out: *'Six-heure ekoki, tika nazonga mboka ahhh au beauté na'milengela...'* He glanced at his cheap Roamer watch to confirm the musician's accuracy of the hour. Midnight precisely. The Muganda had intended to go to bed early. They crossed the road to the car that glittered under the street lamps and reflected their approach like an uneven bent mirror of the deepest maroon colour. The man — six-foot-six of beefy flesh and bone — not an ounce of fat showed, dressed in cream safari suit, eased himself out of the driving seat. Taking steps too nimble for such a hulking giant, he stretched out a large meaty right hand. The left held a thin black cigarette between the thick, long fingers with two huge gold rings.

"Rafiki," the man addressed Ssempa in a low, huskily pleasant voice instead of the coarse grunt the latter had expected. "My name is Sorrozo, Laban Hemed Sorrozo. I am glad to meet you." He threw an eye at La Vedette, a pained look creasing his brows. "Who is playing in there *ce soir*? That band is butchering the music. The original composer is a friend of mine — you must have heard of Le Seigneur Pasquale Rochereau; he simply cannot sing in such a brutal voice. They sound like they were thieves and somebody were running after them! Simply listen to that. How very brutal! I am of a mind to go in there and pay them to silence themselves. Just hear how they are murdering that rhythm; that cannot be *Palmarès, mon Dieu!*" His voice was most gentle in its complaint. "If any of you ever wishes to travel to Kinshasa, to visit Limete and Matonge for the real music, just ask Laban Sorrozo. I am very well known there. Franco himself calls me *patron*. But did my brother Sinzagaya here tell you of my urgent requirement?"

The man mixed Kiswahili, French and English so well you understood him better that way. He was, Ssempa reflected, the exact size of Idi Amin with a few kilograms off his paunch. He was black like charcoal with pleasant eyes. His belligerent, strong-bridged nose flared wide like a bull's at the nostrils and his mouth was as used to laughing as to giving orders. He had a square chin and a lantern jaw and had his hair close cropped so that the scalp showed through. He left no bristle of hair on his face in his daily shaving.

"Yes, monsieur. My friend Sinzagaya tells me you want to go somewhere. But he has not told me where."

"Why," replied the giant, with utmost gentility. "To Butare, to Gikongoro, to Cyangugu; maybe to Kibuye. Why didn't you tell him, my brother, Sinzagaya? See, I am a merchant. I am buying stuff for export."

"Good," said Ssempa. "I had feared it required going out of Rwanda. When Monsieur Sinzagaya told me...."

"But we shall go outside Rwanda, too," said the giant, almost submissively. He stretched out a hand and patted the Ugandan on the shoulder in a comradely gesture. "We might go to Kabare and Bukavu in Zaire, maybe to Kamanyola. And we might perhaps even go to Port Empain and Shabunda, if the need arises. It all depends on the procurers of my merchandise. You will give me your daily costs and I shall provide fuel, repairs and so on."

"It will depend, Mr Sorrozo, on what your cargo is. I myself indulge in some minor trade. But I never touch elephant tusks, game animal skins and pelts. Oh, and anything else that may create acrimony between the Rwandese authorities and myself. I still love to live here."

The last bit Ssempa added because he could not view Mr Sorrozo as a man without some dirty business up his sleeve. It was his clincher, the main bargaining chip.

"Ah, about that," said the giant with a dismissive gesture of his hand. "You won't carry much. There are trucks bringing in the haul that I deal in. But we shall negotiate. You haven't even told me your name yet, see?"

"David Ssempa. I am Ugandan. Mechanic. I transport tourists and merchandise as a side occupation. But you have said nothing about...."

"Yeees, yeeees, about the animal things! Ah, you are a hard man. Actually you are trying to push me off you; you don't like your customer, eh? But I promise you there will be nothing of the game-parks stuff. What else do you do?" Ssempa thought he caught a trace of suspicion in the big man's voice.

"I told you I am a mechanic."

"Interesting, interesting. Meet my wife, Zainab. She is Ugandan herself."

"You are sure?" Ssempa bent into the car.

The woman, Zainab Illeh, was about twenty-three. She had an Afro hair style, and big sleepy — or what many called come-to-bed — eyes, a purple lipstick on her mouth and a terra cotta complexion that appeared glazed in its smoothness. She was a match in size to her husband as she could have measured five-foot-eleven and could have weighed over one hundred kilos. She was clad in a velveteen dress with horizontal frills on the sleeves and chest. It was in the maroon colour of Sorrozo's car. The car smelt of upholstery leather and cigarette smoke. They spoke in Luganda and Ssempa learned that she came from Ediofe, a part of Arua, a northern Ugandan town, and was a product of a

West Nile Kakwa chief and a nomadic cattlewoman from northern Tanzania. You could have easily taken her for one of the Hamitic tribes of the region. She must have inherited of the Kakwa the much rougher of her bodily features and the gentler ones from her mother. He called her a drifter and she called him a vagabond, and they laughed heartily.

"Is that your van?" Sorrozo asked, pointing. Ssempa nodded. The rust-brown Combi stood parked next to a mosque up the deserted, brightly lit street. Inside La Vedette, some vocalist was just saying: 'Ah, Nico; *Dieu de la guitare!*' Ssempa glanced at Laban Sorrozo's face. There was pain there and the giant had screwed his face into a pleasant grimace at the guitar solo. He said: "Ohhh, my God! — Do you hear that, Zainab? Now it is my friend Docteur Nico wa Kasanda, that they are out to massacre. They really believe that is *Pauline*? Even I can play that solo better. Where did they come from, Sinzagaya?"

"You just talked of the place," Ssempa replied for Gakinya. "It is written on the billboards that they are the Kwashamankoi of the African Fiesta, resident in Kinshasa's *zone* Matonge."

"Liars... felons; pretenders. There is nothing like that at all. Docteur Nico's African Fiesta is an entirely distinct jazz band from Kwashamankoi. I will definitely talk someone into throwing them out of the place. They cannot be allowed to brutalise my great friends' music with such impunity. I imagine Roger Izeidi would faint to hear *their* music suffer so. *Pour l'amour de Dieu!* — To travel is to see." He turned to Ssempa. "That Combi of yours appears as good as new. It should do the job. We will drop in at the place of Monsieur Gakinya and then go to my hotel to negotiate the deal. I would pay just anything to be away from this place of the heinous murder of my most favourite music."

They left La Vedette in their three vehicles, taking a darker street behind the mosque. Gakinya lived in Nyamirambo, not a long way from La Vedette, but on the opposite side, down a steep footpath with a deep gully that had to be traversed several times. It was a small, newish house with a zinc-sheet roof painted a dark red, which appeared black in the evening light. The house was whitewashed with a shiny cream oil paint. They had accompanied him there, having left their vehicles at a fuel-filling station, the usual spot when not in use. Zainab remained in the car because she complained of a headache. An Arab woman of about forty, short and rotund and dressed in black *buibui*, doted about them, offering them tea, which they declined, and a homemade orange squash of delicate, nectarine sweetness, which they accepted, along with crisp, hot-spiced delicacies they referred to as *kouskous*. The giant Sorrozo chewed at these, his strong jaws making a rapid, muffled noise like rocks being crushed inside his mouth, which seemed to please the Arab woman immensely.

They watched James Cagney and Humphrey Bogart in a black-and-white Michael Curtiz movie, *Angels with Dirty Faces*, in French, on the very first video machine Ssempa had seen. He would see it again eight years later. Sorrozo wept like a woman, dabbing at his eyes with a large light blue handkerchief.

"To think that most of these men and women, friends to me I tell you, no longer live!" He sniffed in his lamentations. "Such wonderful actors too." He got up. "I cannot stand to watch more of this. I hate sadness and death, Mr David. Come on, Madame," he gestured to the Arab woman while he pulled at his Gitanes cigarette with eyes closed. "I bring along your gift which I promised you last year." And from a breast pocket he pulled out a white, ornately mimeographed leather box that he snapped open with a thumb. Inside it was a glittering that stabbed their eyes like electric welding arcs. "Small and beautiful, and very, very expensive, too. Do you have a wife, Mr David?"

"No," Ssempa shook his head, still puzzling at the man's strange sentiments. "Not yet."

"What a waste," said Sorrozo, slowly shaking his great head with absent-minded solemnity. "Why don't you get our friend here a Munyarwanda beauty of a wife, brother Sinzagaya?"

"I am just learning of his predicament, Hemed," lied the other man. Ssempa had told the former exile all about his troubles in Uganda and why he was a fugitive in Rwanda. "I could do something for him in the near future."

"No; it's nothing. I'll get my dear Zainab to get him some good girl from their own land, not so, Mr David?"

But Ssempa's attention was presently glued to Mrs Gakinya, who was obviously enraptured by her gift. "I can't believe it," she was saying in her quick, breathless Kiswahili. "Oh, I can't believe this."

Gakinya took it from her, looked at the little watch with concentration, weighed it in his hand and embraced Mr Sorrozo. He then turned to Ssempa and said: "Look, Muganda, what Laban does for his friends."

Ssempa took the tiny watch in his hand. Twenty-two carat white gold, studded with half a dozen twinkling white diamonds round its dial, made by Tiffany of New York, as emblazoned on the lid of the white leather box. He thanked the West African for the family and later the two zigzagged their way up the perilous path back to the road, all the time Ssempa wondering why Sinzagaya Gakinya had not told him they were so familiar with the giant. At the car, Sorrozo talked tenderly with great concern to his wife and gave her a tablet he got from a small cluster pack in his wallet. The woman swallowed it with a canned orange drink from a freezer box in a console beneath the dashboard of the Peugeot.

"Mr David... your other name is difficult for me — you will leave your van here and squeeze into the back of my car. We'll then head for my hotel and put a seal to our deal with a down payment after I have talked with my partners and they have had a look at you."

"That is all right with me," remarked Ssempa without much enthusiasm. His mind fretted over the omission by Gakinya over his acquaintance with the giant fellow. According to Mr Sorrozo, the promise of the watch to the Arab woman was of *last* year!

"You puzzle me, Mr David. You don't seem to care much for money."

"You say that because you don't know me. There are quite a few things that I wouldn't do for good money."

"Good money, eh? — I've never heard of such a thing. But why even speculate about it? I pay in cash for all services rendered me. I am rich, Mr David. I am the adopted son of an oil sheikh. No joking."

"Oil sheikh? You are from Nigeria?"

"Nigeria?" Sorrozo turned to look at him with a disgusted scowl. He seemed to be good at that kind of look. "You insult me, Mr David."

"Well, why? You are not an Arab, quite obviously."

"And you are wrong, because I am Kuwaiti. How can a Nigerian adopt me? We Senegalese are not like those knaves in Lagos. My father is Kuwaiti, an oil sheikh. Not a scallywag of an *oga* from Lagos." He swerved the Peugeot into a place off Boulevard de la Revolution. Ssempa had no idea just any people went to the Hotel MDR, which would in just one year become l'Hotel de Cinq Juillet. It stood in beautiful gardens with trees whose foliage whistled with the stir of the evening winds. It was the most secluded place in Kigali though it lay by a busy boulevard. "I am a state guest, see, *oga*?"

"Is *oga* not an insult?" Ssempa asked, coolly.

"It means mister in Yoruba."

"But back there...."

"It is because I don't like our neighbours, uncouth boors — worsened by a half-absorbed English influence. It beats me how you Ugandans could have been saved from being spoiled by your English colonial masters."

"I don't know it like that, Monsieur Sorrozo. Ugandans are some of the worst copiers of imported colonial ways and cultures that I have known. Nigerians are quite the opposite. But even so we cannot be as badly taken in by all that cultural imperialism as the citizens of the ex-francophone colonies. You are so much assimilated to the French, you and my Rwandan and Zairian friends, that, if you must know, you are pitiful. If the English had come into

180

Buganda the way the Belgians and French came to your Senegal, they would have suffered an indigestion they would never have gotten over."

"You think we made it that much easier for the imperialists, do you? And if you think the Belgians and the French were such brutes, you will need to study the English-American and English-Australian histories to gauge Europe and its inhabitants." For three minutes as they traversed the large lawns, the giant taught the Muganda some Western European history packed with the slave trade, Congo, racism and minerals, to which the latter listened detachedly until they arrived at the terraced front of the hotel's main building. "Ah, here we are. Unfortunately, my wife has developed an unprecedented abhorrence for Banyarwanda."

"It is simply a quid pro quo," said the wife. "They started it all. That cabinet minister spat at me first."

"But I need them, for security and procurement of my stuff. In any case, my real friends do like you most tremendously. And they are very powerful. You will go straight to the suite, Zainab — unless you want to chat with Mr David about home. Keep her good company, will you, David."

The other nodded and Sorrozo turned and sauntered off through the hotel foyer moving majestically, almost like a big cat, to seek his colleagues.

Zainab was staring at him when Ssempa turned to her. She said: "They talk of nothing else with his army friends one of whom, the captain, claims to be a great political-history researcher and anthropologist."

"Well, I took him for a wealthy illiterate back at La Vedette tonight. Your husband is a book of records. What happened here, Zainab?" Ssempa asked her in Luganda, when they had got a table on the marble-tiled terrace.

"They spat on me here, at this place. These Banyarwanda people are horrific. The minister of justice asked me which part of Uganda I came from and I told him I was from Masaka, because my mother, who is from northern Tanzania, crossed into Uganda in 1961 and lives there. Then, with heavy sarcasm, the cabinet minister asked me if Masaka happened to be in Gahungye or Nyakivale. He pronounced everything wrongly — deliberately of course. The other two places are refuge camps for Batutsi who fled here a decade ago."

"I know Kahungye and Nakivale," Ssempa explained. "And for him to call it Gahungye or Nyakivale is because of their tongues — and teeth, I guess. It annoys me too, but that is how they pronounce things here."

"Well because I had suffered from their hatred because I look like Batutsi, and was fed up with their haughtiness, I told him I had been picked from Nakivale, along with all the other beautiful women there, by Ugandan princes who thought better of us than the Rwandans did. I hadn't imagined exactly what the minister's reaction would be. But because of my response he directed a lump of his thick spittle at me. He had intended to spit in my face but maybe because he feared the friends of Laban, who looked on at us from a distance, he moved his head in a nodding motion so that the saliva flew in a parabola, to fall at my feet. I could not believe it! And instead of fright, I was filled with rage. He is a midget of a man with a large head and protruding bloodshot eyes, dressed in a very expensive European suit. So, to needle him further, I said: 'Why, *monsieur le Ministre*, do you hate Batutsi so profoundly when you yourself look so much like them? You are so tall you could look a giraffe in the eye....' He must have wished to strangle me right there and then, but the friends of Laban, Colonel Habyara and Capitaine Ndize, had gotten up. One heads the army and the other the intelligence branch. The minister glared at me and left immediately with his small entourage. Both the colonel and the captain winked at me gratefully. Both believe me to be a Mututsi and each of them has told me they have a Mututsi concubine living in a swanky hotel room."

"Don't you know your husband's friends are subordinate to the minister?"

"Not unofficially. Officially yes. But you see my point. I have suffered these insults from them from the moment I set foot on Rwandan soil from Burundi, at Akanyaru Haut. The Barundi in Bujumbura embraced me like their very own, but their cousins here have attempted to make me feel like a leper. I see the leprosy in them instead. You know how much menial labour the nincompoops, Hutu or Tutsi, have groveled in back in Uganda from the beginning of the century. Is that why they hate us?"

"No. They hate you because you look like their nemesis, the Batutsi refugees whom our country harbours as refugees and exiles. The two are cat and dog, just like Arab and Jew. Your embracers in Burundi are unwanted in Rwanda since several of them are actually Banyarwanda-Batutsi exiled there for the past decade. You know recently there was a horrific genocide in Burundi when Batutsi, assisted by President Micombero's army, hunted down and massacred nearly three-hundred thousand Bahutu. They sought out the school-going age for murder. Gregoire Kayibanda, on the other hand, did the same thing here and that time the victims were Batutsi. They are xenophobic idiots, both sides. But do not, please Zainab, try to be the one to solve their ethnic problems. Even after they have written a Bible and a Qur'an chronicling their animosities and belligerencies, they will always be cat and dog."

"A bunch of neanderthal creatures. They need to travel the world; travel teaches you a thing or two about how to live amicably in diversity."

"I don't see that anything will ever cause the two to live harmoniously with each other. I have lived here for a good eleven months, mind you. It is a ploy the Belgians employed and one the British attempted with poor results in our own Uganda."

"What idiots. How glad I am not to be one or part of them."

"That is it. Just keep them at bay; give the radicals a wide berth and associate with the more sensible ones. What you say of travel could be true. Those who have lived outside of this place, like my friend Issa Gakinya, the fellow we just left in Nyamirambo, might rectify the problem in the long run. He has such a universal mind. But you see politicians need to allow them to learn to reconcile. I wonder why the heck Monsieur Sorrozo booked himself here. This is a Bahutu political party hotel. Occupational hazard, you think? An opportunity cost?"

"He did not book himself here. The colonel and the captain insisted on it. It is safer, of course, considering his kind of deals. But it is not so for me, though. I associate my headaches with them. Every Muhutu I see hates me. I think they would poison me."

"Poison your food?"

"Banyarwanda are renowned poisoners. That is how backward they still are."

"Apart from the headaches, do you have any other problem?"

"We have been here for two weeks. But since earlier on this evening, I have felt like dead, in addition to the worsening headache."

"How is that? Do you have a history…?"

"No history of illness. Laban thinks it is the change of weather. I have a gut feeling that Laban is lying. I feel as if my heart were not pumping blood. I breathe with a conscious effort. I feel asphyxiated."

"Well. Except for your saying it, you look so full of life and…."

"I am going to entrust you with something of me, Mr Ssempa. You are a Ugandan like myself so do not betray me. In case something happens to me, I want you to give this to my mother, the address is clear on the envelope. I know you shan't read it unless she lets you."

"In case something…. I don't like people talking like that."

"Ssempa, my brother, there is something quite wrong here. The hatred aside; Laban lost his wife here last September. He was not lying to you; he has citizenship in Kuwait. And so the body was flown there for burial."

Ssempa remembered the Arab wife of Monsieur Sinzagaya Gakinya. But he had learned from Gakinya that she was an Afro-Shirazi woman from Mombasa.

"Was Mrs Sorrozo's other wife Kuwaiti?"

"No. She was a Munyankore from Mbarara."

"And…!"

"She was buried in Kuwait. They had been married three months."

"Three…."

"We've been married eleven weeks."

Ssempa calculated the number of months in eleven weeks: "Silly, Zainab. The man looks... behaves like an angel. Actually, he is a crybaby. I have seen him cry like a ninny over a scene in a movie. Sorrozo could be many other things but I don't see him killing a human being, a wife for that matter! He is no murderer."

Zainab Illeh sighed, tiredly: "I wish to agree with you, Mr Ssempa. I love Laban like crazy. He gives me so much: money, so many gifts. Shame on me if I am wrong, and you return to me my secret letter in the future. But all the same make me a solemn promise...."

"That I shall drop the letter with your mother when... if you are dead. I do pledge that with all my heart. I also know you will live happily with Mr Sorrozo into your old age."

"Of course," said Zainab trying but failing, to place some cheer in her voice and face. "If you have some prayer, say some for me. You have no way, or reason, to know what I know. I pray you don't say a thing of this to Laban, or to anybody else, and especially not to that friend of yours who introduced you to my husband. And also David?"

"Yes?"

"If you can't find my mother in Masaka, she might be at my father's place in Koboko, a place called Nyai, or in Arua at a place called Anyafio, or near the army barracks of Gilgil, at Ediofe. Simply mention her name."

"What is your mother's ex-husband's name?"

"He is also my father, an ex King's African Rifles sergeant and currently a chief. Chief Razak Illeh Amin Lupai, but most call him Illeh. Lupai is the overall family name."

Ssempa could not believe his ears. The family name Lupai could not be such a common name among the Kakwa people of Koboko. Could it be the man he had run away from? In less than a month he would find himself the involuntary guest of the Lupai family and meet yet other Lupais not related to Major Ali Drony Lupai, also known as Rapai. A number of questions were disturbing him. Was the Ugandan security system so good that it had traced him here and planned to kidnap him? Ssempa doubted that, because the woman would first and foremost conceal her identity. All the same, if it hadn't been for curiosity's sake, Ssempa would have pulled out of the Sorrozo deal without further ado. He was of a mind, of walking out of the hotel grounds, up the avenue and into the steeply sloping Avenue de Rusumo to his dingy residence in Gikondo-Magerwa. *'Lupai is the overall family name!'* It could not be a coincidental mix-up of names. The man called Chief Razak Illeh was known to be a very close relative of Idi Amin, so was the major. That meant that

184

Zainab's father, and by extension Zainab herself, were blood kindred to Major Ali Drony Lupai. Ssempa saw himself walking down to Gikondo, picking his few personal belongings, and heading down to Burundi and across that country, to Tanzania, which was the better choice of country to flee to from the Amin regime as its executive president was then the Ugandan military ruler's budding arch enemy. But the curiosity, and greed of course, gripped him when Mr Sorrozo, the two military men and the elderly Madame Thaid, an Iranian woman who operated the largest pharmaceuticals outlet in Kigali, came to where he sat with Zainab. The giant started counting and re-counting a sheaf of dollar bills before their eyes. The other men praised Sorrozo's wife on her bravery in the face of *le grossier tyran et brutal ministre* and exchanged greetings in bad English with Ssempa whom they referred to as Mugande. They exuded a harsh smell like that of a dangerous beehive under the savanna midday sun. When the two burly, powerful men had left with the Iranian woman, monsieur Sorrozo counted out twenty-five notes of crisp ten-dollar bills and handed them to Ssempa.

"That is the deposit. How much more I pay you will depend on you, Mr David. I know you already deem the down payment to be too much."

*   *   *

They went to Kabare, across the most dangerous hairpin-curved pass any driver ever had a nightmare of traversing. In clearer areas Ssempa could see the bottoms of the ravines and the blue, red, white, name it, of motor vehicles, usually heavy trucks, that had tumbled down the hillsides, their cargo and human occupants never to be retrieved. Ssempa still thought there was no place of greater beauty in the whole world. He viewed the world below in all its greenness, the blue waters of Lake Kivu to the north and those of Lakes Nyanza and Lake Tanganyika to the south. They crossed the bridge at Cyangugu around midday and proceeded to the edge of Bukavu where Sorrozo went to a small mosque for Friday prayers. Ssempa waited in the van with Theoneste, a soldier relative of a colonel's wife, with whom they had left Kigali. On coming from prayer, Sorrozo ordered Ssempa to drive nonstop through Bukavu until they got to the sprawling dusty town of Kabare to the south of Lac Kivu. They waited there from two o'clock in the afternoon to eleven in the night. They then returned to Bukavu where they slept at a privately owned house with just the caretaker, a Rwandan man who shared Sorrozo's inexhaustible supply of Gitanes cigarettes. The following day they did the same thing, driving to Kabare and sitting in a hot, humid restaurant belonging to a querulous Lebanese woman. Ssempa slept in the back of the Combi, fully satisfied and at home with the twenty-five crisp green notes in the hip pocket of his blue jeans. He hoped whatever or whomsoever they awaited would fail to turn up and the deal would be called off and he wouldn't need to keep Zainab's letter with him.

On the third day they drove in the night for fifteen kilometers outside Bukavu on the road to Kamanyola, an even rockier mountain pass than they had traversed before and with which Ssempa was unfamiliar. Still the most fearful things were the carcasses of the lorries and cars at the bottoms of the gorges. They stopped at an isolated place at the bottom of a valley. Although it was only five o'clock, and the sun was hidden only by the steep Mulenge hills to the west, the only noises were those of birds and frogs. Here they sat waiting for close to eight hours, and in all that time, not a human soul used the road. Soon it was night. A pale yellow moon in its last quarter rode the heavens. The jungle grew thick around them. Water rippled in a mournful soliloquy. The muffled roar of a waterfall came to their ears like rain spraying tall elephant grass. And meanwhile the mosquitoes fed on their exposed flesh. But only Ssempa seemed perturbed by the little noisy insects. Sorrozo and the soldier slept as if they were in their beds back in Kigali. The green luminescent markings in the dial of the van's clock showed 2:10 a.m, Zaire time. Sorrozo and the soldier in civilian clothes slept, the latter snoring like a faulty diesel engine. Ssempa's heart pumped in sudden apprehension. He debated whether to switch off the white and amber parking lights but deemed it too late. A human being approached the van cautiously and when he or she was six metres away, Ssempa turned on the headlights, shaking Sorrozo awake at the same time. A pale hand went to the eyes of the man in thick greatcoat after anxiously lowering a very heavy weight to the ground.

"Turn off the lights, you fool," Sorrozo growled; in the very way Ssempa had all along expected and wanted him to talk. "They are here at last."

The giant stepped out of the van, followed closely by the soldier who held a heavy automatic pistol in his fist. After a few minutes three other men, black Africans, emerged from the nearby bushes. Soon the two were ushering in the newcomers and helping them carry the two grey metal containers the size of a large packet of cornflakes each. The African men were left there and the first comer boarded the van for the return journey. Sorrozo and the newcomer spoke in Arabic throughout the journey back to Bukavu, where the other man, removed his great coat. An elderly fellow of the cloth in his mid sixties, he was nondescript. He could have been European, Asian, Semitic or even mulatto. The sun had burned him over the years into a bronze-red colour and bleached the hair to a steel grey.

It gets more and more curious, mused Ssempa, still contented with his twenty-five green dollar bills.

They drove back to Kabare and this time found an ochre-yellow Tatra truck with COBAZAIRE stenciled in black letters. It was a compact, short-chassis, heavy-duty vehicle meant for the sort of terrain on which it was found. Its driver was a half caste man with a complexion the colour of the truck. Theoneste, the Munyarwanda soldier, sat in the truck with his well-concealed pistol and they started off on the homebound journey. Towards dawn, Ssempa's Combi brought up the rear of the convoy moving across the mountainous pass back to Butare.

* * *

They arrived in Kigali at five o'clock the following morning, having traveled slowly. The cargo carried by the truck was so heavy tyres burst twice and the good tyres were flattened on the rough murram. Ssempa could think of nothing but a cargo of gold. He had never driven so slowly.

The reverend was dropped off at the Hotel de Kiyovu on Avenue de Rusumo. His metal luggage remained in the van. At Hotel MDR Sorrozo and the soldier carried the two small but heavy metal containers to the Peugeot coupe. Gold or what, Ssempa wondered. It had to be a different mineral even if it were to turn out that Laban Sorrozo was the adopted son of a Kuwaiti oil sheikh rotting with riches. But what of the tyre-bursting cargo in the Tatra truck?

Sorrozo's voice shook him from his puzzlement.

"You go home and have some rest, my friend." Sorrozo appeared as fresh as if he had not been on the same trip. "You must be exhausted. Check on me at midday, after you have rested sufficiently. Here — Rwanda francs. Do not touch your dollars, my dear Mr David."

At a few minutes to nine, when Ssempa had slept for less than three hours, someone knocked at his hotel door. Theoneste, the soldier in civilian garb, said, "Monsieur Sorrozo desires you at L'Hotel *Em De Er*. The wife is very ill."

At the MDR, Ssempa was directed into the spacious bedroom of Sorrozo's suite to find a seriously ill Zainab moaning in fearful agony. Said Sorrozo: "We are taking her to the clinic. And I do not have my car with me. We must hurry. She seems to get worse instead of better."

"What's the real trouble with her, Monsieur Sorrozo?"

"It is the climate," Sorrozo waved his huge hand dismissively, smacking his lips. He added, "Rwandan weather has not been kind to my poor wife. I am very disillusioned my friend, Mr David. She began complaining of it the moment we crossed the border at Akanyaru and despite all the medication we've provided her, she gets worse."

Ssempa's mind was busy imagining the other Munyankore wife now buried under the fiery sands of the Arab world; a world, of endless dry desert and straggly clusters of sagging coconut trees.

They took her to a large manour house, which happened to be a nursing home, on Rue Depute Kajangwe. 'Dr. Qeshmi Elburz', was enameled in white capitals on the green signpost. The qualifications of his associate, Dr Dominique Kabeya Ebende, stretched nearly a yard across the signpost. Sorrozo went into the private building, leaving the wife half lying, half leaning, with her back against the door in the middle seat. Ssempa glanced once at the sick woman and went back to playing a tattoo on his teeth with a ball pen.

"You think I am dead yet?" She surprised him. Ssempa had thought the woman too sick to be conscious. He looked at her open-mouthed. "It is their tablets. They aggravate my illness and it is deliberate. When I don't get them quickly enough I scream for those tablets. I am already mad, Ssempa. And I am going in there; I wonder if it is not the very place where my matrimonial predecessor died. I know I shan't come out alive. We women, my dear friend, will perish because of money. My love of money has killed me." Her sob struck straight at Ssempa's heart.

She was leaning on an elbow, her long, supple limbs bent upward at the knees, her eyes bloodshot. Dark smudges had appeared overnight beneath her lower eyelids. Her once seemingly glazed skin was ashen and her straightened hair was tousled with pulling and scratching. Ssempa wondered about the truth in her suspicions.

"I will watch things. I won't let them harm you." He merely wanted to ease her mind, to reduce her paranoia. "As long as I am not sent away on some errand."

Her face did not hide her doubt of his word. She said: "I know you think I am schizophrenic. I am not. Did you by any chance get to meet a French priest where you went — in Bukavu?"

Ssempa became more attentive: "We stopped in Bukavu, a few miles away on the way to Kamanyola. And we picked up a priest from the roadside in the middle of nowhere there. I could not tell he was French. He must be in the Hotel de Kiyovu still. That is where we left him."

"And a truck — is it not here, this place?"

"I wouldn't know. But we brought one with us to Kigali."

"So their mission is ripe. He is the Reverend Honoré d'Aubervilliers. But he is no Frenchman, really. He is an Arab from North Africa. Tangier, I believe. A Christian Arab of sorts. He owns a church in *Province* Kivu — somewhere. Have you ever heard of the term yellowcake?"

Now Ssempa became doubtful. Zainab Illeh was a very sick woman.

"Well, have you, Ssempa?"

"Zainab, all the cakes I have eaten are always yellow, you would agree, wouldn't you?"

"If Laban heard you mention the word *cake* now, you would know from his violent reaction that I don't rave from my illness. It is what the colonel and the captain you saw at the hotel the other day, and Laban, deal in. The Reverend d'Aubervilliers procures it for them from Provence Katanga."

"Is it a sort of food product?"

Zainab laughed, with effort. "A sort of food? — Be serious for once, Ssempa."

"Well, do you yourself know what these yellow cakes are?"

"It is a mineral. I haven't seen it, but I know it is not stuff you eat."

"I guess it should mean gold. Gold is yellow."

"The gold trade is not secretive in these parts of the world, not in Rwanda or Zaire anyway. And there is a laboratory of sorts in this manour house for processing the thing called yellowcake. I've heard them talk of centrifuges and...."

Ssempa said sharply: "Sorrozo is coming. Lie down."

When he got to the van, Sorrozo opened the door and asked her with profound delicacy whether they ought to bring out a stretcher. But she said she could walk, with his help.

"Ah, Mr David," said the giant. "You can now go for your interrupted siesta. My car will be here in a minute and I will handle my wife myself. She will be all right. Do not leave your hotel, please. You never know I might require your services at short notice. You have money, I am sure, Mr David."

"I am quite okay, thank you." The francs he had received in the morning were the equivalent of ten dollars. "I will be at La Vedette up to midday. Then I will go for my rest."

"You *need* to rest, my friend. You need to rest soundly if you have to drive. *A bientôt.*"

At the entry into the drive to the nursing home Ssempa braked hard to avoid hitting the speeding Peugeot 504 coupé coming in. At its wheel was the Reverend Honoré d'Aubervilliers, with Madame Thaid, the Iranian pharmaceuticals trader he had seen at the Hotel MDR four days previously. That was when he started worrying seriously about Zainab. That was when he gave the word *yellowcake* serious thought.

Yellowcake!

He went to Hotel Moderne where his friends Majuto and Tembo, who had schooled with him in Kampala in sixty-eight, procured a cheap phone. He called his jack-of-all-trades and have-read-it-all friend, Prince Eneriko Kayima.

"Yellowcake?" the man asked. "What are you into these days, David. Has somebody contracted you to build them a nuclear bomb?"

"Let us be serious, Eneriko. I am in Kigali, and in this Francophone country some woman just mentioned the thing in English. Ninety-nine percent cakes I've eaten all tend to be yellow. But this dying woman...."

"Dying! Radiation?"

"Nonsense Eneriko; it's just a nasty headache and...."

"Could be radiation too, if she has played around with yellowcake. I don't know exactly how radiation kills but...."

"Look here, Eneriko, just what the shit is yellowcake? She hasn't eaten any all the time we have...."

"Yellowcake is stuff midway between raw pitchblende, mostly radium that is, and enriched uranium. If you had said you were in Likasi, in Zaire instead of Kigali, I'd warn you to start running as fast as your legs could carry you. The country is a bulk producer of the mineral and supplied the stuff that did it for the Japanese in Hiroshima and Nagasaki in 1945. It is the god-damnedest radioactive substance other than processed plutonium. You never get to know what hit you is its major problem."

"You are saying that yellowcake has something to do with uranium!"

"With nuclear energy and, by extension, nukes. Yellowcake, is a uranium concentrate; an oxide of uranium ready for an enriching plant where it is converted into uranium dioxide. Very dangerous stuff that. It is afterwards compressed into cylindrical pellets and stored for moving in hollow rods of zirconium. Are you still there?"

"Thank you, Eneriko," Ssempa said. "Are you reading all that from a book?"

"If Makerere University ever starts up a nuclear studies program, I intend to apply for a job there as chief tutor. All stuff right here, in my cranium," Ssempa could imagine the prince braggingly knocking at the side of his bespectacled head with the knuckles of his fist.

"They accept two-degree-holder lecturers for assistant lecturer posts there, I am told, you braggart. You don't possess a diploma in anything, Eneriko."

"But you consult me on all nature of things. Am I not the one who enlightened you about the precious stone in the heads of bald-pated men and the rats' teeth from which they manufacture...?"

"Thanks a lot, Eneriko." Ssempa hung up.

He ate lunch at the Hotel Moderne while awaiting Monsieur Gakinya. When he appeared, the Munyarwanda claimed he did not have much time and was required to be close to his place of work, and thus Ssempa drove back up the Boulevard de la Revolution, past Hotel Internationale, and parked outside

Kigali Hospital, a short distance from the central army barracks. As he parked the van, a blue Volkswagen Beetle shot out of the barracks' main quarterguard and sped past them. At the wheel was Colonel Habyara, and his passengers were Capitane Ndize, Madame Thaid and Father Honore d'Aubervilliers. They were crowded in the car; it seemed because of their bulky sizes. It reminded Ssempa of a scene from a Charlie Chaplin movie.

He turned to Sinzagaya and asked with mock shock, "You know them, of course, don't you, Issa?"

Gakinya's unlaughing eyes studied the Muganda a moment. He then sighed and said: 'Everybody in Kigali knows the colonel and the *capitaine*. Everybody *particularly* knows the *capitaine*."

"And the other two in the car?"

"The other what? Ah, I did not see any other two in the car, my friend, Muganda."

"Really? How odd!"

"Those things happen, you know. My eyes fail me as I get older, my friend. It will happen to you too in the long run."

"Really? Well, I am not happy with you, my brother Sinzagaya. You gave me a rotten deal. I don't know why, my brother."

"*Mais pourquoi* — why do you call it rotten?"

"You yourself can answer that. Do you know of any Dr Qeshmi Elburz's clinic?"

"No."

"You don't even know of any Dr Qeshmi Elburz?"

"No."

"And Dr Dominique Kabeya Ebende?"

"Never heard of such names before. What of them?"

"Just like you did not see the two light-skinned passengers of Colonel Habyara! Look, I was at Dr Qeshmi Elburz's off the Rue Depute Kajangwe, early this morning. That is where I took the woman — Mrs Laban Sorrozo."

"She wasn't ill, was she?"

So Gakinya knew even more than Ssempa had thought! His deliberately silly denials were meant to get Ssempa off his back.

"That woman believes she is going to be murdered in that clinic. And I happen to believe her. And I'm helpless in the matter. Why did you decline this Sorrozo deal with so much money being paid? He didn't want to pay in dollars? Give me a break, Sinzagaya. The man does not care for dollars."

Gakinya turned his body round to lean against the van's door, removed the flat cap from his bald pate and used it to dab at its sweaty smoothness. He looked straight at the Ugandan. "You must not be sentimental in these things, Muganda. Do not romanticize. Make money, get out after getting paid the whole package and cease to think of it. Don't discuss Sorrozo's business, his person or his associates, not even with me. And do not attempt to pull out now. It is too late for you."

"Too *late* for me for what?"

"I said to pull out; it is quite dangerous. They don't know that you don't know *too* much already. And any much is too much. Monsieur Sorrozo was praising you for your tight mouth just this morning after you returned from Bukavu. I can guarantee you that once you've taken him across the border, you are as safe as if you had never met him."

"Oh, shit, Sinzagaya, you could have been straight with me from the beginning. What happened to his other wife? — Tell me."

"She died. Migraine headaches. General malaise. And Dr Elburz operated on her."

"I don't understand...."

"Do not my dear brother attempt to understand these things. The less you understand them the better for you and everybody else."

"You said once I've taken him across the border: border to where, Sinzagaya? Back to Bukavu?"

"To Uganda. To Kampala and Entebbe Airport. That is where I took the wife's corpse anyway. Laban Sorrozo is a Kuwaiti."

"To Uganda! Ohhh... what have you done to me? You are not a friend. You could have been fairer to me, Sinzagaya. Don't you know of my troubles back in my country?"

"Fairer? Fairer how? This could be a financial break for you. Your Ugandan friends should have forgotten all about you by now, anyway. Look, you have already been paid two hundred and fifty dollars. You might get an additional one grand. Do not doubt me, please. And future gifts, too. He gave me much less, mark you. There is more money in this than you might make in several years, Muganda. I didn't want to give somebody else to Sorrozo when you were there and could use the cash. You ought to thank me one day."

"Thank you, you bloody idiot! I am pulling out immediately. I hadn't bargained for... for driving your friend to Uganda."

"Hey, hey, hey, don't even consider thinking of it. You cannot hide from them anywhere on this continent. Maybe in America — but not even on the European continent. They have associates all over the place. Finish your contract and vamoose to wherever you want. That is what I did myself. I built myself that house you came to the other night and two more in Nyabisindu, where my other wives live. No regrets. You don't have to like or even live here. I don't like it either, but it is my country. You are more fortunate because if you feel hurt by this deal, at least you won't be meeting Habyara and Ndize — and those Persians — I will. Sorrozo has friends in high places in Uganda, but he does not operate there. Get your money and vamoose, I say."

Ssempa's shock was overwhelming as his face depicted it. He shook his head as though to clear it of fuzziness and asked Gakinya: "If what I am thinking about this fellow Laban Sorrozo is so, can there be a worse man on earth?"

"Eh!" Gakinya exclaimed. "You haven't seen really bad men, Muganda. Just imagine if you had God's ability to look at every living thing on this planet. Stand up there in the heavens and place earth at your feet and look at all the thoughts and the deeds of humanity and single out the worst ever human. Simply imagine the worst of them all, Muganda. Go through a street in New Delhi, a housing area in Los Angeles or a government boardroom in Washington D.C., any area of Moscow, Cape Town, Ankara, Tegucigalpa, any place on earth. What would such a man be capable of? Firstly such a person must be on the move constantly, doing evil deeds throughout, which is not what we see Sorrozo doing all of his living moments. Remember his tears over all those gone actors? But let us look at our other man in any of the cities I just mentioned; it could even be a woman, you know. Does he walk about with a knife, a gun, a rope, some grenades, thumbscrews, acid, arsenic, and perhaps much more and worse? He must have untold malice and spite in his heart, sick to the brain with evil, selfish, haughty. He must pretend kindness and at the same time fake illness when healthy and health when he is sick. When he smiles nicely, he is busy twirling a jagged blade or a chisel in the bowels of a baby. Is such a person in Britain, in China, Colombia, in Rhodesia? Where? That man is everywhere, Muganda. Think of my friend Juma Kasimbi, whom we met last month in Bujumbura, the man who was arrested by the antifraud squad in Mombasa with fake gold and fake cocaine. He was so cunning he bribed his way out, of course. The antifraud cops were arrested the same evening for passing around foolproof forgeries of hundred-bill Kenyan notes gotten from Kasimbi! This same Kasimbi later helped redeem the fellows from gaol by bribing the magistrate with dollars that the honourable member of the judiciary was embarrassed with in the duty-free supermarket. I tell you, Muganda, you have not seen an evil enough human being. You probably will die before meeting one, believe you me."

Issa Sinzagaya Gakinya jammed the flat cap back to cover his pate and jumped out of the van. "See you later when you are much richer." His words were accompanied by an idiotic grin.

* * *

At a few minutes to three, Laban Sorrozo found Ssempa at La Vedette and gave him the sad news. His eyes were teary and bloodshot and his pitch-black face was covered in sweat and was evidently stricken with grief. He pulled continuously on his thin Gitanes cigarette and dabbed at his forehead and the back of his thick neck with a blue handkerchief. His weeping fits were on and off, in a high-pitched but hushed voice, which faltered and got stuck completely at times. Had Ssempa not talked with Gakinya, tears would have sprung from his own eyes in sympathy for the man.

"Zainab has left me, Mr David," Sorrozo cried, hoarsely. "She has stabbed me in the back. No warning at all. Why not warn me? Did she look to you like the person to die, David? Why me — oh, God! — Why me?"

Ssempa looked back at him in silence, a gigantic hand of restraint holding him back from patting the Kuwaiti African with compassion, his own face registering genuine grief for Zainab Illeh Sorrozo.

"I cannot allow the body of my darling wife to decompose in this hellhole of a town. I have worked out the papers. We are taking her to Kuwait. You'll have to drive me to Entebbe Airport. Do you have any problems with the Ugandan authorities?"

Ssempa was tempted to answer in the affirmative. His tongue kept the word yellowcake at its tip. Why should he not ask the giant what he did with his wives. But he knew the big man would immediately alert his military friends and in a few minutes the Muganda would be no more. And as for telling him about his fears about going to Uganda, Ssempa was sure the fellow would insist he had the new military chaps under Idi Amin in his breast pocket. Moreover, he was curious to see how it would all end. He had the letter to Zainab's mother and he knew he would need to provide details when he delivered it.

"I have no problems in Uganda," he lied. "But why not depart from Kanombe International Airport, here in Kigali? — Entebbe is some three hundred and twenty miles and as you know, there is a military government now in my country."

"I know, I know," the giant patted his shoulder. "I know nearly all of those chaps right from the top. But at Kanombe there are Frenchmen in charge of airport control and security. Never attempt to bribe people working under the French, David. They don't rule over a people before assimilating them. Will you drive me, my friend? To Uganda, I mean."

"Our original deal...."

"Ah, I know. Here, another deposit. The other half when we get to Entebbe. You ought to have a wife to whom you can entrust your money. I don't like to travel with such cash on me."

"Five hundred dollars! And another five when...."

"Yes. When we get to Entebbe. My father, the sheikh who adopted me from Senegal, owns several oil wells. Ah, Mr David, do not think of the well where your sisters fetch water with earthen pots balanced on their heads. And do not doubt my word, I did love my wife more than anything in this world."

"I have not doubted your love for your Zainab. I witnessed it at close quarters. When do you want us...?"

"Right away of course, Mr David. I want you to drive to the clinic and park the van where the good Doctor Ebende will show you. The orderlies will then lift in the coffin."

So, mused Ssempa, the chief purpose for the hiring of the van was at hand at last. Any vehicle other than the Combi would have done the Bukavu-Kamanyola trip.

"A coffin! Your wife hadn't converted to your religion?"

"How can you say that of my Zainab? She was a Muslim even before we met. Ah, only foolish Muslims in these parts of Africa turn the Qur'anic teachings upside down — out of sheer ignorance, obviously. Otherwise, Mr David, Islam is the religion, the lifestyle to live. The sharia tells us to inter our loved ones in the cheapest materials available. You don't go in for gold and platinum coffins; see. But what, tell me, is cheaper than wood in Africa. Why, it is cheaper than some of the cloth in which I've seen people bury their dead. In Arabia, where there are no trees for timber, we bury our dead in modern coffins. But we delay with argument. I want to catch the midnight Air-Zaire flight from Kinshasa to Entebbe, which flies to Paris and Brussels via Jeddah."

"You can take any other airline from...."

"On the other airlines I don't have friends like I do in Air-Zaire."

* * *

They left Kigali at a few minutes past seven, when it had darkened and the glittery signal-red lights of the Radio Deutschwelle relay station were brightening up to the north of the city. They took the Kagitumba-via-Rwamagana route, but instead of heading for Mirama Hill, they branched off at Kamagiri, to go through Nyagatare and Kamwezi, where they crossed the border under a slow drizzle. Ssempa used his wipers only when the rain drops fully covered the windscreen. At Muhanga, Sorrozo took over the wheel. It was obvious Ssempa was dog-tired, having refused to sleep during the day, and had caught himself falling asleep at the wheel more than once. In the back of the Combi where the seats had been folded to face down, Zainab Illeh rested in oblivion in the tightly nailed, highly polished mahogany coffin.

Ssempa was dreaming of an immense mine with extremely high yellow walls and a yellowish vapour suspended over Algerians and Kuwaitis wearing white dog collars and shoveling away at yellow earth onto yellow trolleys. A large extraction fan in an abysmal hollow howled like the faulty engine of a car and blew cold air in his face as he tried to swallow the beautiful but tasteless yellowcake that the fat Madame Thaid, also wearing a white dog collar, was stuffing into his mouth. Then Sorrozo appeared and pushed away Madame Thaid — who had now become an emaciated Zainab Illeh. Annoyed that the cake was becoming contaminated, Sorrozo shouted at them in Arabic, his voice swaying the whole mine from side to side like there was an earthquake.

Ssempa was awakened from his nap by Sorrozo's staccato swearing in Arabic. And as he opened his eyes, he noted that some fool had parked a long vehicle — a white Peugeot 404 estate car, as he would realise the next day — across the road just a mile before Rwentobo Trading Centre: the standard highway robbery tactic. But robbers ambushed you at a spot where the road offered them a natural obstacle — a ditch or a pothole or even a small rise where the victim motorist would have to slow down to change gears. But this was a smooth black strip of tarmac road built five years previously by the Israelis, and it sloped towards the awkwardly parked white car. The ambushers, it occurred to Ssempa, did not care what happened either to their Peugeot or the oncoming van. He was beginning to appreciate the length of a Peugeot 404 station wagon when he noticed several other vehicles behind the oddly parked car and a dark red Range Rover on the grass kerb. He was also thinking that had he been at the wheel, even at that speed — the speedometer had been licking the ninety-five mile mark — he would have avoided the crash. And, of course, he would realise much later — he would have died instead. He would, very strictly, have relied on clutch and gear lever. He would never have touched those brakes in such a drizzle for the life of him. He was now quite fully awake.

He would always remember Monsieur Laban Sorrozo's high-pitched lamentations in Kiswahili, Arabic and English — and other languages too: "Ambush, Mr David — ambush. Nobody told me... *ya rabbi mungu....*" He went on in that staccato prayer mixed with curses and swear words. He touched the brakes and the van lost traction on the wet tarmac. It skidded erratically. The coffin shifted and banged into the panel that separated the cabin from the back jarring Ssempa's spine. They hit the long Peugeot sideways and the van seemed to spin in the air. Even so Ssempa managed to see two very light faces and other dark figures in military garb gathered a safe distance from the Peugeot. He would never know what happened to his door... he might have touched its handle subconsciously. He fell out. He knew he was dead because he felt a fluid flowing coldly out of his clothes. The chill of that flow helped him remain conscious.

He realised that the van was lying on top of him. The reason he wasn't flattened under its weight was a concrete gully in which he had fallen. He could see nothing, but he heard everything with great clarity. As he lay beneath his van its insides were savagely ripped out. The fuel tank was hacked out with axes and hammered chisels and split open. Several people heaved the coffin out and threw out the dead body at someone's order, given in English. Then all the tyres were shredded, including the spare one. The Kiswahili they used was Uganda Army, the English Ugandan and Middle Eastern — Arabian or Israeli, with strong rolled r's, fluid l's and soft but abrupt syllabic endings. Ssempa had the presence of mind to wonder that in the past four days alone he had encountered too many foreigners from around that same zone: Algerian, Kuwaiti, Iranian and now Arab or Israeli! After sighs and comments of frustration, a voice said in English: "One-hundred-twenty-eight thousand American dollars, fifty-two thousand in traveler's cheques — all are American Express. Three thousand mint-new British pounds, in fifties-bills. There are also seventy thousand Saudi Arabian riyals in travelers' cheques, and about... nearly one kilograms of raw gold granule. Have you noted all that, Zvi?"

"Yes, sir."

"Our information was correct. Only slightly exaggerated because someone badly wanted to bring in Tel Aviv, of course."

So they were Israeli, mused Ssempa from his tomb.

"But there was supposed to be another man, the owner of the Volkswagen. We haven't made a search for his whereabouts. He could have jumped out... somewhere up the road."

"The thug could even be under the van, you never know. Get me that flashlight; let me see...."

Heavy boots treaded towards one end of the wrecked vehicle. Ssempa could not see him though he heard the strained breath of someone getting to his knees. "I seem to see some.... Let's see... it would have to be a daredevil of a man to be under there, anyway. The place is a small river."

After another minute the man heaved a sigh as he straightened up, beating his palms together to remove dirt.

"You like to waste time, my dear friends," said the Mid-Eastern voice. "There is not a chance in a million, Zvi. Remember we were also told the Ugandan element was meant to be gotten rid of, permanently, inside Rwanda. That's where he will be, poor devil. The brute *himself* was driving."

"Uh hum. What do we do with the stuff then? — Not our kettle of fish, eh, Lev?"

"Hand it over to Paul Owilli's bureau after Ben Gurr has seen everything. I know what will happen to it in the hands of Military Intelligence afterwards, eh Hassani? I already see you demanding a bigger share of the stuff here."

There was soft laughter.

"Be serious, Lev. Do you see your friend Owilli sharing it with anybody? After your Colonel Gurr has seen it, return it to me at brigade intelligence in Mbarara. I will know what to retain in the office as *exhibits* for Owilli. I had wanted to get hold of that Muganda man. Must be an enemy of the state or else what has he been doing in Rwanda all that time we've been informed he has lived there?"

"Never mind, Hassani. Hemed did him in for you somewhere there."

"And these stiffs?" Zvi's voice queried.

"She was big, and heavy too, probably with child. Both Hemed and the woman are Hassani's business. Me, I want the Peugeot loaded onto a lorry. Colonel Gurr will want to assess the damage."

"Assess the damage! You deem it necessary? Your 404 is a complete write-off."

"Yes, Hassani. We do things differently than you in our departments."

"Hemed and his woman and their stolen van will be found by the first taxis in the morning. Accidents are not such rare occurrences at this spot," Hassani said. "We'll leave it the way it is."

"Not with ripped out tank and shredded tyres. Be serious Hassani. We'll set everything on fire."

"Maybe the vandalized van," Hassani said. "My religion bars me from setting fire to human beings. I am neither Hindu nor Buddhist."

"I wouldn't be in for burning this woman myself," said Lev's voice. "She must have been a beautiful African queen. But the giant's body cannot be easily disentangled from the aluminium and steel mess. Most of *him* is beneath the wrecked engine."

"You Jews don't burn your dead either."

"We don't. Not if there is a better choice. I always remind you there are bigger similarities between Islam and my religion than there are between Christianity and us. The Romans had too much of their own cultural influences to add to the latter to render the thing unrecognizable to a Yid like myself. But about burning the brute... does it matter, really? I know it does not. I've been in your country for four years now. Never seen a single serious autopsy carried out for investigative purposes. In this desolate savannah, hyenas may finish the job for you on the woman before daybreak. That is a near certainty."

Hassani's voice ordered the lorry brought up and the Peugeot lifted into it. Hassani wanted it burnt too, but both Lev and Zvi were adamantly against it. "This is our vehicle, not yours. I don't like answering to Colonel Ben Gurr for failing to convey to him his damaged office tool for his own assessment."

While the soldiers hoisted the Peugeot station wagon onto the three-tonner army Bedford, Ssempa crawled from beneath his damaged van and made his way along the narrow concrete gully with its rushing rain water, which he had mistaken for his own blood, until he was a good hundred or so yards up the roadside. Several minutes later, he saw the Combi go up in flames. And then, exhausted, he slept. But it could not have been for long. He awakened at dawn, chilled to the bone and aching in every joint of his body.

The first vehicle to appear on the scene did not come from either side of the highway. It came first as a sound from the grassy savannah opposite where he crouched. There Ssempa saw two grooves left by four-wheeled vehicles. A dark blue Toyota Stout-2000 pickup, emerged from the grassy track as if from beneath the earth and nosed onto the highway. A light-skinned, fat-cheeked man with a Muslim skullcap jammed on his head and a smouldering cigarette clamped between his teeth drove the pickup. At the back of the vehicle were a number of men and several male youths of various ages. They all jumped down to view the scene of mayhem when the vehicle came to a stop. Ssempa, seeing no immediate danger, got up stiffly from his place of hiding and limped over. He knew the man, a Tanzanian immigrant's descendant. And the man, a Hajji Yakaa, knew him too. Rwentobo was the most conveniently un-patrolled gateway to Rwanda through Runara and Kamwezi to Nyagatare and Gabiro. And the hajji had been in trouble with the police and the military on several occasions for allegedly being in charge of those smuggling routes. The hajji was an old friend of his father.

"*Ya rabbil'alamiina,* son of Ssemaganda, what happened to you? The last I saw of you, you were pursuing a course in motor vehicle mechanics, in Masaka I believe, not so?"

"Yes. I finished that course and got a job as a driver in Kampala."

"This was your vehicle, eh?" The short fat hajji queried in his hoarse, breathless, heavy smoker's voice.

"No, it was his." Ssempa indicated the charred corpse of Laban Sorrozo. "He was driving."

"But the curfew! Where were you headed at such ungodly time? I thought I heard noises in the night. Singing of sorts, you know. And I thought it was ghosts of Bacweezi herders lighting bonfires and whistling to their ghost cattle as they graze."

He had heard the singing, of course, thought Ssempa. The soldiers had chanted obscenely as they heaved and pushed the Peugeot carcass onto the truck.

"Well, the fire burnt the van. We were attempting to beat the curfew and this is the result."

"Can we be of any help then? These people were Christian?"

"The man was a Muslim, I am sure. The woman, Zainab, was his wife."

"Aah, we could not leave a Muslim's body by the roadside. We cannot help the man immediately, of course. Islam requires a prompt burial. You think it okay, don't you, son of Ssemaganda? If their families don't like it, they can always come and exhume her."

"They are foreigners. The woman is Sudanese," he lied. He was still scheming a way out of Uganda, back into Rwanda, whose frontier was quite near. Anything could happen at any time. The Ugandan Military Intelligence and its Mossad colleagues of the previous night could come in to make further inquiries; they could remember a thing they had forgotten at the scene, or get information they had not gotten before about Laban Sorrozo. "She was a daughter of a mullah in Juba."

"Save your breath. We will put off the fieldwork for today. We were out to fence off a piece of pastureland I purchased recently. But that can wait another day. Duty to the dead first. Young men, hurry to the job."

From the roadside the land fell away steeply to the south, towards the border, less than half a dozen miles away. Rwentobo is a cattle-grazing zone with nomadic people who prefer to stay away from the roadside. The trading centre was made up of three or four iron-roofed shops with walls of mud coated with grey lime. There was a regular Wednesday cattle market, which gave the place an economic importance. The desolateness was probably why the Uganda Army and its Israeli counterparts had nominated it for its deadly ambush.

From his homestead deep in the hollow area of the valley, the hajji would have heard the singing of the soldiers as they loaded the vehicle onto the lorry — old people lie awake in the small hours in darkness; but even that singing would have been very faint. The homestead had some fine houses, all tin roofed, and a large cattle kraal where milking was still in progress in the crash paddocks. A grove of banana trees was interspersed with large oaks, papaw and avocado trees. Birds shrieked merrily at the risen sun, and dew droplets sparkled on every blade of the blue-green grasses.

The family made him warm with a huge enamel cupful of sugared milk and strong home-ground coffee served with hot roasted sweet potatoes with chalky, yellow insides that reminded Ssempa of his ante-tragedy dream. Fresh clothing from one of the sons of Hajji Yakaa was produced. He was given a place to lie down in the main house. "This is a son of my very good friend," the old man told his people. "You have to rest yourself young man. We'll do everything else ourselves."

Ssempa could not be more grateful. His mind shuttled between torpor and alertness brought on by the strong coffee. Should he walk, or get a lift, back to

Rwanda, or should he go to Kampala and lie low there? He still had his seven-hundred-and-fifty dollars in his hip pocket and could start off wonderfully in a new life. As he lay there contemplating his future, the hajji came to where he lay half awake. He held out a steel grey, tubular metal object the size of a standard police baton in circumference and half in length. Ssempa held out his hand and the old man placed it in his open palm. Ssempa dropped the thing immediately; involuntarily, following it with his eyes to where it had fallen with a heavy dull thud without rolling even a millimetre. He had never imagined that an object so small could weigh so heavily. His mind went back quickly to the Reverend Honore d'Aubervilliers in his greatcoat and his three Congolese men bent under the weight of the two metal containers he had brought out from God knew where! And to Eneriko Kayima's warning about processed pitchblende or radium, or whatever he had called it. He thought back to Zainab Illeh, whose letter the ditch water had partly destroyed and her hinting that there was a laboratory at Dr Qeshmi Elburz' nursing home for processing whatever stuff Sorrozo dealt in there! And he thought of the burnt-yellow compact truck belonging to the Zairian cobalt mining company that had laboured its way across the rough terrain above Bukavu with a tyre-bursting cargo. So that was it; Laban Sorrozo had been a uranium smuggler!

How very simple!

"Oh, my God, Hajji," he swore softly under his breath. "Where did you get the goddamned things from?"

"Don't you know that we Muslims don't bury the dead with the filth in them, son? The women that cleaned the dead wife of your friend found several of these inside her as they did the cleaning. She cannot have died in the accident of course, son. Why didn't you tell me?"

"Because you never asked. And I am really sick and tired of the whole thing. She was in a coffin, but the people that burnt the vehicle — Israelis and Uganda Army soldiers, must have burnt the coffin, somehow."

"Well, well, well. Didn't I tell you I heard singing? You'll tell me later. Your woman was well sewn up — from the back, along the spinal column, not at the stomach. And there is a thin but rigid plastic container in there. I have never seen such plastic before. It was packed in a woolen material where her entrails should have been; quite a number of these." The hajji bent down to pick the cylinder up.

"D-don't touch it again, sir. Oh, my God! What have I brought you? Hurry up and tell them not to touch the things."

"Why is that?"

His mind was engrossed with the image of Laban Sorrozo and the words of Eneriko Kayima on the telephone the previous afternoon. How simply, terribly simple! The amiable giant takes a beauty or two into Rwanda by road, makes his gentle way around, weeping sentimentally at movie scenes, and flies out a body... bodies actually, containing materials for a nuclear bomb!

He looked at the hajji with a painful expression: "Because they kill. They kill you through exposure to radiation. How many people have seen them?"

"Son; the washing of dead women is done by their fellow women only. The men are busy sinking the grave. Only my two wives and my big daughter have seen them so far." The hajji's hands had gone to his temples and his eyes looked around him in worry. "Why did I not drive on my way when I saw the burnt wreck and the blasted corpses? I am comfortable enough with my own troubles. I only stopped to give help to offspring of ibn'Adam. What do you want me to do?"

"I don't know, Hajji. This stuff might be safe. The grey metal looks like a foil covering the real dangerous substance. It is supposed to be yellow, I suspect, not like gold, but like the sulphur used on bad wounds, like some type of soap. But I am not even sure of that. It can be extremely deadly, and they call it yellowcake. I've never seen it myself. Actually, it might no longer be yellowcake. It could be an entirely different colour after advanced processing. It is used in making the type of bombs that were used in Japan during the Second World War."

"Hiroshima!"

"You've heard of it! This is the stuff. It is uranium midway processed, I believe. Whether safe or unsafe, go tell the women to desist from touching it. We'll get a spade and carry these two to join their own ilk inside Zainab Illeh and bury them together. I cannot rest now, though my whole body aches. I must share in your danger. And you must swear to yourself and swear your three women to secrecy. Otherwise, the Israelis and the Iranians may come to your doorstep. They will kill for this stuff. Any of them will kill to possess it and kill to keep it unknown. That is how bad I have been to you this godforsaken dawn, my dear Hajji."

"And Amin's soldiers? — They could return here to investigate things. They make all sorts of allegations against me every now and then. Of course it is because of my being Tanzanian. I've been taken to Simba Battalion barracks thrice already and the last time I spent nearly three months in their filthy cells. They want me dead, son of Ssemaganda."

"Their mission as far as the dead Hemed is concerned ended last night. You are safe from them, particularly if nobody ever mentions what you saw or did this morning."

* * *

A short while later, Idi Amin began expelling Israelis from Uganda. A few months later in July 1973, Major General Juvenal Habyarimana toppled the government of President Gregoire Kayibanda in Rwanda. But even then Ssempa would not sit comfortably in the southern part of Uganda or in Rwanda. He had gotten in touch with Issa Sinzagaya Gakinya through the post and later by telephone from Kampala. The Munyarwanda told Ssempa not to show himself in Kigali or Kampala until he had made sure no one was interested in him. He received addresses in Mombasa where he could live without disturbance for as long as he wished, and Ssempa accepted the idea gratefully. But he knew he would never renege on the pledge he had made to the late Zainab Illeh — to drop her letter to her mother.

A quiet search for the woman in Masaka's Kimanya area revealed that she was in northern Uganda, as the daughter had suspected. He later traced the ageing Zaituni Tazama Razak in Oraba, a border town at the northwestern tip of Uganda that stands at the meeting point of Uganda, Sudan and Congo-Zaire. At that time the town's main trade was in gold and illegal guns vended by ragtag soldiers of the Anyanya Revolution of General Joseph Lagu of southern Sudan in exchange for tea leaves from central Uganda. Oraba is thirty or so miles north of the regional town of Koboko, and about seventy north of Arua. The people of the area are Kakwa, the tribe of General Idi Amin. Most Kakwa live in Zaire. Zaituni Tazama, the mother of Zainab Illeh, had been married to the local chief, Razak Amin Illeh, distantly related to the general, and had bore him children before returning to her Baziba people in the north of Tanzania. Razak had more than twenty wives. He had sent emissaries to Masaka and northern Tanzania for the return of his favourite concubine, Zaituni Tazama, she of the Baziba tribe whose women were feared and abhorred by women of other tribes as bewitchers of and therefore thieves of husbands. Ssempa, on sojourning among the Kakwa people, found no discord in the Razak homestead. The various wives chatted with each other like they were sisters and bosom friends, devoted to just one man, Chief Razak Amin Illeh.

Razak himself, a large, tall man of fifty-six to sixty, was powerfully built like many men from his region. He had read his daughter's long missive, which was in English, spiced generously with Nubian words, and he thanked the Muganda man. The family, deep believers in Islam, attributed their daughter and son-in-law's demise to Allah and thanked the Creator with several *Alhamdu'lillahis*. They made a big *douwah* for the woman's soul and invited Ssempa to stay around. The old man reiterated Gakinya's advice for him not to return to Kigali or even to Mbarara until he was sure no one was looking for him. Idi Amin's regime was two years old and Razak, an ex King's African Rifles sergeant, who had brothers and sons in high positions in the Uganda Army, was being posted as administrator plenipotentiary in Mbarara, where there was a large Nubian community. The community wanted the new regime's power felt as the region was next to Tanzania, the country that had offered refuge to Milton Obote, whom Idi Amin had toppled from the state presidency. In leaving for the south, Chief Illeh left the large hides-and-skins concern he owned in Koboko town to Ssempa under a partnership arrangement reached after Ssempa had shown the old man some of his fortune in US dollars. The Muganda thus soon found himself living between Koboko and Arua, trading in *kitenge* cloth and high-heeled, Gabon or platform shoes, gold, mercury, petrol, tealeaf and even guns and ammunition in the three neighbouring countries. He lived in a Razak Illeh-owned house in Arua for a rental fee, and free of charge in the Koboko residence, where he was treated as part of the family. One of Illeh's daughters, Zakiya, a six-foot black amazon of a woman, had just completed a teacher-training course at a college in Lango and had come to Arua as she prepared for a job outside the teaching profession. Since the president was a son-of-the-soil, she would be assured of a well-paying job.

Even if it hadn't been for her glossy-skinned resemblance to the late Zainab Illeh, there would have been no way for her and Ssempa, to avoid an affair. They lived under the same roof in Anyafio, in the vicinity of Arua Hill. They shared several traits, read the same novelists and went to the movies together along with her brother Aliu Alimakodra, who encouraged the affair, because the Muganda occasionally gave him money. And they loved the booze, which Aliu Alimakodra, a staunch believer in Islamic values, disapproved of. She was soon pregnant with Ssempa's son and would not heed his exhortations to have an abortion. Her mother, a Congolese from Mahagi Port, threatened the Muganda with death if he did not wed her daughter. Ssempa denied responsibility for the pregnancy, because Zakiya had been known to date a customs official at Oraba. She confessed to the affair, but the girl's mother and Aliu Alimakodra insisted he was the culprit for he slept with her the most – on a *nightly* basis, as Alimakodra put it, and therefore it was not possible that the man his sister had slept with less than ten times could have impregnated her. This was silly but everybody else seemed to agree with the illogical notion. The Muganda fled to Mbarara, his hometown — from the frying pan into the fire, so to say, as Razak Illeh reigned supreme there as zone administrator, and was held in greater awe than the regional governor or the officer commanding the Uganda Army battalion quartered in Simba Barracks. Ssempa was arrested and Razak Illeh personally threatened to resurrect the Laban Sorrozo issue and 'extradite' the young man to Rwanda with a 'file.' But for some reason, Razak seemed to have lost interest in the quarrel over his daughter and got Ssempa released after a month in police custody. He did not follow up the matter as hotly as he had done before even though the powerful mother kept up the threat. By now Illeh was acquainted with Ssempa's father, Hajji Sulayman Ssemaganda, with whom they had served in the British King's African Rifles, on different fronts as Razak had been to Burma instead of North Africa. At a *maulid* called to inaugurate entry into an old house Ssemaganda had bought from the Forestry Department in Kaburangire, Razak Amin had told Ssempa in his father's presence: "You cannot deny your progeny forever, Daoudi. Your son resembles this father of yours to the smallest detail: fingernails, nose, forehead, feet — and I believe even penis. If it had not been for Sulayman, indeed, I swear to Allah by now you would be *khalas*." Razak slashed an index finger at a place below his triple chin. "You would be finish," he added in his English.

"I don't know it like that," said Ssempa, without the faintest show of bother. "My saviour is not you but poor Zainab's mother. If you touched my skin she would flay you like a dead goat, with her bare hands. It comforts me that you know it."

The time he had spent with the elderly veteran sergeant of the KAR in Koboko and Arua had taught Ssempa that the chief did not like people who attempted to ingratiate themselves to him or to any other person. He was a man who appreciated and respected boldness and bravery.

He laughed gruffly and said: "I'll not quarrel with you ever again. Why should I harm my son-in-law? Leave Tazama, my good wife alone; they claim she captured my soul and imprisoned it in a tree in northern Tanzania. One day I should go out on a quest for that tree — by Allah, I would never be forgiven if I were to be the slayer of my children's husbands and my grandchildren's parents. You are such a stupid man with the mind of a boy. Why don't you wed Zakiya and make a family? She is not so badly off, is she? I will watch you, of course; I would go mad if I ever heard of you two together again outside wedlock. Girls can be so foolish, you know!"

At that time Zakiya was a secretary of sorts, something to do with espionage, at the Ugandan embassy in Nairobi.

* * *

"So that was the genesis of my encounter with your uncle, the good Monsieur Sinzagaya Gakinya. I only returned to Rwanda at the end of last year; and even then it has been mostly a transit arrangement. Until yesterday I made it a point never to go into Kigali proper. I still wouldn't like to meet that colonel, who now heads intelligence."

205

Julian had listened to the tale most attentively, never interrupting. Ssempa had said nothing about Zakiya and her pregnancy out of consideration for her feelings as a woman and lover.

"Do you weep because of Zainab?"

She nodded: "It is your world. It is a world so full of greed, lies, betrayal and death. And I just became part of it! I only hope — I believe — that you are not as bad as them. You say you fear meeting with the intelligence colonel! Would it be okay meeting with Habyara then?"

"I am told Ndize is a most painstaking intelligence officer. I would hate to find myself answering his questions, especially questions concerning that uranium."

Julian looked at him keenly. "Yes, that uranium. I was wondering — is it still where you left it, do you think?"

"Yes, I think so. That old man is in prison — has been there for the past three years, over a smuggling charge."

"Poor fellow!" Julian rued. "And is the short Algerian priest you picked from Bukavu the Father Honoré d'Aubervilliers to whom we took the letter?"

"Yes. He indeed is."

"But you didn't see him yourself in Rue de Rusumo; how can you be so certain?"

"Ah... but when you took in the letter you confirmed it was a short old priest whom you couldn't associate with the French. And yet you heard Monsignor state he was Algerian, didn't you? Besides, there *cannot* be two Honoré d'Aubervillierses in this region."

"Who then can be any good if such a nice old padre cannot be a saint?"

"Father d'Aubervilliers a saint! They murdered Zainab Illeh, Julian. I was there. One day you should ask your uncle, Issa Sinzagaya, to describe to you the really worst person. There seems to be none. Indeed the worst person on the planet could be so in thought rather than deed. Even Adolf Hitler must have given his killer command reasons accepted as correct. Think of our lieutenant at the roadblock. I am convinced he intended to kill us after whatever crime he would have ended up committing. We as innocent as we were!"

Julian shivered involuntarily and they fell silent for several moments. It was late and cold. The hills to the west cast a deep gloom, a gloom accentuated by the large trees above and around them.

"You haven't told me one thing," said Julian. "Was Mr Sorrozo actually a Kuwaiti or Senegalese?"

"Why do you ask that, Julia? You give the impression you know what he actually was."

206

"He was a Munyarwanda, eh?"

"Yeah. Sinzagaya told me much later that Sorrozo was a Munyarwanda with a family in Nyamirambo — close to La Vedette. But quite a few people in Kigali knew that. Your uncle learned of it all at the funeral of the giant, which took place less than half a kilometer from his Nyamirambo home, imagine. Sorrozo had lived most of his life in Kinshasa and Abidjan. It's through Abidjan that he got such concrete connections with people of the Gulf States and the Middle East. I met his widow and children — quite a set of angels those — two years ago in Kigali."

She yawned and stretched herself out against him: "I am feeling sleepy."

"Let us go inside, then, honey. It is getting chilly, too."

"You have not told me why you were in Kigali in the first place. Even today you don't find many Ugandans in Rwanda. There is a huge divide between Banyarwanda and Ugandans because of the Anglophone-Francophone thing. Of course it would have been much different if you had met my uncle in Nairobi or Mombasa."

They looked at each other in the deepening gloom. He whispered into her ear: "You are tired, my dear. Let us go back inside as I said. It's getting cold out here."

"You are dodging my question, David. Why were you in Rwanda, eh?"

He still held her in his lap and he cupped her breasts in his hands. She stretched out her legs and body allowing him to pat the equally heavy, plump cupola of bulge at her groin, saying softly: "I've been wondering why a nun takes the time to shave her pubic hair, though I believe nuns are never short of time anyway. Besides, yours is like you use commercial hair removers."

She attempted to rise off him in protest but he kept her firmly in his grasp, preventing her from falling sideways.

"You think we have lots of time on our hands, do you? Far from it; we never have enough in the House to do all we are required to do. But at the same time we accomplish all that our Office requires of us. We — nuns I mean, tend to matters of hygiene. But I have never grown that devil hair there or under my armpits."

"Really! With so much thick hair on your head? It is not easy to believe that."

She tried to make out his eyes in the darkness. In a flash of reproof, she said, "You must believe what a nun tells you."

"Julia?" Ssempa spoke with a hurt solemnity. "I did not mean to doubt you. I am sorry. I must never doubt *you*, ever."

"Look; if you won't tell me now what you were doing in Rwanda in seventy-two you must promise you will tell me one day."

"All right," he told her with a doubtful look that she could not discern in the twilight. "I do promise. One day I'll tell you all about it."

Five

Kabale, Uganda, 1976

They spent the following day ensconced in their hut, chatting and playing in between passionate bouts of lovemaking. And all that time both worried about Monsignor Raphael Nyarwaya's reaction if he were to telephone Kyera Catholic Diocesan Headquarters, to find she had not arrived there. The nun wanted to call Father Honore d'Aubervilliers to get him to convey a message to her uncle about the troubles they had encountered. But there were snags. Kabale was not a big town and even if Ssempa was to acquire for her a set of plain clothes, she might be seen and recognized by anyone who had been at Gatuna in Rwanda or Katuna on the Uganda side of the border the night before last. They decided that since nobody had come to the hotel seeking suspicious characters, they should leave Kabale that very evening after dusk.

Ssempa went out once, after sunset that day, to gather news about the military checkpoint that he had destroyed. The general story in Kabale, the town of rusty iron-roofed shops and district administrative buildings that lay sprawled in the flat valley six hundred feet below the White Horse Inn to the south, was that over twenty soldiers had burnt themselves accidentally in an inferno while tampering with gasoline that they had siphoned out of commercial trucks in transit to Kigali and Bujumbura. The soldiers were said to have been habitual collaborators of smugglers of fuel, which they took into Rwanda through the hills of Rubaya and Kivuye, close to the official crossing point of Katuna. Petrol fires killing people, sometimes whole families, were not uncommon occurrences during Idi Amin's times of scarcity. To make a living and not starve, people would hoard the precious volatile liquids in plastic containers in their residences for sale to motorists in search of cheaper fuel. Soldiers procured such fuel by force from transit tankers and at times highway robbers hijacked the heavy trucks en route and emptied — or as they liked to say, 'milked' — them on lonely village paths. Even more commonly, drivers of government-owned motor vehicles, who got fuel straight from government-controlled pumps for official duties that were never carried out, would sell the gas to smugglers and other users. The rumours about the deaths of soldiers near Kamuganguzi were rife and varied in presentation. Other townsfolk talked of villagers having heard explosions like gunfire and bombs but were not sure what the blasts were as the rainstorm had been unusually heavy. The contents of the tent, Ssempa was heartened to hear, had been incinerated completely except for the shells of a Land Rover, empty tin drums and lanterns that must have been the main culprits for the fire. He wondered about the Land Rover's possible presence in the place. He had seen no such vehicle in the vicinity, no vehicle at all. But it perhaps had been parked at the back of the tent.

When he returned to their hut he found Julian at the terrazzo mantelshelf hot-pressing their garments. The sun was setting and it cast an even deeper red hue on things than it had had at dawn. It tinged everything it touched a deep-crimson shade. Outside on the western horizon, Ssempa imagined — just as he used to do during his adolescence — God was busy at the cooking pots, stoking the red ember of fireball against the huge logs, with smoke-induced tears streaming out of His eyes and women dressed like nuns and others like Muslim women in buibui garments, doting over their Husband. Sister Julian Kantarama's dark complexion was tinctured with that golden red tone that appeared to be infused in her skin and the thick curly strands of her unveiled hair. Her face even, seemed to glow crimson, like a bronze or terracotta sculpture pulsating with life. Her eyes, with that nearly impudent look, burned like rubies when she turned them to him. Ssempa felt a little shock go through him when he noticed the likeness of a wimple-like headdress in a lighter, golden carmine hue round her head. He blinked to affirm it wasn't an illusion, perhaps a trick of the setting sunlight. But it sure remained there, the spectre of a golden flame-red light which had developed round the upper part of her body from the shoulders like an aura, a halo. A halo on a sinner, he thought, appalled. He blinked several times so as to view the phenomenon even better.

"What is it? What are you staring at me like that for?" The sacs beneath her lower eyelids were more pronounced, lending an oriental appearance to her facial features, her mouth perhaps swollen, like a ripe red berry.

"There is... there was." He could not say it, for the halo had gone with her query, as if her calm voice had frightened it into flight. In its place there remained the big, tall, dark, long-legged Munyarwanda woman regarding him with that infectious mocking look in her gentle impala eyes. In his mind, the woman he had picked up at Gitarama the previous day would never again be Sister Julian Dominicus.

"What?" She cocked her head to one side, inquisitive, the short curly hair brushed and blown out by a fine-tooth comb. "What? You were staring at something about me. I saw your eyes."

"Nothing really."

"There was... that makes two unsaid things you need to tell me one day when you've decided, not so?"

He remembered his promise to explain his presence in Kigali in 72. "Yes, Julian."

"Will you always call me that?"

"I don't know. I wish it were Julia, or plain Kantarama."

"Then choose. But there was *what* about me? I am a woman remember. And a woman understands her man quickly."

"Your wouldn't know that, Julia."

"I would. I am a teacher. I teach biology in the mission secondary school at Kyera. So tell me what you saw."

"I don't know. I think you are an angel, Julia."

"Ah, you!" she said with mock contempt, taking the electric iron again. "Tell me something that I don't know already."

He took the iron from her and started to press the dusty brown habits.

"What are you thinking?" Julian asked, leaning against the doorframe, arms clasped about her bosom.

"Nothing, really," he told her.

"But you look so pensive. How was your news hunt? Are we going to be arrested?"

"No. We are safe. Their fellow soldiers seem to be laughing their heads off at those four. So are the traders in town. It appears our dear lieutenant of last night, his name was Manuel Musinzi, hadn't been very popular in Kabale."

"How is that?"

"It seems I extinguished a very nasty reputation in the area. Fortunately everybody believes they burnt themselves tampering with purloined petrol."

"So that means we leave for Mbarara tonight — nothing to stop us?"

"Yes. We leave for Mbarara at nightfall. That should be in two hours. I wouldn't want someone getting inquisitive about our shattered windscreen."

"Okay, I will get myself ready."

"Do, please. I am seeing Byangye to find out if there are any roadblocks on the eastern exit. If there are we shall take the longer route through Ntungamo-Rwashamaire via Kisiizi. I hope not because it would be more than twice longer."

"Oh, how I hope not, myself. I prefer entering the convent at a normal hour, now that I am so guilty."

"Please, do not say that again."

"About guilt?"

He nodded.

"I won't. I promise."

* * *

They arrived at Kyera at ten in the evening. When Ssempa stopped the pickup before the poorly lit red brick buildings, several of them three quarters of a century old, the woman touched his hand, holding it in her warm grasp.

"This is home," she said cheerfully, in a low voice. "Look at it, David. My home!"

"It's so... so secluded. So lonely."

"You wanted to say *eerie*."

"Not really...." he began to protest.

"It is, too. It is much beyond compline, when we all must be abed in our cells. I have lived here for close to eighteen years, except the period I was at college in Bwanda and Nkozi and in my teaching practice in Mt St Theresa's, Kisubi. I've delighted in my solitude here so long that I am lost thinking of alternatives. Right from here, the moment you see me enter that brick building, I am to be a true bride of God, serene, strict and austere in all I do. I practice custody of my eyes, mind and entire self. You know what that means, David? That I am going to miss you like crazy. I feel simply silly — and light-headed, and light-hearted at the same time you know. I am not permitted to speak like this, like a magpie. But that is what I have indulged in from the day I met you. And I am afraid my people will notice the change in me. I don't know how I will be able to hide my — restlessness. Sister Gerald will be the very first to notice it, of course. We teach together; did I tell you about her? Now I begin to see why the ecclesia enforced chastity and celibacy and all that go with the two. I feel simply idiotic."

She sounded to him like an adolescent school going girl chattering away to a lover on her very first date. Sister Julian Dominicus Kantarama, the man saw, had been reborn; reborn, at the very juncture she had broken away from the world to take up the unnatural life of the cloister.

"I don't suppose it will be easy for you, Julia," he said to her, having also noted her animation at the realization they were parting. "I am frightened of the workings of your existence, the way you have gotten me to view it. But I will always be waiting for you out here. I will always be there for you."

"Yes. But you don't understand. It is not simply a matter of seeing you from time to time. I want to be with you all the time. In lower school at Kabgaye *ecole primaire*, I used to see the girls, the worldly girls — bigger girls of course — restlessly move about over the boys. I did not laugh at them. I despised their trivial minds. It is silly that I can suffer their worries a whole two decades later. It is, I now know, a worse torment. It is the natural, *human* falling in love. I don't feel like I can let go of the feeling. My good Virgin Mary had always defended me from the agony of being worldly. But I am now in the thick of it; I am filled with the feeling that this is how it feels to be in purgatory, which is a kind of nowhereness. And its worst pain is that this is my home, that you must leave me, and that I won't be with you for all the moments of my unworldly life that I want to be with you. You, of course, must feel the same about me."

"Julia, I am a worldly creature. As you say, you are like a newborn infant to the world of humans who live outside the world in which you have been enwombed. I am not like you."

"Cruel words, but honest words. You will not abandon me in my purgatory, David?"

"Providence willing, I will guide you through the mundane life out there where I live with the likes of Lieutenant Manuel Musinzi and Corporal Bingwa. But I genuinely wish there was a more convenient way out of it for you, Julia. I hate myself for destroying your life — even if it is a life of such solitude, for you. And that destruction is bound to come in the long run, however discreet we shall be. I know how the world out there functions. It is a world of watchful people, of schemers, of rumourmongers. They never rest till they have discovered some skeleton in somebody's closet. If they are capable of inventing some skeletons to show to the eager watchers, what would they do with a closetful of genuine secrets?"

"The Mother of God schemed this; I did not. She must have means of disentangling me from its dangers and tribulations. Do you want to leave, David?"

"Yes. For if they should see us together in such tete à tete, your tribulations won't wait."

"Yes. So we must part, David."

"Your uncle knows how to say goodbye. He simply says *au revoir* — till we meet again."

"There is even a better way to release you from my hold: àbientot."

"You'll check at the garage the moment you get the opportunity, won't you?"

"Can you see me waiting for that opportunity? Seconds will become eons to me. Why do you shiver?"

"This place is not just eerie. It is spooky."

"Yes, I know. On moonlit nights from my cell, pale figures of priests and nuns in white soutanes and habits float among the roses and narcissuses towards our windows." Ssempa let fall his jaw, opening his eyes wide in mock panic. "Don't believe any of that, of course; we love to use it to frighten the toughest of us. We claim those figures are long dead founders of Kyera. But it is lonely now. I've never felt lonelier in my life! This Virigo Kabibi at your address, is she not Catholic?"

"Staunch."

"That is not very good. She could disapprove and start a bad rumour."

"She is not the type to do that. Sometimes I've thought she should have lived in such places as this. But she worships me. I am like her godfather."

"She is not your woman, David?"

"Virigo is old enough to be my mother. Wait till you've seen her. I inherited her from my father with the trade enterprises."

"I am becoming jealous, like the worldly women I have sometimes counselled! I am keeping you long and...."

"Someone could be watching," he finished for her. She had been bending to peer through the top of the space where the windscreen should have been, to view the front of the first-floor windows.

"You are picking at my mind again, serialising my thoughts."

"Can there be someone watching?" Ssempa asked, in genuine apprehension.

"I doubt it. But — yes, someone could be. God certainly is."

She attempted to embrace him but he drew back, hesitantly. He feared for her.

"Nobody is watching, silly. And God has been at it for quite a while now so that it ceases to matter. Hear me talk — oh, Virgin Mary!"

Her breasts heaved against his chest. He sought out her lips in the translucency of the night and munched at her softened mouth, eating at her tongue and at her teeth and her spittle. Mysteriously, his tongue loved to try to force itself into the small gap between her upper teeth and her mouth seemed to love it. They released each other without quenching their unholy hungers. He was engulfed by a powerful urge to drive the vehicle out of the grounds with her and never to bring her back. But as if she suspected his feelings, she opened the door, stepped out and closed it again, fleeing from him as it seemed.

"I could help with your valise."

She shook her head and said: "I don't want whoever is watching to see, to recognize you."

"Do you feel somebody *is* watching?" Ssempa asked, with urgency in his voice.

"Yes. Do you, too?"

"Yes. There is someone, someone somewhere."

She pressed his hand, giggled in a slightly high-pitched yet husky voice: "It is always God, you fool."

"Yes, God's and other eyes."

She opened her eyes wide in that humorous, theatrical way only persons from Francophone countries are able to muster. She said, very softly, "Goodbye, David," and, bending, picked up her valise and walked off to the steps without turning back to look at him in the semi-darkness. He engaged the gear, turned the vehicle round and turned on the lights. He drove down the pebbled slope through the yews and willow trees that lined the drive.

* * *

And the watcher left her perch at the high window beneath the gabled roof of the main building of the convent where she had sat for the past few hours in deep meditation and prayer, as she waited for the long expected arrival of Sister Julian Dominicus. She was flabbergasted by what she had just witnessed. At forty-three years of age, twenty-eight of those years in the service of The Father, Son, Holy Spirit and Mary Mother of God, she had witnessed and experienced much of the ungodly passionate love in the cloister and the cloth. When the prioress had summoned her to say a Monsignor Raphael had telephoned from Rwanda to enquire about Julian Dominicus' safe arrival, she did not think much of it.

Sister Prioress had said, "Reverend Superior wants you to come up together when Sister Julian arrives. Monsignor Raphael was worried about her. He is her uncle — as you know. Superior assured him she was safe. You would know whether she might have gone on to the farm at the river or even to Mabonwa Sanctuary, where she confers with her refugees. And it is you who will inform me when our sister arrives."

They were a set actually. They had been together at Sacred Heart Bwanda Major Tutorial and later on at St Maria-Goretti Trinity College, a Catholic teacher training school in Masaka, for two years. For another year, they had done their teaching practice at Mt St Theresa School, Kisubi, and were regarded as a team. They taught together at Sacred-Heart Hill Mixed Secondary School and, being teachers, freely interacted with the world outside the cloister. Being intellectuals, they enjoyed qualified access to The Marlorec, an exclusive Catholic clergy club in the swanky Kizunguni suburb of Mbarara town.

Sister Gerald Namazzi had fallen to sin three years previously, around the time the mission school procured exotic cattle from Galloway, Ireland, to start a livestock-farming project. The half-caste veterinarian, who was also the father to little Sheba Kavuyo, a favourite student of hers, had come in to demonstrate to them the best way to entice the two crossbreed bulls into mating with the exotic cows. It was the silliest way to get caught into the web of sin that she could think of. The veterinarian, a pencil-thin mustachioed man in his mid-forties, was an expert at his job and in three hours had coaxed the two bulls to inseminate all six heifers. She still felt silly whenever she thought back to the episode. They had entered the old small Fiat Matador lorry that had transported the bulls to the demonstration farm behind Kyera. She was crushed between Sister Remmy Shaw, sixty years, obese, with liver spots all over her hands and arms, and Jimmy Kavuyo, the vet. "You will have to edge in further away, Gerald," said the old Irishwoman, who had arranged for the bulls to be imported. "To create space. I have this spastic numbness in my hipbone that will become the devil of a pain from this pressure. We should have brought along that old Thames Trader truck; it has wider seats."

It was the wrong time for Gerald to sit with a male person and so pressed to him too. She had just come out of her menstrual period and that always left her hot and burning and uncomfortably funny, one of the handful of situations she had never managed to fight successfully. And now the act of coitus between the beasts had awakened a beast within her. Under the guidance of the wiry man now pressed against her, the heifers had, attempted to mount the brutes. Kavuyo had used his own hands to incite sexual arousal. As they rode along the rutted path from the farm, the lorry bucked, dipped and swayed. After several minutes of such driving, she realized her right elbow had all along been pressed into Kavuyo's lap. Consciousness of the man's stiff manhood caused her to jump.

"Do not fidget, please," cried the old nun. "My hip is on fire; I should have traveled in the back where I would stand upright. What do you think, James?"

"Not a good idea, Sister Remmy. It could dislocate your joints. They should grade this road."

The Fiat truck bucked on. Gerald had tried to keep her elbow away but it came back hitting at the hard thing again and again with the violent motions of the vehicle. She had stolen a glance at Kavuyo, quite convinced he was unconscious of what was happening. To her horror, she found his moustache crooked in a mischievous smile, showing a glint of tobacco-stained teeth. She pushed left, away from him, into Sister Remmy, who complained more vehemently about her hipbone. She had looked back at the driver, whose smile became devilishly broader. By the time they got to the convent, her elbow had brushed against Kavuyo's hardened body so much she thought of nothing but the hard, meaty phalluses of the two bulls back at the farm. At the gate to the House, the driver spoke to her in vernacular of which the Irishwoman knew very little.

"I want to get to know you more, Gerald," he had said, cautiously.

"You are the death of me, father of Sheba."

"I would kill you with utmost gentility."

"You've turned me into your bovine beasts and led me into wanting to ride you."

"Shall we be able to?"

"Yes. At the river farm."

"Thank you for not leaving me to suffer alone."

"If I had a way I would not let you near our farms, or let any of our people learn those skills from you."

"Cross my heart and hope to die, Gerald, it was not my intention."

"Lucifer sat with us."

"Not *her*, really," Kavuyo said with his mouth pointed at the old white woman going up the steps of the main building of the convent.

"No, Lucifer the real beast, the one with a tail. A hard tail. Greet Sheba and her mother. Get her to arrive at school promptly after vacation."

"When do we meet at the river farm?"

"I go there daily now that it is holidays. Tomorrow four o'clock I'll be there. Goodbye."

And it had started like that. And the very day she went to the farm by herself, they committed their sin together and afterwards she drove back to Kyera, a fat spoilt wench. That same evening after compline, Sister Julian said to her: "Ah la lah — Gerald, what has happened to you today? Your eyes are too soft. Your mouth is... is strange, and your face is too bright. What have you seen?"

Sister Gerald was shocked. Her heart took flight from its usual cradle into her mouth. Was it so evident that she had sinned? Of course it was. So now what? If Julian, so young, was able to discern it in her, and talk like God to Adam and Eve in the Evangel, what of the older ones?

"What have you done, Gerald?"

"Nothing; nothing, Julian that I can go to Father Confessor for. Maybe I should go to *penetencia* in seclusion. My dear Julian, do pray that what happened to me yesterday never befalls you."

"Yesterday? Yesterday you appeared normal. Today you look like you have seen the bird that contains the bolt of thunder in its wings."

Sister Gerald regarded the younger woman; Sister Julian was twenty-six or seven then. "What happened yesterday inevitably culminated into today." The older nun was impatient. She knew the younger nun knew she would not be the first or the only one to fall — if she were to discover the truth of her sin.

"And you won't go to Father Kajene to confess?"

"Julian," the fat Muganda woman told her emphatically, "you can only go to the confessor in my case to disgrace God. I've not committed sacrilege yet. But it is not like me to remain around here after confessing my present kind of sin; it should certainly reduce our numbers if we were to bend to the worse weaknesses — sin indeed, of lack of foresight, and the Church would consequently cease to be. Now — I've just known a human; I have just known a human in the naked flesh. And the human has known me. And I am tarnished. Just like, well, you know, like Sister Vito, except she is doing it with our brother of the cross; like Valerian, who is dating the history teacher; like Sister Anastasia, who has even become a drunkard and Jesus knows what else. My confession, Julian, isn't the sort that Father Kajene is looking forward to. Know it and you yourself desist most strongly against what happened to me yesterday. I should not even be talking to you of it; you should remain free of such sin, my dear."

"What happened to you yesterday?" Julian's granite-hard eyes battered her.

"You be my curate, Julian. I am fortunate in that." As if she were in a play, the large nun genuflected before the younger. "I wish to confess my faults, dear Sister...."

After she had told her the story of the cows, the bulls, Kavuyo and old Sister Remmy, Julian said, "But your ordeal was over yesterday and you had a whole twenty hours to strangle it inside you. You had ample opportunity to visit Father Kajene then."

Sister Gerald stood up, walking to the small high window set in red brick. "That is why I am warning you against carrying my kind of burden. Some faults are easy to overcome; others are not. I am at that point where sympathizing with Anastasia and her likes instead of chiding her, is much easier for me."

"You are using Sister Anastasia for simply too much."

"I have no other choice or excuse for my faults, Reverend Sister."

"Gerald," said Julian, weeping loudly, "you sound like y-you are telling me that it is not over, aren't you?"

"Frankly, Julian, I don't know."

"No. You obviously do know. Satan has power equal to God the Father, like that history teacher always tells us. You want Bikira Maria's help; the Mother of Christ never fails."

She knew it was her duty to report the grave imperfection of her colleague. But beside her liking for Gerald, a deep liking that had arisen through their work together; and her Kinyarwanda upbringing, could not let her betray a friend closer to her than her natural family. The law of *inaama* or secretiveness was tacitly instilled in her from childhood. She knew perfectly well that things of the homestead were never unnecessarily divulged to outsiders. The two nuns' long association outside the strictness of convent life had in the long run allowed them to indulge in such liberties as free speech, so that they sometimes felt like outsiders, conspirators not only against their fellow nuns but also against the Rule.

The young Dutchman, Wilhem van Gestel, the visiting Mill Hill Fathers dentist who spent some months in the province looking at all the diocesan clergy and nunnery dental formulas, was experienced with African women — having lived in Zaire, Rwanda and Tanzanian. He had told Julian she belonged to Viennese art galleries. "Not bootifool," he had said in his embarrassingly guttural English. "Not bootifool or preetty; just provocatively voluuptuous in innocence. You will come to my abode together both of you and we shall enjoy a good bottle of Burgundy that my dear Brodher Antoine Fasson brought me all the way from Saone-et-Loire for his teeth." They went there, of course, but Julian was determined not to be seduced.

Father Damien Beemereire, called simply Dam, that powerful diocesan education officer, had told her most cruelly that she had no business settled in convents. He taught English and Latin, and was a fine artist. But most importantly, Dam was a master dramatist. He had near divine acting powers. He could transform himself for any role, male or female, with utmost ease. He acted King David dispatching off his general to war as he preyed on the wife; had done the role of Zechariah, the short man who climbed the sycamore tree to view Jesus Christ; and had acted as Jairus of Galilee in Lloyd Douglas' *The Big Fisherman*, with Julian as Jairus' beautiful wife, Aidel — a role she would have given her right arm to swap with that of Tamar, sister to Prince Joseph of Erimathee. But Father Damien had castigated her: 'you don't want to act my wife eh?' — and added stingingly; 'Look, this is mere playacting and shouldn't go to your head.' The priest, more intriguingly, had come off well acting the role of the prostitute that confiscated King Solomon's royal mace at the gates of Jerusalem. This role had earned Father Dam his greatest stage fame in the diocesan secondary schools.

He was a very pushy man who assigned the nuns and the brothers their teaching posts and duties. The two nuns, did not mind or care where they were posted. But Sister Gerald had noted the younger nun's wish to remain posted at Kyera, their headquarters, or Mabonwa, close to the two refugee camps of Orukinga and Kashojwa, which had housed Banyarwanda refugees since 1959. And not to transfer her from Kyera to another place, Father Damien Beemereire, who seemed to know the reasons for Julian's wish to remain within the Kyera zone, had forced the two nuns into a casual friendship with him. He would ride with them to The Martini Lobo Recreation Centre, that beautiful place bequeathed to the Catholic Church by a long gone staunch Catholic Goanese from Bangalore. And he would get them drunk on Rufino wine. Father Damien Beemereire was a very short, light-brown priest from the predominantly Catholic county of Buhweju. His saucer-round eyes had very white irises and very sharp pupils the colour of jet. Sister Gerald believed that if Dam were to fail with Julian then no Lucifer — clothed or worldly — should ever fell her. In the first place the priest was well liked by all who knew of his theatrical flair and it was well known that quite a few women within the cloister and many within the faithful flock had not encountered the great Dam in the flesh. He occasionally made the two tipsy nuns to sleep at his residence. Julian never ceased to indicate to the priest that the scandal would be his if he ever felled her through skullduggery. Thus she never allowed him to get too far beyond her nearly flat but well-rounded breasts with their puffed nipples and naturally ripe raspberry sheen, which she allowed him piecemeal and begrudgingly.

And yet she never let him off either, keeping him guessing like a coquette, a characteristic the Munyankore priest attributed to her ethnicity as a Munyarwanda woman. Being refugees, the majority of Banyarwanda women who were not married off to Arab and Baganda men made ends meet through harlotry and prostitution in the big towns. But they treasured their virginity more than most. The Banyarwanda had more mature virgins than Ugandans. In wedlock, Banyarwanda women had no equals in perseverance to the bothersome headaches of matrimony; all the same even their Banyarwanda men accused these wonderful women usually correctly, of matrimonial disloyalty. Father Beemereire's unkindly reference to Julian was thus simply a typical Banyankore way of snubbing Banyarwanda as an ancient enemy neighbour. 'You can make beddings of a Munyarwanda woman, but not a bedcover as well,' went a Banyankore adage, which implied Banyarwanda women were not marriageable. Yet others said those women were only good for the bed, not for the home! Julian could not recall a single Munyarwanda divorcee and yet she had encountered several divorcees out in the world where she taught.

Sister Julian had kept her place in the diocese and gone on to help the refugees who were her country folk. And she kept Father Damien at bay until he got his transfer to distant Burundi.

Knowing Sister Julian Dominicus so intimately, Gerald tried to distinguish something unholy in what she had just witnessed; some flaw in the chaste Julian whom Providence may have misplaced. There are women, thought the elderly fat nun, whom God, in his everlasting wisdom, never meant for human men. Sister Julian Dominicus was of just that very creation. Gerald was not emotional about it; instead, as she searched for an explanation for what she had seen, she could not discard the feeling that she was dreaming. Lately she had been in the habit of consciously waking herself up from dreams that she did not favour and reeling off the spools of those that pleased her. She had told Julian about it: "I don't know whether this is part of ageing but today I control my dreams. I tell myself I am dreaming and I order myself to wake up or to go on dreaming."

And Julian had laughed at her: "I never dream," she had told the older nun with a child-like simplicity.

So now as she paced reluctantly towards the stairs, Gerald ordered herself several times to wake up. Instead of waiting to hear Julian enter her cubicle, she headed for that staircase to meet her. Was it a bad dream? Yes. And no. Because if Julian had gotten herself a human lover, Gerald would be alone no longer. They would share hitherto unspoken problems. And, yes, a problem it was. A problem whose solving lay between a rock and a hard place as Julian's twin sister, Apollonia Kasangaire, studying in Chicago, liked to say during the time she paid them a visit in Mt St Theresa, Kisubi, some years back. You either kept the problem secret or, in the most utterly humiliating routine ceremony, vacated the cloister. And became a disgraced human!

* * *

They met at the top of the stairs. Sister Julian placed her valise down at her feet and in the light from a street lamp a hundred yards away, through the leafy grey-green atmosphere, looked straight at Gerald and said, almost tartly: "What?"

'For crying out aloud!' Sister Gerald Sebastian chortled inwardly. There was a certain pertness in the younger woman's voice. Aloud, she said: "My dear Reverend Sister, let's go in. God alone knows all and we know nothing. Mother Superior got a call from your uncle and Sister Prioress instructed me to know when you should arrive. I took over Sister Jimminez's place at the duty desk for that, not officially, of course. I will get her to resume at once."

"Sister Prioress will want to see me tonight?"

"Yes. But you *look* okay to me."

"I do? You saw — him, of course. I don't *feel* okay."

"That was a daft, reckless thing to do, Julian, though I would simply take it as a mere goodbye between people who had traveled together. I believe if anybody did notice your arrival, they should take it so."

"I feel awful, Gerald!"

"You feel the way I once felt. Sometimes I have wondered whether they know."

"About you they do not," Julian said. "I know of it because you endeavoured to explain it. I have seen Sister Benedict Bazzekuketta, at her age, look as though she had been struck by lightening. That thunderbird I rebuked you about once, remember? Her eyes dilated, her mouth melted — as if she had just seen a human! But alas, Sister Bazzekuketta has not disgraced herself seeing a man, as you and I quite well know."

"Well, my very dear Sister Julian, welcome to the club."

"Don't bloody rub it in, Gerald."

"Shhh — do not swear."

* * *

She turned and tossed in her bed — a wooden bedstead with a base of dried elephant-grass reeds nailed to wooden struts that crossed the breadth of the bed, one of a few hundred made more than half a century ago, and a mattress of a burlap sack filled with cut lawn grass from various schools in the area: St Josef's, Mt St Helena, St Aloysius, Mount Mary High. The burlap bags, which had contained diverse merchandise when they came from India at the beginning of the twentieth century, had been provided in 1911 by the great Goan Catholic trader, Martin Lobo, and given to the Indian clothier, Jetha Ishmael, to sew into mattresses for the recruit nurses and nuns of the young church at Kyera. Julian had slept in this chamber of cubicles for three consecutive years, which was atypical as it was a tenet of the Rule never to allow a nun to become so accustomed to an item as to perceive it as a possession. A nun, of course, owned nothing. The practice of poverty precluded notions such as 'my cubicle' or 'my bed.' But nuns involved in professional callings outside the convent grounds, Sister Gerald, for instance, had slept in her cubicle for four years. It was a sort of dormitory, partitioned into cubicles containing a bed, a high-backed wooden chair, a wooden table and a thirty-watt electric bulb hooded by a tightly-woven palm leaf shade for use in working at the little pile of books with the pen and pencil and razorblade that were the only occupants of the tabletop. This sleeping quarter, an assembly of some thirty cubicles, was different in many ways from the rest of the convent. Here some leeway was provided in regard to the Rule of Silence at particular hours, particularly hours between vespers and matins. In the sleeping quarters at these hours a nun might speak with another nun about matters that did not strictly concern sanctity. The teacher sisters had to study deep into the small hours and on occasion found it necessary, to consult one another on a mathematical equation, a historical problem or a chemical solution. Of course the nuns knew very well not to indulge in unnecessary diversions or infringements of the Rule. They exercised extreme discipline and only occasionally found themselves at the threshold of Mother Superior's office to confess varieties of faults. The sins of the nuns who never ventured out of the convent as freely as these professionals were never quite as diverse or as frequent.

Julian lay on her side, turned to the other, and then on her stomach. She felt very uncomfortable. She was a sound sleeper, unlike her fellow nuns in the main sleeping quarters, where one chamber was segregated into more than two-hundred cubicles, each closed off at the entrance with an ages-old serge curtain. They could be heard turning and tossing in their cots from the moment the lights went out to the first bell slightly before six o'clock, which signaled them to head, without delay, to the chapel. Sister Odilla, the fifty-year-old cateress was legendary for her sad habit of turning, tossing, crying, and moaning as though in agony in her bed. Yet she would always be found fast asleep even as she turned and tossed and moaned! Julian's mind fixed upon Sister Odilla in search of some hidden thing she associated with the old nun. She realized that the very same silly sounds made by poor Sister Odilla were those she had made in Kabale on two consecutive nights and days! God! She recalled making noises a million times worse. And then her mind went quickly to her admonitions of Sister Gerald some years in the past. Would her confessions ever include the episodes of tonight, yesterday and the day before, episodes she had had it in her power to stop? What good, Gerald might ask, would the confession of her sin do for the refugees charged to her care in Kyera?

She turned on her back and regarded the age-blackened wooden rafters of the high roof. Why had she done it? Why had she continued it? Of course, it was because of that blasted soldier's hand. No; it was because her body had a stronger will than her head. Her body!

In Gitarama she had seen nothing in the driver of the pickup truck apart from a Muganda man with eyes of a habitual boozer. In Mbarara, Baganda were considered colonialists. They had turned up at the end of the nineteenth century with the bazungu European masters. Distrust was contagious as newcomers were made to look at Baganda in the light of usurpers or encroachers on Nkore things. Worse still, most Baganda that had come to southern Uganda were Muslims, and this made the fellows doubly distrusted. Thus Julian couldn't have done what she had done on account of comeliness in a man.

Julian could remember episodes along the way — like bits of discarded scrap paper, from high up in Gitarama; and later the visit to the place of the Algerian priest in the Rue de Rusumo; the dark, grey stormy clouds that had obliterated the sky and the subsequent torrents of rain; the foamy biscuit-brown deluge and the washed away bridge at Murindi. Their hectic, hurtling journey from mountainous Urukomo and the odious countenances of the Banyarwanda peasantry as they regarded her face in poorly concealed antipathy, and their hearty hand in seeing the two out of the snags of the bad roads; and the Muganda's mockery of Banyarwanda's attitudes towards each other. Nothing amazed Ugandans as much as what they saw as wasted energy in the cat-and-dog hatred between the Banyarwanda people and the Muganda, Ssempa laughed at it and considered the actors in these animosities to be bigots. He had hinted so even as he spoke to her uncle in Gitarama, stopping short of calling the monsignor a nincompoop.

But of course, there were animosities even among the people of Uganda, which was made up of hundreds of tribes and sub-tribes. In Rwanda there was only one tribe made up of just three ethnic groupings sharing a common language, the same names, and even a common culture. Well, except that the Batwa ate mutton!

She came to the episodes at Gatuna frontier, where the customs official had, as always, taunted her for having the temerity to return to Rwanda, which, the man seemed to believe, just as Julian perhaps had accepted, was no longer her country and would never be! Never during all that time had she committed sin, even in thought. Even her conversations with the Muganda, though a strict silence should have been observed on her part, were permissible. She spoke to Ssempa as she spoke to her relatives or to the pupils in her class on a study tour. Had she brought upon herself the error at Kyondo? Could she have made it impossible for that soldier, a man wearing a crucifix round his neck, to do to her what he had done? At this point she realised her fingers were touching her delicate body and she quickly withdrew the hand. She had prayed as she had never prayed before the moment she realised the army lieutenant's fixed purpose, which was communicated filthily in his eyes as he looked in her own. '*In nomine Patris...* shield me from this macabre threat to your Kingdom...! You would never let me slip into this sort of evil; you shall always keep me away from all evil. O Mary Mother of the Christ, do not let this happen; do not let the mad man... touch Your body'. But no helpful answers came for her prayer. The profanity appeared to be inevitable.

The dirty hand, a feverish fire in its fingers, had shot between her knees. The hand was large and hard and calloused against the soft skin of her inner leg, and though it did not seem to move at all in its rude grasp as the rain hammered into the canvas of the tent and the pressure lamp hissed and the hard-shelled beetles flung themselves against the hot glass globe, it did move. The Muganda's infrequent admonitions and the silly childish giggles of the three soldiers — sounds that seemed to have occurred at some remote time and space, rumbled eerily through her head. She had hoped that the man might be satisfied with merely touching her naked thigh. But his hand moved on to a spot no hand — not even her own had ever dared to touch. She knew she could banish the shame of that hand by constantly conversing with God. But as the foreign body pushed on and pressed and twirled, a detestable feeling arose in her — detestable because the hand evoked an enjoyable sensation that threatened to spread to her other self, to her inner self! She did everything in her drastically subdued powers to bend that terrible feeling, that frightful hunger, to her will and that of the Catholic God and of the Virgin Mother.

How was she to exorcise that feeling from her body now that she had been contaminated with its corrupting power? Her mind whirled, creating questions that had never before occurred to her! What if that horrific feeling were to arise again? Would she not become like Sister Gerald Namazzi? She knew she had to tame that feeling by all means.

And she might have succeeded but for that coffee mixed with gin. A few sips of the hot sugared stuff had made her sneeze violently and the feeling returned. This time round the burning concupiscence was not exactly in the area of the flesh that the soldier's hand had disturbed. It was centred between the small of her back and the lower abdomen, around the frontal pelvic bone, below her navel. It was a feeling of a steadily rising warmth where nothing could reach to touch! 'To touch'! — she said to herself in horror. If someone were to stab a sharp instrument right there below her abdomen and it probed deep enough through bone, that fire could be touched — and perhaps be extinguished! She wished, her wanton soul wandering away wildly from her, to be touched with a burning rod, to be ripped open there and then.

The *In nomine Patris* prayer still dominated her mind. But nothing happened to the feeling that went on to consume her in its fire.

When later he placed her below him on the wide bed, his body pinning hers under its heaving weight, and a hot hardsoft probe jabbed jerkily at the area the hand of fate had touched, her angry fingers blindly shot out and directed that probe to sate her need. But she was shocked when she found the hard, hot rubbery object to be larger than she had anticipated. It was many times larger than the finger of the soldier at Kyondo. The discovery sapped all her energy to resist whatever Ssempa had in mind for her. She took a deep breath as she steadied herself against him.

In her wooden bedstead, Julian's mind recalled the cries she had made at every jerky thrust of his pelvis toward hers as he trembled and cried as if to take her through her pain. And she struggled suddenly into awareness with a little muted cry escaping her mouth. Her hand had returned to her secret body.

In genuine sympathy, she puzzled over Sister Odilla and her chronic nocturnal moaning!

* * *

A week later Julian and the fat Sister Namazzi arrived at the address Ssempa had given to the nun. It was a motor vehicle garage in an old building with a high roof of soot-blackened corrugated iron sheets supported on heavy angled steel girders and oil preserved timber where spiders, sparrows and wasps nested in groups and swarms and seemed so accustomed to the cacophonous din in the place that it was not easy to notice them unless you looked up deliberately. A series of twelve-foot fluorescent tubes lit the place brightly to give this jungle of noisy activity a semblance of civilization. It was a crowded, noisy area pushed away eastward from the centre of town. Across from the garage's entrance was the town mosque, this beautiful stone and marble building, like the garages themselves, a relic left behind by an Asian-Indian community that Idi Amin had banished from the country half a decade ago. The nuns arrived in a white Nissan Datsun estate car driven by the older of the two, in their dusty-brown habits and dusty-cream head coverings. As the driver parked the car and looked at her wrist to consult her watch, the deep, metallic voice of the muezzin in the taller of the three minarets of the mosque a mere fifty metres away, slashed through the clangour of the garages; the rhubarb of raucous-voiced mechanics and hammers on steel anvils, nearly silencing the clamour in its crackling intensity. *'Allahu akibaru, Allaaaahu, akibaru'!* The two nuns on reflex looked across the oil stained tarmac road, at the men in kanzu robes climbing the few steps to the entrance of the mosque in various degrees of hurry, discarding their shoes and sandals there, the way they had been told Moses might have done at Mount Sinai, their faces solemnly pointed at that entrance with near exaggerated purpose. The two looked at one another, the older woman's face questioningly, as if to say — 'Is this fair'?

The receptionist, whom the two nuns suspected to be the Virgo woman, was a light brown, lean Munyarwanda with severely sharp aquiline features and spectacles on her exquisitely beautiful face. Those glasses seemed not to have attracted the metallic dust that pervaded the place. They studied her together, separately, and differently; placed her age at forty or fifty. She had been too beautiful and too conscious of her skin at one time in her past to expose her age easily to casual observation. Ssempa had told Julian that Virgo was old enough to be his mother. 'Well,' thought Julian. 'Not exactly'. But she was so serious-countenanced, so severe in her looks, both nuns, having known in advance she was Catholic and discussed how they would react to her, were taken disconcertingly aback. They saw in Virgo Kabibi a woman that would know how to treat and handle them instead; after all, thought Julian with some bitterness; they were the sinners, not she. As for her reaction to them, here was a politely formal non-gregarious woman. She offered them seats — two iron frames onto which car's bucket seats had been welded. Kabibi returned to her seat behind the grey iron desk with an old grey Olivetti typewriter and a grey cash till. A film of fine grey dust lay on nearly everything in that amplitudinous, echoic room. She greeted them in the Kinyankore language.

"You want me to call Ssempa?" Not *David*, the two nuns noted. Not *mister*. Just like an elder sister or, thought Julian, even one fit to be a mother, to a close relative rather than an employer. She did not give them the option to respond: "Ssempa?" She called out loudly, in an almost banal, non-sophisticated, car garage-associated voice. "Come." The last one word was spoken in perfect, accentless Luganda and sounded like an order.

"What's it?" Ssempa's muffled voice came impatiently from behind heavy, wall-size steel shutters.

Julian's heart somersaulted at the sound of his voice. She had not heard him talk so loudly and there was an anxious feeling in her body that an altogether different man might emerge from behind those steel shutters.

"Some people to see you," said Kabibi, in fluent Luganda.

"Let them come this way. I cannot leave this thing."

Julian's knees fluttered under her. She felt unable to breathe properly.

"Let's go there." Kabibi addressed them in Kinyankore, as she arose from behind the steel desk.

The two nuns followed as commanded. They were the sinners, not she. The skinny woman heaved the sliding shutter to one side, the opening of which revealed mechanics busy with their tasks. Only a few turned to stare at the nuns; several might not have heard the heavy doors slide open on creaky ball bearings. Ssempa was working on a heavy motor disgorged from the gaping mouth of a big Deutz Magirus tipper truck. He was clad in what seemed to Julian to be the same jeans, sweat shirt and boots he had worn back in Gitarama nine days previously, except that today the jeans and the sweatshirt were caked with grease and oil, which also shone on his biceps and wrists. His fingers were literally dripping with black oil. He stared at the three women open-mouthed.

"Eh eh. *Tobalya banno*!" Virgo said to him reprovingly and then laughed. It meant: 'You look like you might swallow the guests'!

"Ummm! You are most welcome," he managed to blurt out and, wiping his hands on the jeans, came from behind the winch-hoisted motor. "Let us go back to the shop. Virigo?" he asked Kabibi. "Get Sande to bring in two cold drinks, will you. What will it be, Sisters? Pepsi or Coca Cola?"

"Two Pepsi colas," the older of the nuns said.

Sister Gerald's voice somewhat stabilised Julian's body.

"I will get them myself," said Virgo Kabibi, not as a request or offer but as a position taken and not requiring contention. Ssempa did not notice the elderly woman as she pulled a squeaky drawer in the steel desk and picked out the money for the purchase of the sodas. But the two newcomers noted every item, every movement, including the sparrows streaking up in the girders and trying to outdo the garage hands in noise-making.

Kabibi's dress was a flowing, garishly printed poplin with weed tendrils, flower petals and honeybees, with soft pleats that flared from the waist to just above her ankles. The sleeves of her blouse, in the same material as the skirt, snuggled her wrists. It was one of those fashions approved by dictator Idi Amin, who had one morning awoken from a purported dream revelation and banned mini dresses, shorts and thick beards. Her slim feet were as light brown as her face and as long as her neck was slender. She had on cream-to-brown leather strapped shoes with thin high heels that she tap-tapped and clack-clacked on the terrazzo floor like a prancing *runyegye* dancer. Three ornamental rings adorned her long, lean fingers which now held the empty soda bottles for exchange with the filled ones. She walked out, not elegantly, but at the same time not mundanely. Her hips were quite wide below her waspy waist and she swayed those in a sort of dance. When she had turned out of sight, Julia turned to Sister Gerald, whose own eyes were just settling on hers, and both turned in unison to look at Ssempa, who half sat, half leaned on a large, dust-covered BSA Motor Goose motorcycle.

Julian said in Luganda: "This is Sister Gerald Sebastian Namazzi, a colleague and sister, though she is my mother as well. Gerald — David Ssimha."

"You *mu*'sister," Ssempa said, making a threatening face at her. He was mimicking her way of saying: 'You man'! "Only Monsignor Raphael is permitted usage of that name."

"It is Uncle Monsignor's name for him," Julian said to Gerald. "I suspect he loves it."

"Who — your uncle?"

"No. Yourself, don't you, now?"

"How can I; when you saw me quarrelling over it in Gitarama? Anyway, names are names. Gerald reminds me of one of the mechanics in there." Ssempa liked the mood of their conversation and did not want anything changing it. He had feared a tongue-tie. "He is an old man too, but neither a Muganda nor as a result, from the Mpologoma clan. Or are you a mumbejja?"

"Who is of the Mpologoma or Bambejja clan?" Julian asked, looking at both Ssempa and Sister Gerald suspiciously. "I know her simply to be a Muganda."

"That is true, Sister Julian, but she is also of the Mpologoma clan, the clan of the lion if not of the Bambejja princesses of the Balangira royal clan of Buganda. I am sure you are one of either, Sister."

"As sure as you must be of the Nte clan if your name is truly Ssempa; I am of Mpologoma."

"Guilty," stated Ssempa, beaming. "I am a great, great grandson of Katongole in Mulema."

"What is *nte*?" Julian asked, exasperated. "All along I thought I knew you." This was directed at Gerald.

"Nte is obviously cow. In my case it is a particular cow with a particular brownish-black colour and a much darker line of hair running along the ridge of its spine. It is a clan that originated from among the Banyoro people of western Uganda, bordering Lake Muttanzige to the west and the Kyoga to the northeast."

"And which is Lake Muttanzige?" Sister Julian's brow was furrowed in curiosity.

"Ah, the *bazungu* christened it Lake Albert." The fat Sister Gerald Sebastian Namazzi supplied this answer.

"How did you learn all that, you a nun like me?"

"I am a Muganda. A Muganda learns these things from childhood. I joined the convent at the age of fifteen."

"I joined at fourteen," Julian said this. "And how do names come into clans?"

"Ask him," Gerald indicated Ssempa.

Ssempa, who was suspicious of the elderly nun, was pleased that they had opened up a good easy conversation so promptly. He had in the first place not expected Julian to reveal their secret; he doubted she could. Now that they had come in a pair, not knowing how to address them together, he had feared a dumbfounded atmosphere. He looked in Julian's ever-alert, mocking eyes and said: "Ask me."

"Well, come on," she commanded. "What are you waiting for?"

"For your soda," Ssempa said, irritating her.

"Ah la lah! She's returning so soon?" Julian expressed exasperation.

"We are mortified by her presence," put in Gerald. "She is a strong Catholic woman."

"The gentlest creature God ever cared to create, too," said Ssempa.

"Oh, I hope so. So, how did you know Gerald was of the lion clan — and she that you are of the clan of cows?"

229

"Baganda have three types of name. They have clan names that rarely deviate to other clans but also have several which are shared amongst their fifty-two clans. Then they have the the proverbial names, which refer to events, deeds or abilities. Then there are the names of Buganda's *lubaales*, our angels, which humans do sometimes share. Baganda have no new names and cannot create them. I have noted the same thing amongst your Banyarwanda. There has always been Kabibi and there has always been Kantarama, and Gakinya. But it isn't the same for the Banyankore or the Bachiga and the Banyoro; or the so-called Bafumbira, who are actually Banyarwanda caught and marooned on this side of the frontiers by colonial border demarcations. These people, probably because of a low opinion of their own cultures, have embraced biblical, religious or European names liberally. They have even turned local adjectives into new names, an indication that their cultures are still evolving. I said you couldn't invent new names in Buganda. Nor can you create them in Rwanda, Gikuyuland or Burundi. But the opposite is the general trend — say here in Nkore. You can no longer find a parent naming a child after its ancestor. They refer to such ancestral names as pagan or ugly or dirty, in compliance with imperialist ideology. They have created an excuse from one of their proverbs: 'A bad name influences its possessor to its likeness', a proverb with no truth in it. At the time I went to primary school in the late 50s, you found men with names of obscure meaning like Kyamanianga, Rwankujungu, Machoro, and those with pointed meaning like Karyarug'okwo — which is like a husband telling his wife that their offspring's negative traits can only be imported from her family to his; Kishetsya or Kashetsya both of which denote jests and Kazini which means 'the ace dancer'. My first headmaster was called Kicere. It means toad or frog. He later changed it to Baguma, which means 'tough'. If he had been tough enough he would have stuck to the name his father gave him. It appears that the colonised Kicere was encouraged to hate his name. What, if I may ask, is so bad about a frog? They swim in the water we bathe in and drink unboiled. Mind you, the French and the Chinese regard them as a most delicious diet. The Kicere I am talking about wasn't an ugly man or toad-like, mark you, but I believe he was concerned about how the opposite sex might consider his name. Even Kadori, which means chamber pot, was a schoolmate's name. As for women — Nkoobwa, a shared sweet potato; Nyambiro, the first female of a pair of twins; Kibotsize — not necessarily with a meaning or Mahitsi, a female name denoting the ways of hyenas; all were immediately changed the moment a girl enrolled for formal education. Banyankore had other names coined after flora and fauna: Nyangongi the otter, Kentwiiga the giraffe, Kenturegye the zebra; Kenyonza the sweet-voiced robin, Kanyamuteete of the savanna dental-cleaning grass. Or those names given after places and events like Kekikomera, which could denote the day she was born, or Kenturire, born the day her father got drunk on potent banana beer. Alas, it is no longer possible to find such beautiful, meaningful cultural names in Mbarara or even in the entire range of western Uganda today. Today the Banyankore want to name their brethren with titles — not names — and nearly all refer to Jesus, or the Arabo-Hebraic rendition of God. They have coined names like Kansiime, Mwebaze, Tumukunde, Muhairwe and Agaba, all of which give thanks and praise, or exult the intruder lords. Tumwesigye — trust in Jesus; Atukunda and Atwiine to praise the same for sustenance. When those fellows toting Jewish and Arab names and cultures arrived here, did they find us barren or starving, so that we must thank their gods for our existence and sustenance to the extent of replacing our names with theirs? Did they find us killing each other the way they have taught us to do? Did they find us killing our fauna without necessity, the way they have done on their devastating hunting safaris? So there you are. These days, for every ten words the Banyankore speak, four are in English, three in Luganda. They are discarding their natural language with such disconcerting ease that unless they take drastic measures, Kinyankore might vanish completely. That is the cultural gospel according to Ssempa, son of Ssemaganda."

"Okay, Ssimha, son of Ssimagan'ha," Julian said, deliberately mispronouncing the names the Kinyarwanda way. "But must Namazzi be of the lion clan and Ssempa of the cow clan? That is what I want to know."

"They should be. You see Ganda names are not merely clan names; the fifty-two clans of Buganda are actually fifty-two different tribes or nationalities amalgamated as one and united under a single monarch. Ah, the monarch is out for the time being, but Baganda do seriously consider their kingdom to be intact. On studying them closely you see each clan's unique traits, mannerisms, behaviours, names, and even physical and physiognomic differences. The Mmamba clan are good at trade and are the most numerous; the Lugave — that is pangolin clan — are, besides the Nseenene — grasshopper clan — the best dramatists in the land and produce the most shrewd and pushiest scholars and legal advocates. The Balangira, that royal clan, are poor in formal schooling but make the best fighters in the armed forces alongside the Ngabi or bushbuck clan. They are also — along with Nkima or monkey clan — adept conmen. The cheetah clan people, known as Abaakasimba, and those of Obutiko mushrooms are renowned night dancers and are even known to be very recent cannibals. When in Buganda, never accept a casual invitation from a man called Kabazzi or Kiyemba or women with the names Najjuka and Nakawoza; you could end up in someone's cooking pot. They say that the Mutima or heart clan is full of rumourmongers. I forgot to tell you that the bushbuck clan people are the best bonesetters. As for names Namazzi, which translates as 'of water', is purely a clan name. Nakkazi, denoting 'big, strong woman' is generally a name of the Mmamba — or lungfish — clan. The Nakazzi spelled with two zeds, means 'of the small water-well', and is of the Nnyonyi — or the bird clan. Another clan may infringe on these names out of ignorance or out of kubbula, or copying. If I have had a great friend from a different clan I may decide to name my son after him. But I should give him my own clan name in addition because he will always be questioned about where he got the other non-clan name, usually to his discomfiture. Another thing: offspring never named themselves after their fathers as it is done nowadays. Such a thing was taboo among the Banyankore because when a person died his name was not to be uttered by friends and family for years.

"Let me touch on your own turf. You have several clans in Rwanda. The Banyiginya are your royal clan like the Balangira in Buganda or the Babiito and Bahinda in Bunyoro and Nkore. These provide the monarchy with kings. In your case the chief royal names there are Ntale, Rudahigwa, Rwabugiri, Rwaagasore, Ganyonza. The names Kigeri — warrior king — or Mutara — the peacemaker king — accompany whoever gets to your throne. If you don't belong to the Banyiginya clan, I don't see your parents naming your brother Ganyonza, Ntale or Rudahigwa. Do you now understand how I know Sister Gerald's clan by merely hearing her name? To me, though a fellow Muganda, Namazzi belongs to another tribe under some entity called Buganda, which word itself comes from *Obuganda*, meaning items brought together to make one unit or, in terms of human beings, to practice one culture."

"Gosh! And what is the use of all that?"

"It prevents incestuous conjugal relationships on one hand; I'd know a woman of my clan or of my mother's clan as soon as she told me her name and thenceforth refer to her as sister or aunt. Names ultimately ensure a ban on intra-clan matrimony. I mean, I wouldn't wed a woman from my father or mother's clan. For your information even veterinarians greatly discourage incest among livestock animals because it produces inferior stock. The uses of this protocol are many. For instance I would receive or assist someone of my clan differently, even if he were a total stranger than I would a stranger from a clan other than mine. My clanmate is automatically my relative, you see, and I can identify him simply by knowing his name. It is certainly a form of sectarianism. But a positive sectarianism, since it is all united under a kabaka, a monarch who, by the way, belongs to his own clan and will have to marry from any of most of the remaining fifty-two clans to which his own mother is not directly or matrimonially related."

Of Saints and Scarecrows

"It is all so confusing," said Julia. "And now you even teach me about my own people of Rwanda! Yet somebody once told me that my ancestors were Bacweezi. How do you know all that? You are not an anthropologist?"

"I don't even know the meaning of the word. But you see the majority of us are descendants of the Bacweezi except that historians enjoy mixing things up. This district we live in, Nkore, is deemed to be the true Cweeziland. Cweezi descendants are more related to the Ganda and Nyoro monarchies than Kore's. Neither Buganda nor Bunyoro have ever been part of Nkore and yet all Cweezi capitals and historical sites are in Buganda and Bunyoro. Come to that, Baganda and Banyoro continue to name their children with Cweezi appellations yet the Banyankore don't. Take purely Cweezi names; names of those past peoples' kings, princes, princesses and commoners but which the Baganda and to a certain extent the Banyoro give to their offspring unconscious of the Cweezi connections. Names such as Ndawula, Ssimbwa, Kagolo, Kyomya, Namata, Nakayima, Wamala, Mukasa, Nabiryo, Mulindwa, Nanteza. The Nyoro counterpart-names are Ndahura, Isimbwa, Kagoro, Mugasa, Wamara. There are no Nkore equivalents for these names. In their oral and written histories, the Banyankore mention a Mucweezi called Murindwa, who was murdered in a conspiracy by two women called Nyabiryo and Nyanteza. All three names are rare in all Nkore and yet they are common Ganda clan names. The Banyankore have claimed they glorify the Bacweezi too much to give their names to simpler human offspring, a poor pretext, of course. Thus the history of the Bacweezi is a Ganda-Nyoro, not Nkore, thing. But, of course, language is the only difference among all these peoples, Nilotic or Bantu. There isn't much difference between the peoples of Rwanda or Congo and the people of Uganda, Kenya or even Maniikaland in southern Africa. The Bacweezi, as you will find, are associated more with the Luo than with the Bantu peoples. All the monarchs of this area — the Great Lakes area — were originally Luo or Nilotic and more specifically Acholi. We share all our cultures with freak differences. Like the Middle Eastern religions we inherited from the Europeans and Arabs with so-called holy books covering our eyes and gun muzzles pointed at our temples, our own frontiers are false creations by the same Bible-toting Europeans. Our artificial frontiers are strategically meant to have us notice irrelevant differences and uniquenesses. Chantal Nzaza — Monsieur Gakinya's former wife and Gakinya have educated me a lot on Banyarwanda cultural history. And I have Virigo with me here. She is a walking encyclopedia on matters of Rwanda and Burundi and says she got it all from childhood folklore. Well, talk of the devil!"

Kabibi entered at that very moment with the two bottles of Pepsi cola and waxpaper straws.

They conversed easily, Ssempa unable to rid himself of the suspicion that Julian might have been caught, made to confess and volunteer to lead the elderly nun to him to elicit a confession or a confirmation for the diocesan headquarters. He never let down his guard and he watched the elderly nun scrutinise him whenever he pretended to have his attention elsewhere. When he had introduced Virgo Kabibi, Sister Gerald had commented, "What beautiful names! Virigo! Befits the owner too. It is Catholic, certainly!" she wondered aloud as if she did not know already.

In Uganda there were Catholic and Protestant names. The Catholic ones usually ended in vowels and sounded Latin or Roman, and the Protestant ones — since that sect of Christianity was brought in by the British colonisers and was indeed called the Anglican Church — usually Anglicised. The Catholics baptised Maria, Eneriko, Margarita, Joanita, Antonio and Francisco whereas the Protestants used Mary, Henry, Margaret, Jane, Anthony and Francis. The Catholics had appellations that the Protestants dismissed as unorthodox; names like Remigio, Anastasia, Fulgencio or Gonzaga. You wouldn't meet a Catholic named Wilson, Wilbur, Sarah, Joy or Dinah.

"Yes," replied Kabibi, brief as always. "I am Catholic through and through."

"I did think so. Virigo must be for Virgo, of course. Virgin, eh? We'll be good friends, you and I."

"You've found a true candidate." Kabibi's voice sometimes irritated Ssempa. She spoke as if Sister Gerald was one of the more familiar of the area's mechanics. "I will sometimes come and sleep in the convent."

"You don't say," laughed Gerald, mirthfully. "You cannot be Catholic and not know that that is not allowed."

"Who will prevent me? — Abbess Sister Valerian or Monsignor Fabiano Mpagi? Why, I have always visited Kyera. But we mostly drink from The Marlorec."

"Shhh," that was Gerald, enjoying herself. "You'll get Mr Ssempa to think that the church has turned into a free-for-all tavern. Do you know of The Marlorec, Mr Ssempa?"

"Who doesn't? Except you are telling me what actually goes on there." He was wondering: 'if she has not been dispatched to spy on me, could she also be a sinner? Is she a lesbian — or might she even be a succubus'? He had been told lesbians could easily identify each other and get along; but was Kabibi a lesbian? No. Not a chance in a million. As far as he knew Kabibi had never had a man in her life. And about succubae — He had read a great deal about how those interesting creatures could become the scourge of a monastery or convent, enjoying of nuns and priests alike in their constant sex mutations.

"Where do you live?" Ssempa was sure the question was directed at Kabibi. He turned his eyes away from Sister Julian to find Gerald's on his face. "Is it far from here?"

"Um   er, yes," he blurted out, apprehensively. This time he was convinced the elderly nun was a spy and that was the reason Julian wasn't contributing much to the exchanges. "Four kilometres from here in Buremba. My house is right on the River Rwiizi."

"Are you sure? Four kilometers would be... you aren't talking of the former Forests house!"

"It could be the one, though I doubt you would...."

"That is near Kidofoori's boat, isn't it? — At the crossing. That is Kaburangire, not Buremba. The old timber house."

Ssempa tried to show he hadn't been caught off balance by the nun's precise description of his home. His mind shot back to the roadblock episode of the previous week, when a lieutenant had hinted about the Catholic Church being a hotbed of espionage. Should he deny it was his house? Why had she gone there to view it? What would his answer to her question entail?

"Yes," he said, bravely. "Have you been to the place?"

"Yes. Several times."

"That cannot be true," protested Ssempa. "Even though I spend most of my time away from there, it is where I reside whenever I am in town. I have people there who would tell me of you."

He glanced at Julian whose eyes laughed at him: 'squirm and fidget all you can', they seemed to say.

"The livestock farm across the river belongs to the Franciscan Sisters. It is on the other side of the graphite hill. I started managing it four years ago."

"Oh, I see. Now I remember; you must be the nun who crosses that bridge in a white Datsun station wagon — I've heard about you."

"The very car is parked outside there. Let us go out and you have a look at it."

Alarm bells rang in Ssempa's mind. What was there in looking at a station wagon?

"Look at it?" he asked the nun.

"Yes. Have a look at it. Do you have some aversion to looking at station wagons driven by veterinarians?"

"You are a vet?"

"Yes. Became one four years ago. Well?"

Ssempa now realised the nun might want to keep Kabibi out of any further conversations.

"Why not, anyhow? Maybe it needs repair, though we specialize in European makes of vehicle. Sister Julian, you are not talking."

"You know me," the latter replied at the entrance. "I am a woman of a few words."

As they walked out they faced the mosque, and men in white and cream kanzu robes and tarboushes, fezzes and skullcaps on their heads were streaming out of it. A smaller number of fat women with headdresses and bulky costumes emanated from the less elegant back of the stone and marble building.

"As you know," said Gerald. "She is a professional nun."

They laughed at the joke. The day Major General Idi Amin took state power in a bloody military coup d'etat he had said. 'I am a professional soldier'. His voice had boomed on the radio loudspeakers across the nation. 'And a man of a few words'.

"And she fears nothing except God," Gerald finished off.

Idi Amin had said that too.

"Don't be deceived by Gerald, David," Julian said. "Julian is only human. She fears other things too."

"Things like what, Julian?" asked Gerald as they got to their car.

"You yourself know what. Things like Virigo Kabibi."

"Oh, oh, oh!" Gerald said, in Luganda. "Don't tell me. A Catholic if any ever breathed this air," she touched the air between index finger and thumb and then released it, following it with her laughing eyes as it went. "How much do you trust that woman, Ssempa?"

"Besides adoring her, I trust her infinitely."

"That is very gratifying. We want to see your place. Julian tells me you aren't married, but I know town folk better than she. I grew up on Martin Road in Old Kampala, where my father guarded St Matia Mulumba Memorial Shrine — did you know that is where he was captured by Ssekabaka Mwanga's men and put to death?"

"Your father! You mean your father was a martyr?"

"No. I mean Saint Matia Mulumba the martyr. So, being city-born, I tell Julian to take great caution with humans — when I say 'humans,' I mean.... what should I call you? — civilians... men of the material world. Julian is my most beloved... how should I say it to you? — Most beloved daughter. You, townsfolk of the world can destroy our folk. You can destroy her. You have no fear for scandal. You actually could show her off to other worldly men, and say: 'hey, here I am; I am dating no one less than a bride of God! Don't you think I should kill you then?"

"I should rather.... I wonder what you mean!" Ssempa was fumbling about for responses.

236

"You see, Ssempa, my brother, we are nuns. And at the same time we, too, are human beings, with human bodies… human feelings. But we are trained, indoctrinated actually, to discard all normal human feelings. We learn, in the long run, to kill normal feelings within us. It is not as hard as you may think. Julian only needs to immerse herself in prayer and penance through the doctrine of the liturgical soul of silence and sacrifice, and wham! — Out Ssempa, in Jesus Christ. Totally. Just like that. It is actually harder to return to the normal human world from the cloister, with the murky deeds that go on in the world out here. But human beings in body and heart we remain all the same, as you may have discovered. The heart can control the brain even though the brain is the wiser. The heart is the stronger, the harbourer of sentiment. Thus the reasons we are here are for matters of the heart. And Julian here has had the toughest heart of them all. If it should ever happen that you may laugh at Julian! — If ever you make a laughing stock of her…." She left her threat hanging. "And so, if you are a married man, tell us right here and now so that we can devise means of meeting other than at your house."

Ssempa felt lost. His responses to the elderly nun could turn out to be the undoing of the silent Julian. He kept a smug face and said: "If you are enquiring about my marital status, I am fully wedded to machinery, grease, oil, coffee beans, whisky, matches, dry batteries, cigarettes, cars — they are my wife and my soul. Without them I would try to find another world in one of the stars that shine in the night heavens. Of course, when I brought her from Rwanda, I explained that I am divorced from matters of organised religion. I am not even secular, as that would make me political; I am just me by myself."

"That is not true. You are more for others than for yourself. That I do know from the affection Virigo Kabibi has for you. And from what Julian told me. All the same you know we cannot always come here. Not even to repair our car since you said you are specialists. We are teachers and enjoy certain freedoms that poor Mother Church has to tolerate. Your river house is most convenient, of course. Julian must never ever return here to this place."

Ssempa was silent, his head cocked slightly to one side in a listening manner. When he opened his mouth to speak, Sister Julian spoke instead: "Oh, Holy Mother! — He thinks you are spying on him, Gerald." The truth of her statement startled Ssempa. "Did you… you did term it a survival what? Oh, boy! Dear Gerald, David is right now scheming how to outwit you and your assumed collaborators at Kyera — who, obviously, include myself. Have you heard him utter just one word that would commit him to me? Have you heard the fool say a single meaningful thing?"

"Come to think of it, no!" Sister Gerald said, laughing. "Is it true you suspect me of spying on you?"

"No."

"You do," said Julian.

"Umm — yes. I suspected, at first. But when you spoke out, I saw some light."

"Well," said Julian. "She told you she is more or less my mother. Trust Gerald with me, and entrust me to her for you. We are one with her. You can take us to your house now without a fear in this world."

"When? …Now?"

"You are too busy?" Gerald queried. "Of course. I know the place anyway. Julian has never visited the farm because it caused my downfall from the grace of Our Mother. She hated it so much she did not want to be associated with anything that goes on there. She even decampaigned my efforts to get novices to become vets. Let Virigo take us there."

"What do you want to do there?" Ssempa asked.

"I want to gauge its safety as far as Julian is concerned. To assure myself that when Julian — she has just been appointed procuratrix, in charge of all procurements for the House — that when she comes, there won't be problems. Being procuratrix, apart from the teaching and the occasional cooking at Marlorec, gives her lots of freedom. She happens to be above suspicion where we come from. I want it that when she goes to your house by the river, prying eyes and minds there will be minimal."

"And you need to go inside, of course?"

"Bluntly," said Gerald in a teacher's voice, "Julian must view all that she is going into. And she won't return to this place, ever."

"Alright, then. I'll give Virigo the keys."

"Yes. And I wish you could get her not to mind. She is highly committed if, as she says, she is acquainted to Abbess Valerian — she is our Prioress — and to Monsignor Fabiano. But as to you, hers is not mere love. Virigo is not even your elder sister. She thinks she begat you. She would die before seeing you suffer. You will give us your telephone number, of course. And ours will be with Virigo. She can call the school and ask for either of us."

"Good arrangements," said Ssempa, wondering at his newly acquired taciturnity.

"Don't be so smug. You have an unasked question disturbing your conscience," said Gerald, in Luganda.

"What?"

"You want to know where I stand! Do I have a man?"

"It did cross my mind."

"Don't bother your head about that. Send us that Virigo woman, Mr Ssempa, will you?"

* * *

And so it came to pass that Sister Julian Dominicus Kantarama would ring
the workshop and learn of Ssempa's work schedules from Kabibi. The two
women, both being refugees from Rwanda, had inevitably struck an intimate
friendship so that they were frequently to be found together at the exclusive
Catholic Secretariat Marlorec, with its flowery greenery, red brick structures,
excellent chefs, Italian and French wines, local and visiting prelacy, and flocks
of the more affluent religiose and various humanity that Kyera had shepherded
into the faith. In due course, Julian got to know the ways of the world. She
could drive herself in the station wagon to the river house to which she had
acquired spare keys. The isolation of the timber house allowed no prying eyes.
There were few local folk in the vicinity of the pine forest and only child goat
grazers swimming in the grey currents of the river in the evenings. It was fine
for her for the time being.

Six

Mbarara, Southern Uganda, 1976

In their third month of sin, Sister Julian Dominicus told him she and others of her Order were going on a month-long trip to Poland, Italy and the Holy Land. This was much to be desired. Ssempa had been bracing himself to announce to her his own people's religion in order to explain his impending pilgrimage to Mecca, a journey he had undertaken annually for the past three years. It was a trip from which he made as much money in a few days as in two months of risk coffee bean smuggling. To Arabia he took sapphires, rubies and garnets that he procured from Mbuji Mayi and Mbandaka in Zaire through a mineral trader introduced to him by Issa Sinzagaya Gakinya. He returned with cash dollars and electronic merchandise from Jeddah to sell on the steadily developing and quite lucrative *magendo* black market. He had found the need to expose to her the part of him that he had kept quiet about not only because of his impending absence but also because of the grand Islamic festivities that would welcome him from the hajj. He had no idea how she would take the revelation, but he was determined to tell her.

It was surprising that neither she nor Sister Gerald had found out so far, say from Kabibi. The latter had recently queried him: "Does Kantarama know you are Muslim?"

"Ha! — Great question that. Am I a Muslim, really, Virigo?"

"You aren't a Christian, anyhow."

"Muslim is not the opposite of Christian, Virigo. I'm a Muganda with some belief in a God who rules and sustains us through the sun, the planets, the other stars and the various essential gases that ensure our mathematical, chemical, biological and physical being. Surely, you know that for I have always striven to explain that pet subject of mine. It happens I am much older than Islam and Christianity."

"You infuriate me so!" Kabibi pursed her mouth. "I always tell you that people belong to their parents' religions; you just want to be a stubborn exception."

"I am above the age of belonging to my parents' spiritual beliefs. Only four decades ago my mother believed she was a Christian because her parents had been converted to that culture. Then she met my father and now believes — as he does — that she is a Muslim. The only condition that does not change for them is that they are both Africans who were enticed away from their time-tested faiths by glib tongues. Because of that, all the Baganda people I

240

know — Christian or Muslim, lay or clergy — occasionally return to ancestral shrines for spiritual cleansing. You know that, surely."

"You want to start your own faith; you believe that's possible?"

"No, I don't think it easy. Possible yes. Actually Islam and Christianity are the religions that were *started* — some nineteen hundred years ago. They are both too young to affect me the way my ancestral beliefs would. They cannot affect me at all. I am not one of those who believe we had no God to profess our faith in, or that our beliefs were inferior to the new, or that God above Africa is spelt with a smaller *g*, since *He* is the very same universal God."

"You are going to Mecca...."

"You very well know it is for trade, Virigo...."

"Kantarama will not know that; she will want to know why."

"Oh, I see. Now that you mention it and we indeed discuss the issue, I will explain it to her. I had never bothered about it before."

"Why not before your pilgrimage... before she asks?"

"Because I have nothing to explain."

"You know what she is, but she does not know what you are, Ssempa."

"Julian knows pretty well what I am. We sleep together every now and then, mind you. Her Catholicism is a mere by-the-way and likewise she should find my Islamic background another fickle *by-the-way* and...."

"Not all people find things as simple as you make them out. If Catholics cannot stand Protestants who are fellow Christians, what will it be like for her to realise, as she certainly will in the end, that the only man she has in this world goes on annual pilgrimages to Mecca? All the angels and all the devils will rain here from heaven and hell will rise from the depths of the earth. Why didn't you tell her about yourself in the first place?"

"There wasn't the need for it, I keep telling you. She and her uncle had taken my foreign name to be Christian, I assume. Gakinya should have told his brother-in-law; he might even have done so for all I know. They are extremely sectarian too; though Julia hides her own ethnic biases well, having grown up here. I have sometimes wondered whether Gakinya might not have told the monsignor about my background!"

Kabibi sighed. "He may not have found it relevant. The two women will discover it by themselves. They are happy you aren't Catholic; of course it makes them feel less of sinners. Gerald has a man too, you know. The proprietor of In-Café Breeds! They have been together at it like wife and husband, imagine; I mean, three years like that and not a whisper of it in public! Even his wife does not know."

"But you do!"

"Kantarama confided in me. The man, being Catholic and rich, is always at The Marlorec. His flirtation with Gerald has long been taken as the innocent result of prolonged acquaintance. If Kantarama hadn't told me of it, me I'd have taken it for granted they were merely shepherdess and sheep."

"Ewe and ram sounds more to the point. Lucky bastard! Makes one wish he were Catholic too. He should be a real cancer, eating away at the setup from deep within."

"Any other one should say that about wishing to be Catholic. But you?" Kabibi shook her head. "You are a heathen through and through. What will happen when she finds out — or may be you don't care?"

"What do you take me for, Virigo? I know I am an atheist, in terms of your foreign, organised religion. But I have a heart, too. I have feelings. I, too, love."

"You — love? Tell that to the birds. It would have been futile for me to attempt to divert her feelings for you, to have her shun you like you were the plague. And you are saying to me that you have love! You? In that heart?" She prodded his chest. "Have a heart."

"It will shock her to death, my poor innocent virgin, when she finds out I not only am *pagan*, but a purported Muslim too. We are in a world where even love must be pegged on imported, false, and malicious faiths. If love exists, Virigo, it is what I feel for Julia."

"Love has existed for eons of time for you, Ssempa. You told me you solemnly loved Jessica, then Kaburunga, then Chandiru, and Djamila Abbo the Jopadhola police driver, and Joy Kabenge! Ah, how you loved Joy Kabenge — do you remember the day Abbo very nearly injured her with a pistol shot? And Zakiya Razak, and Nyte Basuuta, and that Alur, whom you told me had been a married woman! Who didn't you love and feel sorry for? When I remember the fashion in which you dumped Joy Kabenge, I know you are a real man. Macho mixed with masochism. Is Kantarama any better than Kabenge? — Or Basuuta?"

"Yes. Julian is virgin."

"Still? Ah la la la la! Stop talking to me the way you do when drunk, Ssempa."

"Okay, okay, Virigo. Help me marry Julia. Just help me in that and you will be a better godmother to me than old, long-gone Nyirandegeya."

"Do not bother me, idiot," Kabibi said with a skeptical look creasing her brow. She said, almost with kindness — as though speaking to a foolish child — "Ssempa, you can never love. Period. Sleep with the nun and dump her. I know your heart. You aren't bad. I know you won't follow her with bad language and rumour the way the men here do when they fall out with their women. Let her go back and heal, eh? Though, I hasten to add, I don't see Kantarama healing. Did you know that if you were to ask her to leave the convent today she would do so without giving it a second thought?"

"I know."

"Like hell you do! Do me a grand favour, Ssempa, and I will never ask you for a bigger one. You ask me to help you marry Kantarama. Thank you for that. Help me and don't just marry her. *Wed* her, for my sake." There was a genuine note of appeal in Kabibi's voice and her eyes.

"Virigo...!"

"Yes. She is willing. She would ask you to move away from the town. Away from her diocese, so that she may not shame her faith — her people."

"You have forgotten the other consideration...."

"Wedlock would get rid of all those. It would make the gross disparity between your purported religions the triviality it deserves to be. Kantarama has come to view foreign religions the very way you yourself do. By the way — 'never tether a bad goat next to a good one,' as the old adage goes. She laughs at what she calls 'the antics' of the clergy that visit The Marlorec. She has told me she had not noticed what went on there until she met you, and that that was mostly unholy stuff."

* * *

Sister Julian left for her own pilgrimage in the middle of February and Ssempa left for Saudi Arabia at the beginning of March. He arrived back in Mbarara two days before her.

* * *

She would later narrate her shock to Virgo Kabibi at The Marlorec where they sat alone under a cluster of date palms imported and planted by the man that should have deflowered her chastity instead of Ssempa, the Frenchman, Father Antoine Fasson. She recalled driving the station wagon to River House, eager to see, touch and hold her worldly inamorato.

Julian was mildly surprised to find the telltale remains of a just-ended festivity. A large makeshift marquee with an expansive blue-and-white striped tarpaulin spread over its top as a canopy was erected in the three-acre courtyard. There were charred areas in the recently mown lawn, where big fires had licked barbecuing meats and the bottoms of large copper *sufurias* of cooking food. Clusters of large bare bones, cow horns and dried lumps of cooked *matooke* lay scattered all over the place and cow and goat hides stood stretched out on scaffolds to dry. Chicken feathers of various colours lay piled in several small mounds, the wind blowing at them all over the compound. Mountains of banana peelings at the edge of the pine forest were beginning to reek with traces of alcohol, and goats and sheep nibbled them, oblivious to the recent mass killing of their brethren. And men, women and children were bent to some task wherever her eyes went. There had quite evidently been a grand banquet that had involved much feasting.

A wedding! *That* had been her initial foreboding.

Mother of God! — Was that possible?

Her heart reeled. Her arteries and veins burnt, tickled and itched with the pain of boiling blood. She felt faint. She was uttering a series of Holy Marys as she opened the door to step out of the car. 'Holy Mary, Mother of God, blessed above all women you are, harrowed is your name ... let it not be.' She buttoned and belted the dusty brown mackintosh she had bought in Florence. The workers paid her little attention as she donned a pair of dark sunglasses. She had an uncomfortable feeling that those hordes of people would identify the worries by looking at her face and general stature. She had placed a yellow, brown and lavender bandanna over her head and tied it gingerly at the nape to conceal the cream veil.

A wedding! A wedding festival for sure. And who else's? Gerald would kill him, she thought. The elderly nun had insisted she knew the townsfolk well. They were loose and unserious in all they did. Julian had been away for thirty-eight days only and Ssempa had gone on to.... She laughed at herself. She knew he could *not* do that to her. She had no doubt he felt for her the way she did for him.

The workers turned to look at her as she walked towards the entrance: four white terrazzo steps yellowed by time, wide and semicircular, which took you to the door — a pair of dark, heavy *mvule*-wood shutters with thick glass panels in their top halves. She felt their eyes on her, knew they scrutinized her attire. She felt heavy in her limbs, light in the head. 'If David has gone and wedded! — Have mercy on me, Holy Virgin.'

She stepped into the thirty-foot square hall, which had always been bare of furniture but had been maintained tidily and smelt strongly of honey-scented floor polish. But today, large and small cartons of all description were piled on top of each other all over the room. Kodak, Ilford, Fuji–photo chemicals, Olivetti typewriter ribbons, Nippondenso spark plugs, Hitachi, Toshiba, Mitsubishi, Sony, Matsushita–transistor radios, Lockheed brake fluid, Toyota, Saab Scania, Volvo – motor spare parts; trademarks were emblazoned in various letterings and colourings wherever her eyes went.

A new puzzle entered her mind. She realised that all the women were attired in the Kiganda *busuuti* costume: bulky garments that flowed below the ankles in rolls of printed fabric and headdresses that covered the ears. In Nkore such attire was more religious than tribal. Julian's eyes went to the men, two wore that skullcap that was the trademark of those that professed the religion of tongues that nobody spoke on the streets or casually in the homestead.

Had David sold the house? He was a smuggler and a mechanic. Their family owned other buildings in Mbarara. But he had seemed to adore the river house. She didn't imagine him bargaining it away easily. And he had told her it belonged to his aged father who had retired to his rural farms, away from the hustle and bustle of man-eat-man trade that Idi Amin's Economic War had brought with it. She climbed the stairs and when she had reached the first landing, chanced to see through the round porthole where five vehicles and Ssempa's blue Peugeot pickup were parked by the disused seedling beds to the southeast of the house, which you could not view from the front. As she got to the top of the staircase, in the hall off which opened the two bedroom doors and the one to the living room on her right, the strong fragrance of burning frankincense hit her nostrils.

Incense!

Had David died? For when someone dies in Uganda food is cooked in plenty and animals are killed for their meat to feed the hundreds of mourners. But why the presence of the Muslims?

'If he dies,' Julian declared, 'Mother of God, I shall also certainly die.'

Then as the living room door opened while she stood hesitantly at the top of the stairs, two dozen feet emerged from it, her own mouth fell open. Four men, big and beefy, followed each other out of the big room trailed, like flies, by the strong frankincense. All were clad in snow-white *kanzu* robes with gold embroidery at the necks or breasts. Three wore red fezzes and one, a snow-white skullcap with tiny holes in it. He was as black and hulking as Idi Amin, the president of the Republic of Uganda. Another one was obviously a high-ranking military man; he had tribal markings slashed savagely in his cheeks, like the people of the West Nile region of Uganda. They all wore expensive-looking sandals and reeked of perfume.

'Had David been arrested'? Her mind flew back to Kyondo and the destroyed tent and the dead soldiers.

But that was answered quickly. The men looked at her cordially and politely saluted her without taking her hand. She had pushed both hands into the pockets of the mackintosh in an openly unfriendly manner. One of the men asked her business in the place and that relieved her because, the men, who spoke Luganda and Kiswahili, would have said to the stranger as a greeting: '*Nga kitalo,*' which would have been a commiseration. It meant: 'What ghastly tidings!'

And now she was hopeful and wishful at the same time that Ssempa had sold the house. It was the first idea to enter her heart as an alternative to his frightening demise. These men were nothing like David. They were all Moslems.

"Does David — Mr Ssempa — still live here?"

"Oh, certainly, madam — er, Sister." One of the men, shortish, light-complexioned with an acne-infested face and protuberant eyes, had looked at her headdress and down at the opening in the lower front of the mackintosh. "He is inside the sitting room. You go right through the door."

Her heart pumped a great deal more, in disdain. She had been unmasked. That unpleasant man might have noted the brown Franciscan habit through the inverted V opening at the lower front of the mackintosh. The men descended the stairs slower than she thought they should have. She wished that she had called Virgo Kabibi before venturing here. She wished like she had never wished before that she had come along with Sister Gerald. Gerald would probably have pushed these over-polite men out of the way and gone in to lambaste David for having invited them to the house without informing Julian! She nearly left. But the four men in long white and cream *kanzu* robes were going down those stairs with all faces curiously turned back at her. She was reminded of swiveling gun turrets on tanks. She disliked the men and she feared their stares. She would not walk on the same stairs with them. She pushed the door and stepped into the big living room.

Ssempa was seated cross-legged on a small oval, cream, red, deep brown and pale yellow Persian rug placed on an expansive green, blue, red and cream one that had not been in the house before. The furniture, heavy-cushioned sofas, ottomans, coffee tables, lamp stands, sideboards and glittering-wood Blaupunkt tape recorder, were pushed to the far end, towards the dining room, against a wall. Seated in the same fashion as Ssempa were three other men, all elderly and one of them obviously a sheikh! The burning incense was issuing from a pale-brown clay bowl with a small pile of smouldering charcoal. Plumes of white smoke floated towards the high pine ceiling. Around the seated men, cartons of merchandise were piled.

He looked up at her and she became, at least seventy-five percent sure it was him! But what on earth was this?

Did she see guilt in his eyes? What devil had propelled her through the lounge on the ground floor, up that long staircase, past those funny kanzu-clad men, through the door behind her, to this hellhole? Curiosity!

She heard the faint strains of Zairean music coming out of the bedrooms' mahogany door. Franco was singing *Catherine Ndoki*. Julian had learned most of the meaning of the lyrics from Ssempa. Catherine wanted to punish her husband because she felt he wasn't being faithful to her. She went to a cultural consultant for action and that doctor asked her what she wanted done. *'Catho alobi nganga boma mari, eh.'* Kill my husband, said Catherine. And the *nganga* turned his eyes to the ceiling and clapped his hands once in exasperatiom. He said, 'I don't kill people': *'Kobebisa ngai te; tika mobali ooo.'* He was appealing to her not to contaminate his practice by demanding the unorthodox. He advised her to divorce her husband instead. So witch-doctory wasn't all about bloodthirst! What would have been in it for Catho — revenge? And, of course, she would keep the deceased man's property! Her mind returned to her present plight.

The bastard fool had converted to Islam!

Why? What could have happened?

Ssempa, she noted, was dressed worse than the sheikh. That is to say, his Arabian attire was even more elaborate than the others'. Julian had seen Israeli Jews dressed like that in Megiddo and she had enquired to know what Muslims were doing on a Christian pilgrimage and was told, to her astonishment, that very few Jews were Christian. And that Arabs and Jews were a Semitic people who dressed the same and shared similar cultural and religious values not shared by Christians. What was taboo to Arabs, like, the consumption of alcohol and pork, was taboo to Jews too, but not necessarily to Christians. Arabs had their chief weekly prayers on a Friday. Jews, like the Adventists in her own country, had theirs on Saturdays, which they termed the Sabbath. To travel was to see! She had not known before what she was being told. She only knew of the rabid antagonism between the two Semitic peoples; today, to be anti-Semitic meant being pro-Arab. Semite no longer meant Arab but Jew only. As far as the Semites' identical dress was concerned, here in Uganda only devout Muslims dressed so — so detestably. She never easily discarded the notion that that dress in Megiddo and all the places she had visited in the Holy Land was enemy dress. Ssempa's *kaffiyeh*, woven in golden yellow and black thread and with a square open casement to hold down the white wimple-like headdress made him look like a black King Faisal ibn Saud of Arabia.

In spite of the fact that he appeared powerful and enigmatically beautiful in the dress, she felt sick. Her stomach churned. She was dazed by the alien and almost chaste appearance that the Semitic garb lent the man she thought she knew.

To confirm and exacerbate her worst fears, Ssempa spoke in the language not meant for the street or the homestead: "*Yaah swahhab'ah*, Sheikh Maulaana," he prattled. "Colonel Lupai, Mr Reisch, you must now excuse me. I must talk to Julian. *Wa hadha assalaam aleikoum.*"

How could Ssempa speak in this godforsaken Arabic language?

She was glued to the spot where she stood. This, surely, was a dream! Was it Gerald who had said she knew how to awaken herself from dreams she didn't enjoy! The old sheikh and the two other men, one of them a very wealthy fat half-caste whom she knew to own several M.A.N lorries, coffee and hides and skins stores and a big section of Mbarara town, got up as the nails of Julian's right-hand fingers tried to inflict pain to her upper thigh, just below the hip. No amount of the sharp pinching would change the scenery.

The man with deep tribal slashes in his cheeks was just saying to Ssempa: "That man convinced me he knew your face from 1971 or 72; one day I will show him to you."

"What is his name, Colonel?"

"Warrant Officer Class-Two Tretre Juma. A man from Maracha, in West Nile. But he is an ageing soldier. Brain goes saw-dusty in such men, you know. He can't have seen you in Kampala in 71 when you were far away in Rwanda. That big Toyota man, Silas, told me you put up his mega-workshop in Kigali. One day you will see this Tretre Juma."

"Sure I should like to see him one day, Colonel," Ssempa had responded after a brisk hesitation. Seeing that particular man, the man that had caused the death of Zoe Atimango, was the very last thing he would want. "*Salaam aleikum.*"

The exchange came to her faintly, as if it took place in another place at another time. The Ssempa who spoke strange tongues stood up nimbly and planted himself before her with a look she might have punched him in the mouth for, if her heart had not hoped he would grasp her and keep her from falling! She watched the men shuffle out of the room one following the other, the way white ants did after their flight when they had shed their wings. They left the door ajar; Ssempa closed it.

"Ah la la lah." He mimicked the exclamation she always used to express consternation. "You are going to kill me now."

He was attempting a smile that did not come off. He had the notion that his Islam was like granules of sugar your parents found stuck to your mouth when they pulled your head out of the cupboard, where you were eating it illegally. His guilt was in the notion that it would appear he had deliberately hidden his religious leanings from her.

She glowered at him, her eyes dark pieces of flint, which threatened to ignite the crisp atmosphere. Her trip had made her flesh much smoother, fresher. She was, he was realising, the most curvaceously smashing beauty, the most dazzling woman, he had ever beheld.

"Well, you are not dreaming, Julia, and I am not a ghost. I am sorry for never having had the guts to warn you about this religion thing. I knew — all along I knew it might tarnish your perception of me. Now I cannot continue to run. You've caught me in my true colours and here I am, stark naked before you. I, David Ssempa, do belong to the Muslims. It is partly through my belonging to them that I became associated with your uncle Gakinya in Kigali in 1972. But it was due to my unconcern for religions which keep brother and brother at bay as foes that I never found it worthwhile to explain my religious background." He touched his *kaffiyeh*.

Her disbelieving eyes never left his face.

"Let me pull this piece of relic off my head." He pulled down his headdress and then carefully removed her own bandanna that covered the cream vestal veil. "And this other museum piece on your own head." He placed *kaffiyeh* and vestal veil opposite each other on the Persian rug, tossing the bandanna aside. "Instead of you and I killing each other with hatreds foreign to us, let them tear each other into pieces as we look on. Let us witness what they are capable of on their own. After all they both, in their separate ways, represent the great God of Abraham, of Ishmael, of Isaac, of Moses, of David, of Israel, of Jesus of Galilee, of Muhammad and his Arabs, of the Middle East, Rome, Great Britain, America. Mine here belongs to the Arabs' deity while yours here belongs to the Romans' god." Ssempa prodded both pieces of cloth with his index finger. "Tough, powerful little things these two, Julia, eh? You are a Munyarwanda, and I am a Muganda. We both live in Nkore in a town called Mbarara — a mere one-hundred-and-fifty miles midway between Kigali and Kampala." He ran an index finger across the soft glossy skin of her arm. "The apparent difference in the textures of our skins is only due to our sexes. But you are no more a relation of Jesus Christ and his mother than I am of Muhammad of Mecca and Medina. To the Arab and Jew, to Jesus and to Muhammad, your purported Christianity and my supposed Islam are local traditions while to us they are sheer religion or *diinih*. Faith! Powerful word that. *Diinih* is the Hebraic and Arabic word for culture or way of life, see? To us, their tradition is a cutthroat *faith*. And our Africanness — our religious values, ancient and humane as they are, are heathenness to them. No matter how we attempt to become humble converts, we remain kaffirs in their eyes because of our colour. We strive to learn their *diinihs* and lifestyles in their tongues and manners through much difficulty and financial depravation so that we may use those faiths to learn to hate each other. They hate our colour and culture and yet we are prepared to tear each other apart in suspicion and anger for those two bastard Semites instead of agreeing on the issues that concern our lives. We lie in our hearts that we don't belong to our own ancestors, whom we disown as heathen atheists. Why, Julia — whose real name is Kantarama *ka* Sebwitabure because you have nothing to do with Julius, the Roman seventh number — won't these two modern-ancient relics of cloth made of cotton and silk probably gotten from Africa by trick or from vast China, which has no God — why won't these two relics fall on each other and slug it out? If they won't — and they cannot! — why must you doubt my profound feeling; my great personal African love for you, my very dearest sweetheart?"

Without saying a thing, she gripped him, her fingers digging into the bones of his shoulder blades, her intense eyes prodding at his like needles. She forced him to sit down and she knelt before him as he sat cross-legged the way she had found him.

"But your name, David? It is a Christian name."

"You must come out of their past, Kantarama, and enter into ours. I love the name David because, like a fool, I also think he was a hero. *Whose* hero, though, was he? Some Jews fighting Philistines? It is all archaic. David is a Semitic name shared by the Arab and the Jew, who know its meaning, and I know it not. It could mean *nte*-cow, for all I know, which, as you already know, also happens to be my clan totem. It might mean that particular cow that I wouldn't knowingly touch for the life of me. David and Julian are silly names that we have adopted, like foreign headdresses, table manners, languages. Come to think of it, would you imagine Pope Paulus Sextus hating your Bahutu with that enthusiasm that you and Monsignor Raphael share? No. He would bless them. I seem to remember Rome assisted them to chase you out of Rwanda. He would, rightly of course — but to your utter discomfiture, wed you to them without a thought. Please, count me out of such a club of mediocre people. I told your uncle in Gitarama the first time we met and stressed it to you in Kabale that organised religion and I were true divorcees. One of the reasons I really hated that lieutenant was his persistent reference to me as a priest."

"Don't continue philosophising, David Ssempa. You will tell me why you are dressed like this and what the banquet here was for. Whose wedding was it? You Muslims are renowned for multiple polygamy."

"Polygamy is not that Islamic. I happen to have lived with Muslims all my life and have had the opportunity to travel a bit. The majority of Muslim Arab men I have met have just one wife. Polygamy is an African thing and Africans who practise Islam only indulge in polygamy out of their lustful wishes, laying the blame on the weaknesses in their Quran. Europeans would practise it but for their economic selfishness — not morals, mark you. Polygamy is a positive thing when the number of women in the land surpasses that of men. Where do the rest of the husbandless women go? — To the convents? Or do they go to the streets to sell their flesh? Don't you see the master plan to keep our numbers in check? Is an army of lesser numbers stronger than that of multitudes?"

"Those Westerners you so much love to criticize wed one wife.

"We need numbers to match their technologies."

"Well, did you or did you not just wed, Ssempa?"

"There was no wedding. I just returned from a pilgrimage to Mecca."

"A pilgrimage to Mecca! And yet you say you aren't a devout…!'"

"These days, my dear, pilgrims to what you think is the Holy Land travel to purchase duty-free merchandise for resale back here at great profit. The Mecca trip is even more profitable because all purchases there are not only duty-free but subsidised."

"Do you love money above all else?"

"Even in the convents, Julia, there is nothing nearly as crucially important as money. Those with the bigger heaps of it control the churches, the mosques and the reins of state. Governments are operated on nothing else. The Vatican and miniature vaticans like the one at Kyera, are some of the richest establishments on Earth. Their inhabitants wallow in money-based luxuries. Simply look at The Marlorec."

"I cannot argue with you of course because your worst rhetoric always makes sense to me. But listen to my own philosophy, David. You could have had the courtesy to prepare me for this outrage, to tell me you were nothing but a goddamned Mohammedan. All along I took you for a goddamned Protestant. It would have been the goddamnedest lesser evil of the two since the latter are Christian — albeit a confused type. All along I consoled myself with the illusion that we had done this thing by coincidence. It was never an accident to you, was it? Had I known you were a Moslem, I wouldn't have fallen for those cheap, dirty tricks. Your gin-in-coffee was not a remedy for my high fever — it was… was — ooo, you!"

"You are grossly unfair to me. I am irreligious and I told you so. All the same I don't know Islam to be an evil faith. If I were to choose between the two, I would take the one that took your *Old Testament* to the letter, which Islam, like Judaism, does. After all, I was brought up in the thick of Islam. The first commandment of the Bible — the most fundamental one since that book defines God as a jealous God — is to desist from the worship of graven images. Your church's foundation is built on that worship. No wonder you were assured that to read the Bible was a sin so that you may not question those figurines to which you pray. Muslims remove their shoes to go to prayer — the way Moses did the day he met God in person at Mount Sinai. The way the Bible tells it is the way Muslims supplicate to God Almighty. The daily Muslim dress is that of your priests and priestesses at the altar. What Muslim women wear as their daily street attire are what nuns like you don to claim holiness! And the tricks you accuse me of! I realised late you needed a man to take your body when you yourself cajoled me into that bed."

"Because I was drunk;" and then she added, emphasizing each words, "You ... knew ... I ... waaas ... drunk. You made me drunk *intentionally*."

"Then you insult my wisdom, Julia. And you accuse me unfairly. You may not have heard yourself saying it over and over as we fornicated our very first time. You kept lamenting that officer's actions, that officer's hand. You tricked me into that bed, Julia."

She fell silent in disbelief.

"Is that what you say?" Julian asked huskily.

"Yes; that soldier — that soldier's hand, made you do it."

"Oh my God — *David*! If you repeat any such words, you will never ever see me again."

"I shall never repeat those stupid words."

After a brief silence she said: "But you knew I had a Muslim uncle and I thus wouldn't hold such silly prejudices."

"That is filthy, detestable hypocrisy. You hate me right now — for nothing but a faith I make fun at, a religion in which my ignorant father believes as faithfully as your hopeless uncle, Monsignor Nyarwaya, does in his. But the Monsignor is neither ignorant of nor oblivious to the fickleness of foreign religion because he's paid a fat salary to spread it. His elegance in God's dress also shows me a man of God who knows what women want in a man. Why does he not exchange that large solid gold rood at his breast for a wooden one? Why are his vestments so rich in texture and, obviously, so expensive? Why...?"

"Will you, please, leave my uncle out of this?"

"He, like you, like my father and my uncle — and worst of all like all the people who don special regalia to lead others to doctrines that divide us and insult our values — are evil and greedy felons pretending to be saints. Their musical utterances and their rich dress are like scarecrows in the millet and sorghum fields; they are meant to eternally bar us from discovering the truth that would free us from bondage and salvage us from hunger."

"I am not that ripe yet in your dark evangelism...."

"That's it! Doing your best to scare me away from my freedom, to keep me in bondage to foreign dogma by demonising my faith as dark — as black evangelism, and yet you are so black. Look, I hate to see you this joyless. We are calling it quits. Go back to your convent, confess your sins and go into penitence. Turn back to your dictatorial Christ, that great bloke who was honest enough to tell all to hear that his gospels were never meant for non-Jewish *dogs*. You are the one who has something to lose. Me, I have no apologies to your foreign gods and prophets and their mothers. *Virgin* mothers my foot! A mother and at the same time a virgin? Why do you teach biology, Julia?"

Ssempa shook his head in irritation. "Yet for you I would do anything. To you I have apologised because I've destroyed your freak sanctity. If you say you forgive me, I will release myself from my guilt and live a happy man. If you don't, I shall not rest. Not because of your false god of Christ but because of your sanctified person. Because for any woman to live for three decades without knowledge of a man can be nothing but sanctified. Remember we had such sanctified men and women here ourselves before Europeans and Arabs came here to destroy our religio-cultural heritages. Go back, Julian, please, and leave me to pick up the pieces of my life."

"I cannot go back. I have become a worldly woman. I see things differently now. I sat on jetliners and thought of no Jesus but you, David. In Polish Zakopane I sat in the ancient church and thought of nothing but you. In Brindisi I dreamt of us together in the pine forest yonder. In Capernaum, in the Holy Land, I filled the pages of my notebook with your name — goddamn you. And now you send me away, like a Muslim man tired of his umpteenth wife."

"If you won't go back, I will not wait to wed you; I know you know what that means. We travel to Kampala, or to Mbale, or to Nairobi, and get two nice witnesses and the books of those Arabs and Hebrews between us to swear upon. And metal bands on our fingers to keep reminding us we are wed. Our people never required such relics to keep reminding them of their matrimonial responsibilities. Our people were tougher — more serious — until the scourge of Jesus and Mohammed arrived here in the hands of Arabs, Frenchmen and Englishmen. Personally I would prefer seeing the Monsignor Raphael Nyarwaya and my father, Hajji Sulayman Ssemaganda, outside of their foreign regalia, blessing us as spouses."

"If you will always find things as easy as you say them, I will be your ever-loving happy wife. After all you are a good solver of dicey problems. I do realise the things you claim, too. For one those headdresses haven't moved an inch towards each other. I have not fallen dead with my initial shock at your funny dress! Not even God or *Bikira* Maria is killing me yet or I'd already feel it in my gut. I have for the past several minutes attempted to hate you. I've wished I were dead for not finding that hatred deep inside me. I wish to find the whole thing horrendous but a dense screen of corruption and confusion stands between my heart and my brain. I cannot even say I don't know what you have done to me, because I know. You have loved me and loved me in a way that no other human being can be allowed to love me. Virigo is my indemnity in this, just like Gerald will be yours. I am going to be your wife and be a mother of your children. And I am not drunk on gin coffee."

"Oh, Gerald! What will that woman say?"

"Let Gerald alone. Uncle Monsignor will strangle me."

"Then I shan't allow you to go there."

"Oh, David, husband mine! Man of final, steadfast solutions. Did you know you hadn't welcomed me from my pilgrimage?"

He stood up, went to the door and latched it, turned back and gave the two discarded headdresses a sidelong look: "Poor devils," he shook his head. "Stuck for action. Mere scarecrows passing for saints' representations, transplanted from their more convenient cradles in Arabia and Rome to seek recognition and even solace in our lands and in our loving hearts, to subtly poison us. But caught out in time, aren't they? There they lie, unmasked." He picked up the two headdresses and cast them to one side without ceremony and sat down again, cross-legged. "If you forgive me for this, Julia, for not having unmasked these spies for you, you'll never catch me in any other wrongdoing."

"Spies — and intruders. *Agents provocateurs*! I was just wondering, are you circumcised?"

He looked at her with stunned delicateness. She wouldn't know that, even. He held his hands to her smooth cheeks and said, gently: "I am guilty of harbouring that other intruder."

She changed her kneeling position and sat cross-legged, before him, their knees pressed each to the other.

"I know what worldly love is now. To forgive — to feel no ill will towards you for this, which I will get accustomed to as I did my first sin. You should know that what I loathed most in the past minutes was to discover that you had wedded another woman! Swear to me, David Ssempa, that even though you are a Moslem, you won't do that."

"Do... what? Marry another —! Oh, my dear, Julia. I am not that kind of Muslim. I don't even think God himself is in the process of creating another woman for me."

"On my part, David, I love Jesus, you know. Believe it, Jesus can make love to you: sacerdotal love. But it leaves you empty. Perhaps even emptier than before! Like it was a mere fragment of passion. But with you, it is so stupendous, so physically gratifying. I don't know what to say."

"That makes two of us. As I said, God isn't yet ready to create another you. When he does, let Him do so for our first son."

"Oh, how I know you mean it, David. I promised my mother I'd go to see her in Kabgaye when I returned from the pilgrimage. I want to travel to Rwanda next week and stay with her for a fortnight."

"You don't want me to accompany you?"

"Yes, I want you to. I am afraid of the border."

"I will take you through Kisoro and Cyanika-Kidaho. Or even make as if we are going to Zaire through Bunagana and make a tour of Kivu through

Rutshuru. There we have an option to go into Rwanda through Goma-Gisenyi. I have a wonderful old touring car. We could even go round the Lake Kivu to Bukavu and come into Rwanda through Cyangugu-Kibuye to Gitarama. It's the most difficult terrain I have ever driven through, and at the same time, the most breathtakingly beautiful land in the world."

"You have been to all those places?"

"I told you of my ordeal with the late Laban Sorrozo. Besides a relative of mine owns buildings in Bukavu and I lived there when I was a teenager. Why, I could return to Burundi and see my Senegalese associates for whatever new thing they have on market. Care to travel to Bujumbura with me? Very humid, hot city on the shores of Lake Tanganyika."

"Look, I am not used to all that. A nun professes to live a life of humility, poverty, frugality and chastity among other things. You offer me luxury only."

"I intend to make you my business assistant. You have to learn the ropes. One of the most effective ways to do that is to know the routes."

"From the cloister to the highways! What a metamorphosis!"

"You would love it. Nearly eighteen years of no life — just like you were back in the womb. The remainder must recompense your lost naturalness."

"True too. Once you get a whiff of nature, there is no turning back to fragments of passion. I am tired. Let us go to the bedroom. I need to rest. Do you still listen to *Soley Soley*?"

"We shall listen to it together. As for that rest, these carpets and cushions are yet unused. We will rest here," he bowed forward, hefted her and sat her in his lap, her long supple legs and thighs straddling him, the knees touching his ears.

"On the prayer mat!" Julian gasped in protest, breathlessly.

"*Carpet*. We shall pray to have that baby boy, too."

"Oh, David! That's blasphemy." She breathed, huskily.

"Yes; sure." Grunted he.

And the strong ripe *kassukussuku* scent of her loins awakened in him a frenzied desire punctuated by whispered groans, moans and sighs.

Seven

Kigali, Rwanda, April 1977

They left Mbarara towards Easter holidays in Ssempa's ten-year-old, six-cylinder, bone-white Jaguar MK2-340, which he had bought from an old army captain, a Sandhurst Military Academy graduate, who was replacing it with the newer XJ6 model. They decided to evade the Kabale-Gatuna or even the Mirama Hill-Kagitumba frontiers where they did not want to be seen again, and went through the Kisoro-Cyanika customs point through Ruhengeri. They crossed the border at Cyanika at high noon and headed for Kigali where they arrived at four, Rwanda time. Ssempa went into a clothier's shop on Rue de Lac Bulera and bought dresses for her. He never ceased to marvel at the way she appeared in secular clothes. Julian was a *woman* God had made for giving birth.

Two large planeloads of Libyan officials, most of them military, had arrived at Kanombe in the late afternoon and there were no suites in any of Kigali's best hotels: the Hotel Belge or the Milles Collines. A Muganda mechanic friend of Ssempa with connections to *les mannequins* spies of the defence ministry secured him a suite in L'Hotel de Cinq Juillet which, half a decade previously, he had known as L'Hotel MDR. At that time the late Laban Sorrozo had resided there under the wings of a Colonel Habyara and a Capitaine Ndize, now a colonel heading the military *les mannequins*. Ndize's spies and the even more efficient spies of the Ministry of Justice were, deceptively harmless individuals who noted and recorded everything they saw for *La Présidence*. Banyarwanda popularly pronounced *les mannequins* as *les mannehko* and simply called all government spies *ba'mannehko*. Ssempa did not find it easy to convince Julian to sleep in the Cinq Juillet, an MRND party-owned hotel. The MRND party was the military ruling junta of Juvenal Habyarimana, who created it when he overthrew the Gregoire Kayibanda regime on the fifth of July 1973.

"We could have slept in anything, David. The Hotel du Kiyovu on Avenue de Rusumo is a good place. Even the Moderne, opposite the Tanzanian embassy, is a better place to bring a Mututsi lady to than this dump of murderers."

He had had to lie to the concierge that Julian was a Muhima woman rather than a Mututsi and made her, against her will, to speak Kinyankore rather than Kinyarwanda. In her angry reasoning, the Bahutu of the Cinq Juillet did not own Kinyarwanda any more than she. She accused him of attempting to recreate the Sorrozo-Zainab scenarios.

"I respect your argument in this respect. You are belligerent over your own language — your culture. If it weren't for the Libyans taking over all available hotel rooms, this would not be happening. I will never bring you to such a silly place ever again. But always remember that you have an equal right to enjoy every place in your own country without any MRND diehard preventing you. You have a right to access every place in Rwanda."

"You will show me where they spat at that poor Sorrozo's wife, won't you?"

"I'll show you where she sat with me as she told me of your cat-and-dog animosities."

The Hotel de Cinq Juillet was even swankier, in its simplicity, than the Hotel des Milles Collines. Gold spoons were used to stir sugar into teas and coffees brewed by French, Congolese and Lebanese cooks.

In the early evening they walked out in the cool winds of Kigali Hill to the only cinema in town and watched Julie Andrews and Rock Hudson in *Darling Lili*. Like Laban Sorrozo half a decade ago, Julian cried throughout the beautiful musical.

* * *

Her mother's house stood on a knoll behind the missionary *enseignement secondaire* to which had been added *l'école normale* for training teachers and, fenced off most harshly, le *Sacré Collège*, at Kabgaye. Sabina Mukamuhizi's was an old zinc-sheet roofed house, probably built in the early 40s, which stood under giant white-stemmed eucalyptuses that oozed a resinous substance and emitted a heavy, balmy scent. A local company called Trafipro was busy hewing trees and demarcating the passage of the new road to Akanyaru Haut border via Butare.

Ssempa parked the old Jaguar in front of the house and an eight-year-old boy cannoned himself into Julian's offered bosom. She lifted the boy up and walked with him to the door. Her mother, a Julian Kantarama with the features of Monsignor Raphael Nyarwaya, put a hand to her forehead like a visor, the way her elder brother the monsignor had done the day he handed Ssempa his niece. Her old eyes took in the driver of the ugly white car with the large ugly Ugandan number plates and the unusually fat tyres. She openly winced. The big black, fleshy-faced man with a dark-blue baseball cap had remained seated behind the wrongly placed steering wheel of the car. She came down the two steps rather slowly, her long flowing skirt sweeping the crisp dry leaves of the eucalyptuses. Her heart performed somersaults on taking a second glance at her daughter.

"Kantarama *weh*?" Sabina Mukamuhizi cooed to her daughter fondly. "The Mugande carried you off to Bugande and now he brings you back! How generous! He is the *one*, isn't he? *Musenyeri* Rafaeri will be pleased." Because Banyarwanda, like Banyankore, don't have L in their language she referred to Raphael as Rafaeri and to monseigneur or monsignor as *musenyeri or munshenyere*, which, among the Banyankore, means 'fetch me firewood' and hints at labour exploitation by the clergies that prepared the way for colonialism. "He thinks much of you, Mugande," she told Ssempa in Kinyarwanda. "He has talked well of you from the time you took my Kantarama away to Bugande. *Wiiriwe Mugande weh*?"

"*Uraaho*, Mama?" Ssempa returned her salutation in her own tongue, wondering how she had discovered he was a Muganda — *the* Muganda that had given her daughter a lift so many months previously. They had not met!

"*Ngira nkugire, sheh,*" mother said to daughter, and they embraced passionately.

"*Umwanzi aganye,*" returned the daughter, winking at Ssempa over her mother's shoulder.

"Ah," the matriarch sighed after releasing her daughter. "Bring our guest into the house, Kantarama. You are most welcome, Mugande."

Julian looked back at him, doubtfully. She said with her eyes: 'You'll give us away,' and aloud she said to her mother: "David is going on to Bujumbura. You know he is a trader."

"I know he is a *mucuruuzi*, too. But I should give him something to eat — and to drink. Some milk?"

"*Arikwo mama....*" Ssempa began, apologetically.

"No buts. Don't argue with me, Mugande. You are my son, too. I have no other, Mugande. You will come in, no?"

You could not reasonably decline an offer from such an old, genteel lonesome mother.

She served him warm milk that smelled and tasted of eucalyptus fagot smoke, which he found agreeable as it evoked memories of the teas he had drunk before his father had acquired the town businesses left behind by Asian traders. There was charcoal-roasted veal and well-prepared Irish potatoes with black beans. The mother of the nun sat for a while, exchanging a word or two with the Muganda man before she stood up and took her daughter by the hand and led her through the door to the backrooms. She had exhibited no emotion to the Muganda stranger.

She conducted her daughter to the kitchen house, which was separated from the main house by twenty yards of reddish-brown soil scattered with sickle-shaped, biscuit-brown, olive and yellow leaves of eucalyptus. The kitchen house was papyrus-thatched and made up of three rooms: two small ones that served as stores for dry foods and garden implements, and that opened off either side of the central one in which they stood. This room consisted of three small hearths, three-stone affairs with smouldering grey embers in them, and discarded furniture — old green synthetic leather chairs and a threadbare grey canvas chaise lounge that appeared to be the nightly perch for domestic fowls. The old woman used a rag to beat the dust off but realized her daughter would not take the seat and so she threw the rag aside wearily. Rodents squeaked restively somewhere under the jumble of discarded furniture and other bric-a-brac. Mother stared at daughter. She then took a step back and flapped her gout-disfigured hands at her sides, uttering a bunch of Kinyarwanda swear words in grim agitation. One hand went to her mouth, thumb pressed to one side of the mouth and index finger with the rest of the fingers pushing into the cheek on the other side. The daughter waited.

"*Ai weh*, Kantarama!" Mother spoke at last.

"What is it, Mother?"

"*Ai weh, uranyise*. What have you done to me?"

"Why? — What's wrong, my dear mother?"

"I invited him into the house to see…. Just to be sure, and to see his reactions…. Oh, Maria Mother of Christ!"

"See what, Mother? Sure of what? What are you exclaiming about? Don't frighten me."

"Kantarama, in the name of Christ, you cannot stay here! Rafaeri, your uncle will see you! He will notice!"

Julian's heart sank and her whole body felt weak. A fright she had never experienced engulfed her entire body. Had her mother noticed her sin?

"Uncle Raphael will notice what, Mother?"

"Look at you." The mother's eyes rested at a point below her chin, above her breastbones, at the cleft in her throat where, unknown to the nun, a pulse fluttered. "What am I going to say, Mother of God?" Her eyes betrayed disdain, disbelief and shock. Was her carnality so obvious? … thought Julian. She slumped onto a wooden seat but her mother pulled her roughly to her feet. Julian waited for the blow to her face with tightly closed eyes and when it did not come she opened them cautiously. She was prepared to confess everything now. But just then, an extraordinary thing happened. Her mother's face twisted into a slow grimace, the eyes crying without tears. She made fists of the hands she had so recently flapped at her sides in agitation, and pressed them at either side of her mouth as if in preparation for an earsplitting scream. The daughter made to grab her — to hug her quickly so she might not tumble down. But Sabina Mukamuhizi stepped back. Uncurling her fingers, she spread them out tautly, crooking them into talons and, as if in a trance, took a step towards her daughter, who remained frozen but unafraid now. The mother grabbed her daughter, pulling her into a bear hug, her talon-like fingers digging into the younger woman's shoulder blades, verily hurting her. As her mind went to the Ssempa they had left marooned in the main house, to an episode at River House back in Mbarara where she herself had wished her own tautened fingers could sink into the raw flesh of the man, to kill him for his sins, her mother pushed her away and spoke.

"Kantarama *weh,*" she cried in a hoarse whisper. "God have mercy on this house. Kantarama, my darling daughter! Kantarama! — You have known a man!" She took hold of the daughter's face, kissing her cheeks, forehead, chin and finally, her mouth, forcing her teeth open with her own and, forgetting herself, immersing herself into that sensual contact as the daughter's protesting hands pushed at her forlornly. Julian was shocked by the savage act but was unable to stop herself from being mauled by her mother in such pagan, ritual-like passion. Both women sobbed in great emotion as mother pushed daughter off again, but held her at arms length. A smile exposed her upper front teeth. She again studied her daughter's face as if to find new things there, things she had perhaps not seen in the thirty-two years since she had pushed Kantarama from between her legs at a Belgian hospital in Astrida. Then she pulled her to herself once more in an embrace that took the nun's breath away in its crush.

"Kantarama, Kantarama, Kantarama!" Sabina Mukamuhizi was sobbing with a mixture of mirth and exasperation. "Ooo, how I love you. How I do love you more than I thought myself capable of at this sunset hour of my life! I believed I had lost you all. First your father gets murdered — along with your four brothers. Then Ngoga, your sole surviving brother, gets killed in a freak bicycle accident in Bugande. Gakinya loses all his sons and a daughter in the same way your father and brothers did, and he becomes sterile! You become a nun! Poronia goes for the same in America, as if God had lost His wisdom! Ooo, Holy Mary, Mother of Christ, blessed above all women, have mercy on my child. She has sinned against you for me. Kantarama, you have sinned for God!"

She then released the daughter suddenly.

"Mother, how...?"

"Kantarama," Mukamuhizi interrupted her daughter. "Tell me I am right, am I not? It *is* the Mugande. I'd hate it if it were a priest."

"No, Mother," Julian said, beaten. "It is David, the Muganda. *Arikwo,* Mama, how did you know about it?"

"I am your mother, child; that is mainly why. Any person with eyes can see. You are too plump. I noticed that as you stepped out of the car. No more antelope wildness about you. No more innocence to your gait — your hand brushed at your habit to remove creases, subconsciously, of course. Since when did good nuns become so self-conscious? I wondered and wondered. And I confirmed it when I embraced you, Kantarama, my child. Since when did I greet you so fondly with my very rare *ngira-nkugires*, my girl? And that pulse at your throat…. I hope not too many have noticed the pregnancy yet."

A gasp escaped from the nun's open mouth. She looked aghast and sank to the floor. Her mother kept her from knocking her head against the wooden seat. She gently pressed her daughter's nose between index finger and thumb. Julian opened her eyes, spluttering and murmuring unintelligibly. The mother gave her two gentle slaps to either cheek and Julian sat up. Her mother helped her onto the seat that she had dusted clean.

For a time the nun sat back in the old chair with the look of one lost to the world. She sighed and asked her mother in a husky voice: "What did you say, Sabina?"

"*Ai weh*, Kantarama," wailed the old woman. "You don't even know!"

"Not *know*, Mother? It cannot be true!"

Mukamuhizi stared at her with sad eyes. She then grabbed her daughter once more and roughly undid the buttons of her dress. "I want you to look at your breasts, Kantarama. Should you see no large dark circles round the teats, then I am not your mother. Hmmm! — You are not wearing a corset even! My daughter… you are a nun no more!"

The nun peered at her firm round breasts, which appeared to have grown, and, without covering them, cried out in desperation: "Oh, Sabina! Oh, my God!" She wailed like one threatened with a sharp dagger at the throat.

She got up unsteadily, patted her clothes, and, remembering her mother's words, restrained herself from straightening them out. "What have I done to you, my very dear mother? I don't deserve to live. I must do away with my blasted sinning life! I am such a disgrace to everybody. I am not worthy of life."

"No. You deserve to live more than ever before. Have courage, my poor child. Your father and grandfather's blood will not perish. It won't perish with me. For many years it appeared as though Gakinya, Poronia and you were the very last. And the ancestors would never have looked kindly upon me for being the last wife of the last man in the family. You will have a baby boy, through dire difficulties. I will succour him myself. And he will take the Sebwitabure name. Nobody has noticed then?"

"Ooo, Mother, I wouldn't know. But on hindsight, I seem to recall Reverend Superior General looking at me with more scrutiny than usual when she was releasing me. She said, 'have a whole month with Sabina. And take good care of

261

yourself too.' I may be mistaken about her attitude, of course, but now, thinking back, I don't know what she thought of me or meant by those words."

"Ah, now I see. She has noticed. Since you are a Perpetual, she trusts you will do the needful — the only logically reasonable thing to do. She thinks you are aware of the pregnancy and she does not want it to be the business of the Franciscan Order."

"You are saying that Mother Superior expects me to have an abortion?"

"If she did not want you to do so she would not have released you. She would have sent you along with an emissary to your Uncle Rafaeri, with a sealed letter. She would have given you a whole two years. That is what is usually done. You would only return to Kyera after your baby was out of danger. And the baby would grow as an orphan of the church under Rafaeri, in your case, or to whomever it was entrusted under the Faith."

Julian said, emphatically, "I *cannot* have an abortion, Mother."

"I would never let you, Kantarama, or forgive you for it. But it still means you cannot go back to Kyera. And that was why I would not allow that Mugande to leave you behind here. If your Reverend Superior did not wish to involve Monsignor Rafaeri, then Rafaeri must never know. He's my brother and I know his temperament. He might say hard things to you that could not be forgiven until your deaths. Better for him to hear of it away from him so that his curses don't reach you directly. A curse that travels long distances does less harm to its target. In his profound kindness, Rafaeri is also very unforgiving. And he must not find you here."

"But, Mother," exclaimed Julian in consternation. "You mean I can't...?"

"Out of the question. You cannot stay here. Your uncle cannot find you here. He will notice your condition immediately. I know him only too well. You will go away with your Mugande to wherever he is going. In the long run he will need to hide you — from the church. Is he a Catholic by any chance?"

"David is a Mohammedan."

"A *mo*-what? God have mercy on me! — A *musulman*?"

"Yes, Mother."

"Was it rape, then — that day he drove you away. What happened, Kantarama?"

"Mother, I don't know how to express it but... well, to say the truth, I kind of raped him."

Her mother slumped in the seat opposite her, awaiting further explanation. When none came she said: "But like all Bagande he is not even handsome. What happened to you when you left this place? Did he pretend to have a mechanical problem with the vehicle? They do it to trick good people into spending the night on the journey."

"God Himself tricked us instead. The day we left here there were heavy rainstorms in Byumba and Rubaya. The road was washed away at Murindi and we had to make a long detour through Urukomo. We arrived at Gatuna very late and you know how nasty those *manehko* can behave toward Batutsi. We were delayed. And there was a curfew on the Ugandan side, but David — he is a very stubborn man — wanted to get me to Mbarara by beating the curfew. He didn't believe the soldiers about the curfew anyway. We found a roadblock inside Uganda, soon after Katuna. Four soldiers there. Their leader attempted to rape me. He defiled me with his hand using the pretext of searching for a pistol in my undergarments." Her body shuddered in a shiver at mentioning this.

"And then? — Then what happened?" Her mother's face was tense with apprehension, her voice, indignant.

"David — Mugande, killed them. He shot them all with one of their guns. I don't know how he did it. It was still raining and the bullets had shattered our windscreen, I think. There can be nothing worse than being fired at with guns — at very close range too, Mother. We got to Kabale, to a hotel where David was well known, and got a suite. I was ill with a high fever — from the heavy cold thunderstorm and the fright of the roadblock. He... David, got me hot coffee, which he mixed with liquor, for my fever. David himself looked dead on his feet. He has unbelievable energy, but he looked battered then. I needed comfort. He had done all those things that endangered his own life to save me. I felt sympathy for his plight. I felt like he needed nursing — needed a mother, you see? — To give him the warmth he required for us to continue our journey the following day."

"Save me the nonsense, Kantarama. Sweet nonsense it is, of course. The *musulman* intended it with the liquor. *Musulmans* are subtle bastards. Did he drink the concoction himself?"

"You are always right, except this time. Yes, he drinks. He drinks a lot. He is outright irreligious, Mother. I know he knows of no God but an African God. But he had no hand in what happened. He refused to give me the alcohol and I insisted on it. I did insist, too, that we share the hotel bed. I was frozen to the bone. I wanted warmth and comfort; I wanted us to share those. I had had a hell of a scare at the roadblock... the frightful banging away of guns and the dead bodies. And David looking so beaten!"

"Did the soldier rape you?"

"He did defile me — with his dirty hand."

Her mother studied her critically, a dry smile frozen on her face: "So? So you felt — ah, I see now. You wanted the defilement completed for you. You wanted someone to complete the sin for you, eh? You would have died without that consummation, or so you felt!"

Julian looked at her mother steadfastly and said: "Yes, Mother," the way she would have said it to a curate behind the confession screen.

"Yes. I understand, Kantarama. I should imagine that a young woman who has just gone through such experience is a very vulnerable woman. There cannot exist anything like it," she smirked, in what appeared to be annoyance, and asked: "And why did he accompany you here? An escort! As would be expected of a jealous *musulman* husband?"

"*Oya-a*, Mama! Be fair to David. He is not like anyone you have ever met."

Her mother laughed, light heartedly: "Tell me quickly — do not hesitate. *Aragukunda?*"

"*Cyane* Mama. He loves me as much as I need him to love me. I know he would marry me."

"Would? *Would* leaves a void — some doubt!"

Julian looked at her mother with eyes that almost expressed adoration, appreciation and gratitude: "*Shall*, Mother mine."

"*Etes-vous bien sûr? Uragihamya?*"

"*Ko-ko*, Mama. I have not had the opportunity to tell him how deeply I love him, but he has professed his love for me in many ways. I am quite certain of David's love for me. I ask your forgiveness, Sabina."

"I forgave you the moment I opened that door and saw your state, Kantarama. Remember, Rafaeri will never forgive you; neither will Poronia. You are twins but you took to your father and Sinzagaya Gakinya. Free and outgoing. But Poronia is your Uncle Nyarwaya through and through; subtle even when they are with their very own. I always saw Poronia as the nun and you as myself — the wife of your father. Hurry. I will see you to your man's car and pray for you with my heart all the time. If I die today, I will die happier than if I had died yesterday. Remember to bring me the boy. *Au revoir ma chérie petite.*"